AMONG THE HEATHER

SPECIAL EDITION

THE HIGHLANDS SERIES
BOOK TWO

SAMANTHA YOUNG

Among the Heather

A Highlands Series Novel

By Samantha Young

ALSO BY SAMANTHA YOUNG

Other Adult Contemporary Novels by Samantha Young

Play On

As Dust Dances

Black Tangled Heart

Hold On: A Play On Novella

Into the Deep

Out of the Shallows

Hero

Villain: A Hero Novella

One Day: A Valentine Novella

Fight or Flight

Much Ado About You

A Cosmic Kind of love

The Love Plot

On Dublin Street Series:

On Dublin Street

Down London Road

Before Jamaica Lane

Fall From India Place

Echoes of Scotland Street

Moonlight on Nightingale Way

Until Fountain Bridge (a novella)

Castle Hill (a novella)

ABOUT THE AUTHOR

Samantha is a New York Times, USA Today, and Wall Street Journal bestselling author and a Goodreads Choice Awards Nominee. Samantha has written over 50 books and is published in 31 countries. She writes emotional and angsty romance, often set where she resides—in her beloved home country Scotland. Samantha splits her time between her family, writing and chasing after two very mischievous cavapoos.

ACKNOWLEDGMENTS

For the most part, writing is a solitary endeavor, but publishing most certainly is not. I have to thank my amazing editor Jennifer Sommersby Young for always, *always* being there to help make me a better writer and storyteller. Thank you for working extra hard with me to make sure Aria and North's story concluded the way it was meant to.

Thank you to Julie Deaton for proofreading *Among the Heather* and catching all the things. I'm so glad you loved Aria and North and are excited for what's next!

And thank you to my bestie and PA extraordinaire Ashleen Walker for helping to lighten the load and supporting me more than ever this year. I really couldn't do this without you.

The life of a writer doesn't stop with the book. Our job expands beyond the written word to marketing, advertising, graphic design, social media management, and more. Help from those in the know goes a long way. A huge thank-you to Nina Grinstead, Kim Cermak, Kelley Beckham and all the team at Valentine PR for your encouragement, support, insight and advice. You all are amazing!

Thank you to every single blogger, Instagrammer, and book lover who has helped spread the word about my books. You all are appreciated so much! On that note, a massive thank-you to the fantastic readers in my private Facebook group, Samantha Young's Clan McBookish. You're truly special. You're a safe space of love and support on the internet and I couldn't be more grateful for you.

A massive thank-you to Hang Le for creating a beautiful cover that literally made readers gasp when it was revealed. You are a tremendous talent! And thank you to Regina Wamba for the beautiful couple photography that brings Aria and North to life.

As always, thank you to my agent Lauren Abramo for making it possible for readers all over the world to find my words. You're phenomenal, and I'm so lucky to have you.

A huge thank-you to my family and friends for always supporting and encouraging me, and for listening to me talk, sometimes in circles, about the worlds I live in.

Finally, to you, thank you for reading. Funny, how as a writer, I find myself unable to express just how much it means to me. It means everything and the moon, dear reader. Everything and the moon.

For Sam's Clan McBookish.
Thank you for reading my stories, and for your tremendous kindness and support. It means the world to me.

Fly we to some desert isle,
There we'll pass our days together,
Shun the world's derisive smile,
Wand'ring tenants of the heather
— Robert Tannahill, *Fly We to Some Desert Isle*

PROLOGUE
ARIA

Ardnoch Estate, Scotland
July

Sitting on my porch, sipping my morning coffee, I gazed out at the North Sea. Waves gently lapped at the shore below, seagulls squalled in the cloudless sky above, and I felt ... content. If not happy, then content. The heat wave that hit the rest of the Western Hemisphere had found a home in the Scottish Highlands too. The early-morning sun turned the waters of the North Sea a Mediterranean turquoise along its shallow depths toward the beach. A slight breeze offered a cool caress against what was an unusually warm temperature for this time of the morning. Thank goodness my father had thought to fit the house with air conditioning, despite being advised it was pointless in this part of the world. If he'd listened to that advice, I wouldn't have slept last night.

Last summer, my first as hospitality manager at the exclusive members-only club in the Highlands, was a roller-coaster ride of weather. This summer, the film and television professionals who paid a fortune to have access to one of the most secure estates in the world had spent much of it outdoors because of weeks filled with sunny days. I'd never seen so many members take advantage of our private beach or require security to protect them as they enjoyed guided tours of the Highlands. Not to mention, the use of the spa doubled. In fact, I'd hired extra seasonal staff this year, more than Ardnoch had ever required.

Ardnoch Castle was meant to buzz with life and energy ... but, honestly, I wanted Hollywood to return to work. I longed for September to arrive so they'd hurry home or onto their next project in whichever corner of the world it took them to. As long as it wasn't here.

The estate could never be like LA, but fill it with people from LA and it became uncomfortably close.

Glancing at the elegant Rolex my mother had given me for Christmas, I quickly threw back the last of my coffee and hurried into my house. It was technically my parents' house, but I lived in it year-round while they (mostly my mother) visited for the summer. Spotting Mamma's jewelry scattered over the breakfast nook, I hurried quietly through the downstairs. I didn't want to wake her.

My mother had descended upon Ardnoch weeks ago, and even though I was busy at the castle with work, she still wore on my last nerve.

Grabbing my purse, phone, and car keys, I tiptoed toward the front door so the sound of my heels wouldn't echo upstairs.

"*Buondì, coccolona.*"

My mother's husky voice stopped me in my tracks. I'd inherited that sultry huskiness, but not the sultry Italian accent that went with it. Taking a deep breath, I turned and watched Mamma descend the staircase like she was on a photo shoot. Her silk robe billowed open, flashing her long, perfect legs. Dark hair that she'd been dyeing since she was thirty to cover premature gray was tied up in an artfully messy bun as she frowned at me. Because of the fillers she had injected into her lips every few months, it seemed as if she was perpetually pouting. To be fair, she usually was.

"Morning, Mamma," I answered, straightening instinctually. My entire life, my mother, the supermodel, had drilled it into me to keep my shoulders and spine straight.

"No daughter of mine will have a hunchback."

"Coffee?" she asked as she stepped down into the hallway and crossed the distance between us.

"There's some in the kitchen."

Her dark eyes narrowed. "You're leaving? Again?"

I sighed inwardly. "Mamma, you know I work here."

"All you do is work. Do you not get a break?"

"Summer is our busiest time. You know that."

"I've hardly seen you."

Biting back a response, I took a second to control my irritation. Snapping at Mamma only led to days of drama. However, I found it ironic that my mother wanted to spend time with me only after I became an adult and no longer needed her in the way I used to. As a child, I spent a lot of time with nannies and overworked personal assistants. My dad was Wesley Howard, legendary movie director, and he spent a lot of time away from home when I was a kid. My mom, a famous Italian supermodel, was always off in some exotic location shooting for a magazine or an ad campaign.

When they were home, I wouldn't say they weren't involved because they were. My parents did their best to show that they loved me and my sister, despite how busy they were. But the truth of the matter was, they didn't raise me. And when Allegra unexpectedly came along when I was ten years old, I—and not our absent parents—raised my younger sister.

I'd sacrificed going to the college of my dreams and stayed home in Malibu to commute to the University of California in LA so I could be there for my little sister. After my first two years at UCLA, my mother retired from modeling. With her home, I'd suggested I transfer and head to the East Coast. Mamma had such a dramatic meltdown at the thought of me leaving that I stayed for Allegra's sake.

Our mother had never been more involved in our lives. I was grateful that Allegra got that time with her (even if it hadn't stopped her from going off the rails), but it frustrated me to have to deal with Mamma's constant calls and texts now, too many years after I actually needed her.

"I should get to work." I finally settled on a calm reply.

Her eyes washed over my outfit. "Oh, darling, cover your arms. You haven't used those weights I gave you at all, have you?"

For the whole twenty-eight years of my life, I'd put up with my mother picking apart my appearance. She thought it was her way of showing she cared. I was pretty sure she probably fretted over my cute baby-fat rolls when I was a newborn.

This morning, she was referring to the sleeveless silk blouse I wore tucked into my pencil skirt. "It's hot out," I said.

"The castle has air conditioning. Wait here and I'll get you something to cover up, okay?" Mamma patted my shoulder with a loving smile. "You need to look your best if you are ever to catch a handsome man's eye."

"Mamma, please join the rest of us in the twenty-first century."

"Oh, pfft." She waved a manicured hand as she turned, her robe billowing behind her. "Just because a woman thinks romance and companionship are important does not mean she's not a feminist."

"Coming from the woman who sees her husband a few times a year."

"Exaggeration," my mother threw over her shoulder, "and distance does make the heart grow fonder. Your father and I still cannot keep our hands off each other."

"Tell me something I don't know," I muttered under my breath. My parents' passion for each other was not something I'd ever questioned. "I'm going!"

"No, coccolona, I'll be just a minute!"

"And don't call me that!" My patience ended, and I hurried out of the house before she could stop me.

Coccolona translated to *cuddly*. I was my mother's cuddly one. It was her affectionate way of referring to the fact that I was a pudgy child. As a teenager, I'd eaten small meals and never snacked, so I could maintain an impossible weight for my bone structure. I spent most of my time in class holding my belly so people wouldn't hear it rumbling. And even then, my mother still made comments about my weight. Finally exhausted by the constant dieting, I gave up and embraced the fact that I was born to be a little overweight. Maybe if Mamma wasn't always pointing out the things I least liked about myself (like my arms!), I'd be more comfortable with my body. I'd be proud of my "tall voluptuousness," as Allegra called it.

Catching sight of my arms in the reflection of my BMW's window, I fought the urge to go back into the house to change. It was hot, goddamn it! So I didn't have slender, toned arms like my mother and Allegra. So what? I'd inherited my figure from my father's maternal side of the family and that was that.

My mother couldn't leave soon enough.

Slamming into my car, I accelerated away from the house with more speed than necessary. Our house was one of only a few large, private, member-owned homes along the estate's coastline. My father was on the board of Ardnoch Estate and had called dibs on one. The anti-drone perimeter that encapsulated the entire estate protected us. The main lodgings for the rest of the members were in the castle itself.

The ancestral estate of Hollywood actor Lachlan Adair, he'd turned his family home into a lucrative business and haven for Hollywood's elite. Lachlan had retired from acting to run the Ardnoch and his other business ventures, but when his wife gave birth to their daughter Vivien, he'd stepped back from his duties to be a hands-on dad. I respected the hell out of that decision and appreciated it because it gave me a job to escape to when I'd desperately needed it. I'd never expected I'd love the Scottish Highlands so much. While my job title was Hospitality Manager, I'd taken over for Lachlan and was running the place. I didn't mind. It kept me busy and fed my love of organization and bossing people around.

While the castle hosted most of the rooms, dining area, and entertainment spaces, separate buildings housed the spa, gym, and swimming pool. The property also offered tennis courts, a golf course, two small lochs, a private beach, and luxury lodges for members who preferred more privacy.

Including having to liaise with the head butler, a maître d', head chef, head housekeeper, and all of their staff, I had to oversee beauty therapists, personal trainers, physical therapists, masseuses, a yoga, Pilates, and mindfulness instructor, golf and tennis coaches, lifeguards, and one of the best private security teams in the country. Never mind that I was also the person members wanted to talk to when there was a problem.

Moreover, I was the welcome wagon, and today we were expecting our latest member. North Hunter, a renowned Scottish actor. I'd seen him in a couple of meh rom-coms he'd made. What? So I was kind of a film snob. I could say without bias my dad was one of the greatest directors of all time. Blame him for my film snobbery.

However, I had caught an episode of North Hunter's TV show, *King's Valley*, that had catapulted him to fame these past few years. He played a serial killer and won a Golden Globe for his performance last year. I'd been surprised by his acting chops when I saw *King's Valley*. I hadn't expected him to go from cocky, charming Scot to intensely charismatic and complex sociopath.

After I saw the show, I reached out to his management to see if he'd be interested in a membership. Part of my job was to bring fresh blood to the estate, and I wanted that fresh blood to be the cream of the crop. North had just bagged the lead role in what was sure to be the next big spy action movie franchise. Rumor had it filming started at the end of the year. It thrilled me when North paid for a membership without even coming to tour the estate. He'd apparently heard enough about Ardnoch through the grapevine and understood that membership here was gilding for credentials. Yes, that sounded elitist and pretentious, but it was the truth. There was a long waiting list for membership to Ardnoch. To bypass that waiting list meant you'd made it.

It was a five-minute drive through woodland to the castle, and I was one of the first to park my vehicle in the staff lot. I liked to be early to work. Hurrying into the castle's cool interior, I nodded hello to the staff who had just arrived or were coming off the night shift, and greeted Wakefield, our head butler. He wore his formal black-and-white butler uniform of tailcoat and white gloves. In the year I'd been working at Ardnoch, I'd never beaten that man to work.

"Good morning, Wakefield."

He gave me a small bow. "Ms. Howard. Mr. Hunter has arrived."

I stumbled to a stop on the edges of the opulent reception hall, my heels squeaking on the parquet flooring. The room was empty. No sign of North Hunter. A grand staircase descended into the center, fitted with a red-and-gray tartan wool runner. It led to a landing where three floor-to-ceiling stained glass windows spilled sunlight. Then it branched off at either side, twin staircases leading to the floor above, which I could partially see from the galleried balconies at either end of the reception hall. It was too hot for a fire in the huge hearth on the wall adjacent to the entrance and opposite the staircase. Tiffany lamps scattered throughout on end tables gave the space a warm glow, as it wasn't the most light-filled space.

Opposite the quiet hearth sat two matching suede-and-fabric buttoned sofas with a coffee table in between. This was usually where new members awaited my arrival.

"Already?" I asked, turning back to Wakefield. "Where is he?"

"I took the liberty of showing Mr. Hunter to the dining room. Chef has provided breakfast for him."

"Good. Good. He's very early." We hadn't expected North until this afternoon. I had a meeting this morning first thing with Jock McRory, our head of security. "Wakefield, can you tell Mr. McRory I have to postpone our meeting until nine thirty and have Mr. Hunter brought to my office as soon as he's finished breakfast?"

"Of course, Ms. Howard."

"Where is his luggage?" I asked.

"Mrs. Hutchinson recalled you wished to have Mr. Hunter stay in the Bruce Suite, so I had his luggage delivered to his room."

My lips twitched at the thought of our head housekeeper. "I swear that woman has supernatural abilities." Agnes Hutchinson seemed to know everything that went on at the castle and had my schedule memorized.

"Indeed." Wakefield's eyes glimmered with amusement.

"Thank you, Wakefield. I'll be in my office."

"Shall I have coffee brought to you?"

"Yes, please."

Wakefield was the best.

My office was Lachlan's "stage office," as he'd called it. His real office was in the staff quarters and was a dismal, dreary little room next to Jock's office. This stage office was where he took meetings with members. He'd insisted I take it as my own, and I did not argue. The room was like a smaller version of the estate library. Wall-to-wall dark oak bookshelves, an impressive open fireplace, and two comfortable armchairs situated in front of a captain's pedestal desk. A floor-to-ceiling window adjacent to the desk let in light so it didn't feel too dark. Tiffany lamps aided in chasing off the gloom too. Luxurious velvet curtains at the window pooled on the wooden floors, most of which were covered in expensive carpets.

I rounded the desk and took a seat in the ergonomic chair that was specially designed to fit in with the room's traditional opulence. My small keyboard sat on the leather top of the pedestal desk, and I stared at it and the blank screen on my computer for a second.

No doubt a million emails awaited me as soon as I switched it on.

So I took a breath and let it out before I reached over and woke up the monitor.

Not a minute later, there was a knock at the door, and Wakefield arrived with hot coffee and a breakfast pastry.

"Mr. Hunter is just finishing up. Would you like me to ask him to wait in the reception hall for a few moments?"

"No, just bring him in." Although he was early and it wasn't my fault, he'd been waiting long enough.

As per usual, nerves threatened to take over. This happened anytime I was meeting someone new. But I'd learned to pour on self-assurance like it was a role I was playing. Glancing down to make sure I was presentable, I frowned at the sight of my bare arms and cursed my mother for bringing them to my attention. I suddenly wished I was wearing anything but the silk blouse. Truthfully, I was probably too busty for silk. Mamma always said silk was for elegant figures. My breasts wouldn't know how to be elegant if they were strapped down with a mile's worth of boob tape.

Stop it.

I straightened my shoulders just as the knock came at the door.

"Come in."

Wakefield entered. "Mr. North Hunter, Ms. Howard."

"Thank you, Wakefield." I stood as the Scottish actor entered the room.

Our eyes locked and I was barely aware of Wakefield leaving the office as goose bumps suddenly prickled across my arms. Penetrating, beautiful gray eyes stared intensely into mine and awareness shivered down my spine.

The entire room seemed to shrink in North Hunter's presence. He was tall, perhaps six feet two. Dressed in a black fitted T-shirt and dark blue jeans, I noted the broad shoulders, the hard, sculpted biceps, the long, lean, athletic physique. Dark blond hair cropped fairly short.

Angled jaw, thin, serious lips, and a strong, straight but sharp nose. High cheekbones.

My feet felt stuck as he held my stare, his expression changing from surprised to curious to smoldering in an instant.

North Hunter was a rugged, beautiful man.

I'd met many beautiful men, but I'd only been attracted to a few. Usually, it took more than several seconds in their presence for that tingle between my thighs to let itself be known.

Then North smiled. A wicked, boyish smile that made my belly flip like I was a freaking teenager.

Fear scored through me and I stiffened, dismay chasing away the fear.

My tone sounded brittle even to my ears as I rounded the

desk and reluctantly held out my hand. "Mr. Hunter, welcome to Ardnoch. You're early."

The last sounded accusatory.

His smile only deepened, causing his eyes to crinkle sexily at the corners. "That I am." His gaze leisurely moved down my body in inappropriate perusal. My hand wavered. I knew from my research that North had been dating British pop star Cara Rochdale for two years. So when he finally deigned to drag his attention back to my face and there was no mistaking the heat in his eyes, I struggled not to hide my distaste. I wondered how many women he'd cheated on the English beauty with.

North took hold of my hand, his grip tight. "You look different in real life," he mused in that lilting accent that was unfairly attractive.

He looked different too. Or rather, his magnetism was muted in film. I could practically sense his energy vibrating up my arm, and as he held my hand for too long, I felt a tightening in my breasts.

Sucking in a breath, I yanked my hand out of his.

I'd been fooled before by hot looks and charisma. Never again. Ignoring the comment that suggested he'd googled me (there were a few red carpet shots online of me with my family, but the last one had to have been taken at least four years ago), I moved back behind my desk. I'd put a key card for North's room in my drawer last night.

"As you know, I'm Ms. Howard, and I run Ardnoch when Mr. Adair is otherwise occupied. However, we have a full staff who are at your disposal. There is information in your room regarding spa treatments, personal trainers, physical therapists, golf lessons, tennis lessons, yoga, Pilates, mindfulness, tour guides, and things to see in the area. If you have any questions, please don't hesitate to press zero on the telephone in your room to be connected to our liaison service." I grabbed the envelope with his key card and rounded the desk again to hand it to him. "Welcome to Ardnoch."

"You said that already." He took the envelope and glanced inside it.

I waited for him to leave.

Laughter twinkled in North's eyes. "Is that it, then? Is that my warm welcome?"

I tried not to let my discomfort show. "Is there anything else you require, Mr. Hunter?"

"Well, I'd love it if you'd call me North."

Since that would be inappropriate, I didn't respond.

A furrow appeared between his brows. "Have I done something to offend you, Aria?"

"Ms. Howard," I insisted gently. *And maybe stop looking at me like I'm something you want to eat.* "Of course not. However, I am late for a meeting, so if you'll excuse me." I crossed the room and pulled open the door.

When I glanced back over my shoulder, North's eyes were on my ass.

Indignation filled me and I cleared my throat, even as I wondered if he was looking at my ass because he liked it or because its largeness surprised him.

He didn't appear even a tiny bit sheepish about being caught as he strolled over to the door. "Thank you for the short and not very sweet welcome." North halted inches from me, and I fought the urge to step back. He searched my face like I was a puzzle he couldn't figure out. "I do feel as though I might have offended you somehow, and that bothers me more than I like."

He sounded sincere.

That was the thing about actors.

They were very good at pretending.

"Of course you haven't offended me, Mr. Hunter. We've never met until today. It's just a busy morning here at

Ardnoch." I noted Max, one of our valets, waiting outside. "Max here will show you to your suite. I took the liberty of procuring the Bruce Suite for your stay. It has a wonderful view of the North Sea. If, when you return to Ardnoch, you would like us to reserve a particular room or lodge, please give us plenty of notice and we'll do our best to accommodate." Even as I spoke, I fought the invisible pull to lean closer to him, to breathe deeply of his sandalwood and citrus cologne.

A coolness entered his expression at my crisp formality. "Very good, *Ms. Howard*." He strode out of my office without looking back, and I quickly shut the door.

Resting my forehead on the wood, I exhaled shakily.

What the hell was that?

Whatever it was, my alarm bells were ringing. The last time I was attracted to an actor, he ripped my fragile self-esteem to shreds.

And this actor was one of my members.

I needed to stay as far away from North Hunter as possible.

ONE
NORTH

December

The driveway led through woodlands for what felt like forever before the trees disappeared to reveal grass for miles around a mammoth building in the distance. Flags were situated throughout the rolling plains of the estate—the golf course. Only a few months ago I stood on that grass with my mate Theo Cavendish, pretending like we knew what the hell we were doing.

Carefree. Confident. Celebratory. Assured my life was about to change in the best way.

Oh, aye, it had changed all right.

In the worst fucking way possible.

Ardnoch Castle was a rambling, castellated mansion, six stories tall and about two hundred years old, situated on thousands of acres of estate. When Aria Howard had reached out to my management to ask if I was interested in membership, my publicist Annette was on at me to buy it. I thought it was a bunch of pretentious, overpriced nonsense. But they said it would be good for my image, and I liked the idea that the club was in my homeland. I hadn't expected to fall in love with the place. I hadn't anticipated that because of its security, I'd need it as a haven to run to.

The low winter sun hovered over the horizon, making the windows of the castle glint in welcome.

Wakefield, the butler, appeared out of the large main entrance before the Range Rover had even pulled to a stop on the gravel. The weirdest part of the transition from impoverished nobody to famous actor was the way people wanted to do everything for me. It chafed a bit. Wakefield opened my door as soon as the car stopped.

"Welcome back to Ardnoch, Mr. Hunter," he said with warm professionalism.

No hint of accusation or judgment in his voice.

"Thank you, Wakefield," I replied, even though I didn't want to speak to anyone.

"Any luggage, sir?"

No. As soon as my team told me what the papers would publish this morning, I jumped on a plane to Scotland. I'd been in LA, getting ready to fly back to London to start shooting *Birdwatcher*, the spy movie that was going to change my life. With a director as infamously brilliant as Blake Forster at the helm, it was set to rival James Bond.

A knot twisted in my gut.

Annette told me to flee to Ardnoch to ride out the coming storm while my agent, Harry, warned me this might wreak havoc with the film and its schedule. That's all I needed. To be the reason the studio lost money on delays because the tabloids were fucking savage animals who didn't give a shit what they put anyone through.

"My luggage is arriving separately," I told Wakefield. "I don't know how long I'm going to be staying at the moment."

"Very good, sir. Let me show you to Ms. Howard's office."

I groaned inwardly. "Can't you just show me to my room?" It was like being taken to the head teacher's office. A tantalizingly sexy head teacher. But I wasn't in the mood for Aria Howard's disdain today.

"Ms. Howard would like to speak to you, sir," Wakefield said carefully.

Oh, aye, right. I had a feeling I knew what she wanted to say, and honestly, I wasn't sure my frayed bloody nerves could take it.

Usually, I got a kind of perverse satisfaction out of her aloof and caustic reaction to me. It had been like that between us from the moment we met, and I had no clue why. Today, however, I just wanted to hide in my fucking room and have no bugger bother me.

Reluctantly, I followed the butler to Aria's office.

She spoke with Wakefield before I entered the room and I knew I was in a bad way because her husky voice did nothing to me. Her voice normally made my cock twitch. I didn't think the woman realized she had the bedroom voice to beat all bedroom voices.

The butler withdrew as I stepped inside, and he closed the door behind us. Aria stood, drawing my attention. I didn't want to look at her, but I couldn't stop myself.

Women had fallen at my feet my whole life. Aye, that sounded horrifically arrogant, didn't it? But it was the truth. I'd never had to work hard to get a woman in my bed. In fact, since becoming famous, I'd even found them in it without invitation. Problem was, I couldn't do casual sex. It wasn't something I talked about a lot because my mates would probably look at me like I was off my nut, but casual sex left me feeling empty. I enjoyed being in a relationship. Enjoyed feeling needed. I was in a long-term relationship with Cara Rochdale the first time I'd met Aria, so the fact that another woman made my blood hot beyond bearing incited some major fucking guilt.

But after what Cara did to me only fourteen hours ago, I no longer felt guilty about my attraction to the estate manager. I didn't know what it was about Aria Howard that excited me. Aye, she was beautiful, but I'd dated beautiful women before, Cara among them. I think it was the dichotomy of Aria's overtly sexual, physical appearance to her cool, efficient manner.

My gut twisted as our eyes met and held.

Aria had striking eyes. Mossy green and so light and clear against her olive complexion and almost black hair. Everything about her made a man want to sink into her. Plump lips, spectacularly large tits, and full hips. She was tall, almost my height in heels, and her length stretched her voluptuous curves, but thankfully not enough. Her waist drew in, giving her that perfect, exaggerated hourglass. I'd overheard an actor gossiping with another on the estate a few months back and Aria had come up in conversation. She'd called Aria fat. Jealous cow. Aria was perfect.

Unfortunately, she hated me even before today.

I waited for her disgust to twist that knot in my gut even tighter.

She rounded her desk to face me, and I insolently drew my eyes down her body and back up again, provoking her. Her lips pursed for a second, and she crossed her arms over her chest. I wondered if she knew her body language gave her away. She was always crossing her arms over her chest in my presence. Guarding herself. Defensive. I had no idea what I'd done to this woman, but I didn't have my usual energy to figure it out.

"Room key?" I held out my hand.

Her eyes flared at my abruptness. "I put you in the Bruce Suite."

I didn't say thank you. Any other day I'd appreciate it, but I wanted to disappear.

Aria drew herself up, her arms dropping to her sides. "I want you to know that security here at Ardnoch will protect your privacy. You're safe from the tabloids, and you can come and go across the estate as you please. If you wish to leave the estate for any reason, we'll assemble a team to escort you."

Shock rendered me speechless. For the past few months, I'd dropped in on Ardnoch for a few days here and there, and anytime I met Aria, she was antagonistic as fuck. The conclusion I'd come to, since as far as I knew I had done nothing to warrant her disdain, was that she knew of my background and thought I was beneath her.

However, today a story broke in the news that I was complicit in the murder of a homeless man when I was thirteen years old ... and she'd decided to be almost welcoming. It made no sense.

"Is there anything else you need, Mr. Hunter?"

I sneered. "No judgment today, sweetheart? I thought you'd be salivating over this?"

Her eyes widened at the nastiness in my voice, and I tried not to drown in them. "I was reminded this morning that I should never believe what I read online."

Her kindness, for some reason, made everything worse. "A man *did* die," I bit out.

"Yes, but I don't know the circumstances. I do know that you were a child when it happened, and the man standing before me saved my friend from an assault and an experience she would never have gotten over."

I stiffened. Aria was referring to an event a few months ago. I'd been talking with one of the security guards on the estate, Walker Ironside. He was well known in the biz as a top private bodyguard. Elite military background. And he was Scottish. I'd been trying to lure him away from the estate to work for me when we'd heard a scream from one of the rooms. It turned out a housekeeper, Aria's friend Sloane, had warned Walker of a member's untoward behavior. He'd been keeping an eye on the situation and thankfully had a key to the bastard's room. Byron Hoffman was the son of a studio head and considered himself untouchable. When Walker and I burst into his room to find him suffocating Sloane while attempting to rape her, I'd wanted to tear the evil son of a bitch to shreds.

News had just broken that Byron Hoffman had been arrested for multiple counts of rape. Rumor was that the owner of the estate, Lachlan Adair, was responsible for finding his victims and convincing them to come forward.

"One has nothing to do with the other." I stuffed my hands into the pockets of my jeans and shrugged with a smirk. "A man died. Turns out I'm the scum you thought I was."

Her lips parted in surprise. "I never thought you were scum, Mr. Hunter."

"Don't worry about it, sweetheart. You think I'm scum, I think you're an uptight, frigid, elitist snob. That's life. Now, do you have my room key or not?"

Aria's eyes flashed, her jaw clenching seconds before she whirled and marched around her desk. She threw open the drawer, snatched up the key card, and strode back to me to slap it in my open palm. Then she crossed her arms over her chest and lifted her chin toward the door in a silent *get out*. Buried behind the anger, I saw her hurt.

That knot in my gut twisted again.

I opened my mouth to apologize, but the words wouldn't come. What I said was true. And I didn't want her fucking sympathy or understanding.

Karma had caught up with me. Maybe I did deserve this.

I was an orphan from Falkirk, a commuter town between Glasgow and Edinburgh, where the socioeconomic divide was vast. I could anglicize my broad Scots accent and mask my origins, but there was no scraping off the poverty or dirt that clung to the soul of that wee foster kid who chased after boys who'd had humanity beaten out of them from the start. They'd done things I was brutally ashamed of. *We* had.

Maybe dangling this life in front of me was part of Karma's punishment. It wasn't just enough to have the past catch up with me. She wanted me to feel the pain of knowing what it was like to come out the other side ... only to have a better life ripped away from me.

Aria Howard was the daughter of Hollywood legend Wesley Howard and world-renowned supermodel Chiara Bellucci Howard. She'd met the fucking president of the United States. Lived a privileged life in Malibu. And every inch of her was immaculate. Not a hair out of place. Nails perfectly manicured. Makeup subtle and perfume expensive. Rolex on her wrist, diamonds in her ears. Clean and luxurious all the way to her soul.

She'd never known dirt. Never waded near scum.

She was ... Not. For. Me.

I'd known that from the moment we'd met. And I didn't need the goddamn reminder now.

Without another word, I turned and slammed out of her office.

TWO
ARIA

February

From: Ariella Branch <ariellathelion@gmail.com>
To: Aria Howard

Hey, honey! How are things? Long time, no speak. I tried reaching out before, but I think my emails must be going into your spam. I was out with Marissa and Ana the other day and we bumped into Allegra. She was kind of weird with me. It hurt my feelings. We used to be so close. What's with that? Anyway, word on the street is that you're managing Lachlan Adair's members-only club in Scotland. That sounds fancy. I'm still the hospitality manager at Curiosity, but I'm so in the mood to get out of LA. How about it? Do you want to hire your old friend? It would be so great to spend time with you in Scotland! My new number is 213-555-3890. Call me, honey. I'm kind of losing patience, lol.
Ariella xoxoxoxo

· · ·

"What the actual fuck?" I muttered under my breath, indignation heating my skin. "How many times do I need to block your ass?" Along with my anger, I felt a familiar pang of unease. There were very few people in this world I disliked as much as I disliked Caitlyn "Ariella" Branch. I thought fleeing five thousand miles and ignoring all attempts at contact would send a clear and concise message. However, it was like she couldn't hear it. She was delusional. And was there something a little threatening in her tone here?

I hadn't seen Caitlyn's unstable behavior at first. Allegra had. I'd waved off my little sister's concerns. Until one night my blinders came off, and I realized Allegra was right about my clingy so-called friend.

"Ugh." I clicked on the email and blocked the new account she was using.

Trying to distract myself from the sudden churning in my gut, I pushed away from my desk. The PA of longtime member Angeline Potter, a British actor who was kind of annoying, had called to inform me that Angeline would arrive in two days' time for a three-day stay. Grabbing the list of treatments she wanted, I headed out the door to inform Wakefield and Mrs. Hutchinson. I felt like stretching my legs, so I planned on walking the five minutes to the spa building to have the team pencil Angeline in for her massage, hair, nails ... the list went on.

As I strode toward the staff quarters intent on finding Mrs. Hutchinson first to discuss Angeline's room for her stay, I spotted a housekeeper, Sarah McCulloch, coming out of the staff elevator struggling with two champagne buckets filled with empty beer bottles.

Sarah had worked at Ardnoch for seven years and was the granddaughter of local farmer Collum McCulloch. I knew from her payroll information she was thirty-one years old, but if I didn't know that, I'd think Sarah was only in her early twenties. Yes, she was young looking, but her painful shyness also made her seem younger than her years.

"Let me help." I hurried over, my heels clacking across the floor.

"Oh no, Ms. Howard, I have it." Sarah looked mortified by my offer of assistance.

I smiled at her. "I can carry a bucket." As the beer bottles clattered around in it, I frowned at the sight of the whisky bottle jammed in between them all. There were two whisky bottles in Sarah's. "Where did these come from?"

Sarah met my eyes briefly before looking ahead as we walked toward the housekeeping department. "Mr. Hunter left them and some empty food trays outside his room. Frannie told me she'd deal with the trays." She referred to her new housekeeping partner. After my good friend Sloane quit last week to pursue her bakery business dream, we reorganized the teams.

Irritation made my jaw clench. I took a minute and then calmly asked, "Has Mr. Hunter refused you entry to his room?"

"For over a week now." Sarah bit her lip, expression uncomfortable. "Mrs. Hutchinson isn't happy."

"I'd think not."

Two months. North Hunter had been hiding out at Ardnoch for two months since the story broke that he and his friends were responsible for the death of that homeless man all those years ago. In that time, Cara Rochdale dumped him over the scandal, giving weight to its veracity. Then he was dropped as the face of a well-known designer's brand. North's sexy ads for their cologne had driven a dramatic spike in sales, so that must have been a difficult decision for them. And, of course, the studio producing his upcoming spy thriller dropped him. I'd gotten a little info from my dad, who knew everyone in Hollywood, and apparently, the studio had paused the film. The script had been written specifically for North, and they were struggling to find a new male lead.

I wasn't sure North was aware of that information. I wasn't sure he was aware of anything but his self-pity. The man had been wallowing. At first, he'd left his room every day to attend the gym and/or swim. He'd hidden in his room during the New Year's Eve party, which I understood. Two weeks ago, however, he stopped leaving his room entirely. I'd kept an eye out and knew there was a lot of alcohol being sent up during this period too.

Enough was enough.

I didn't know if North had many friends beyond Theo Cavendish, but I knew from my research when I first reached out to his people that North was an orphan. He didn't have a family to flee to. He didn't have a family to kick his ass and drag him out of the dark hole of a pity party. The last person I wanted to be was the one yanking North from his misery, but we needed to clean his room. And he needed to return to his life.

I followed Sarah into the utility room and slid the bucket onto a counter. "Have you got this?"

"Of course, Ms. Howard. Thank you for your help." Her eyes held mine for once and I was surprised to realize they were a beautiful green. Not mossy green like mine but a striking jade green, clear and startlingly pretty.

"You're welcome." I gave her a kind smile, and her gaze lowered with shyness again. It was a shame she hid like that, but I knew a little something about wanting to hide.

Thoughts of Sarah disappeared as I hurried toward the secure room where we kept spare key cards. It was time to boot North Hunter out of the Bruce Suite. At least for a few hours so we could clean the place. I worried about what I'd find in there.

"Ms. Howard?" Walker Ironside stood slowly from the table of monitors. Another security guard accompanied him. "What can we do for you?"

Walker had joined Ardnoch a year ago when Brodan Adair, Lachlan's brother, retired from Hollywood. Walker had been his bodyguard. In that time, he'd fallen in love with Sloane, and only a few months ago he took a bullet to the gut trying to protect her from a man hired to kill her for the inheritance left by her father. It was a scandal still being discussed in the media. At six foot five, Walker was a rugged, intimidating specimen who worshipped Sloane and adored her daughter Callie. For that reason alone, he was kind of my favorite among the staff. But I'd never let that show. He was also stubborn and insisted on returning to work as soon as possible. I'd demanded he return to reduced duties only until he was fully healed. Sloane thanked me for that.

"I need the spare key card for the Bruce Suite."

Understanding crossed Walker's face. "Would you like me to accompany you? Perhaps I can talk to North?" So everyone knew the actor was holed up in there, huh? I guessed Walker felt he owed North for helping him stop Byron Hoffman from hurting Sloane all those months ago. However, I worried that the feeling of gratitude would make Walker too soft on the guy. North Hunter needed a firm hand in this.

"I can handle it," I promised him.

"Of that, I have no doubt." Walker's mouth curled at the corners. Before Sloane, I'd never seen the brooding Scot smile. Since her, he'd melted a little. The first time I saw him grin at Sloane, I nearly fainted with surprise ... and a small amount of envy. It must be spectacular to have someone love you so much that you change them for the better. Make their world a world worth smiling for.

Dismissing a pang of longing, I thanked Walker once he handed me the key and then I strode in the direction of the staff elevator. Determination rode that elevator with me.

The Bruce Suite was on the second floor and was one of our best rooms. Its windows faced the North Sea, and it comprised a large bedroom, a small sitting room with a writing desk beneath the window, and a luxurious en suite.

I dreaded to think what state it was in.

Attempting diplomacy, I knocked hard on the door. When no answer was forthcoming, I rang the doorbell. Not even a whisper of a footstep. I rang the doorbell again.

"Go away!" a belligerent male voice yelled from inside.

Charming.

"Mr. Hunter, it's Aria Howard. Please open the door."

No answer.

"Mr. Hunter!"

His muffled "Piss aff!" heated my skin with indignation.

I swiped the key card and strode inside, letting the door slowly shut behind me. Blinking against the dim light spilling in through the half-closed curtains, I allowed my eyes to adjust.

"Whit part eh piss aff dae ye no understand?"

My eyes moved over the unmade bed, the half-eaten sandwich molding on the bedside table, the clothes strewn everywhere ... to North. He was slumped in an armchair in the sitting room, a bottle of beer dangling from his fingers. He was also only wearing pajama trousers. They hung low on his hips as his legs sprawled out, and I noted the carved definition of his obliques. North didn't have massive broad shoulders and bulging biceps. But I was momentarily stunned to notice the hardest six-pack I'd ever seen in my life. The man looked sculpted from stone, not an inch of fat on him. Surprising, considering the amount of alcohol he'd consumed this week.

"Did ye jist come here tae leer at me?" He slurred his

words, his eyes low-lidded as he watched me like I was prey. His accent was so thick, I could barely understand him. But I understood enough.

The smell of stale beer and sweat filtered into my nostrils, and I grimaced. "I came here to ask you to vacate the room so we can clean it."

North scoffed. "Dae ye no mean so the wee maids can get in tae clean it? Ah doubt ye even wipe yer ain arse."

"Housekeepers, not maids," I answered stiffly, not responding to his last comment. Striding past the bed toward the window, I could feel him watching me as I reached for the curtains and drew them open in jerky, annoyed movements.

"Fuck!" he snarled, and I turned to see he'd dropped the beer bottle, which was thankfully empty. North covered his eyes. "Get oot ma room, ye she-divil!"

I smirked, taking malicious pleasure in his discomfort. "You are incredibly Scottish when you're drunk. Did you know that?"

He blinked rapidly, somehow scowling at the same time. "Ah'll gee ye incredibly fuckin' Scottish, ye pain in the utter arsehole. Gee a man some warnin' before ye burn his fuckin' retinas aff."

"It's called daylight." I swiped up clothes as I wandered around the musty space. "You should try walking around in it. Sober. But first, take a shower. You smell as bad as the room." Dumping his clothes at the door for housekeeping to collect, I said, "We'll wash and dry-clean these for you. Do you have anything to wear in the meantime?"

"Who needs clothes?"

I glanced back at the sullen purr in his voice. It wasn't anger in his eyes but something else. Tension stiffened my spine. "This isn't a nudist resort, Mr. Hunter. Clothes are a requirement."

"C'mon." He winked at me as he patted his abs. "Ah saw ye lookin'. Ye prefer me naked. Admit it."

Oh, dear God. "I'd shut up before you say something you regret."

"Maybe Ah'll shut up if ye shut up with me. If ye get ma drift." He winked.

"I'm going to pretend I don't."

"Because ye think am beneath ye?"

Surprised by the bitterness in his tone, I huffed. "Absolutely not. But I do think right now you're acting like a self-indulgent playboy wallowing in self-pity. Take a shower, get dressed, and go for a walk." I turned to stride toward his door but was startled at the sound of hard footsteps behind me. As I glanced over my shoulder, I saw North was almost upon me, and I spun to face him, eyebrows raised. Nervousness skittered down my spine, but I lifted my chin, not letting him think for one second he intimidated me.

Beer reeked from his pores, and I wrinkled my nose. Just how drunk was he?

North leaned into me, his face almost touching mine as he whispered harshly, "Huv ye always been sae coldhearted? Whit's the problem? Whit wid it take tae melt yer frigid fuckin' heart?"

Refusing to let him see his words hurt, I said sternly, "You stepping back might be a good place to start."

"Why? Afraid ye'd like whit ah could might make ye feel?"

A shiver cascaded around the curve of my breasts and between my legs. Furious that even when he was drunk I could be attracted to this asshole, I was rendered momentarily speechless. He seemed to understand my silence.

North cupped my hip, drawing me against him as he murmured silkily in my ear, "Ye wouldnae let me near ye wi' a barge pole, wid ye? Aria Howard, ice queen. Dae ye even like men?"

Angry with him, with myself, I stepped back, curled my hand into a fist, and punched it between his legs with as much force as I had in me.

North's knees buckled and his lips parted in an *O* of pained shock seconds before his eyes widened and he fell to the floor, holding himself. His expression turned mottled with agony as he nodded frantically, fell onto his back, and gasped, "Aye. Ah deserved that. Ah deserved it."

With one last look of disgust, I marched out of the room and walked straight into Theodore Cavendish.

"Mr. Cavendish." I nodded and moved to step aside.

Theo gestured to the now closed door. "Has he finally arisen?" he drawled in his incredibly posh British accent. Theo was an English screenwriter and director. He wrote and directed the TV show *King's Valley* that had launched North into superstardom. They'd both won awards for the show. Theo was also the second son of a viscount. Good-looking and urbane, I gathered most people found Cavendish charming. But there was an underlying hardness and superiority about him that made me wary. Very few people intimidated me, but Theo Cavendish was one of them. Not that I'd ever let it show. His friendship with North surprised me. They were from completely different backgrounds.

"Right now, he's on the floor clutching his balls." It was unprofessional of me, but I had no doubt North would tell Theo about the encounter, anyway. "Maybe you can get him to shower, sober up, and stop being such a cliché. I'm sending in housekeeping to clean his room in two hours, and if I have to, I'll send security with them."

Theo smirked but nodded.

"Oh ... and tell your friend that if he ever insults me again, I'll make sure his career isn't the only thing that's canceled this year." I swiped the door lock with my spare key card to let him into North's room.

Theo bit back a bark of laughter and tapped two fingers off his head in a salute before he pushed inside. Before the door closed, I heard him say, "Look at you, old boy. This is the most animated I've seen you in weeks."

"Ah think she broke ma fuckin' balls."

"Well, to be fair, you haven't been using them much lately." The door closed behind Theo just as an unexpected burst of laughter swelled in my throat.

Realizing I was struggling with a complex mix of pity, concern, annoyance, satisfaction, and amusement, I shrugged my shoulders, trying to shake it off. North's emotional state was none of my business, and beyond doing my job, I didn't want his world to affect mine.

THREE
NORTH

L et it blow over.

That's what my agent suggested.

To give it some time, stay at Ardnoch for a while, and let it blow over.

Yet it had been two months since the tabloids leaked that dreaded fucking story and it felt like at least a year. Why did it have to be that story? The one that raised ghosts and the guilt I had to work every day of my life to compartmentalize. I hadn't been doing a very good job with compartmentalizing lately. Instead, I'd drowned myself in alcohol.

Shame prickled my cheeks as freezing cold air surrounded me. It was a calm winter's day, the water lapping rhythmically at the shore as I stared out at the gray expanse of the North Sea. The sound slowly soothed my frayed nerves.

After Theo helped me off the floor of my room, I was so fucking ashamed of myself that I didn't dare go against Aria's orders. The things I'd said to the woman made my fists clench at my sides. It had taken ages for the throbbing to dissipate after her triumphant punch, but I welcomed the ache. I deserved it.

Theo had forced copious amounts of water down my throat, and then I showered. When I emerged, he'd laid out clothes for me, followed by a sandwich he goaded me to eat. Afterward, he slapped me on the back and said, "Go take a bracing walk, old boy. Let the staff in to clean this midden."

Now the sea called to me as I stood on the estate's private beach, isolated, a speck against the vastness before me.

Aria Howard was right. I'd spent the last few weeks wallowing in self-fucking-pity. She was also wrong. It wasn't just self-pity. Guilt had wrapped its hands around my throat, and I wasn't sure how to loosen its grip. But I couldn't go on like this.

Lying low didn't mean giving up, and that's what it seemed like I'd done.

My parents would be ashamed.

Of course, I didn't know that for sure. But I liked to think the parents I remembered would be the kind who gave a shit about my life choices.

Without thinking (and in hindsight, probably stupid when I wasn't totally sober), I stripped to my boxer briefs, feeling the icy air prickle over my skin. It cut through the numbness.

I marched into the water, feeling the dichotomy of the gentle tide pushing around my ankles and calves against the burning, needlelike sensation of its wintry temperature. Gasping, I allowed my body a minute to get used to it before I dove into its depths. It was black under there, and I popped back up to the surface and did the front crawl until I was a hundred yards or so from shore. The pull of the waves was stronger here, but in my regular life, I swam every day if I could. Even still, a week of eating very little and drinking a shit ton made my limbs lethargic. The burn in my muscles as I fought against the strength of the water was satisfying as I swam to shore and then back out again, doing laps until I felt completely awake but heavy with physical exertion. Knowing when tiredness would become a problem in a place as unpredictable as the sea, I swam toward shore and trudged out onto the beach.

My chest heaved as I strode over to my clothes. But the swim had been worth it.

I pulled on my T-shirt and jeans and took my phone out of the rear pocket.

Aye, I was stuck at Ardnoch for a while, but that didn't mean I couldn't do something with my time here. For example, getting my bloody career back. I shot off a text to my agent, Harry, asking if it was too soon to send out feelers for other parts. So I'd lost *Birdwatcher*. That didn't mean there wouldn't be other opportunities. I had to believe that I wasn't entirely canceled. My publicity team handled my social media, and they'd posted to my Instagram a statement I'd approved. It was a denial of the allegations the tabloids had made and a reiteration that no charges had been laid against me.

It made me feel like shit even though, rationally, I knew it was the truth.

My PR team suggested I go silent for a while, so they hadn't posted anything lately. After a quick look at the comment section of the statement, I decided not to look again. Diehard fans sent me love and offered their faith. But there was a lot of condemnation and disgust in the comments too. Someone had suggested I donate all my earnings to homeless charities. If only they knew I'd been donating a percentage of every payment I'd ever received since I'd started receiving wages to a charity in Scotland that fought for housing rights and helped house as many in need as they could. But I couldn't say that without looking like a prick or providing an admission of guilt.

Soul heavy, I trudged back toward the castle, shivering in my wet clothes. Just as I reached the main entrance, my phone buzzed in my back pocket. It was a reply from Harry.

Just keep holding tight. I'll be in touch.

Disappointment soured my gut alongside the remnants of the alcohol, and I typed out a quick *OK* and let myself into the building.

The grand reception hall was empty, though a fire crackled invitingly in the enormous fireplace at its center. Most of the members had left after New Year, which I was thankful for. Anytime I left my suite to go to the gym or pool, I was met with compassionate or curious looks that made my skin crawl.

Just as I was about to take the stairs to the second floor, I heard footsteps up ahead. Theo descended slowly toward me. "Fancy joining me for lunch? This script is fucking killing me, and I need a break."

"Writer's block?" I asked as we met.

My friend nodded, expression tight. "I need a scenery change." He took in my appearance. "Did you swim in the sea?"

"Aye. Let me change."

"You are insane." He turned to follow me back up. "You'd have been quicker asking me to throw several buckets of ice water over you, and I could have taken perverse pleasure in your discomfort."

I smirked as we ascended. Never in a million years would I think I'd be mates with someone like Cavendish. Second son of a viscount, his father and brother were members of White's, an exclusive centuries-old gentleman's club in St. James, London. King Charles and Prince William were members of the same club. Theo had grown up in a world so far removed from my own. Yet when I was cast in his show *King's Valley*, we'd gotten along and had remained friends since. Despite outward appearances, I got the distinct impression Theo disliked the society he was born into. I'd noted most of his acquaintances were from diverse backgrounds while few were from his own.

"Cold-water swimming is good for you. I already feel better."

He eyed me. "You do look less like you've spent months in a cave being buggered by a stalker."

I grinned even as I retorted, "How the fuck did I get canceled when you go around saying shit like that?"

"Because I'm a charming Englishman." He flashed me a humorless smile. "My accent makes everything less offensive."

Shaking my head, I reached to pull the key card out of my back pocket just as the door swung open and a housekeeper stumbled out of my suite and into me. She held a bundle of sheets in her arms, so she had no way to stop her momentum. I quickly caught her by the biceps and steadied her.

The blond blinked up at me with stunning jade eyes. She was quite beautiful. So much so, it shocked me I'd never noticed her before. She swallowed, staring up at me in embarrassed horror as her cheeks flushed the brightest red I'd ever seen. My eyes drifted over her and I noted her name tag.

Sarah.

"Sorry, so sorry," Sarah mumbled, lowering her eyes as she pulled out of my hold and moved to pass me.

Unfortunately, Theo was standing in her way. My friend gazed down at her with a sardonic expression, and I noticed her neck was flushed too. Sympathy filled me as she shimmied past him with a muttered apology, dumped the sheets on a trolley opposite the door, and darted away.

"Good God," Theo drawled as we strode into my now extremely clean and tidy suite. "I can't remember the last time I saw a grown woman blush like that. How mortifying."

At his mocking tone, I cut him a look. "Be kind."

"What?" Theo raised an eyebrow as he lounged in an armchair in the sitting room. "I just stated the obvious. If she can't deal with celebrity, she shouldn't be working in a place like this. I don't want to imagine my housekeeper getting her rocks off cleaning my room."

His arrogance irritated me. "I hate to break it to you, man, but no one outside the industry really knows who the fuck you are. You're just jealous because she blushed for me, not you."

"Jealous over that little mouse?" Theo sneered. "Please."

"Sometimes you're an utter arsehole, Theo," I said conversationally as I grabbed fresh clothes out of the chest of drawers.

"Tell me something I don't know."

Not long later, I left the bathroom showered, dried, and fully dressed. I half expected Theo to give me shit for making him wait while I showered again, but I found my friend waiting, scowling, with a sheet of paper folded between his fingers. He gestured with it and then turned to point at a pile of letters on the writing desk.

My mood soured.

"What the hell is this?" he demanded.

I snatched the letter out of his hand. "You're a nosy bastard, Cavendish. What? So bored with your own life, you need to get to the arsehole of mine?"

"Oh, fuck off, you insolent prick. I was looking for a pen." Theo stabbed a finger at the papers I was now pushing back into the drawer they'd been in. "I was joking about the stalker. Apparently, it isn't a joke. How long have you been receiving threats?"

"Years." I slammed the drawer shut and straightened. "They've been coming to my P.O. box since the first movie I was a lead in. Police can't do anything about it, and frankly think the threat is benign because I've had a few different ones over the years."

"These are clearly from the same person."

"Aye, I know. But I stopped looking at my fan mail years

ago until this happened. My management forwarded everything here for me to go through on my downtime." That was the word they'd used. *Downtime*.

What a joke.

"Is this why you were so eager for Ironside to work for you?"

I glanced back at the drawer. The truth was, I'd be lying if I said the threats didn't play on my mind. That they didn't bother me. Especially as it seemed they'd escalated this year. The author had gone from wishing bad things would happen to threatening to kill me. They were all typewritten in the same format, font, and font size but were usually only a few sentences. The last one read:

It isn't enough that they all know WHO YOU really ARE. I still want to see you DEAD DEAD DEAD.

Theo looked surprisingly concerned. "North—"

"It doesn't matter." I waved them off, not wanting to think about them. "I'm safe here."

"And when you return to the real world?"

"Why, Theo"—I patted him on the shoulder—"a person might think you cared."

He grimaced. "I'm just afraid if I spend any more time with you, I'll find myself in your stalker's crosshairs."

"Aye, aye, keep telling yourself that." I chuckled and strode toward the door. "Let's eat. I'm starving."

Thankfully, Theo didn't mention the threats again as we strode downstairs. Instead, I asked what was causing the block in his script and suggested he talk it over. Before I became an actor, I was convinced I'd be a musician. I'd borrowed guitars from the music room at school and spent hours composing songs and writing lyrics. Even now, I wrote songs in those previously sparse moments of free time. Maybe I should have one of my guitars shipped to Ardnoch.

Theo was describing the journey he wanted his leading

lady to take as we turned the corner toward the dining room and almost walked into Aria.

We halted as she drew up short.

Guilt from what I'd said earlier sat uneasily on my shoulders.

She pursed her lips as her gaze darted between us. "If you'll excuse me."

Theo made to move, but I didn't. I held up a palm to stop her. "About earlier ... I apologize for my behavior."

"Accepted," she replied coolly and moved to walk past me.

Irritated at her dismissal, I jabbed, "My balls are fine, though. Thanks for asking."

Aria flicked me a look beneath those thick dark lashes as her perfume tickled my senses. "I was surprised you had any to hurt."

I turned as she strolled away. "Charming as always, Ms. Howard."

She waved a manicured, ring-bedecked hand without looking back. "Enjoy lunch, gentlemen."

Aria was totally unaffected by me.

And I couldn't drag my eyes off her curvy arse as her hips swayed from side to side in her tight skirt. My skin felt too hot, my mouth dry.

"Yes." Theo stepped beside me. "She is rather luscious, that one, isn't she? Frigid around men, though. I'd bet my fortune she's gay."

Despite having implied the same thing earlier, Theo's words pissed me off. He would also lose that bet. I'd already googled the estate manager, and her last few relationships had been with male actors. "Just because Aria doesn't fall at your feet doesn't mean she's frigid or gay, Theodore."

He cut me a dark look for full-naming him. "No woman is immune to my charm unless they're gay. I'm a spectacular lover, and everyone knows it."

"That's because you've slept with everyone."

Theo narrowed his eyes. "Some of us don't attach feelings to the sexual act like infatuated teenage girls."

"I'm never fucking telling you anything ever again." I marched toward the dining room.

"Oh, don't be sore, old boy. Your serial monogamy is adorable. Really."

He was such a prick. "You're wrong about Aria." I changed the subject as a waiter stepped forward to lead us to a table.

"What? That she doesn't have a trail of gorgeous girl-friends in her past? God, there's fantastic masturbatory imagery."

Seeing the waiter flush at Theo's comment, I shot the young bloke an apologetic look.

"We'll have water for the table, with fresh-cut lime," Theo directed.

As soon as the boy left, I replied, "She doesn't have a trail of girlfriends in her past and if you even think about wanking off to her, I'll cut off your dick."

His grin widened. "Did you fuck her? Is that why she hates you?"

I wanted to punch *him* in the balls. Hard. "No."

"Shame." Theo perused the short menu the waiter had placed in front of him. "That woman needs a decent fucking. Maybe I should offer to bed her. Like I said, I've had no complaints."

Something like fury clawed at my gut, but my tone was quiet as I looked over the menu and warned, "Try anything with Aria Howard, Theo, and I'll break that pretty fucking face of yours."

Silence fell over the table and then my friend murmured silkily, "We are territorial, aren't we?"

I glared at him.

Theo chuckled and raised his palms in surrender. "I hereby promise to stay away from Aria Howard. And I'll even be a good friend and not press you about why you're so protective of a woman who punched your balls only a few hours ago."

Good.

Because I honestly wouldn't know how to answer that question.

FOUR
ARIA

Someone else could have gone to the main gates to receive the delivery. Wakefield. Jock. But no, I had to go. And Walker insisted on escorting me when he could have gone himself.

Why was I such a nosy parker when it came to North Hunter?

The delivery was for him and since he was still lying low, we'd agreed to sign the package. *I'd* agreed.

He was waiting up at the castle for it and ...

I should have just let Walker handle this.

Especially when the delivery guy passed over a large box with an item that shook around inside it. Jordan, one of our valets, hurried out of the castle to collect the package. I practically ran inside to get out of the cold after him and Walker and then halted at the sight of North hovering over the valet.

"Can we just unpack it here?" he asked Jordan. "Are you able to recycle the packaging for me?"

"Of course, Mr. Hunter," Jordan replied.

North studiously avoided my eyes as Walker produced a Swiss Army knife they could use to open the large box. My cheeks felt hot as North continued to ignore me. Asshole. Despite his apology, maybe he hadn't forgiven me for punching him in the junk.

To my shock, a leather guitar case came out of the box. While Jordan strode off to dispose of the packaging, North laid the carrying case down on the floor and kneeled to open it. His fingers stroked lovingly over the acoustic guitar inside.

"It's a guitar," I said inanely.

He pulled it out and plucked a few strings. "It's not just a guitar. It's a Builder's Edition Taylor."

"I didn't know you played." Walker echoed my thoughts.

The corner of North's mouth curled. "Few people do." With that, he patted the guitar and placed it gently back in the case.

Again, he didn't look at me.

He hadn't looked at me once.

Irritation warmed my blood as North stood with the case in hand, ready to depart for his room without a word. "I assume I don't need to tell you to keep the noise down with that thing. Our members don't pay for the privilege of listening to amateur music."

I regretted the comment as soon as I said it.

North finally turned, but it was only to glare at me like I was a slug before he stalked off, taking the stairs two at a time.

I could feel Walker's attention. Daring to glance at him, I almost winced at his penetrating stare. The man didn't need to say a word to make me feel bad for my unnecessarily mean comment. I already felt bad without his judgy eyes on me.

As if he knew that, Walker's expression flattened. "Still on for lunch Sunday?"

He referred to the lunch Sloane had invited me to at Walker's house. While Sloane rented a cottage in the middle of the village for her and Callie, I knew they'd been spending a lot of time at Walker's because it was bigger. I doubted it would be long before that man had his girls moved in with him. I was over the moon for Sloane. No one deserved happiness more. She was one of the few people in this world I trusted.

"Of course. I'll be there."

Ola Q's manager had a nasal, monotonous way of speaking that made it hard to concentrate. I waited for him to shut up about Ola Q's significance to the world, and cut in as soon as he took a breath. "I understand all that, Mr. Paulson, and that's exactly why we'd love to hire her to perform at our summer solstice party here at Ardnoch."

Ola Q was a sexy Australian pop star who'd had a tremendous year of global number one hits two years ago, and while fervor for her had died down a little, she was still a big enough star to make my event special. We hosted a Christmas party and extravagant New Year's Eve event at Ardnoch every year, and I felt like we were missing a trick during the summer. Summer was our busiest time, with most of Hollywood taking a break between June and September. As much as I hated parties, I felt we should host a special summer event for our members. Lachlan agreed, and I told him I'd take care of it.

"Ola has a gig in London that week."

"I know. Which is why it's perfect. We'll fly her up here if you'd like."

"I just don't think this kind of thing is her thing, you know."

He was lying. He wanted me to beg. To offer ludicrous amounts of money. Thankfully, when you had a business as successful as Ardnoch Members-Only Club, you could afford to pay people only what they were worth. "Oh, well, I understand. There are other performers who recognize what a singular opportunity it is to perform for the crème da le crème of Hollywood, so I'll bother you no more. Thank you for your time, Mr. Paulson, I appreciate it—"

"Well, wait there," he cut in flatly. "I should talk to Ola first."

A knock sounded on my office door seconds before it opened and Wakefield appeared. I held up a hand with a small smile as I spoke into my phone. "Oh, excellent. If you could respond to our request by the end of this week, that would be wonderful."

"Yeah, yeah, okay."

"Goodbye." I hung up before I had to listen to his toneless voice again. I noted Wakefield's bemused expression. "Problem?"

"Your sister has arrived unexpectedly," he announced. "She's coming up the driveway as we speak."

"What?" I practically screeched. Pushing my chair away from the desk, I hurried and followed Wakefield from the office. "How? When? What?"

"She just arrived at the gate with no explanation, I'm afraid."

What the hell was my baby sister doing in Scotland when she was supposed to be at her fancy-ass art school? Pulse racing with the anxiety that seemed to hit me whenever my family became part of my daily equation, I rushed out into the wintry day. Shivering, I watched the cab in the distance as it followed the gravel driveway through the manicured lawns toward us.

My sister Allegra had just turned nineteen and was supposed to be in attendance at Otis College in LA. Fear that she was on yet another downward spiral held me stiff as the cab drew closer.

Wakefield strode out to open the back passenger door and out popped Allegra. A rush of love and homesickness hit me at the sight of her, mixing with all my worries.

"Oh, don't look like that!" my little sister called as she

hurried over the gravel. "Everything's cool, I promise. Happy Valentine's Day!" She threw her arms around me before I could say a word. I returned her embrace, and thanked the universe that she was safe and here with me.

"You're okay?" I asked hoarsely.

"I promise," she repeated, squeezing and then pulling back to meet my gaze. Her eyes were as watery as mine. "Missed you, big sis."

Clasping her beautiful face in my hands, I pressed a kiss to her forehead. "Missed you, too, Ally."

She beamed like a little kid and hugged me tight again. I laughed and stroked her hair. "Come inside out of this arctic cold so you can tell me what the heck you're doing in Scotland."

MY SISTER HAD dark hair and the same olive skin we'd inherited from our mother, but that's where the similarities ended. Allegra was a few inches shorter than me, and while she was slighter than Mamma, she had the same overwhelming beauty that made me worry about her.

This world liked to use up beauty until there was nothing left.

Allegra sat in the breakfast nook of our family home on the estate, a mug of coffee between her hands. "It gets dark so early here," she noted, glancing out the window behind her.

After she arrived, I got her settled at the house and then promised I'd finish work early so we could talk. Valentine's Day was not a holiday we celebrated at Ardnoch unless we received individual requests from members. A few married couples had arrived at the estate for the long weekend, so I coordinated with the chef, housekeeping, and Wakefield to make sure their requests were ready for smooth execution. Then I returned to my baby sister.

Now here we were, with food the estate chef had prepped for me heating in the oven.

"Are we going to talk about sunset or are you going to tell me why you're here?" I'd returned to the house just as the sky darkened to find Allegra had made herself at home. Four pairs of shoes now sat at the front door. Her laptop was on the coffee table, her e-reader plugged in near the couch. The fireplace was roaring and there were crumbs all over the kitchen island.

I'd spent most of my day distracted and worried about why she'd come.

"Do Mamma and Dad know you're here?"

"Are you just going to fire question after question at me?" Allegra's large dark eyes glimmered with amusement, but I saw the weariness buried in them too.

"Ally."

She sighed heavily. "No, they don't know."

Our mother was staying in our New York apartment because she loved the city at this time of year. Dad was on the set of a movie in Vancouver.

It was my turn to exhale slowly. "So ... what brings you here without telling our parents?"

"Will you sit?" She patted the bench beside her. "I have something to show you."

Warily, I padded over in bare feet. The first thing I usually did upon arriving home was change out of my constricting pencil skirt and button-down shirt. But I'd been too impatient to talk to Allegra. I shimmied in beside her as she lifted her phone off the table and tapped the screen.

"I've been keeping a secret." Her voice trembled with nervousness, and I felt answering butterflies in my belly.

"Okay ..."

Allegra licked her lips and clutched her phone to her chest. Our eyes met and hers almost pleaded with me. "I created a social media account under an alias and started sharing art on it."

"Okay," I repeated.

"And the account kind of blew up." Her eyes widened. "Like, I've been selling my stuff online and making an absolute mint."

Surprise rocked me, along with pride and relief. "But ... that's amazing! Let me see."

My little sister seemed to deflate, her sweet smile slow but growing bigger by the second. Finally, she shoved her phone at me. I took it and scrolled through the feed of her alias, Lucy Stella.

"The name is a take on Italian for *starlight*," she explained. *Luce stellare.*

And I understood why when I saw her work. "Is this glass?"

"Yeah, and mixed media."

Awe filled me as I looked at piece after piece of the most exquisite glass art. She'd used paint, metallic foils, glitter, and precious stones on glass to create abstract pieces that shimmered and glimmered like pieces of the universe. "I want one," I said immediately. "I've been looking for a piece for the living room." Gesturing to a blank space near the entrance to the sitting room, I continued, "A framed piece of glass would look perfect there."

"Really?" Allegra bit her lip even as she grinned. "You like them?"

"Ally, how can you even ask?" I waved the phone at her. "This is extraordinary."

"Galleries in San Francisco and Seattle approached me."

More pride swelled. "I'm not even surprised."

"My larger pieces have sold for five grand."

My jaw dropped. "Are you kidding me?"

Allegra shook her head. "I'm making real money from my art, Ari. That's why I'm here. I ... you know your opinion means more to me than Mamma's or Daddy's. The whole point of art school was to learn how to do this—make a living from my art. And I'm already doing it. I want to quit school and concentrate on my art."

Anxiety suddenly crushed my swelling pride. "Oh. Oh, Ally ..." I handed back her phone. "Look, sweetie, it's amazing that you're doing so well and I'm so proud and in awe of you. Really."

Her expression fell as her eyes lowered. "But you don't think I can do this."

"No, not that." I gripped her free hand in mine and ducked my head so she'd have to meet my gaze. "Sweetie, art, in all its forms, can have a brief shelf life. Nothing goes through trends more than art."

"So you're saying people might not want my stuff in another six months?"

"No. I'm ... ugh, obviously I'm saying this all wrong. I just ... this beautiful glasswork could stay popular for a few months or years. No one knows, and that's my point. Art will be a career of ups and downs. Most people don't have careers like Dad. Look at Mom. She could only book particular kinds of jobs once she hit a certain age. Do you see what I'm saying?"

"Yeah." Allegra looked annoyed. "You're telling me something I already know. But whether I finish college, I'm going to be an artist, so I already know I'm looking at a career filled with peaks and valleys. What's the difference?"

"The difference is, if you graduate from a college like Otis, you could apply for more stable positions within the art world if you need to."

My sister looked at me as if I was naive. "What stable positions? Ari, I don't intend to do anything but be an artist."

I knew that.

And a part of me understood what she was saying. But the risk-averse side of me wanted my kid sister to finish college. Seeing me waver, Allegra pushed, "I want to travel and be inspired. Being here only a day has my mind whirring with ideas. I saw all this beautiful purple heather on the drive over, and I'm desperate to go out and pick some and incorporate it into the glass."

"Right, but—"

"And I hate LA."

I shut my mouth.

"Everyone at school seems so young. Like, they think they're worldly, but I listen to them drone on about things they don't even understand and they're so privileged and immature. All they care about is how strangers view them. We go out to eat and I can't even dig into my burger because they're all snapping photos of the food for five fucking minutes. We go out for a drive and a picnic on the beach, and no one's experiencing it because they're too busy setting up the perfect shots for their social media. It makes me want to scream. And I know that sounds crazy coming from me because I know who we are. I know I'm privileged. But I don't feel young, Ari. I feel old. And tired. And lonely. And I don't want to feel like that. Getting on the plane to come here is the most excited I've felt in months."

Well ... shit.

What could I say to that? I hated LA, too, for many of the same reasons.

"Okay. You can stay for a week or two until we figure this out."

Joy flooded her face. "Really?"

"Yes. But no promises," I warned her. "Mamma and Dad need to know about this, and I don't know what they'll say."

Allegra threw her arms around me, hugging so tight she

almost choked me. "Thank you for always being there for me. And for being my Valentine this year."

I smoothed a reassuring hand down her back, already dreading the conversation we needed to have with our parents. I didn't let her see that, though. "Happy Valentine's Day, Ally. No one I'd rather spend this miserable holiday with."

She chuckled and tightened her embrace. "Me neither."

FIVE
NORTH

"I'm like this discarded bottle of whisky," I sang under my breath as I strummed my guitar, "worthless now that it's empty. And you can't get drunk on this guy everyone thought they knew …" My last strum echoed through the room as I stared at the notepad in front of me. Humming the music I'd just written, I grabbed the pen off the bed and scribbled "Instead you should run for your life before they empty you too."

I replayed the verse I'd just written, the sound heavily inspired by the country music my parents had loved. We'd only had seven years together, but I remembered things from the early parts of my childhood I imagined other people didn't.

Over an hour in, my neck was tight from the way I'd been sitting, so I rested my Taylor on the bed and rubbed at the spot. Early winter light poured in through the room. I'd tried to keep my playing low, even though I knew for a fact I didn't have a neighbor on either side of me. The club was quiet. Even Theo left yesterday, off to guest direct a few episodes of a popular new streaming show. Despite being an arsehole some-times, I was friends with Cavendish because, underneath his droll wit, he gave a shit about the people he allowed into his inner circle. He'd never admit it, of course. Having someone around who didn't judge or throw me pitying looks helped bring me out of the pit of depression.

Now that he was gone, I was relying on music to do that.

And the gym.

With that thought in mind, I threw some gym clothes and a towel into a bag and made my way downstairs to a side exit. One of my favorite things about this place was the state-of-the-art gym. It was housed in a larch-clad building a five-minute walk from the castle. Next to it was a spa and salon, and I contemplated walking in after my workout to see if they had a spot open for a massage. Might as well take advantage of everything I could at the club, because if my career didn't pick up, I might not be able to afford to stay. Which would be a crying shame since I'd already dropped forty grand just on the club joining fee. From there I paid a smaller annual fee, but I also paid for my accommodation, like I would at a hotel. The annual fee covered the exclusivity, privacy, security, food, drink, and all the facilities but not accommodation fees. Though Lachlan had authorized to give me a discount for my prolonged stay, it was still costing me a fortune to live at the castle.

This was why some members had purchased property on the estate. I'd thought it a ludicrous idea, considering we wouldn't even own the land our home was on, but I hadn't expected to need a safe haven.

I poured all my worries into working out. One of the gym's personal trainers spotted me while I did some weight training first. If this scandal did eventually blow over, I wanted to be in peak condition for the next job. That's the mindset I needed to have. Things were going to turn around for me. There was no other option.

Moving on from the weights, I did a ten-minute sprint on

the rower, then moved on to the running machine. My eyes were on the TV screen above me, watching what seemed to be a replay of last November's game between Celtic and Motherwell. Growing up in Falkirk, I was loyal to my home team, but they didn't play in the Scottish Premiership. They were League One. Celtic was my team in the premiership. Nostalgia hit as I watched them. It had been years since I'd paid any attention to the sport, and yet as a young lad, I'd dreamed of being the next Ronaldinho.

"I don't understand the fascination with soccer."

I startled, catching myself before I faltered on the treadmill as I looked to my left. A young woman I hadn't even been aware of getting on the machine next to me gave me a cheeky smile. I flashed her a grin. "It's called football."

Despite her large brown eyes and smaller build, she looked too much like Aria Howard not to be related. Her dark hair swung in a ponytail as she ran alongside me. "Soccer, football, tomato, tomahto. I liked your TV show," she announced abruptly and with familiarity. As if we knew each other. "It's absolute bullshit what the industry is putting you through. We've all turned into spineless assholes, afraid to stand up for each other in case we get canceled too." Her eyes widened. "Not that you've been canceled."

Though her words stung, her friendly rambling amused me. "I might have been canceled." I returned my attention to the television. Sweat slid down my back beneath my shirt, and I welcomed the burn in my thighs and calves. "You don't believe I killed a man?"

"I don't know, did you?"

I cut her a dark look. "I didn't."

"Yeah, despite being scarily good at the sociopath role, you don't look the type."

I snorted.

"I'm Allegra Howard, by the way."

"Aria's sister?"

"The very one. You wouldn't know it since she's a sexy badass and I'm ... me ... but yeah, she's my big sister."

Hearing the pride in her voice, I wondered at the differences between them. Perhaps it was Allegra's youth, but she seemed a lot warmer and friendlier than her sister. "Just visiting, then?"

She nodded as she jogged at a far more sedate pace than me. "Taking a break to figure things out, you know."

"Oh aye, more than I'd like to."

Understanding crossed her pretty features. "It'll get better," she promised me. "You're too talented for this shit to last long."

She was very different from her sister. "Thanks."

"I only speak the truth." Allegra beamed. "Even when you were in—"

"Ally!"

Both of us looked sharply toward the voice that cut through the gym. My already pounding heart seemed to race a little harder at the sight of Aria strutting across the quiet space toward us. I hit the speed button on the treadmill and slowed to a stop as the woman approached.

Every day she wore a calf-length tight skirt with a shirt tucked into it. The skirt accentuated the voluptuous curves of her hips and fantastic arse, while her shirt buttons always seemed to strain a little across her impressive tits. If her body wasn't appealing enough, she genuinely had one of the most beautiful faces I'd ever seen.

Now, I liked to think I wasn't a shallow man. Aye, all my previous girlfriends would be considered conventionally pretty. But I'd been attracted to their personalities too.

This attraction to Aria Howard was driving me crazy because she was a termagant shrew.

Case in point: glaring at me ferociously as she stopped in

front of our machines. Like I was contaminating her precious baby sister just by being near her.

"She's nineteen," Aria seethed.

Hot indignation boiled my blood. "Meaning?"

"You know what I mean." She crossed her arms over her chest.

"For fear of being kicked out, I'm going to refrain from telling you to do something to yourself. I'll give you a hint, though, it's not 'go *luck* yourself,' but close."

Allegra choked on a shocked snort.

Aria's gorgeous eyes narrowed. "Say it for real," she taunted. "Go on. I dare you."

"Oh, whoa, okay." Allegra stopped her machine and jumped off. "*I* started talking to *him*, Ari. *Talking*. That's it."

Aria cut her an impatient look before turning back to me. "I'm here at your disposal, Mr. Hunter." Her tone suggested the complete opposite. "What exactly is it you really want to say to me?"

What the hell was this woman's problem? Yes, okay, I had been offensive when she came into my suite when I was drunk, but I assumed her punching me in the balls had cleared the air between us. But no. She was still being a harpy every chance she got. "I wonder, do you treat all the members to this delightfully caustic attitude?"

Uneasiness flickered over her face as she dropped her arms and straightened. "I am just protecting my sister, Mr. Hunter."

"From *me*?"

I saw the moment she remembered I'd helped save her friend from that arsehole Byron Hoffman. Something like shame glimmered in her eyes, but it was gone in an instant as she tilted her chin in defiance. "She's my little sister."

Like that excused her behavior. "Was it your little sister when my guitar arrived?"

"Well, I—"

"Or when we met? Or all the times in between when you've treated me like shite on your shoe?"

"I do not." Aria glared up at me. "You're just sensitive."

"*I'm* sensitive." I leaned over the top of the treadmill, enraged now. "Better to be sensitive than to be so zipped up the back I can't feel regular emotions."

Her lips parted in outrage. "Are you saying I'm unfeeling?"

"If the shoe fits, sweetheart."

"Don't call me sweetheart."

"My mistake. Spock."

"Well, actually, Spock had feelings," Allegra threw in.

"Very true," I agreed and turned back to Aria. "Agent Smith."

She scowled at me. "Agent Smith?"

"*The Matrix*."

"You're a child."

"That's exactly what he'd say."

Aria's hands clenched into fists at her sides, her knuckles turning white, and I took a perverse pleasure that she couldn't hide how much I annoyed her.

"I don't have time for this nonsense." She gestured to her sister. "Get your butt out of this gym while he's in here."

Genuine anger filled me. "I resent the implication, Aria."

Perhaps it was my use of her name, but she stiffened. "I didn't mean it that way. I don't want my sister bothering my guests."

"Oh, so now I'm a guest?"

She sucked in a breath like I was fraying her patience, and I tried not to smile. Cutting her sister a look, she ordered, "Finish up in here. Now." And with that, she marched out of the gym without looking back.

Feeling Allegra's gaze, I turned my eyes from her retreating sister to her. She grinned mischievously at me, and my lips twitched. "What?"

"What the hell did you do to her?"

"Me? Nothing."

"Well, she's usually the epitome of professional and cordial with the club members."

"Her? Cordial?"

Allegra nodded, still grinning like a madwoman. "You pissed her off, didn't you?"

Jumping off the machine, I decided I was done for the day. "By breathing, sweetheart. I pissed her off merely by breathing."

"Uh-huh." She didn't look convinced, but I wasn't about to protest my innocence. "Seriously. What did you do to her?"

Swiping my towel and water bottle from the floor, I strode past her and said, "If you find out, let me know."

I attempted to brush off the encounter with Aria as I showered and changed back into my regular clothes. Still, her comments played around and around in my head, driving me to distraction. What was it about that bloody woman?

Thankfully, a better distraction came in the form of Harry.

As I walked back to the castle in the cold, my phone rang and my agent's name appeared on the screen. The urge to answer it was real, but I forced myself to let it ring a few times before I picked up. Thankfully, I didn't sound desperate when I did.

After we exchanged pleasantries, Harry got down to it. "Here's the situation: The studio is in contention with Blake and Lisa over you." Blake Forster, the director, and Lisa Helman who'd written the script. "Lisa wrote this part with you in mind."

Shock halted me. "I didn't know that. She never said."

"Well, she probably wanted to keep your ego in check. But

she sold the idea of you as the leading man to Blake when he came on board, and neither of them can see the movie without you in it. But the studio is looking at the response online from the public and thinks you're a bad investment right now."

I flinched.

"However, the fact that there's no movement here is a good thing. I think we need to hang tight a little longer and hope the studio will see that this was just a blip and it'll all blow over." He exhaled slowly, as if hesitant to say the next part. "It would help if we could maybe get you on a talk show or do a serious interview with a big media outlet where we get the full story from the horse's mouth."

At the thought of sharing that part of my life with the world, a terrifying tightness squeezed my chest. "I'm not ready for that," I bit out.

"But you'll think about it?" Harry pressed.

I promised him I would.

But we both knew it was a goddamn lie.

Six

ARIA

As I swung the BMW X7 out onto the main road toward Ardnoch, I waved in my wing mirror to Jamie, the guard on duty at the staff entrance, then focused on the road ahead.

"Look at you driving on the wrong side of the road on the other side of the car," Allegra teased, her eyes wide with admiration. "Seriously. And in an SUV, no less."

I grinned at her playfulness. We'd decided to give ourselves a week before we called our parents about the art school situation, and I'd never seen my little sister so happy and relaxed as these last few days. "What do you mean?"

"Back in LA, you drove convertibles."

"True." I chuckled. "Convertibles are for LA. SUVs are for the Highlands."

"Well, you're a badass. Does it not get confusing driving here? There are a ton of traffic circles."

"They call them roundabouts. And you get used to them."

"When you're scarily adept like you?"

I snorted. "Scarily adept?"

"Your ability to learn something new within minutes is scary, yes."

Shaking my head at her teasing, I asked, "Are you looking forward to seeing Sloane?"

"Very much." Allegra nodded as she stared at the passing trees. "So, now that I have you trapped in a car, maybe you can tell me why you acted uncharacteristically immature to North Hunter?"

My back stiffened. I knew it. I'd thought it was weird she hadn't mentioned the encounter in the gym yesterday. She'd been biding her time for the right opportunity. Sneaky girl. "I don't know what you're talking about." Yesterday was the first day of my period, and seeing him flirt with my baby sister ignited my menstrual wrath. The first two days of my period, my cramps were always so bad and I was always so tired, which led to impatience and snippiness. I did my very best to rein it in and not infect people with my bad mood. Sometimes I didn't succeed, which would lead to self-flagellation of the worst kind.

"You were pretty mean to him."

"First day of my period," I explained.

"Okay, that might account for your impatience, but there's something else going on with you and this guy. The air between you practically crackled. Did you sleep with him?"

"No!" I objected loudly. "With that man-child? Puhlease. He's just like every other so-called charismatic, charming actor we've ever met. It's all lies and bullshit and you never know what they're really thinking because they're so good at pretending."

Allegra huffed. "Uh, North was none of those things to you."

"He was at first. Believe me. He tried to be all smoldering and sexy the first time we met, and he was dating Cara Rochdale. She probably didn't even dump him because of the scandal. I bet she found out he'd cheated on her a million times."

"Hmm."

"What?" I threw her a dark look as I pulled my SUV into the parking lot outside the Gloaming.

"I just think you're making a lot of assumptions about the guy based on ... what? Your experience with Preston? Your horrible experience with Lucas? North Hunter isn't Lucas."

Heat scored up my neck at the mere mention of his name. "Don't talk about him." Before she could respond, I practically jumped out of the car.

Allegra hurried to follow me, and I locked the car as I strutted down the street toward the cobbled lane that housed the florist. Usually, I'd buy wine from William's Wine Cellar, but Allegra was sober.

"I'm sorry for pushing." My sister fell into step beside me. "I just worry about you. I don't want you to be lonely."

Softening, I wrapped an arm around her shoulders and ducked my head to hers as I pulled her into my side. "You don't need to worry about me ever. I'm—oof." I stumbled with my sister as my other shoulder bumped into something.

A female voice cried out, and we turned to see an older woman clutching her forehead as bags of groceries spilled onto the ground. She was a tiny woman, and I realized I'd walked into her head with my shoulder because I wasn't looking where I was going.

"I'm so sorry." I kneeled in my jeans and began gathering her groceries into her bags. Allegra scrambled to help me.

"Och, it's awright." The woman assured me. "It happens."

Once we'd gotten her shopping back in the bags, I offered to help her to her car.

"Ahm stayin' in a wee flat 'roond the core-ner." She brushed me off. I wasn't familiar with all the villagers yet because I spent so much time on the estate, but I didn't recognize her roughened face. She had the kind of skin that spoke of a hard life. And she didn't sound like she was from around here. In fact, her accent made me think of North and his strong brogue when he was drunk. When I googled him, I discovered he'd grown up in a town I'd never heard of set between Glasgow and Edinburgh.

Ugh.

Why did everything make me think of that damn man?

Assured the woman was okay, Allegra and I continued on toward the florist.

"You're distracted," Allegra said in a singsong voice. "I wonder by what or whom."

"Don't push me on this, dear sister."

"I think the lady doth protest too much."

"I think the lady doth better shut up before she gets my foot in her ass."

Allegra burst into delighted laughter, and I couldn't stay annoyed with her. If anyone wanted to know what my weak spot was, they could look no further than my baby sister. I was worried about telling my parents of her desire to drop out of college, but I was even more worried about forcing her to stay on a path she didn't want. Problem was, as much as I loved her, my sister could be a little spoiled and impulsive. Was dropping out just another spur-of-the-moment idea, or was she serious about how unhappy she was there?

The last time Allegra was miserable, we almost lost her. She was on the honor roll, had offers to attend some of the finest art schools in the country, and yet she was a chaotic ball of teenage emotions and anger. It was a testament to her intelligence, talent, and multitasking ability that the crap she'd gotten into at sixteen hadn't derailed her education.

At first, she partied with an older Malibu crowd, and that was worrying enough. But then she started partying with a rougher crowd, which led her to drinking and experimenting with drugs. When it all came to a head the night she met Sloane, we tried to get her to explain what had sent her down this path. She wouldn't tell us. However, that night with Sloane terrified her back onto a better road. Allegra had started seeing Sloane's ex-boyfriend, who just happened to be a high-ranking "soldier" in a criminal gang that traded in drugs and chopped cars.

The night Sloane went to a house party looking to talk to her ex (he was the father of her child), she found Allegra in a room with him. An argument ensued. He tried to assault my sister, and Sloane helped fight him off. Allegra grabbed his gun and accidentally shot Sloane, and he started beating Allegra to death for it. If Sloane hadn't gotten a hold of the gun, shot him, and then rushed my sister to safety (all with a bullet hole in her arm), I don't know what might have happened. I did know that same psychopath was rotting in jail, awaiting trial for kidnapping his own daughter, kidnapping Sloane, and attempting to murder her.

My family will be forever grateful to Sloane for saving Allegra. That's how she got the job as a housekeeper at Ardnoch, and my father arranged a skilled worker's visa for her so she could stay in the Highlands for at least five years. Now that she was madly in love with Walker, I couldn't see her and Callie ever leaving Scotland.

As for Allegra, she still hadn't told me what set off the wild partying and uncharacteristic anger. I worried every day that it was something traumatic, but I didn't want to push her. Instead, I was grateful that the scare with Sloane and her ex got her into rehab, where she talked with a therapist every day. She still had a therapist now. And she seemed better. Wearier, a little more worldly wise than I'd like, but happier. Nowhere near as angry.

Ten minutes later, as Sloane and Walker let us into Walker's bungalow, I noted Sloane's relief to see Allegra looking so well and happy.

"Oh my God, you're getting so big!" Allegra exclaimed when she saw Callie.

"I'll be eleven this year," Callie announced proudly. "Next year I start high school."

Allegra's eyes rounded. "Are you some kind of genius?"

Sloane chuckled as she tucked Callie against her front. "They start high school earlier here."

"But I'm still kind of a genius, right?" Callie grinned cheekily up at her mother.

We chuckled as Sloane agreed she was.

"Look at this place." Allegra surveyed Walker's bungalow. The living room flowed into a beautiful, modern kitchen. "Nice. Kind of masculine, but nice. You need to put your stamp on it, girl."

"Allegra," I chastised with a snort of laughter.

"What?" She winked at Walker. "Walker knows what I'm talking about."

Amusement gleamed in Walker's eyes, but he didn't smile.

A flush brightened Sloane's cheeks, and she looked slightly flustered by my sister's implication that she and Walker should move in together. "Okay, who's ready to eat?"

If we weren't ready, it would be a shame because Sloane had laid out a buffet in the kitchen.

Taking in the array of delicious finger sandwiches, pastries, vol-au-vents, cakes, chips, dips, and salad, I cracked, "Are we expecting more people?"

Sloane grinned sheepishly. "I might have gotten a little carried away. Come on, dig in."

Soon we were all seated around Walker's dining table, Allegra, Callie, and Sloane doing most of the talking as Walker and I listened and added commentary when required. It didn't surprise me that Allegra confessed to Sloane about her art alias and showed off her work to her. She seemed to trust Sloane in the same way I'd grown to believe she was one of the few people who could truly be trusted. I'd add Walker and Lachlan Adair to that list too.

Sloane oohed and aahed over Allegra's art and seemed as genuinely impressed as I was. "So what does this mean?"

Allegra glanced at me. "We're going to talk to our parents about me dropping out of art college."

"Is that wise?" Walker asked quietly.

"I don't know," my sister *wisely* answered. "I just know I'm not happy in LA."

"Seems to be a family trait." Sloane smiled sympathetically at me. She knew I would be worrying my ass off about Allegra's decision.

"I don't want her to stay somewhere she's not happy," I admitted.

"Though I don't think I could stay here full time," Allegra said after swallowing a bite of cupcake. "But only because I'd get fat on your baking."

"You could just not eat my baking."

I huffed because I'd lived with Sloane and Callie for a few weeks and put on about ten pounds from all the delicious baked goods she left lying around.

Sloane grinned mischievously because she knew exactly what I was thinking. Allegra watched the silent exchange and announced, "I'm so glad you guys have become friends." She patted Sloane's arm. "Between you and me, I worry about Aria here."

Irritation cut through my contentment. "Ally," I warned.

"What?" She raised an eyebrow. "You're allowed to worry about me, but I'm not allowed to worry about you? I'm just saying, I'm glad you've made a friend here."

"Oh my God, I'm not in first grade."

"Speaking of friends, how is North doing?" Sloane swiftly changed the subject. To the wrong one.

I groaned inwardly.

"North?" Allegra's ears perked up like a puppy hearing the word *treat*. "What about North?"

Sloane gestured to Walker. "Walk and North have become quite friendly. As friendly as macho men can become," she teased. Her boyfriend barely reacted as he popped a mini choux pastry into his mouth. "But he's kind of holed himself up in that castle for the past few weeks."

"Months. Past few months," I corrected.

"Did he really hurt someone?" Callie suddenly asked, wide-eyed. "That's what they're saying at school."

It horrified me that ten-year-olds were gossiping about this stuff.

"No," Walker assured her. "He's a good man."

"You believe that?" Allegra asked.

"Absolutely."

Walker's conviction in North's goodness only raised my hackles. And maybe a little guilt.

"A good man." Allegra stared pointedly at me. "Imagine that."

"Though I'd like to know what he did to upset you?" Walker directed his question my way. I got the feeling he wasn't accusing me. Instead, I sensed the question came from a place of protectiveness.

What *had* North done to upset me?

Truthfully? Nothing.

His only crime was to remind me too much of the men who had hurt me.

I'd been horrible to him. Looking down at my empty plate, the plate Mamma would have taken away three sandwiches ago, I answered stiffly, "Nothing. He's done nothing wrong."

ALLEGRA WAS quiet in the car as if she knew I'd locked myself inside my head. Distracted, I barely remembered the drive back to the estate and to our house. It wasn't until we'd let ourselves inside the warm home and kicked off our shoes that Allegra spoke, offering to make herbal tea.

I lit the fire and settled down on the plush corner sofa, the view of the sea already masked by the dark sky outside. A few minutes later, Allegra brought me a steaming mug and curled up next to me. Pleasant silence fell between us. You couldn't hear the waves outside unless you opened a window because my father had the house built with the best materials to withstand its coastal position. That included triple glazing and self-cleaning glass.

"I didn't mean to embarrass you at Sloane and Walker's."

I looked at my sister. "You didn't."

She winced. "I think I did, and I'm sorry. I just ... I was so relieved to see you and Sloane had grown closer. That you're letting yourself trust someone. After what Lucas and Caitlyn did, I was afraid you'd stop trusting *everyone*."

The urge to change the subject was real, but that would only make Allegra worry more. Plus, I didn't want my sister to think I didn't trust *her*. "It wasn't just Lucas and Caitlyn. It's been a long stream of people using me for who Dad is and betraying me when they don't get what they want." I stared at my sister. She looked so young, huddled up on the couch. "I don't want that to happen to you. I want people to see you and not our father's name. Maybe getting out of LA is really what's best for you. I'll tell Mamma and Dad that, too, I promise. You know you could go places and not need to tell people who you are until you trust them. You could have a sense of anonymity outside of California."

Allegra nodded, expression grim. "That's the price of our

privilege. I have to hide who I am from people until I can trust that they're hanging around because they like me for me. And you ... you learned that lesson for me, so I don't have to. But now you have so many walls up, it's a miracle you're friends with Sloane."

I didn't know how to respond because she spoke the truth. A lot of truth.

"And what about men, Aria?" Allegra pushed. "Are you going to spend the rest of your life pushing guys like North away because you're afraid to be hurt?"

"What is your obsession with this guy?" I huffed.

"Your reaction to him. There are plenty of guys who come through those castle doors who are flirty, charming, cocky actors, and I bet you don't speak to any of them the way you speak to North."

I tried not to show in my expression that she was right.

She still seemed to know she was right, anyway, because a smugness glinted in her eyes.

Irritated, I blurted, "You don't understand. It wasn't just one guy, Allegra. It has been almost every man I let myself get close to. They've betrayed me, one after the other. Do you know what that's like?" Tears burned as the buried hurt tried to uncover itself. "If our mother didn't do a good enough job of shredding my self-esteem, those guys finished her work. And it hurts too fucking much to keep letting them in. So yes, I would rather be alone than feel every day the way they made me feel."

Allegra's eyes grew shiny and round with emotion. "I want to kill them all. And I want to shake Mamma so badly for all the things she's said to make you not like yourself. Because you're, like, the best person ever. I'd give everything to be you, Ari. I wish you could see yourself how I see you. And I won't stand by and let these assholes ruin your future. All you do is work. You've isolated yourself. Sure, it's a beautiful place. But you're lonely, Ari. I won't let you wither away. I'm going to force you to be brave and truly live again."

I blinked in surprise at her passionate speech. Love for her filled me until I felt like I might burst with it. And it was enough. To have her affection and admiration was enough. Shimmying along the couch, I wrapped my arm around her and she snuggled into me, resting her head on my shoulder like she used to as a kid. "You, my sweet girl, are going to stop worrying about me because I'm fine. Let's just focus on you and your future."

Allegra didn't protest.

So I stupidly assumed that meant she agreed.

SEVEN
NORTH

I f something didn't change soon, I was afraid I might lose my mind.

The hiding had begun to feel more like imprisonment. Sure, nicest prison in the world if so, but Ardnoch's walls were closing in on me.

I needed something different to happen.

Preferably for my career to come back.

Shipping my guitar from my apartment had only helped for a bit. The feeling of restlessness and lack of productivity was making me so bloody angsty. And I couldn't bear to think about how abandoned I felt by this thing—acting—that had brought me so much joy.

My pen swept over the page as I committed these feelings to paper. When I was thirteen, after what happened with Gil MacDonald, a child therapist had suggested I write everything down. For a boy who had been hoarding his anger and pain since he was seven years old, the act of unleashing at the end of every day into a journal was shockingly helpful. It was a way for me to voice everything I bottled up but where it was still safe. Where I only had to be vulnerable with myself.

I didn't grow up in a very forward-thinking area. Boys didn't talk about their feelings. We just took the piss out of each other and if it all boiled to a head, it usually ended in a brawl. There was always one arsehole who brought a knife to the fight, though, and I'd had a few lucky escapes.

By the time I was fourteen, however, between what happened to Gil, talk therapy, and my newfound self-therapy in journaling, I was a different wee boy. I moved to a better foster family in a village west of Falkirk and started a new school where I could reinvent myself. I studied harder and by chance fell into acting when my girlfriend, Donna (who I fancied myself in love with at the time), begged me to join the local youth theater with her. If my mates from my old life had seen me, they would have kicked the utter shit out of me. And at first, the acting classes were mortifying. But it turned out, I was a natural.

Somehow, I just knew how to channel all my young angst and trauma into my performances. Ms. Anderson, our director, mentored and sent me off for auditions. I starred in a couple of local TV ads, and I landed a few episodes of a Scottish soap. Between that, my theater work, and my grades, I could audition for the Royal Conservatoire of Scotland. It's one of the top performing art schools in the world. And to my awe, I got in.

Because I was eighteen with no financial aid from a parent, they even provided a scholarship and bursaries to help with the fees. I worked my arse off to get my BA in acting, and I was a working actor during my studies there. While performing at the school, an American producer saw me and asked me to audition for her upcoming rom-com. I had to do it with an American accent, and I got the part. From there, I landed a stream of rom-coms until I grew worried I was being typecast. Most of the world didn't even know I was Scottish. It used to surprise the hell out of talk show hosts.

But I did that.

I clawed my way out of poverty. I was a discarded child. And I shattered what should have been my fate and gave everything to my pursuit of betterment.

Now the world wanted to take it away from me.

How fucking dare it.

I whipped the journal across the bed and braced my head in my hands.

I needed something to change.

An abrupt hammering on my suite door brought my head up. Reaching for my phone, I saw it was nearly midnight. What the hell?

"North, you in there?"

The female voice was familiar.

Hurrying across the room, I threw open the door to find Allegra Howard standing in the hall. "Something wrong?"

She gave me a pained smile. "Sorry to disturb you at this hour, but Aria sent me to get you."

Worry scored through me. "Is she okay?"

Her eyes rounded. "I'm not sure. She just asked me to come get you. She said she really needs to talk to you."

What? I scowled. "At midnight?"

Allegra shrugged. "That's all she told me."

Finding it all a bit strange, my guard was up. But my curiosity was also pricked. What if she needed to cancel my membership? And to save face, they were booting me off the estate in the middle of the night, so there were no witnesses to my humiliation. Bloody great. That would be the icing on the worst fucking cake. Well, if so, I wanted my goddamn membership fee back.

"One second." I closed the door on Aria's sister and impatiently shoved on socks and shoes and grabbed my key card.

Allegra seemed to sigh in relief when I reopened the door,

her eyes darting over my body. But not as if she were checking me out. "You didn't bring your phone, did you?"

"No, why?"

"Aria has some ... privacy issues."

"Among many others," I muttered as we walked down the hall.

"I heard that."

I chuckled darkly. "I meant for you to hear it. So, why is Her Majesty commanding me to meet her in her office at midnight?"

"Oh, not her office. She asked me to bring you to the library." Allegra stared up at me, wide-eyed and confused. "And like I said, I'm as clueless as you are. In fact, I'm kind of worried."

What on earth?

Tension settled between us as my concern grew. Allegra seemed anxious. If I had any dignity, I'd tell the sisters where to stuff their cloak-and-dagger games, but honestly, I was bored out of my mind. I'd probably have agreed to listen to one of them read from Proust's *Remembrance of Things Past* at this point.

The castle was eerily quiet. Last summer, it buzzed nightly until one in the morning, but there were fewer guests this month and as we passed the dining room and lounge, they were dark. There was no sign of Wakefield or any of the under-butlers.

"Aria told everyone to finish up for the night at eleven," Allegra whispered. "She said it's the quietest week she's ever seen at Ardnoch."

"So why the hell is she still here?"

"Hey, that's what I asked." She wrinkled her nose. "I'm beginning to think she truly is a workaholic. In here." Allegra pushed open the large, heavy library door and ushered me past her.

Frowning, I strode in.

To an empty room. I spun around. "Where is she?"

Allegra whispered again, "She's in her office, but she told me to bring you here. I'll go tell her."

"Why are you whispering?"

But she left without replying.

Bloody hell.

This was not how I wanted to spend my night.

Liar. You asked for something to change.

I exhaled heavily. How low I'd been brought to find excitement in a clandestine meeting with a woman who hated me for the mere fact that I was born.

The sound of high heels on hardwood made my pulse race. My blood pumped as anticipation filled me. It was emasculating that she could make me feel this way. It really was.

"What do you need at this time of night, Mr. Hunter?" Aria swept into the room, her beautiful face pinched with annoyance.

Indignation riled me. "What do *I* need? What the fuck do you mean, what do I need? You're the one who hauled me from my room to meet me for some mysterious reason."

Her brows almost met she frowned so hard. "Why on earth would I ask a club member to meet me at midnight?"

A bang filled the room, and we both jumped, startled. Aria whirled around as I gaped at the now closed library door. The snick of a lock turning echoed through the room.

"Allegra?" Aria squeaked.

Then she was running across the room with hilarious difficulty in her tight skirt. She turned the handle, but the door didn't budge. She pulled harder. Then she slammed her palm against the wood. "Allegra Howard, you open this door right now."

What the actual fuck?

"No!" Allegra called back. "You're both going to stay in there until you work out your shit."

"Have you lost your mind?" Aria yelled.

"Clearly," I huffed behind her.

She shot me a dark look before turning back to the door. "Allegra, there's no way out of this library. That's not safe."

"I know you're in there. And I'll let you out once you two have made nice."

"What do you mean, there's no way out?" I strode toward the windows. The estate grounds were lit up outside so I could only make out my reflection in them. They were tall and narrow, and I couldn't see a latch anywhere. Surely that was illegal?

"Most of the windows are just one long sheet of glass. There's a second smaller pane at the top. It has the latch on it," Aria explained behind me.

I looked over my shoulder to find her standing in the middle of the room, hands on her hips. "You're shitting me?"

"Oh, how I wish I were."

Craning my neck, I looked up at the out-of-reach latches. "Please tell me there's a ladder hidden somewhere in here."

"Only the ones on the bookshelf rails, and they're not tall enough. Even if they were, you'd break something jumping out at that height."

"I'm going to kill your sister," I announced as I spun to face Aria.

"You'll have to get in line."

"See, you're agreeing already!" Allegra called out.

Aria's expression darkened as she half turned to speak to her. "You have no idea how much I'm going to make you pay for this, darling sister."

"I'll be back in an hour to check on you." At that, we heard footsteps moving away.

"Is this actually happening?"

At my question, Aria growled and stormed across the room to the only desk. "Is there a phone in here? Please say there's a phone."

My eyes swept the desk and then the walls, just in case. "No phone. And I didn't bring my mobile. Did you?"

She shook her head in exasperation. "I left it in my office."

"Can I ask why this is happening?"

"Because of your attitude toward me, that's why." Aria ran a hand over her head, smoothing her ponytail, the delicate gold rings she wore on every finger glinting in the low light. Even with a scowl on her face, she was fucking gorgeous.

Damn her.

"My attitude? Sweetheart, I've been nothing but polite to you since we met."

She faced me fully. "Uh, I beg to differ. Or do you not remembering getting junk-punched for your behavior?"

"I was drunk, and you quite rightly punched me in the balls for the transgression. And yet still, I'm treated to your contempt and suspicion." I lowered my gaze from hers, afraid I'd say something I regretted if I let my anger boil over. "Fuck. Please tell me there's at least some alcohol in here."

Aria shifted ever so slightly, and my hyperawareness of her pissed me off even more. My attention moved to her against my will. She sighed and pointed to a cabinet to my left. "In there. Whisky. The good stuff."

Thank God for small mercies. I crossed the room and lowered to my haunches to open the expensive walnut cabinet. Inside, I found five bottles, including an eighteen-year-old Macallan. "You sure? This is expensive stuff."

"Yup. And pour me a drink. A big one."

I grinned where she couldn't see and reached in for the bottle and two crystal glasses.

EIGHT
ARIA

Eventually, the words *I'm going to kill my sister* stopped running through my head as we finished the entire bottle of Macallan. Allegra did not return after an hour, so that one glass I'd had to calm my nerves had turned into several.

Despite the alcohol, tension stretched between me and North like a guitar string. One pull too many and it would snap.

"So ..." North's deep voice cut through the room after what felt like hours of strained silence. "It doesn't look like your sister's coming back. How long have you known she was a psychopath?"

Maybe it was the whisky warming my belly, or maybe I was bordering on hysterical from exhaustion and the pending need to pee, but laughter burst from my lips.

"Fuck, are you drunk?"

At North's disbelief, I turned to look at him from my place on the chesterfield sofa. He slouched in a library chair, his long legs sprawled up on the large reading desk. "I'm buzzed," I admitted. "And trying not to think about peeing."

"Right?" North threw his legs off the desk and stood. "I've been trying not to think about it since that she-devil locked us in here. Where is she?"

"The little brat probably fell asleep." I threw back the last of my whisky and got up to pour the remaining Macallan. I gestured toward the drink cabinet. "You can open another if you want. I'll replace them using my sister's trust fund."

North smirked before he crossed the room to lower in front of the cabinet. His T-shirt stretched across his muscular back as he leaned in. He wasn't a beefy guy, but he had deceptively broad shoulders.

The whisky was working its magic because rather than the usual stiffness that seemed to take over my body in his presence, I felt warm and languid. Relaxing my ass against the desk, I sipped at the drink that had long ago lost its burn and watched as North opened the 1995 Lagavulin.

"So how does one come by a name like North?" I asked, swirling the liquid in my glass.

He glanced over his shoulder at me, and I felt a whoosh of butterflies in my belly as I took in his handsome face. What he saw in my expression made him turn around and lean against the drinks cabinet, his gaze assessing.

Finally, just as I squirmed, regretting asking a personal question, he answered, "My dad was a professor of astronomy at Edinburgh Uni. My mum had been one of his students."

I raised an eyebrow, and he grinned ruefully. "I didn't know that until a few years ago when I went digging into their past. She fell pregnant with me, and he married her. I was ... I was only seven years old when they died, but I remember a lot and how they loved each other. I remember them dancing in the kitchen while they cooked. Always kissing and cuddling."

The memories he described made me smile even as my heart ached for the little boy who'd lost so much.

"Anyway ..." He exhaled slowly. "I remember coming

home from primary one, crying because the other kids made fun of my name. And my mum told me I was named after the North Star because they knew I was all they would ever need ..." North suddenly swallowed hard against emotion. "To find their way. That I'd brought them together on the right path. I was their true North."

Unexpected sadness hit me in the gut, and I could feel it choking me as I watched North throw back an entire glass of whisky. He turned to pour another, his shoulders bowed with sorrow.

I forced words through the thickening in my throat. "I'm so sorry. I didn't realize you remembered so much about them."

North turned around again, seeming more in control. "I wouldn't have it any other way. I couldn't have gotten through the shit show that was my childhood without knowing better was possible."

Admiration thrummed through me. "Some people might have turned bitter to have lost it."

"I did for a while," he admitted.

"Is that what drives you? The memories of your parents, those good times?"

"Mostly."

"What else drives you?"

He considered me, his eyes narrowing slightly. "What drives you?"

I sipped at my whisky before replying, "I never want people to think I have what I have through nepotism. There's no getting away from the fact that I have what I have through privilege ... but I always want to work hard. To prove that I've kept this position, or any position, because I'm smart and hardworking."

"No one would doubt that." North strolled over to an

armchair and lowered into it. His eyes remained on me. "Is that why you work until midnight?"

I tilted my head and smirked. "Answer my question first."

He frowned like he couldn't remember.

Snorting, I repeated, "What else drives you?"

"Oh. That." He swirled his glass just like I had done, his eyes on the amber liquid inside. "By the time I reached thirteen, I'd lived in three different foster homes where there were so many kids, the parents barely had time for us. Two of them were fine, if a bit negligent. One liked to slap us around."

"Jesus."

North shrugged. "It is what it is. They're no longer fostering."

Meaning he'd gone back to check.

"We grew up in a deprived area of our town. Parents weren't educated, they didn't know how to educate us, and we fucked around. I pretended like I wasn't smart and that I hated school, and I followed a gang of lads around that liked to get into trouble." He leaned forward now. "Some of these lads were from pretty shitty backgrounds. One of them, our so-called leader, if you like, Darren Menzies ... his dad had been out of the picture since he was a baby, and we all knew his mum's boyfriend was beating the shit out of him and his mum. I was the only one who knew he was doing other horrific things to him. That was a very angry young man. Darren was cruel because of it. I used to let him get away with terrible shit. We got into it with each other a few times, once when he tried to torture a dog we'd found."

My hand flew to my mouth in horror as North continued grimly. "I took the beating of a lifetime, but I saved the dog."

"Wow." It seemed like a life so far removed from my own, I was almost ashamed.

"Anyway, we were fighting more and more as his destructiveness escalated. Until Gil MacDonald."

"Who is Gil MacDonald?"

North looked into my eyes, and even in the dim light, I saw his pain. "The homeless man the media dragged up from the grave."

Without thinking, I crossed the room and took the armchair opposite him. "What really happened?"

North scrubbed a weary hand over his face. I didn't think he was going to tell me, but when he dropped his hand, he spoke. "We were messing around one evening. It was just after dinnertime. We came across Gil in his sleeping bag behind an express supermarket. Darren taunted him, agitating him, and Gil shouted foul things back. So Darren started beating on him and screaming at the rest of us to get in there. The other lads ... it was like he turned them into animals." Anguish darkened North's expression. His voice turned hoarse, his accent thickening, as he continued, "I tried. I yelled at them tae get off him. When that didnae work, I pulled Darren off him and we fought long enough for Gil tae run away. But the wee shits chased after him, and I chased after them. They chased him right intae traffic and he was killed."

It was unimaginable to me he'd witnessed something like that as a child. Just a child. What an event to carry the weight of for so long. I'd never been angrier at the media for dragging it up and twisting the story. "God, North. I am so sorry you went through that."

"Nothing compared to the terror that man must have felt running from a bunch of wee pricks."

I heard it. The guilt. He still blamed himself, even though he'd tried to stop it. "What happened after?"

"Darren threatened us all tae stay quiet. I didnae. It didnae matter, anyway. Witnesses saw us chase him intae traffic. We were all arrested."

"But you weren't charged." I knew that from the newspaper articles.

"There was CCTV behind the supermarket. They saw me trying tae stop it."

"Oh my God."

"The lads were done for manslaughter and sent tae Young Offenders. Our version of juvie. Which is in Falkirk. So those who had parents didnae have tae travel far tae see their boys."

"Your accent slips when you talk about home," I whispered.

North raised an eyebrow. "It wasn't home. My home was with my parents."

"Right." Heartache filled me.

"Don't look at me like that. Things got better," he promised, and I noted his accent had smoothed again now that he was aware of it. "It motivated me. What happened to Gil fired me up. Because I knew that if I stayed there, I'd end up in prison at some point. As it was, another boy killed Darren before he ever got out. One of the other lads got out and was put away a few years later for aggravated assault. The other two got jobs, seemed to settle down a bit. But they're just scraping by like their parents did. I didn't want that. I didn't want to disappoint my parents. They'd be so fucking ashamed if I didn't try to find the life I wanted."

I stared at North, seeing him in a whole new light. There was a lot of depth to this man, and I was ashamed of assuming so much about him. More curious than I knew was good for me, I pressed, "What happened to you after they went to juvie?"

"In exchange for my witness statement at court, social services agreed to move me out of Falkirk for my protection. They placed me in a village near Edinburgh with a couple who only fostered three kids at a time. Emma and Nick were nice. Wary of me at first, I think, but then once I showed them I was willing to work hard, to improve, they were very generous with their time and money." He smiled softly, and I felt another wild flutter in my belly that I attempted to ignore. "I tried to pay off their house for them when I got my first big check, but they were having none of it."

"They sound like nice people."

"They are. Don't get me wrong, I'd stayed with nice foster parents before, but they just had too many kids under their roof. Emma and Nick could give us the attention we needed." He went on to tell me about how he buckled down at school, earned excellent grades, and how his high school girlfriend got him into theater.

"And then you got accepted into RCS?" I was super impressed by that when I was researching him for membership because it's such a prestigious school.

"Aye. And the rest, as they say, is history." North sipped at his whisky and lounged back in his chair. "So now that I've spilled my guts, tell me the truth."

I frowned, confused. "About what?"

"You obviously knew about some of my background before I came here. Did your research. Is that why you treated me like a foul smell from the moment we met? Because you thought I was scum?"

Indignation flooded me, and I was so agitated I stood up. "Is that what you think? That I think I'm better than you because I grew up with money and you didn't?"

He shrugged lazily, and I wanted to throw my whisky in his face for his assumptions. Yes, I knew that was hypocritical, but this guy really got under my skin. "What else am I to think?"

"Not that." I marched across the room and poured the Lagavulin into my glass.

"I'll have some more, thanks."

Grumbling under my breath, I strode over to him with the bottle and snarled, "You're lucky I'm not pouring it over your head."

Amusement glinted in North's beautiful eyes as I filled his glass. "Then tell me why."

Later, I'd blame it on the whisky and the fact that he'd lowered my defenses with his brutal honesty about his past. Settling back down, I locked eyes with him and admitted, "I don't trust actors."

Surprise slackened his features. "At all?"

"Except for Lachlan, and perhaps Brodan Adair, yeah. I don't trust actors."

"Why the fuck not?"

His boyish ire made me smile, but I smothered it since he looked so piqued. Then he shook his head. "No, that can't be it. You are far nicer to other actors here than to me. It's a 'me thing.'"

With more nonchalance than I felt, I confessed, "You're kind of my type. And I have a terrible record of dating actors like you who treated me like shit."

Stunned, North stared at me for a second too long and too fiercely. Heat crawled over my skin, and I could feel my body reacting to his focused attention. "Are you ..." He cleared his throat. "Are you telling me that you're attracted to me and that's why you hate me?"

That tension stretched between us again, but this time it was straining to snap for a different reason. Like, if it snapped, it was because we'd jumped each other.

Wrenching my eyes from him, I looked down at my glass. My cheeks burned hot, and my body thrummed with need. Oh, shit. "I don't hate you." I forced out and then said as a reminder to myself, "I just don't trust you."

"That's nice to hear after what I just confessed."

I winced at the slight hurt in his voice. "Sorry. I really am. It's not your fault. But I can't change how I feel."

"Well, that's not good enough." North shook his head. "I

want to know why, when you know so little about me, that you've decided I'm untrustworthy."

"I'm sure you're great. But I have a no-actors rule because of my unhealthy attraction to your type."

"To my type?" My explanation seemed to piss him off more.

This was going so well.

"I'm not being judged for myself? I'm being lumped together with a bunch of guys you think are exactly like me? Well, that's wonderful. That's what everyone wants to hear—how not fucking special you are. One of many! Just like all the others."

I rolled my eyes. "You're being a drama king right now."

"Fuck you. See how you'd like it if I lumped you in with a 'type.'"

Hmm. That would hurt my feelings. Why did I always say the wrong things to this man? And why couldn't he be an asshole who bottled up his feelings and didn't tell you what he was thinking? For the second time, I apologized. "I'm sorry. You're right."

"Not good enough," he repeated. "I told you my sob story. Now you tell me why you've treated me like crap for the misdeeds of others."

God, when he put it like that ... I groaned and rested my head back on the armchair. "I have been kind of a bitch, haven't I?"

"Terse and unfriendly, yes."

My lips twitched. He couldn't even call me a bitch. I melted a little more. And then thought, *what the hell?* North had just laid out some pretty vulnerable stuff about himself.

Guess it was my turn.

I lifted my head to meet his inquiring gaze. "Guys have hurt me a lot. Not just guys. Friends too."

He scowled unhappily. "In what ways?"

I shrugged. "I grew up in Malibu where everyone knew who my dad was. My first boyfriend, Montana, was cool. His dad was an actor so Montana didn't give a shit who my dad was. We broke up because he went to college on the East Coast and I stayed behind to look out for Allegra. I guess I didn't realize that a guy might use me because Montana was so sweet." Feeling my skirt dig into my side, I unzipped it without thinking. "That's better."

North's attention zeroed in on the area where my skirt had loosened, and I felt a shiver of insecurity. Could he see my belly rolls? Could he tell that I did not have a flat stomach and never would?

"Continue," he forced out, his voice sounding hoarse to my ears.

"What is there to say?" I replied with a false insouciance. "My next boyfriend was a struggling actor who fucked me until he realized I would not get him an audition for my dad's next movie. He said to my face when he broke up with me, 'What is the point of sleeping with you if you won't help me out?'"

"That motherfucker," North fumed, leaning forward in his seat, his glass held so tight in his hand I could see his knuckles straining.

I smiled at him for taking umbrage on my behalf. "Yup. And he wasn't the last. I dated Preston Holden for three years."

North's expression shifted. "I've met Preston. He seems like an all-right bloke."

It didn't surprise me they'd met. Preston won an Oscar two years ago for Best Supporting Actor. "Oh, yeah, he's just dandy." Preston had worked a lot during those three years, so we probably only saw each other for the equivalent of one. "He was talented, so I helped him get an audition for my dad's movie and he got the part. I surprised him by showing up to the set one day and found him fucking his costar in his trailer."

"Jesus."

"Oh, it gets worse. He dumped me while he was still inside her." I raised my glass, hiding the pain that sliced through me at the memory. "Cheers to being told that you were no longer of use and that I was getting fat while he's literally inside his beautiful costar."

North stood slowly, visibly agitated. "Please tell me you are fucking kidding."

I stared up at him owlishly. "Goodness, we haven't even gotten to Lucas yet."

"Lucas?" he seethed.

"My last boyfriend." I nodded and gestured back to his chair. "Sit."

"I'm too enraged to sit." He enunciated each word as he paced. "So what the fuck did this Lucas do?"

I watched him pace, surprised he was this indignant on my behalf. "Uh ... well, it was my fault, really. I promised myself no more actors after Preston, but Lucas Grant was all charming and cocky and sexy." I waved a hand at North as if to say *like you*, and he scowled even more ferociously. "He'd been in a few small movies, and he'd written a script that he wanted my dad to see. I explained I couldn't get that in front of my dad, and he seemed to be understanding. At the time I was working as the hospitality manager for my friend's new restaurant, Curiosity. We hired a girl named Caitlyn Branch to run the social media. And she was kind of overeager and sweet and seemed fascinated by me, so I took her under my wing. She changed her name to Ariella and started dressing like me and following me everywhere, and it became suffocating. I tried to distance myself from her a little, and I don't know if that pissed her off, but she sent me a video of her fucking Lucas."

North stopped pacing to stare at me, dumbfounded.

I nodded, the terrible ache I'd buried threatening to take hold. "When I confronted Lucas, do you know what he said?"

"I'm afraid to ask."

I couldn't hold North's gaze any longer. "He said that I was fat and bad in bed, but he didn't want to break up with me in case it hurt his future chances of working with my father."

"Fuck." North exhaled harshly. "Aria." He sat in the chair across from me, and I forced my attention back to him. He seemed as if he was in pain. "Please don't tell me you believe any of that shite."

I gave him an exasperated look. "If people repeat a pattern with you, you kinda start to believe what they're saying. Friends have tried to use me to get to my father. I've been used by different boyfriends to get to Dad, and all of them cheated on me and all of them made it clear that I wasn't sexy to them, that they didn't enjoy our time ... in bed."

Suddenly, North slammed his glass down on a side table and lowered himself to his knees in front of me. I gaped at him as he braced his hands on the arms of my chair and leaned right into me. The smell of his cologne mingled with the scent of whisky and heat. There was nowhere to look but straight into his beautiful eyes because our noses almost touched.

"They were callous, ruthless wee pricks who couldn't admit that they were scummy, callous, ruthless wee pricks, so they laid the blame at your feet."

"North." I pressed a hand to his chest but didn't exert pressure. "Don't."

"What? Tell you the truth? I could give a rat's arse who your father is. You're Aria. A woman so sexy and beautiful that I felt guilty for checking you out the first day we met because I wanted you. A lot. And I had a girlfriend who I cared about. I wouldn't have done anything, but just wanting you that much made me feel like a bit of a bastard." His eyes lowered to my mouth, and my body tingled to life under his stare, at his proximity, at his words. "But she dumped me because I no longer made her look good." His eyes returned to mine. "It's not the same, but I understand a wee bit."

"North ... I have serious trust issues," I warned him. "I can't date anyone."

Determination hardened his gaze. "Then at least let me show you how beautiful I think you are. Let me prove you're dynamite in bed. Let me take away what the arseholes planted in you."

"Why?" I whispered hoarsely.

"Because it's a fucking travesty that a woman as charismatic and sexy as you would think otherwise."

I wanted to.

I wanted to push him to the floor, unbuckle his jeans, and ride him until there was nothing but the pursuit of pleasure.

But fear pushed in, icing the heat in my blood.

No.

Somehow, I knew if I let him, North could hurt me worse than all the others.

Patting his chest gently, I eased away from him. "I think we've both had a lot to drink. We should try to get some sleep until Allegra remembers we're in here."

North didn't hide his frustration or disappointment, but he moved away from me. Scrubbing a hand over his unshaven cheeks, he gestured to the couch. "You take the sofa. I'll push two chairs together."

Nodding, I waited until he'd moved out of my path and then I reclined on the couch, bending my knees to fit. I gave him my back and murmured, "Good night, North."

His deep voice made me shiver as he replied, "Good night, gorgeous."

NINE
NORTH

I'd wanted a distraction.

I'd wanted something to change.

Well, wish granted.

Now I was infatuated with Aria Howard.

My wrist hurt from writing about the night in my journal. I wanted to commit every moment and every feeling to paper before I finally got some sleep. It was not Allegra who saved us from the library, but Wakefield. The butler didn't say a damn word about finding us locked in the room. Both Aria and I had barely slept, though she did at some point, because she snored a wee bit. We were desperate to use the restroom after all the whisky we'd consumed, and even so, Aria asked Wakefield to give us a minute.

Once the butler had departed, Aria turned to me with those stunning green eyes. They were filled with apology, sincerity, and a softness I didn't know she was capable of until last night.

"I want to say how sorry I am for the way I've treated you. It won't happen again."

I was surprised by the relief I experienced. "Thank you."

Unable to leave it at that, I lowered my voice and said, "I'm not drunk."

She raised an eyebrow.

"And I still want you." I leaned into her as I moved slowly past, and her lashes fluttered, her breathing shallow. Aye, she wanted me too. "You know where to find me if you decide you want to prove those bastards wrong."

Then she tortured me by nervously licking her plump lips. I seemed to have rendered her speechless, so I nodded with a slight smile and walked away.

Now she was all I could think about. I wanted to erase all the shit those arseholes had planted in her head. How the fuck could they? Cheating on her was one thing, but to say such cruel drivel to her? The next time I saw Preston Holden, he'd be lucky if he didn't walk away with a broken nose.

I got up off the bed and pulled the curtains closed. I'd already put a Do Not Disturb sign on my door. But as soon as I rested my head on the pillow, I pictured her. Damn, I wanted her. I'd told her things about my past that I hadn't spoken about to many people. She'd listened like she gave a damn, and I'd felt a weight releasing from me to have her know the truth about Gil. Aria didn't look at me with pity, but empathy. She didn't judge me, but seemed to admire me.

I had to admit, I could get high on Aria's admiration.

Hell, I could just get high on her. I wanted to let her hair down and undress her and have her melt under my hands. Now I knew why she was wound so tightly. She was wrapped in steel armor to protect her from arseholes. Her trust issues were a problem, which meant I'd have to tread carefully. Take things slowly.

Aye, I knew I had major life problems at the moment, and my sexual attraction to a Hollywood princess should not take priority. But why not? Whether she knew it, Aria Howard needed me. If it was the last thing I did, I'd help that woman get her confidence back. Preferably by giving her many, many orgasms.

Groaning as I hardened at the thought, I turned on my side and tried to switch my tired brain off. The decision was made. As much as I'd love to explore something real with Aria, she couldn't handle that.

So I'd give her whatever little piece of me she would take.

Now I just had to convince her that an unforgettable night in my bed was exactly what she needed.

TEN
ARIA

Having to work on very little sleep and with the worst hangover I'd had in ages was less than preferable. Going home to shower to find Allegra passed out on the couch had made me so furious that I had to ignore her or I'd lose my shit. She was still asleep when I left to return to the castle.

Her barging into my office a few hours later was the last thing I needed.

"Oh my gosh, Ari, I am so sorry I fell asleep. How did you get out?" she asked without preamble, all cute and wide-eyed.

I glowered, wanting to blame her for my fragility this morning. And not just the fragility brought on by my hangover, but because I felt stripped naked now that I'd confessed all that stuff to North. Private feelings I had not shared with anyone.

All because Allegra was bored? "You should leave until I've had some sleep and don't want to skin you alive," I told her calmly.

She winced. "I am so sorry. I didn't mean to leave you guys in there."

"Well, you did. All night. Wakefield, a member of staff that I respect and who, until this morning, respected me, came in to dust the library and found us locked in there. Christ knows what he thinks we were up to, but the two empty bottles of expensive whisky probably have him putting things together I don't want him putting together."

Her eyes rounded, a slight smile curling her mouth. "Did something happen between you and North? I knew it! I knew there was a spark there."

Fury shot me to my feet, and Allegra's expression instantly changed. "You locked me in a room with one of my members. There was no fire escape, no restroom, and neither of us knew North very well. You locked me in a room with a strange man who you are lucky turned out to be a gentleman. Do you understand?"

My sister suddenly looked so very young as tears brightened her eyes. "I'm sorry. I didn't think. I just didn't want you to be alone here."

"Whether I am alone is entirely up to me. Not you. And what you did last night proves to me you are not mature enough to venture out into the world doing whatever the hell you want." My stomach knotted with my coming words. "I will not help you convince our parents to let you drop out of college. I don't think you're ready." She was still way too impulsive and irresponsible for my peace of mind.

Her lips trembled as she lowered her gaze.

I felt like a giant bully. Guilt crushed in on me, but I forced myself to stay firm. "You were accepted into several excellent art schools around the country. I think if LA is the problem, then the better solution is to transfer schools your junior year."

"Are you going to tell Mamma and Dad what I did?" She met my eyes, anger, disappointment, guilt all there for me to see.

"No, of course not."

She relaxed marginally. "I really am sorry, Ari."

I sighed heavily and sat back down in my chair, feeling light-headed. "I know."

A FEW HOURS LATER, a knock sounded on my door and I braced myself, knowing who it was. "Come in."

My boss and owner of the estate, Lachlan Adair, strode inside. The Adair siblings were all tall, blond, and blue-eyed, suggesting a line of Viking blood in their ancestry. Lachlan, the eldest, was also one of the tallest among them, and his impressive height and good looks had helped him on his path to stardom. For about fifteen years, he'd played the game in Hollywood, making a name for himself as an action star. However, he'd retired early from the movies to return home to Scotland and open Ardnoch.

Smart man.

Straightforward, fair, honorable, even, Lachlan was a good boss, and I appreciated he entrusted me with his club. When his wife Robyn gave birth to their daughter, Lachlan wanted to be home more. I made it possible for him to do that. Especially now that he'd gone into business with two of his brothers in separate ventures.

It irked me to no end that I had to have this conversation with him.

"Are you all right?" Lachlan asked as he sat down. I leaned against my desk, my hands curling tightly around the edges. "You look a bit pale."

"I've barely slept." I exhaled shakily. "An incident occurred last night."

He straightened in his chair. "Is anyone hurt?"

I gave him a tight-lipped smile. "Just my reputation."

"What?"

At his confusion, I sat down in the chair next to him. "My younger sister has come for a visit, and unfortunately, last night she played a prank on me and a member."

"Prank?"

"I was working late, and she lied to me and to North Hunter to get us in the library together after the staff had been dismissed. Then she locked us in. All night."

"Why?"

This was the embarrassing part. Well, another embarrassing part. "She was trying to play matchmaker."

"With you and North?"

"Nothing is going on between us," I reassured him. "I wouldn't cross the line with a member."

Lachlan grimaced. "Aria, not that I'm encouraging you to sleep with our members, but I'd be a bloody hypocrite if I enforced a no-fraternization rule between you and them. I married my head of security's daughter. And before that, I'd had relationships with club members. It's different for us than for other staff members. We run in the same circles as our members. Attraction happens."

"Nothing is happening between me and North Hunter," I insisted. "But we drank some whisky that I will replace, I promise."

Lachlan's lips twitched in amusement.

"And, um, Wakefield discovered us this morning and let us out, and I haven't explained to him what happened."

"No need." My boss waved off the suggestion. "Wakefield is the soul of discretion. He won't mention it to anyone."

"You're not mad?"

"That depends on North Hunter's response."

"He is ..." I felt a pang of emotion I didn't quite understand. "An easygoing guy. He didn't seem to be put out by the situation."

Lachlan grinned. "Oh, I bet not."

I could feel my cheeks heating and was glad my olive skin didn't blush. "Well, I was thinking we should compensate Mr. Hunter for his night. Maybe even a few nights."

"Make the entire week complimentary." My boss peered at me. "Is this why you called me in?"

"Yes, in part. The other thing is that there was no way out of the library once we were locked in. If there was a fire and someone got locked in there, it's a problem."

Lachlan nodded. "It came up when we were refurbishing the castle, and the windows were enough to pass fire inspection. Plus we'd thought the likelihood of anyone getting locked in there was slim." I flushed again at his dry tone, cursing my sister to hell. "What do you suggest?"

"I think the least intrusive idea has some expense to it."

"Go on."

"I think we should convert one of the windows into a door."

Lachlan nodded again. "Aye, that sounds logical. I'll deal with it."

"Are you sure? I can handle it."

"No, it's fine. I have a contact who helped refurbish some windows years ago. I'll call you to let you know when they'll be out to measure. Is there anything else?"

"That's it for now."

"Great." He stood, towering over me. "Now go home."

I gaped up at him. "What? Now?"

"Aye, now."

"But I have work."

"I'm here. I'll handle what needs to be handled. You go home and sleep."

"But—"

"No buts. Go home."

"OH MY GOD, please tell me you did not get fired?" Allegra asked as soon as I walked through the door.

"No," I grumbled as I kicked off my heels. "Lachlan sent me home because I haven't slept. I had to tell him what you did in case North complained."

"Why?" Allegra whined. "Now he's going to tell Dad."

Our father was on the board of the estate, and he and Lachlan were good friends. "I swore him to secrecy."

"North wouldn't have complained."

"Oh, and you know this from the five seconds you've spent in his presence. If he didn't complain, Wakefield might have felt obligated to tell Lachlan. Anyway, it's done."

"Like I'm done," she said forlornly.

"My head hurts," I whimpered, striding past her into the kitchen for a bottle of water. My pulse was racing before I even said, "But it's time to call our parents." There was nothing I hated more than playing referee in the middle of Allegra and Mamma and Dad. But I'd taken on that role a long time ago, and as mad as I was at my sister, I couldn't let her deal with them alone.

"Now?"

"Now."

"While you're in a mood?"

I spun on my sister. "Just because I'm pissed at you doesn't mean I'm in a mood." I was so in a mood. "What you did crossed a line."

Allegra tilted her chin defiantly. "I'm sorry if I got you in trouble at work, but I'm not sorry for trying to push you out of your comfort zone."

I will not strangle my beloved sister. I will not strangle my beloved sister.

Instead of answering (because I was afraid I might eviscerate her with my words), I took a massive chug of cold water and then strode over to where I'd left my purse. Grabbing my cell out of it, I intended to video call Mamma first.

Allegra wrapped a hand around my wrist to stop me, her eyes pleading. "I know I made a mistake. But I still really don't think college is the answer."

I studied her face, the tired eyes, the weariness in them that scared the hell out of me. "You're nineteen. Legally, you're an adult. If you want to drop out, you can. But that's a conversation you'll need to have with our parents on your own."

"They don't listen to me."

"If you're mature enough to drop out of college, you're mature enough to handle Mamma and Dad on your own."

Allegra glowered at me for what felt like five minutes. Then she threw her hands up. "Fine! I got into the Rhode Island School of Design. Maybe I could transfer there my junior year."

I narrowed my eyes. "And you'd be cool with that?"

She considered it. "It's not like I have to give up Lucy Stella, right?"

"Nope. You can still do it. I hope you do. Your art is beautiful, Allegra. I just ... want you to experience what other kids your age are experiencing. Maybe the East Coast will be good for you."

Allegra blew out a beleaguered breath. "It *would* be easier for Mamma and Dad to swallow that over dropping out. And it might work."

"So, that's a yes?"

"Yeah." She still didn't look a hundred percent happy, but life was about compromise, right? "Call them."

Mamma picked up on the fourth ring. Her beautiful face appeared on the screen and it looked like she was in our kitchen in the New York apartment. "It's early here, coccolona. Is something wrong?"

"I'm going to try to connect Dad, okay?" I said instead.

"Oh, something is wrong. Just tell me."

"Nothing's wrong. We just need a family meeting."

"Family meeting?"

At that, my sister appeared at my side and waved into the camera. "Hey, Mamma."

Our mother scowled. "Allegra? Why are you in *Scozia*?"

"One second, Mamma," I insisted as I invited Dad into the call.

Wesley Howard might be a legendary film director and super busy guy, but unless he's in the middle of filming a scene, it was rare he didn't pick up when his daughters called. Sure enough, after five rings, my father's rugged face appeared. "Hey!" His eyes widened in surprise. "All my girls? Wait ... what are you doing in LA, Ari?"

"I'm not in LA."

"Allegra, what are you doing in Scotland?"

"Good morning to you, too, husband," Mamma called, pouting childishly.

Our father grinned. "I said *good morning* to you an hour ago."

Allegra and I groaned at the innuendo in his tone and our mother's consequent purr of approval. Good lord! I did not need to know that our parents had phone sex.

"Anyway." I took a deep breath. "We're calling for a reason."

"Why are you so pale?" Mamma cut in. "Ari, you are the face of that estate. You cannot walk around looking like a dead girl."

"Mamma!" Allegra's tone was chastising.

"I'm used to it," I muttered, squeezing her hand. We needed our parents on Allegra's good side.

"And don't mumble. A lady does not mumble."

"Chiara, give it a rest," Dad suggested with a bite in his

tone. The one point of contention between our parents was the way my mother picked at me. "Look, girls, as happy as I am to see you, I have to be back on set in five minutes, so what's the deal?"

Just spit it out fast. "Allegra came to visit me to explain how unhappy she is in LA, so we've been talking about it and think it would be best if she transferred to Rhode Island for junior year."

Dad started speaking first. "Well, I think—"

"No!" Mamma cried out unhappily. "I finally am home to spend time with my *bambina*. No way are you moving across the entire country from me."

Allegra huffed. "You're in New York right now. You didn't even know I wasn't in LA."

I squeezed my sister's hand because antagonizing our mother would get us nowhere.

"That's beside the point. I want you home with me. Why do my daughters insist on leaving me?"

"Chiara, they're growing up," Dad interjected. "I think it might be good for Allegra to go to the East Coast. Rhode Island is a top school."

Mamma's eyes filled with tears. "I just lost so much time with them when I was working and traveling. I want to make up for that."

"I know, baby."

God, give me patience. Not that I didn't love my mother or see her goodness. But she was kind of, well ... utterly and completely self-involved. It was always her first instinct to think about how a situation affected her, but thankfully, she could also be talked into seeing it from someone else's perspective. "Mamma, what's important is Allegra's mental health and emotional well-being. If Rhode Island would make her happier, then I think it's smart we all support her in that move."

As always, my calm words seemed to hit home. Her expression softened. "I suppose that is all that matters. It will give me an excuse to stay in Boston more. I do love the Four Seasons there."

Allegra sagged into my side with silent relief.

"So that's a yes on Allegra transferring?"

Mamma sniffled dramatically. "I suppose so."

Dad grinned. "It's yes from me. Let me know if you need me to make any calls, sweetheart," he said to Allegra. "I gotta get back on set. Love you, girls."

"Love you, Daddy."

"Love you, Dad."

"*Ti amo*, Wes."

I hung up before my mother could start in on my paleness again. Turning to Allegra, I gave her a reassuring smile. "This will all work out."

She nodded slowly, still not entirely convinced. "Yeah. I'm sure it will."

My little sister had locked me in a library all night with a guy I barely knew at my place of work, and yet somehow, I ended up feeling like the bad guy. While she promised we were okay, she disappeared into her room and didn't come back out.

The guilt worsened the next morning when I got ready for work, only to discover that Allegra was already up and packed. She'd booked a flight from Inverness to London to catch an afternoon flight back to LA. She'd also already called for a car on the estate. Even though we hugged and said we loved each other, things felt strained.

Pulling back from the hug, she looked me in the eye and said, "I hope you wake up, Ari. I hope you wake up and start living again."

I knew she hadn't meant to hurt me with the words, but still, they stung. Watching her get into the SUV to head home,

I worried I'd made the wrong decision by suggesting she stay in college. And as I walked into the house, it echoed with emptiness again. Striding through, I noticed the absence of her belongings. Her sketch pad, tablet, phone cables, makeup, jewelry. She was so messy.

I missed the mess.

Grabbing a coffee and yogurt, I sat down at the breakfast nook and stared out at the gray sea beyond. Then I looked back into the open-plan living space.

To all the emptiness.

My vision blurred as tears quietly fell down my cheeks.

Eleven
NORTH

Just checking you're doing OK. Haven't
heard from you in a while.

The text from Emma, my ex-foster mum, made me feel
both grateful and guilty. She'd sent it an hour ago.
Emma and her husband Nick were two of the first people to
reach out to me when the tabloids got hold of the story about
Gil MacDonald. Considering they knew the truth, they were
concerned about me. I'd assured them I was fine and staying at
the club for a while, but that was the last I'd spoken to them.
A look at the texts above this new one from Emma reminded
me she'd texted while I was in my drunken stupor phase. And
I hadn't responded.

Shit.

I was on my way to collect mail. Usually, the underbutlers
brought us our mail, but security had requested I pick it up
from them and I was trying not to overanalyze why.

The inquiry from Emma was a pleasant distraction. I tried
calling her as I made my way downstairs from where I'd been

playing my guitar in the castle turret. The turret was as you'd expect—a small, cylindrical room with narrow, medieval-style windows. It had been transformed into a snug library with built-in bookshelves and a comfortable armchair. Carpeted, it didn't have the best acoustics, but the walls were thick and it was built up and out from the rest of the building, so I knew I wouldn't disturb anyone with my music.

I'd written a song about Aria.

The call to Emma would distract me from the woman who was currently tormenting my every waking thought. Unfortunately, it went to her voicemail.

"Hi, Emma, it's North. I'm sorry I didn't get back to you. I was ... aye, admittedly I wasn't in a very good place when you texted a few weeks ago, but that's no excuse. I'm doing better now, though. We're just sitting tight, hoping the studio might change its mind about the Blake Forster movie. I'll keep you posted. I promise. And I hope you and Nick and the kids are all well. Let me know. Love to you all." Hanging up, I felt mildly less guilty.

This morning I'd locked myself in the turret to avoid several emails from different members of what I called my management team. Charlie, the bloke in charge of the houses I'd invested my money in, wanted me to let out my London apartment. I let out my loft in Brooklyn because maintenance costs were so high that it only made sense to rent it when I wasn't using it. But my London flat was a place I liked to know I could go whenever I needed it. It was my home base, if you will.

Fuck.

I didn't want to rent it out, but with the future so uncertain, I might just have to. Even with the discount Lachlan Adair had offered me for the week in recompense for Allegra Howard's prank, Ardnoch was costing a small fortune.

The second email I didn't want to deal with was from

Annette, my publicist. Apparently, the designer who'd dropped me as the face of their brand had alluded to the possibility of us working together if I made a public statement about the scandal and apologized. If all went well, they'd welcome me back with open arms.

It was a lot of money. Great publicity.

But they—like Cara who texted me ten times last night telling me she loved me, missed me, and would be open to seeing me in secret—could fuck themselves with a trident.

Passing Aria's office, I fought the urge to knock on her door. We hadn't seen each other since the morning Wakefield let us out of the library.

Frowning, I made my way into the staff area of the castle, striding past staff who looked surprised to see me there but nodded deferentially. I'd been in the small department that housed security before when Byron Hoffman attacked Sloane. Finding the CCTV room, I knocked on the partially open door.

Walker looked up from watching the screens, saw it was me, patted the shoulder of the guy next to him, and murmured something as he stood. He opened the door all the way and stepped out. The security guard was one of the few men I'd ever met who made me feel physically diminutive. Not an easy feat when I was six two. Walker technically only had three inches on me, but the bloke was built with powerful shoulders. It was more than that, though. He gave off an intimidating *don't fuck with me or anyone I care about* vibe without even saying a word. I intended to study him and channel that part of his persona if I ever got my role back in *Birdwatcher*.

"So, what's up?" I asked, stepping back to let him out of the room.

Walker lifted his chin, silently gesturing for me to follow

him to another room. Inside the small office, he rounded a desk and pulled a few envelopes out of a drawer.

"These are yours." Walker handed them to me.

I frowned, my stomach tightening as I recognized the font of the address on one of them. "Not that I mind, but why did you need me to collect them?"

"Theo Cavendish had a word with me last time he was here. He said you've been receiving threatening mail for months now."

"Theo did?" The same Theo who pretended not to give a fuck about anyone?

"Aye."

Sighing, I ripped into the first envelope and scanned the page. Indignation flushed hotly through me. "Another letter from an angry member of the public telling me I should be ashamed of myself." I balled it up and threw it into Walker's wastepaper basket. The other envelope I dreaded opening. But I did it.

Do you think if you hide you can escape? You'll NEVER escape me. I'm coming. You'll never SEE it. But I'm coming for you. I won't stop until you're DEAD. DEAD. DEAD.

Fuck my life.

I handed the letter to Walker. "When I asked you if you were open to becoming my private security, this prompted it. I started getting these after my first movie took off. They were accusatory. Offensive. But in the last year, they've turned into death threats."

Walker scanned the letter and murmured, "And there's not a lot the police can do about it."

"Nope."

"Do you have all the letters?"

"Not with me. I have a few."

"I'd like to see them."

Studying Walker's difficult-to-read expression, I asked, "Why?"

"Because there might be something in them to go off. There might not. But you're a club member, and we're tasked with your security. And I owe you. For Sloane."

"Walker, you don't owe me for that."

"Aye, I do."

"How are things going there?" I knew he'd been dating Sloane for a few months now.

A softness entered his eyes. "Better than I deserve."

I grinned, understanding completely. "Glad to hear it."

He waved the letter. "Well?"

"Aye. I'll get you the others." I saw no harm in letting the man have a look. Doubtful he could do much, but all I was doing was low-level worrying about them.

"And if you get a minute, I'd like a list of names of people you might have seriously pissed off in the past. Full names, last known address, if you have them."

Stunned, I jerked my head back. "You're serious? You're looking into this?"

"Somebody needs to."

Grateful, I told him I'd get the information to him as soon as possible and left his office feeling a wee bit lighter. It would be nice to solve the mystery of the death threats and tick one more thing off my worry list.

As I rounded the corner toward the members' area of the castle, my pulse jumped at the sight of Aria. Her step faltered a bit when she saw me, but she straightened her shoulders and continued walking, the sway of her hips mesmerizing. Nervous anticipation rocked my stomach and I felt the skin on the back of my neck grow hot. When we reached each other, the smell of her perfume drifted over me. My fingers twitched at my sides and I clenched them into fists to stop myself from reaching out to touch the bloody woman.

She stared into my eyes. A man could drown in hers. I think I might have been—drowning, that is—because it seemed to take me too long to find words. "Aria."

Wonderful.

Scintillating stuff.

Fuck.

She looked down before reengaging. That's when I noticed she was subtly shifting from one foot to the other. Was she nervous? "How are you?" she asked, sounding calm.

Her husky voice caused heat to pool in my dick because it made me think of what she'd sound like coming.

I scrubbed the back of my neck. "Aye, I'm doing all right. You?"

"Fine."

Scowling at her nonanswer, I hated things were so awkward between us. We'd told each other deep, dark secrets in that library, and now she was treating me like a stranger. "How's Allegra?" I pushed. When Lachlan offered complimentary rooming for the week, I'd worried that Aria or Allegra, or both, had gotten into trouble for the incident. But Lachlan had insisted not. He'd been very professional about the whole thing and hadn't speculated on my feelings about Aria or being locked in a library with her all night.

What could I have said, anyway?

I spent a night talking with a woman, no sex, not even a kiss, and now I couldn't get her out of my mind. In fact, I was probably fifteen the last time I'd been this obsessed with someone. She'd turned me into a bloody teenager.

Aria smoothed her hair, something I noted she did when nervous. The delicate rings on her manicured fingers glittered in the light, and I suddenly imagined shoving her against the wall, pinning her hands above her head, and kissing the hell out of her. "Oh, Allegra's fine."

At her forlorn tone, I shook off my wicked thoughts and frowned. "Are you sure?"

She seemed surprised I'd pushed. Then her shoulders slumped. "Things are weird between us. I'm more than a big sister to her. I have kind of a parental role in Allegra's life. And I don't like it when our relationship is strained."

Hating the idea of anything upsetting her, I took a step closer. "Do you want to talk about it?"

Aria's eyes moved over my face, perhaps searching for my sincerity. Then, to my triumph, she leaned into me and opened her mouth to say—

"Ah, Ms. Howard, there you are."

She startled, stepping away at the sound of Wakefield's voice. The butler marched determinedly toward us, and if I could fry his arse with my mind, I would have.

"Wakefield?" Aria inquired.

He stopped and gave me a small nod of acknowledgment before turning to his boss. "The member you were expecting has arrived at the gates. Her car is on the way up."

"Thank you, Wakefield. I'll be right there." She watched the butler nod again and walk away before turning back to me. Her smile was tight-lipped. "Good afternoon, Mr. Hunter."

Mr. Hunter? I didn't bloody think so. "Aria—"

But she was already walking away.

As much as I enjoyed being in a relationship, I'd never chased a woman before.

Yet it seemed some degree of latent caveman masculinity was coming out because I wanted to live up to my name. I wanted to chase Aria Howard, hunt her down, and drag her back to my cave to have my dirty fucking way with her.

Thankfully, I'd evolved somewhat and knew that most likely would not end well for me.

The sexual restlessness rushing through me, however, needed to be dealt with. So I returned to my room, grabbed the letters for Walker, along with a change of clothes, and after dropping the letters by Walker's office, I hoofed it to the gym.

I worked out until sweat lashed from my body, until my muscles burned and my limbs trembled in the shower afterward.

It still wasn't enough to work Aria Howard out of my system.

TWELVE
ARIA

Despite the biting March chill blowing off the North Sea, the beach wasn't entirely empty. A few people in the distance walked the shoreline, their dogs running in and out of the freezing water.

It had taken my Californian blood some time to get used to a winter-like spring in the Scottish Highlands, but I was acclimating. Last year I'd worn a coat someone might wear in Antarctica with a scarf half covering my face while an oversized woolen hat took care of the rest of my head.

Now, I strolled at Sloane's side, looking more like a local in my lightweight but überwarm hiking jacket, scarf not covering my face, and jeans and hiking boots. Sloane pretty much wore the same thing. We were both hatless, our hair blowing back in the breeze as we walked in silence, enjoying the lulling sound of the dark sea roughly caressing the shore. Seagulls squalled in the gray sky above us. The golden, smooth sand of the beach followed the curve of the coast; grass-covered hills sloped down toward the sand but jutted out over the sea in the far distance.

I grew up by the beach, so it made sense that I felt at home living in a beach town. Malibu's beaches were beautiful, but Ardnoch Beach could compete. Sure, it didn't have the weather, but it was unspoiled and peaceful.

For the first time in weeks, I found myself relaxing.

"I can't imagine living anywhere else now, can you?" Sloane asked as if she'd read my mind.

I looked into her pretty brown eyes that reminded me so much of Allegra's. However, that's where the similarities between my sister and friend ended. "I can't."

Sloane must have sensed something in my tone because she cocked her head and inquired, "But?"

I'm lonely here.

I wanted to force out the words, to admit the truth to my only real friend in Ardnoch. But I was afraid Sloane would take it personally. She was such a good human, she would make it her life's mission to fix my loneliness, and she had enough on her plate to deal with.

"No buts." I gave her a tight smile and turned back to the sea. "Hey, any news about your evil stepmother or Nathan?" I referred to the fact that Sloane's stepmom had hired Sloane's psychopath of an ex (Callie's dad), Nathan Andros, to kill her and prevent Sloane from inheriting her father's fortune. She'd been estranged from her dad and had no idea he was dying. Unfortunately, he passed away before Sloane could be reunited with him. Her stepmom was charged with conspiracy to commit murder, and Nathan was charged with multiple counts of kidnapping and attempted murder, along with his friend Kyle Brixton, who'd tried to finish the job when Nathan couldn't.

"We're just waiting on trial dates. My lawyer said it could be another six months to a year before dates are set."

At Sloane's weary tone, I asked, "And how are you coping with all that?"

She gave me a smile that reached her eyes. "I have a lot in

my life to be thankful for. It took me a while to get out of my funk over Christmas—"

"You were grieving," I interjected. "That's not a funk."

Nudging me playfully, gratefully, Sloane nodded. "I know. I just hate Callie seeing me like that."

"What? Human?"

She chuckled. "I guess. Our lives are so weird right now. Dad's money came in a few weeks ago, and we're about to close on the bakery." Walker had secured a rental agreement from Gordon, a retired businessman who still owned a lot of property in Ardnoch, for Sloane's birthday. Now that she was an independently wealthy woman, however, they'd convinced Gordon to sell the building to her. "I've been worrying about money since I was sixteen years old and not having to is taking some getting used to. In a good way ... plus ..." A very specific kind of smile touched her lips, and her eyes gleamed in the gloomy daylight.

"Plus?"

Sloane full-out grinned in giddy excitement. "My rental agreement is up on the cottage, and Walker asked Callie and me to move in with him."

I stopped in the middle of the beach, joyful for her. If there was a part of me that experienced a pang of envy, I ignored it. "Sloane, that's amazing. I take it you said yes?"

She nodded rapidly. "I'm a little worried about us invading Mr. Bachelor's space, but when Walker makes up his mind about something ... He said he wanted his girls with him always." Tears of happy emotion filled her eyes, and she blinked them rapidly away.

"I would never guess that man was really just a giant marshmallow."

"No one would. And don't tell anyone. He doesn't like anyone to know."

Laughing at her teasing tone, I started to stroll again. "So your life is kind of crazy right now. Pending criminal trials, launching a new business, moving in with your boyfriend. That's a lot."

"It is. And it would be perfect if it weren't for the pesky criminal trial part."

I was glad she could make fun of such a dark situation, and I said as much.

"Well, that's enough about me." Sloane nudged my arm again. "What's going on with you?"

"Where are Callie and Walker today?" I hedged.

She gave me a knowing look. "Walker took Callie and Lewis swimming. Now stop changing the subject."

"Everything's fine. Same old."

"No." She pulled on my arm to halt my steps. Her dark eyes swept over my face. "Something is definitely up."

Had Lachlan blabbed to Walker? I couldn't picture it. But Walker incited a kind of trust. I could see Lachlan telling the security guard things he would never tell others. Especially because I knew Walker had a close relationship with the Adairs through Brodan. "Did Walker say something?"

Sloane's eyebrows shot upward. "What would Walker have to say? Has something happened?"

Damn it.

Realizing Sloane wouldn't give up until I told her (and honestly, I needed someone to talk to about it), I filled her in about Allegra locking me and North in the library. Then I told her what I'd told North. And like he'd been, she was furious at my moronic exes, particularly Lucas.

"North shared things too. Things he told me in confidence that I can't tell you."

She waved a hand in understanding. "I get it. So, whatever he told you, it made you like him?"

My heart raced at the thought. "I'm attracted to him. That's been the problem from the start."

"There are lots of hot actors at Ardnoch. Why did North make you so prickly?"

I shrugged. "Don't you think there are just certain people who you feel an extra spark with? Like, you're more aware of them for whatever chemical reason?"

"Oh, yeah." Sloane grinned cheekily. "But I've only ever felt that way about Walker."

"Really?"

"Yeah. Have you felt it for multiple people?" She seemed surprised I might have.

Hating that it was true, I practically snarled, "I felt it for that asshole Lucas. I mean, I was attracted to my ex-boyfriends, but Lucas just has that thing that North has. That extra quality that makes your skin tingle when he's near."

"But North isn't Lucas."

"I know." Sort of. "I understand rationally that North is not Lucas. And that he might even be a really good guy. But my gut is still screaming 'Danger, Will Robinson.'"

Confusion marred her brow. "Danger who?"

I gaped at her. "*Lost in Space*. 'Danger, Will Robinson.'"

She looked no less confused.

"The TV show. The robot that warns Will Robinson whenever there's a threat?"

Sloane chuckled apologetically. "I don't know that show."

I shrugged. "It's originally from the 1960s, but they remade it a few years ago."

"Like I have time for TV."

"I don't have time for TV either, but I grew up with Wesley Howard. If it's about movies and TV, it's trapped in here." I tapped my temple.

Sloane chuckled. "Okay. Anyway, back to what matters. Basically, your head is saying North might be a good guy, but your gut is telling you to run?"

"Exactly."

"I think you've got it confused. I think your gut is telling you North is a good guy, but your trauma is telling you to run."

Maybe she was right. But I wasn't in a place where I could take the chance to find out. I told her as much.

"Not even for one night of great sex that might give you your confidence back?" Sloane suggested.

The thought of North seeing me naked made me cross my arms over my chest. Right now, I liked that he was attracted to me. It made me feel good, even if it was confusing. The idea of him looking at my naked body and it repulsing him freaked me out. My throat tightened.

"Aria, what's going on in that head of yours?" My friend pushed.

I was ashamed that I was so ashamed of my body. It wasn't who I wanted to be, but there was only so much a person could take before they started to believe the shit others said about them.

At my silence, Sloane continued, "I always knew I wanted more with Walker than just sex. But I also thought it would never happen because he was such a bachelor. And I thought, what if I never feel this physically attracted to someone again? Did I want to give up the possibility of amazing sex just because it wouldn't last? I didn't. I decided I wanted what I could get from him. And even knowing that I was falling for him, I was still glad I took that chance because the sex was unbelievable." She laughed. "And it keeps getting better. If Walker had decided we were done, I wouldn't have regretted him."

"What are you saying?"

"You could take this chance with North. One night. Be in control of the situation and take what you want from him because he's offering."

I stared out at the water as we slowed to a stop. Unable to

meet Sloane's eyes, I confessed, "I used to have some insecurities about my body because my mother was always on my case about what I ate. But my high school boyfriend loved my body, so he helped me learn to love it too. Then after we broke up, my next boyfriend made little comments like my mom did about the things I ate. Like, 'Maybe you shouldn't have that cake for dessert.'"

"Asshole," Sloane spat.

I smirked sadly at her fierce loyalty. "And you already know what Preston and Lucas said. Over the years, those small insecurities have kind of grown to ..." Frustration and sadness fought to overwhelm me, but I pushed those emotions back. My voice was brittle with that fight. "I don't even like looking in the mirror if I'm in my underwear. So how can I get naked with North? Or any man, for that matter? And I hate that I'm letting them win by making me feel that way, but it's an ugly self-loathing I can't move past." The awful words rang out between us and I desperately wanted to take them back.

Sloane wouldn't let me.

She grabbed my hand and tugged, forcing me to look at her.

Tears of empathy gleamed in her eyes. "If I could hunt down every one of those guys, I freaking would. Or I'd sic Walker on them," she seethed. "I wish you didn't feel that way about yourself. And I won't tell you I think you're gorgeous, even though you're genuinely one of the most physically beautiful people I've ever met in my life, and I'm dumbfounded you don't know that ... but because I have a feeling it doesn't help when something is this deep-seated in your mind."

That was the thing. Sloane wasn't the first person to tell me I was beautiful. Mamma's modeling agency had even approached her about adding me to their plus-size roster, but I had never been interested in modeling, much to my mother's chagrin.

So why was I, a successful, independent woman, letting people ruin how I saw and felt about myself?

"Look, it's going to take more than a guy to help you feel confident again. You're going to have to find that place within yourself. But that doesn't mean North can't guide you to it. That he can't help you see yourself clearly again. And maybe you won't ever trust another actor to be in a relationship with ... but do you want to be alone forever?"

The thought of sitting all alone in that big empty house over the water filled me with icy dread. The word was hoarse as I pushed it out. "No."

Sloane squeezed my hand again. "Then let North be your guide. He was the one who suggested one night of no-strings sex."

"And you really think one night will magically fix me?"

"No. But it might be the first step to finding yourself again. And from there, maybe you'll let some future Mr. Aria Howard into your heart."

Her words percolated through my mind as we stared out at the water in perfect silence. The thought of stripping myself bare for North caused a strange mix of anticipation and anxiety.

I had a choice.

I could stay in this lonely fortress I'd built around myself where I'd locked away my sexuality to keep me safe from my and other people's ugly thoughts ... or I could be brave.

Could I be brave?

THIRTEEN
ARIA

I had never tried to sneak into the castle before, and I was shaking with jitters trying to do it now. Deciding to park my car at the spa and gym building so no one would come looking for me if I parked it at the castle, I walked the five minutes to the main building, glancing around like I was being followed. Or up to no good and didn't want to be caught.

The latter was true.

After talking with Sloane yesterday, I hadn't been able to get North out of my mind. The idea of being naked with him still made me feel sick with nerves, but I didn't want to go through life hiding anymore. Every action I'd taken throughout my entire existence had been because of someone else. I hadn't gone to an East Coast college because I wanted to be there for Allegra, and that was fine. I didn't regret that. But then I'd stayed in LA for her and my mother. Finally, when I left like I'd always wanted, it wasn't because I was ready to be brave and make a decision for myself. It was because I was humiliated and needed somewhere to escape.

It was way past time to start making decisions based on what I wanted.

So instead of leaving work at eight o'clock, I'd parked my car at the spa building and made my way back like a sneaky little sneak. It was kind of pointless to slink into the castle because there were cameras everywhere in the public rooms and at all the entrances and exits. Security would know I was there as soon as I walked in. However, I didn't want to bump into any of the staff because I didn't want to explain what I was doing there.

What could I tell them?

Oh, I have self-esteem issues and North Hunter agreed to fuck them out of me, so I'm going to go let him do that.

Yeah, that would sound great coming from the boss.

Some members were drinking in one of the public rooms, but I skirted the edges, sticking to the shadows until I reached the staff elevator. I practically collapsed into it once the doors closed and it carried me upward. Sweat gathered under my arms, which was not a good look for seducing someone. I was already terrified about getting naked in front of North.

Oh my God, this is such a bad idea.

I froze with sudden indecision as the elevator doors opened, revealing a thankfully empty hallway.

Maybe North had been kidding about a one-night stand. Maybe he'd say yes out of pity.

Goddamn it. I hated that voice in my head. My intention was to make my way to North's room. However, when I stepped out of the elevator, the faint stir of music caught my ear. I halted and tilted my head to listen.

Wakefield had mentioned that North was using the castle turret to play his guitar. Heart racing even harder, I followed the strain of guitar music to the turret. Trying to be as quiet as possible, I opened the door, and North's deep, smooth voice reached me.

My breath caught.

The man could sing.

Of course he could.

Entering, I gently closed the door behind me. It was a tight squeeze at the bottom of the turret. Narrow, carpeted stairs spiraled to the circular room above, where North played a song I didn't recognize.

Did he write it?

It had a slight folksy, country sound to it as North sang about being obsessed with a melody he couldn't get out of his head. As my body responded to the timbre of his singing voice, tingles awakening between my thighs, I leaned a palm against the cold brick and took a deep breath. Why wasn't he doing this for a living? The man's talents were apparently boundless.

I had to hope they were because I was somewhere between fleeing the castle, and perhaps Scotland altogether, and running upstairs to throw myself at him.

He's not Lucas, I reminded myself.

To my shock, my legs trembled as I forced them to climb the stairs. I wanted to shake the nerves out of them, but I couldn't force myself not to be anxious as hell. My heels didn't sound on the carpet as I climbed, so when I appeared at the top of the stairs, North didn't notice me at first. He sat on the edge of the armchair, guitar braced on his knee, his head down as he sang. There was a notebook on the floor in front of him with words scrawled in messy handwriting.

He had written this song.

My cheeks heated at lyrics that masked just how sexual they were. There was a playfulness to them that didn't surprise me as he talked about a woman who he wanted to lick like his favorite ice cream.

Jealousy scored through me as I wondered who the song was about. Did he write it for Cara Rochdale? His fascination with the pop star made sense. They had music in common. The thought depressed me.

Suddenly, he looked up and startled so badly, the guitar fell out of his hands. "Fuck!" he yelled, as the guitar hit the carpeted floor. "Fuck, fuck." North half glowered, half grinned. "You scared the shit out of me."

My lips twitched with humor. If only the fans of *King's Valley* in which he played a charismatic sociopath that terrified people could see him now. "Sorry about that."

North shook his head, as if a little dazed, and grabbed his guitar off the floor to check it over. "How long have you been there?"

Just as abruptly as I'd been laughing at him, my nerves returned. Did I really want to initiate sex with a guy singing about another woman? I didn't think that would help my self-esteem much. "Uh ... not long. Long enough to hear your song. You have a great voice."

He scrubbed a hand over his head and gave me a rueful smirk. "Did you like the song?"

I stiffened. Why would he ask me that? "Yeah, sure."

His expression flattened at my less than enthused response, and I felt like the world's biggest asshole.

"It's a great song," I hurried to say. "Catchy. Playful. Is it about your ex-girlfriend?"

North looked horrified. "Why would I write a song about a woman who pretended to love me for two years and then dumped me when I needed her? Though, to be fair, if I'd loved her back, it would probably sting a bit more and I wouldn't be writing songs about another woman."

I knew it.

He was writing songs about another woman.

I was such an idiot to believe his interest would last more than that night in the library. Feeling my chest ache with rejection, I gave him another tight smile and nodded. "Well, good night, then."

"Hey, hey, hey." North stood to his feet, his frantic tone stopping me midturn. He searched my face as if looking for some kind of answer. Then he let out a little huff as he rubbed the back of his neck. "The song is about you."

Stunned, I gaped at him.

His lips turned up at the corner. "You didn't know?"

"H-how could I k-know?" I stuttered in shock.

North's smile stretched into a sexy, wicked grin. "It's about a melody I can't get out of my head."

I frowned, not understanding at all.

He chuckled. "Aria ... your name is Aria."

And an aria was a song. A melody. Oh my god. I felt my cheeks burn with embarrassment and annoyingly, I was flattered. "Oh."

"Right. Oh." He smoldered at me and my heart rate picked up. "So, why did you really come here?"

It took me a minute to answer because I was running the lyrics through my head, and they were definitely about sex with me. Specifically, going down on me.

Arousal flushed through my body like liquid lightning, and when North's expression turned fierce and alert, I knew he could see my chest heaving with shallow breaths.

He looked at me like he wanted to eat me alive.

That, along with the song, bolstered my confidence. "Let's do it. Let's have one night together."

North's eyes flared and the muscle in his jaw flexed as he stared at me until I wanted to melt into a puddle of embarrassment.

"Or not." I shrugged like I didn't care.

Holding my stare, North bridged the distance between us, and my entire being seemed to hum toward him. My legs trembled so badly I wanted to rest my hands on his shoulders for support. Instead, I tried to stay as composed as possible.

"You sure it's what you want?"

Insecurity pricked at me. "If you want. I mean, if you don't, we're cool."

"Oh, I want," he growled, and I felt a rush of tingles between my legs in response. "But I want to know exactly what you're asking of me."

The thought of laying myself bare to any man would usually have me running in the opposite direction, but North already knew about the insecurities planted by my exes. "I ... I want one night. To ... to see ... I mean ... I just ... I want to prove to myself that I'm not a terrible lover. That I can feel attractive and s-sexual again." My cheeks were on fire.

North's pupils dilated as he leaned into me, his cologne tickling my senses. "We're going to prove that to you many, many times tonight."

I sucked in a breath, excitement and nerves thrashing in my stomach.

"Let's go." He nodded toward the stairs.

This was it.

I was really doing this.

WE THANKFULLY MADE it to his room without bumping into anyone, and now I wanted the floor to open up and swallow me. After carefully returning his guitar to its case, North turned around and asked me to take off all my clothes.

Swallowing hard, I hid my hands behind my back so he couldn't see my fingers nervously threading together. "Uh ... maybe we could do this without getting undressed."

"Fuck no," he said with casual but forceful resolve. "I want you naked."

I glanced around the room, looking for a means of escape.

North cursed under his breath and then crossed the room to me, drawing my skittish gaze back. Was he already regretting this?

To my surprise, he clasped my face in his palms and shook his head. "I'd like to skin those bastards alive," he murmured, and I gathered he was referring to my exes. "How can you be so confident in everything else you do but this? It pisses me off."

"Maybe we shoul—"

"Don't." He caressed my cheek with his thumb and then slowly slid his hands down to rest on my neck. Goose bumps prickled in the wake of his touch as he stroked my throat. There was a gentle dominance in his touch that my body definitely liked. "Don't say we shouldn't do this. Not if you want it."

I swallowed hard, and I knew he felt it beneath his hands. "I do want to. I just ..."

North leaned in so close his lips almost touched mine. I shivered as he whispered, "Talk to me."

Be brave.

Be brave!

"I'm afraid if I get undressed, you ..." I suddenly wanted to burst into tears, and that wouldn't do at all. "I can't." I pushed away from him and turned toward the door. "I'm sorry, I can't do this."

But North was in front of me, blocking my exit. His expression was patient, worried. "I will get out of your way if that's what you want. But I don't think it is."

"North ..."

"Talk to me, Aria. Whatever you say won't ever leave this room. I promise."

I would not cry. I rarely cried, and I wasn't about to start now in front of North Hunter. "I'm a mess. This isn't sexy.

Who wants this? No guy wants this." I moved to shove past him, but he grabbed hold of my biceps, tugging me close. My tears spilled over with no warning, horrifying me. "Let me go!"

"No, I will not let you go when you're upset." He crushed me against him, tucking my head into the crook of his neck. "We don't have to do anything. Okay? Just don't cry. I can't stand seeing you cry." His voice broke with hoarseness, and the sincerity in his words cut through my embarrassment. My fingers clenched into his T-shirt, and I shuddered against him as I tried to get a handle on my emotions.

I didn't know how long we stood there, but it was long enough for our breathing to slow. North just held me, running a soothing hand up and down my back until I was calm.

"I'm sorry," I whispered.

"You've nothing to apologize for."

There was something about being held by him, feeling his powerful arms around me, and not having to look him in the eye that made it a little easier this time to admit, "I'm afraid if I get undressed ... that you won't find me attractive anymore."

North's arms tightened around me, but he said nothing.

Oh, God, just saying those words had made me unattractive, hadn't they? "North?"

"I'm sorry. I'm just talking myself out of hunting down your ex-boyfriends and leaving them without the ability to procreate." His voice trembled with anger.

I smoothed a hand over his hard chest. "They're not worth it."

"You're worth it."

Surprised by the intensity of his tone, I lifted my head. His expression was so fierce, fury and longing roiling there for all to see. For me to see. "Christ." His voice was gravelly as he reached up to cup my face. "You don't even know how beautiful you are, and it kills me."

Did he really mean that? I fought against the insidious voice in the back of my mind that told me he was tricking me. That his words were a ruse to lower my guard. I mean, what guy would put himself through this for one night of sex? North was a disgraced actor, desperate to get his life back. Finding a way in with me to get to my father, who was influential enough to help him, made much more sense.

I instantly squirmed with guilt at the thought.

A good guy puts himself through this, another voice fought through my panic. *I think he might be a good guy. And if he's not, what's the worst that could happen? It's one night, not a relationship.*

Summoning what thread of bravery I had in me, I admitted, "I want to try again."

North swallowed hard, the crest of his cheeks flushing with arousal. It was kind of adorable. I suddenly was fully aware of the sensation of my breasts pressing against his chest and I knew North was, too, because I felt him harden against my belly. Tingles reawakened in full force between my thighs.

"Let's start slowly, then," he suggested gruffly, before taking my hand and leading me toward the bed.

My nerves played skip rope in my stomach again, but I forced myself to follow him.

Then North surprised me by sitting on the edge of the bed. His erection bulged against the zipper of his jeans. That didn't look comfortable. But he ignored it, staring boldly up at me as he leaned back on his hands. "Just take your hair down first."

My hair.

Yes, okay, I could do that.

Hands shaking a little, I reached up and tugged out the plain black hair tie. My hair was one of the few things I genuinely liked about myself. That and my eyes. Thick and dark, it spilled down around my shoulders as I released it. North seemed fascinated for a few seconds before his gaze returned to mine. "Now your shirt."

I found myself in a strange state of arousal and fear at his instructions. Pushing past the fear and leaning into the arousal, I tried to be courageous and held North's gaze as I slowly unbuttoned my shirt. He broke first, his eyes dipping to follow my hands. When I got to the last visible button, I tugged the hem out of my skirt and released the last few. Taking a deep breath, I shrugged out of it, letting the silk drop to the floor.

"Fuck me," North breathed as he took me in, eyes lingering on my full breasts cupped by my dark purple bra.

I wanted to slide my arms around my belly to hide the little of it that was exposed by my high-waist skirt, but I urged myself to refrain.

North's fingers clenched into the duvet behind him and his breathing seemed a little shallower. "How can you not know how fucking sexy you are?"

Wait until the skirt comes off ... Or not. "Maybe we could just do it like this?"

He looked into my eyes, understanding in them. "I want all of you."

It was almost a question. Taking in a shuddering breath and releasing it slowly, I nodded in agreement.

I could do this.

"Take off your bra," he commanded, voice thick with sex.

My nipples peaked under the satin before I reached behind to unclasp it. Before I could talk myself out of it, I pulled down the straps and let the bra fall to the floor on top of my shirt. Cool air prickled my skin, tightening my nipples into hard points. North's hungry stare made my breasts swell with anticipation.

Then his hands were on my hips as if he couldn't stop himself, drawing me between his thighs as his ferocious eyes drank me in. He smoothed his hands up my waist, goose bumps chasing his touch ... then he cupped my heavy breasts in his hands and gave them a gentle squeeze.

I moaned while he groaned and kneaded me.

"Fuck me, fuck me," North muttered, staring like he wanted to eat me alive. "You're so sexy it might actually kill me."

My skin flushed at the compliment.

Suddenly, he was on his feet and hauling me into his arms. "I need to kiss you."

It was only then that I realized we hadn't.

Kissed, that was.

Before I could respond, his mouth was on mine.

It wasn't a soft, sweet, gentle, coaxing kiss.

North's kiss was devouring.

I gasped into it as he kissed me like he wanted to fuck me. And it was exactly what I needed at that moment. Heat and desire exploded through me, sweeping my doubts and overthinking from my head until there was nothing but the feel of his hands on my body, the scent of him all around me, his lips bruising mine.

North broke away, panting, staring at me, a little stunned. "Jesus," he murmured, his hands on my hips, squeezing gently. "I knew it would be like this between us."

Relief eased through me. I wanted this with him, and maybe I could do it without overanalyzing his every word and touch.

But then he demanded, "Skirt off. Now." And all that sexy fire filling my belly flickered out, doused by the very thought of being fully naked in front of him.

FOURTEEN
ARIA

"Talk to me."

North was back on the bed, a wrinkle of concern between his brow.

I covered my naked breasts with my arms, feeling vulnerable and irritated. "Can't you just take your pants off?"

He gave me that gorgeous, lopsided grin. "Eventually, aye." Then he was serious again. "But first I want to know why the very mention of taking your skirt off turned *you* off?"

A memory seared through me, a painful flash that made me wince in remembrance. I hated that memory had power over me. I hated it was the reason I couldn't bear to look at myself for more than a few seconds in the mirror.

God, I didn't think I could do this. And didn't that make me the worst fucking tease in the world? I covered my face with my hands, ashamed and furious all at once. "I'm so sorry, but I don't think I can do this after all," I apologized hoarsely between the gap in my fingers.

"You were with me until I asked you to take your skirt off ... Christ, Aria, did ... did someone *hurt* you?"

At the horror in his tone, I dropped my hands. The look

on his face verged on devastated and realizing why, I hurried to assure him, "No, God, no, nothing like that."

North seemed to slump with relief.

A pang of affection cut through the vulnerability. Covering my chest again, I looked down at my feet and admitted, "Not long before we broke up, Lucas and I got into a fight because he ... oh, hell." I felt a little sick. "We were in bed. We'd just had sex, and he put his hand on my stomach and told me I'd be sexier if I did some sit-ups and lost some weight. That he liked a flat, toned stomach on his woman." I remember how hurt I was ... how repulsive I'd suddenly felt lying naked in bed with him. How I'd wanted to hide from him and the world. Instead, I'd told him to go fuck himself. Then I dressed and stormed out. He sent me flowers to apologize and begged me to forgive him. But I didn't want him to touch me after that and only two weeks later, Caitlyn sent me the video of the two of them together.

When North said nothing, I finally looked at him. The muscle in his jaw ticked, and I knew he wanted to pummel Lucas. He slowly stood, as if he were approaching a skittish animal, and moved around to stand behind me. His heat licked up my body as he leaned his chest against my back and took hold of my wrists, gently moving my arms back down to my sides. He trailed his fingertips up and down my arms, a caress that was soothing and arousing at the same time. My nipples peaked as he swept my hair over onto one side, revealing my neck.

A shiver cascaded down my spine when North rested his lips against my ear, his voice rumbling through me. "Not all men are made the same." His hands dropped from my arms and I felt a tug on the zipper of my skirt. I tensed as he continued, "Men like me appreciate women in all their glory." Slowly, he lowered the skirt zipper as he brushed a soft kiss against my neck. "And my brain and my cock happen to think you're the sexiest woman we've ever met."

It's a trick. Lies. He's just saying what he thinks you want to hear.

North pressed his lower body against mine as his hands slipped inside the skirt, and I gasped at the feel of his hard heat. If it was a lie, his cock was in on the deception.

I tensed as the skirt loosened and North pushed it down my hips. Then it dropped around my ankles.

"Step out," he demanded, brushing his knuckles down my back.

Trembling, I stepped out of the skirt, and North made a choked sound. "What?" I glanced over my shoulder to find him looking down at my legs.

He's repulsed by my wide ass, hips, and thighs.

"You're telling me that every day I've been here, you've been walking around wearing lacy fucking stockings and suspenders under your skirt?"

Oh. I let out a little laugh of surprise and relief. "You like?"

"I more than fucking like." He slid his hand over my ass and squeezed. Desire slickened between my thighs. Wow. Okay. "Let me look."

"You are looking."

But now he was walking around to sit on the bed in front of me. I moved to cover my breasts again and North shook his head. "Don't."

You can do this.

Feeling awkward, I dropped my arms and tried not to shift uncomfortably as his gaze traveled up from my shoes. My legs were one of my best physical assets. Long and well-formed, but my thighs were a little bigger than I'd like, and, of course, they led up to curvaceous hips and my dreaded belly.

My awkwardness, however, dissipated beneath North's

ravenous eyes. I swear to God, no one had ever looked at me like he did. Like he wanted to throw me on the bed and fuck me like there was no tomorrow.

"Jesus, woman," he huffed out hoarsely. "You're a walking wet dream."

I think he means it.

Even if he didn't ... he did at least want me. His dick straining against his jeans was proof of that. And this was just one night.

This was happening.

No more stalling. No more hiding.

Once I was naked, he'd either want me or not.

Deep down, I didn't feel those brave words. But I was determined to live by them, anyway. So I kicked off my heels and unclipped my suspenders.

Before I could begin rolling off the stockings, North lowered to his knees in front of me and took over. Instead of the efficient speed I would have used, he rolled each stocking down slowly, his lips following them, whispering across my sensitive skin. Sensation dipped and swooped low and deep in my belly. I shivered, growing wetter. Then his lips returned to my naked thigh and I spread my legs, inviting him upward until I was undulating into his kiss.

"North," I pleaded, running my fingers through his hair.

So distracted by lust, I wasn't prepared for the quickness with which he removed my underwear. Abruptly, they were around my ankles and North was staring up at me in all my nakedness.

I moved to cover my lower belly with my hand. It wasn't flat. It protruded a little and it rolled when I sat. North grunted with disapproval and gently pushed my hand away to caress me.

"Don't—" I moved to stop him and he shook his head at me.

"You're beautiful. Every fucking inch of you is beautiful," he promised seconds before he brushed his lips over my belly.

Tears brightened my eyes as he scattered kisses all over my stomach, his hands caressing every part of me he could reach, as he worshipped me with his lips.

It didn't feel like a trick.

And then he nudged me toward the bed until I was on my back. North stayed on his knees on the floor and cupped my ass in his hands as he draped my legs over his shoulders and buried his head between my thighs. He made a guttural noise of desire seconds before his tongue touched my clit.

Need slammed through me, and I undulated against his mouth. His fingers dug into my thighs, and his groan vibrated through me seconds before he feasted like a starving man. Lust overcame all insecurities, all doubts. There was nothing but North and the way he suckled my clit, pulling on it hard, then gentling, licking and lapping as if he had all the time in the world. Then he slid his tongue down in a dirty, voracious lick before pushing inside me.

"North!" I cried, thrusting against his mouth as I climbed higher and higher toward breaking apart completely.

Feeling my desperation, he returned to my clit and sucked and laved at it until I was nothing but a mindless, flushed thing that needed release.

But then he lifted his head, his eyes glazed with arousal. "You taste amazing." His voice was rough. "I could eat you all fucking night."

"Don't stop," I begged, reaching for him. "Please."

My wish, his command, apparently. He returned to torment my clit.

"North!" My orgasm hit like an explosion of fireworks, release sliding deliciously through me as I shuddered against his mouth and lights flickered behind my closed lids.

Feeling like melted butter sliding off toast, it took me a

minute to come back to myself. To remember that I was sprawled completely naked on North's bed, and I'd just been very, very loud as I came. My eyes flew open and North was now standing. I should have been afraid of the fierce intensity in his expression that told me I was about to be fucked six ways till Sunday, but the muscular body he revealed as he quickly undressed distracted me.

Of course, I'd seen him half-naked before, but somehow I'd forgotten just how phenomenal his body was. Every inch was sculpted to perfection. Lean, hard muscle. Muscles in places I didn't know there could be muscles. He also had the most dramatic V-cut obliques I'd ever seen, and most of my boyfriends had been guys who stayed in shape.

He was perfect.

And I so was not.

I pushed up onto my elbows, about to halt things again, when he shoved down his jeans and boxer briefs to reveal a very hard, throbbing cock already dripping pre-cum, standing to attention between his muscular thighs. No wonder he walked around all cocky with that thing between his legs.

I was suddenly parched.

Okay ... there was no faking that kind of turned on. And I hadn't had sex in what felt like forever. My inner thighs trembled with anticipation.

"Like what you see?" North teased as he whipped a condom out of his wallet, dropped said wallet, and then ripped the package with his teeth. All the while he held my gaze with this sexy confidence that made me want to jump him.

How did he do that?

How did he so thoroughly distract me from my insecurities?

"Very much." My words came out in a whisper that made

something like tenderness soften the harsh need in his expression.

North rolled on the condom and then he leaned over, took hold of me under my arms and slid me up the bed like I weighed nothing. I only had time to gape up at him in surprise for like a second before he kissed me breathless.

I widened my thighs, letting him settle between them, feeling his cock brush my belly as he kissed me until my lips felt swollen. As we kissed, he explored my body. His fingertips were calloused from playing the guitar, and their roughness sparked tingles of sensation as he caressed my soft skin. I moaned and arched into his touch. Ripples of desire undulated low in my belly as he played with my breasts, sculpting and kneading them, stroking and pinching my nipples. His kiss turned rough, hard, desperate, and his groan filled me as he pinched both my nipples between his forefingers and thumbs. I gasped with want, and his growl of satisfaction made me flush with pleasure.

North broke the kiss, but only to scatter more down my throat, across my chest until he reached my breasts. I cried out, eyes on the ceiling as his hot mouth captured my nipple and tugged. He worshipped my breasts until my nipples were swollen and my inner thighs turned slick with my arousal. No guy had ever taken this much time with my body. It was like his patience stretched to breaking, but he got off on it. He got off on drawing it out until we were both mindless with want.

So much so that I didn't even flinch as he kissed his way down my stomach, nuzzling me, murmuring how sexy and sweet I was, how soft my skin was. And then his mouth was between my legs again. North licked me and let out a curse. "Fuck, you're ready."

"Yes," I muttered, dazed, reaching for him. "Come inside me."

But he didn't. Instead, he tormented me, kissing his way

down my inner thighs, moving from leg to leg as he learned every goddamn inch of me with his lips.

By the time he trailed kisses around my ankles, I experienced a mixture of desperation and gratitude. He showed me with his mouth, his touch, that he enjoyed all of my body. Tears pricked my eyes. "North ..."

Whatever he heard in my voice had him crawling back over me. I knew he'd reached his breaking point, too, even though he'd caused this wild frenzy. He gripped his cock and guided it between my legs.

I arched as sensation scored down my spine at the hot feel of his tip pushing in.

North grabbed my thighs, his grip tight, forceful, and he spread me as he thrust inside. I gasped at the feel of him, overwhelming, full, right. Like there was an emptiness inside me for so long, but now he'd filled it. He held my eyes, his teeth gritted, as he fucked me with sure, steady, powerful strokes. I could do nothing but take him, my hands clenching the sheets beneath me as the tension built with every thick drag of him in and out.

"Oh God, oh God," I cried out over and over. I was going to come quicker than I'd ever come in my life.

Sure enough, the tension tightened to breaking, and I soared over the precipice I'd been building toward, exploding in voluptuous waves of sensation that made North bark out, "Fuck!" seconds before he fucked me harder, faster. His features strained taut with lust and, to my shock, I could feel the tension building again.

"Oh my God. North!"

"Aye, that's it. Come on me. You can give it to me again." The last words were hoarse, his grip bruising as he tried to hold off his orgasm, deliberately slowing his strokes. "Come around me again, Aria. Fuck, baby, come on me."

His words set me off and I shattered, giving up control.

Blood rushed in my ears as I shuddered around him. North's eyes flared as his hips stilled for just a second and then he let out a hoarse yell of guttural pleasure as he climaxed.

North shook as he came hard, his hips jerking as the last of his orgasm drained from him.

He slumped over me, his head buried in my neck even as he held his weight off my body. He still throbbed inside me as my inner muscles pulsed every few seconds. I wrapped my arms around him, running my hands down his sweat-slickened back.

Holy. Shit.

Holy fucking shit.

I'd just had the best sex of my goddamn life.

Totally worth the embarrassing beginning to get to that, I mused.

Then North Hunter ruined it by lifting his head. He stared deep into my eyes and declared, "If you think for one second we're a one-night-only deal, you're very, very wrong, Ms. Howard. Because I plan to do that to you many, many fucking times."

FIFTEEN
NORTH

I knew immediately it was the wrong thing to say.

I knew it because the hands that had been stroking my back fell away and Aria froze beneath me.

Oh, bollocks. I braced myself over her as she refused to meet my eyes. One second she'd been flushed, warm, and inviting. Now every part of her silently screamed *Get off me!* "Aria—"

"I better go." She pressed a hand to my chest. "Let me up."

"Aria—"

Her eyes flashed to mine, angry and hard. "I said let me up."

Gritting my teeth, I reluctantly eased out of her. She pushed up and covered her tits with her arm as if I was a stranger who hadn't sucked her nipples until they'd swollen. *Bloody Nora.* I slid an arm around her waist, halting her.

The look she gave me would have felled a mountain lion. She was adorable. I wanted to throw her back down on the bed and make her come all over again. Sensing that grinning at her like a lovesick fool would send her running, I kept a straight face as I leaned in. "Talk to me."

"There's nothing to talk about. We said one night. Now I'm leaving."

"Technically, the night isn't over."

"North—"

I squeezed her waist, loving the feel of her lush warmth beneath my hand. "Don't run away from this." And by this, I meant the spark between us. There was something here. We'd just had the most mind-blowing sex of my life. Aye, I definitely got off on making her loosen up and share herself with me, but it was more than that. It was the electric chemistry present between us since the start. Aria Howard excited me beyond reason. I hadn't lied when I said she was the sexiest woman I'd ever met, and now that I knew how phenomenal it was between us, there was no way I could live with the idea of onetime only with her.

Or just sex.

I wanted to know her. All of her.

Unfortunately, her gorgeous eyes narrowed with suspicion. "Run away from what? It was just sex."

Irritation simmered. "Just sex? We both know it wasn't just sex. It was fucking tremendous sex that comes along rarely, if ever."

Then she gutted me with a scoff. "Oh, God, you don't have to lay it on so thick to make me feel good. We had sex. You took my mind off my insecurities. Let's call your job done and then call it a day."

Furious, I released her. "Lay it on thick? My job done?"

Instead of answering, she shoved away from me and scrambled off the bed. I only had a brief glimpse of her magnificent sweetheart-shaped arse before she shimmied into her skirt with impressive speed.

I launched off the bed as she yanked on her shirt. I grabbed her wrist.

"What are you doing?" she huffed in annoyance as I dragged her into the bathroom with me.

"I have to deal with this fucking condom, and I don't want you running out while I do."

"Oh, you're being ridiculous."

"Am I?" I released her hand to take off the condom and watched her glance down and then look away like a school-marm. If her olive skin could blush, I bet she'd be a hundred shades of red.

"Was that necessary?" she asked once I was done. She glared as she buttoned up her shirt.

Still annoyed but wanting her to feel safe, to know I would let her go without (too much of) a fight, I batted her hands away and began buttoning it for her. Aria sighed in irritation but let me.

"First, if I'd treated you the way you just treated me after sex, I'd be considered a momentous prick of the highest order."

At my admonishment, she stiffened, then slumped as her agitation disappeared, replaced with obvious guilt. "You're right. I'm ... I'm sorry."

"Apology accepted. Even though it was really shitty to say what you said," I told her calmly but honestly.

"What did I say exactly?"

I searched her face, seeing the anxiety creep into her eyes. "To make it out as if I wanted to have sex with you again out of pity. That's what you were alluding to, right?" Sighing, I gave her a knowing look. "It says more about you than me, but it still makes me feel like crap."

She lowered her gaze, and an ache swelled in my chest as I studied her stunning face. I could feel the blood traveling south as my body reacted to her. Why her? Why was she so beautiful to me in a way that transcended physical beauty? I barely knew her. But I really, really wanted to know more.

And I knew I was in trouble. Because if I let her, this woman could hurt me.

"I'm sorry." Her eyes flew to mine as she apologized again. "Trust is hard for me."

At that moment, I regretted we hadn't met sooner. Before those arsehole ex-boyfriends had time to shred her, to have broken her so badly she'd built mile-high walls around herself. "Woman, no one can fake what we just experienced," I told her gruffly instead.

To my relief, a glimmer of heat and amusement entered her eyes. "I guess not."

Stepping closer, I pushed, "Then stay with me."

Indecision played across her features, and I held my breath, waiting.

She shook her head. "I would prefer to leave it as it is. You made me feel really good, and you helped me prove a point to myself. For that, I'm grateful. But I know that if we made this into anything more, everything we just had"—she gestured around the room, toward the bed—"would get poisoned by my trust issues."

Frustrated, I scrubbed a hand over my face. My tone was sharper than I intended as I demanded, "Do you just plan to stay alone for the rest of your life?"

Aria frowned. "No. I don't. But I also never intend to be ..." Something like an apology softened her expression and her voice gentled. "I won't ever be in a relationship with an actor or anyone in the industry, ever again."

Part of me understood. She needed to know there was no motive other than wanting to be with *her*.

However, it fucked me off after everything I'd told her that she could ever think I'd use her to get to her father. "You know I don't want that from you."

She understood my meaning. And she didn't agree. Seeing

my frustration, she placed a hand on my chest. "North, I believed every second between us was about us. And after Lucas, I didn't think I could ever say that again with another actor. But let's just leave it at that. Leave it at a place we both feel good about."

What did I expect? That my cock would magically make her trust me?

Fine.

I nodded and stepped back. "All right."

Aria seemed relieved by my acquiescence. Her smile was soft and too gorgeous for my own good. "Thanks again."

She walked back into the bedroom, and I followed her. The room smelled of sex, and I could feel myself growing hard, so I quickly pulled on the pajama bottoms folded on the nearest armchair. Aria tucked her shirt into her skirt, grabbed her underwear, and slipped into her heels.

My eyes traveled over her legs, and it just made me harder. The woman had the most fantastic pair I'd ever seen. I wanted them wrapped around my back.

When she was ready, she looked at me and quirked an eyebrow when she saw my arousal. "Oh."

Her surprise made me smirk. She still wasn't getting it. "I told you I still want you."

She visibly swallowed. "Uh, huh."

I tried again. "You could stay. Help me take care of it."

For a moment, my heart sped up at her obvious indecision. Then, as if snapping herself out of a daze, she spun toward the door. "I have to go."

Letting out a slow exhale, I took a second before I crossed the room to open the door for her. "Thank you for an unforgettable night, Aria."

Her eyes widened ever so slightly, her lips parting in surprise. "T-thank you. Too."

I gave her a small smile, forcing myself not to touch her.

Not to kiss her. Only to watch her as she hurried out of my room, darting down the hallway without looking back.

Finally, I shut the bedroom door and leaned against it.

Plotting.

My life was a disaster at the moment, and the last thing I needed was to jump into another relationship. But I didn't care. There had to be a way to get Aria to agree to see me. I just had to figure out how to convince her I couldn't give a flying fuck who her father was. That all I wanted was to get to know *her*. And to make her come a million times more while I was at it.

Reminded of my arousal, I glanced down. It was time to take a shower and relive every glorious bloody second of my night with the one woman I apparently couldn't have.

Apparently being the operative word.

Aria had been living in Scotland for a while, but she obviously hadn't figured out the one thing that many Scots had in common. We were a stubborn bunch of bastards, and I was the biggest stubborn bastard of the lot.

When I wanted something as much as I wanted Aria, I never stopped until what I wanted was mine.

Sixteen
ARIA

Despite the emails in bold declaring themselves unread and stacking up in my inbox, I ignored them temporarily as I tried my sister on the phone for the third time that day. For the third time, it went to voicemail.

The pit in my stomach grew as I laid my cell on the desk and stared at it. My feelings about Allegra were so complicated, and I wondered if finally she felt the parts I never wanted her to feel. There was a place inside me that resented the fact that I'd loved her enough to sacrifice what I'd wanted to parent her in a way I'd never been parented. On the other hand, I couldn't have lived with myself if I'd left her to go off to college on the East Coast. But clearly I fucked up, anyway, because she went off the rails for a bit, and I was constantly worried it would happen again. And I resented her a little for that too. But I loved her more. The idea that she hated me for not backing her plans to drop out of college made me feel restless and hollow.

It was almost enough to distract my thoughts from North.

My phone pinged and I jolted, eagerly reaching for it as I

saw a text come in from Allegra. Swiping the screen, I let out a breath.

> Sorry, can't talk now. Got class. Will call you.

The stilted tone, no x's and o's instead of the dozens she usually sent, didn't make me feel any better. But what would I say to her if we actually talked? *Oh, by the way, I know I decided you weren't mature enough to drop out of college because you locked me in a room with a strange man for the night, but I just slept with that guy. Don't you feel vindicated?*

Not that I thought she should feel vindicated. What she did was still wrong. But I knew she'd be hurt and annoyed to discover her plans came to fruition, despite what she saw as punishment.

I just needed to know she was emotionally okay.

> I get it. Hope classes are good. Love you xo

I waited five minutes, and she didn't respond.

It hurt more than I liked because it made me feel used. Like I wasn't lovable to her unless I helped her get what she wanted out of life.

Now I was just being maudlin. I tutted at myself, turning the phone over to stare at my screen. The clock on my desktop told me it was almost eight o'clock in the evening. Today had been *a day*. After I got home from my evening with North, I'd showered and barely slept a wink. Then I'd spent the day vacillating between worry for Allegra and daydreams about North Hunter's heated gaze and boyish smile.

I still couldn't believe that he'd so obliterated my thoughts with undiluted lust that I'd had sex without overthinking everything. In fact, I'd been thinking only of one thing, and that was North + orgasm = YAY.

Remembering the way he'd kneeled over me, powering into me, I couldn't believe that I hadn't been thinking about the way I looked beneath him. When Lucas took me in that position, I always worried that my belly jiggled with his thrusts, so I always maneuvered him out of it.

Not with North.

I hadn't cared with North.

He'd made me feel so wanted and attractive I could almost cry thinking about it now. If someone had told me a single night with that Scot could soothe wounds I'd been nursing for years, I never would have believed them. He hadn't miraculously made me trust men, but I trusted he found me attractive. That he liked my body. And that feeling was addictive. The emails I'd usually use as an excuse not to return to my lonely beach house held no appeal. Instead, my skin flushed at the thought of sneaking upstairs to North's room.

I hadn't seen him today. He'd stayed away. Maybe he wouldn't want me again, anyway.

I should go home.

But the thought of those big empty rooms, my empty bed, filled me with dread. When instead I could have North's hands on my body, his lips ... making me feel good. My pulse raced and I throbbed between my legs.

Oh, hell.

"Suck it up," I whispered hotly to myself, trying to talk my body into calming down. "Go home, put on a TV show, and forget about him." He was a disaster waiting to happen.

Decision made, I shut down my computer and grabbed my stuff. I couldn't help but glance at my phone again to see if Allegra had texted back. She hadn't. Another pang of hurt flared in my chest. There was an unread text from Mamma, but I left it unread for the night. She'd tried calling me earlier, yet I wasn't in the mood for her today. Not exactly a pleasant thing to think about my mother, whom I loved dearly, but North had put me in a good mindset about self-esteem and I didn't want my mother ruining it so soon.

Wakefield had finished for the day an hour ago, and the night butler was most likely hovering near the dining room where I could hear the murmur of guests having a late evening meal. I'd eaten dinner at my desk, trying to catch up on work that would have been done earlier if I hadn't been so distracted.

The sound of my heels was muffled on the Aubusson carpets as I strolled toward the hallway that would lead me past the grand reception room and into the staff quarters. Before I could reach it, my attention caught on the staff elevator.

The one that would take me upstairs.

To North.

A deep tug in my belly took me by surprise, but I forced myself to keep heading in the opposite direction.

I was almost past the elevator when suddenly my feet changed direction.

Oh my God, what are you doing? My breathing grew shallow with excitement as I hurried to the elevator and hit the button. The doors opened and I hopped inside before I could talk myself out of it.

You're insane. This will only end badly.

"Probably," I muttered to myself.

But I needed another hit of whatever drug North Hunter was, and until I got it, I knew I wouldn't be able to think of anything else. And being with him tonight sounded so much better than going home alone to the house.

Despite my confident decision to give into this potentially dangerous addiction, my legs trembled as I hurried off the elevator and down the hall to North's room, hoping desperately not to bump into another member. When I reached his door, that fear stopped me from hesitating.

I knocked without overthinking it.

At the sound of his footsteps drawing near, my pulse raced and the throbbing between my legs intensified. Then the door opened, and he stood with damp hair that told me he'd just showered, jeans, bare feet, and a white T-shirt that hung perfectly on those deceptively broad shoulders.

Sex on legs.

North's beautiful gray eyes rounded ever so slightly at my appearance.

I stated quietly, "Just sex? No strings?"

At the hesitant, wary expression on his face, I felt suddenly vulnerable.

Oh my God. He'd changed his mind.

One night had been enough.

I opened my mouth to tell him to forget about it, but the squeak of surprise that popped out cut me off as North took hold of my arm and hauled me into his room.

A WHILE LATER, I felt so warm and relaxed, my limbs sunk with perfect heaviness into North's mattress as I stared up at the ceiling and caught my breath.

He lay naked at my side, his arms sprawled above his head as his breathing finally relaxed too.

As soon as the man had closed the door on us, he practically ripped off my clothes and vice versa. We didn't say a word. We just attacked each other with our bodies and commenced a round of epic sex that proved last night was not an anomaly.

North + Aria = hot sex.

"I'm taking you fucking me into tomorrow as an agreement for a casual sex arrangement?"

I didn't have to look at him to know he was smiling. I could hear it in his response. "Caught that, did you?"

I giggled with postcoital bliss and suddenly, North rolled onto his side, drawing my gaze. At his cheeky grin and penetrating stare, I asked, "What?"

"I've never heard you laugh like that. It's fucking cute."

I rolled my eyes. "We both know there's nothing cute about me."

"That's where you're wrong." He moved over me, pushing between my thighs as he bent his head to trail kisses down my chest. I arched into his kiss, feeling my body light up again. So quickly. So needy.

Definitely addicted.

"You are many things," he murmured between kisses, "including cute."

"Oh?" I grinned at the ceiling and then gasped when he playfully bit my nipple. Meeting his cocky gaze, I spread my legs wider, inviting him to play more.

North's eyes darkened, and his voice deepened. "You are smart, sarcastic, brusque, and intimidatingly beautiful. But they're just the closet doors hiding all the sweet and kind and sexy inside. Oh, and cute. Don't forget the cute."

An ache spread across my chest. "Just sex," I whispered, reminding him. Reminding me.

Understanding gleamed in his expression seconds before he dipped his head to take my nipple in his mouth. I whimpered, threading my fingers through his hair while he played me as well as he played his damn guitar.

AFTER ROUND TWO, I gave myself five minutes to recover. When North got up to deal with the second used condom, I hurried out of bed to dress before he returned.

I was so fast, I was already buttoning up my shirt by the time he sauntered out, completely at ease and confident in his nakedness.

He should be.

The man's ass was the stuff of gods.

At the sight of me preparing to leave, he scowled and came to a stop, hands on his hips. "Not this again."

I bit my lip as I eyed his hot, naked body and the semihard cock between those sculpted thighs. "It's very difficult to take you seriously when you're standing there looking like that."

"Aria."

At the warning note in his voice, I assured him, "I'm just heading out so I don't get caught doing the walk of shame in the morning. I don't want the staff to gossip."

"You do know security might have seen you come to my room on the CCTV system."

I did know that, and while it didn't make me entirely happy, I shrugged. "The security guys are not gossips. It's part of their job to keep their mouths shut."

He sighed in exasperation and crossed the room to stop me as I picked up my shoes. North drew me into his arms, sliding his hands to grasp my ass. Pressed to his hot, hard body, I trembled with renewed desire. This was getting out of control. I'd never been this turned on by a guy in my life. Stroking my fingers over his smooth shoulders, I insisted, "I have to go."

"But—"

"You could come to the beach house tomorrow, though." The words blurted from me before I could stop them.

North raised an eyebrow. "Really?"

Well, it was out there now.

And I liked the idea of not coming home to an empty house. "Yeah. You could drop by my office tomorrow and I'll give you a key. Hang there if you need a change of scenery. Play your guitar to your heart's content. Maybe write a song about how good sex with me is."

He squeezed me tighter against him, grinning like a sexy, smug bastard. "Good? I think you mean fucking phenomenal."

Chuckling, I shrugged. "Maybe."

North gave me a pretend scolding look. "I guess tomorrow I'll just have to prove how phenomenal it can get. And if we're all alone in the beach house, you can scream through your orgasms as loudly as you want."

I raised an eyebrow as I pushed teasingly away from him. "Scream? I doubt it."

"Oh, gorgeous, you just set a challenge I intend to win."

Shoving my feet into my heels, I met his smoldering stare. "Well, if you lose, I win, and if you win, I win, so I'm looking forward to the trying."

North laughed as he followed me to the door. But as I opened it, he leaned in and whispered hotly in my ear, "There's no running away tomorrow night. You're mine all fucking night, and I intend to keep you busy coming until dawn."

A shiver of need so powerful rippled over me I almost slammed the door shut and jumped him. Instead, I turned to find his lips an inch from mine, his expression deadly serious.

My answer was to close the distance between our mouths and take his in a deep, slow, wet kiss that promised I was up for that challenge too.

A few minutes later, I let myself into the staff elevator, hoping I didn't bump into anyone because I had sex hair, swollen lips, and I was pretty sure my nipples were hard enough to poke through my bra.

I felt alive.

Awake.

I felt like the girl I'd lost years ago. The one who'd been excited by her sexual awakening before those men came along and made her want to hide.

North had done what Sloane said he might. He'd guided me back to myself. I wasn't all the way there yet, but I was inching closer.

I just had to keep in mind that this was all it was. My sexual reawakening and a bit of harmless no-strings sex for him.

It was nothing more.

More would hurt us both.

Seventeen
NORTH

Thunderous clouds above had turned the North Sea gunmetal gray as rain battered it, dancing off the water's surface like oil hopping off a hot pan. I shivered from the safety of the Howards' beach house porch, admiring the force of nature. Waves crashed onto the shore below, the rhythmic sound, while more aggressive than usual, soothing.

I envied Aria this home, its position, its sanctuary. But only from here. Inside, while stylish and comfortable, it didn't feel lived in. There was no sign of what Aria's life consisted of outside work. No hobbies I could see. I imagined her returning home here late every night to no one to hold her and listen about her day and help her decompress.

The idea was miserable, and it agitated me.

She was living half a life here, and it was a damn travesty.

Dictator's "Moonlight" rang in my arse pocket, and I pulled out my phone to see Theo calling.

Stepping back inside, I closed the porch doors and marveled at the silence that followed. The beach house windows had to be made with special noise-reduction glass.

Heat licked my chilled skin as I answered my phone and lounged down by the fire.

"Cavendish, you sneaky bastard," I answered casually.

He drawled, amused. "What the hell have I done now?"

"You sicced Walker on me about those letters."

"Oh, that. I just mentioned it in passing. It's not like I give a shit about you, mate."

I grinned. "Right. How are you?"

"This lead actor is killing me. I walked into 'a situation' when I agreed to guest direct. Viola Stewart, his costar, got a lot of attention for season one, and now he's acting like a little prick. Late to set, questioning lines, questioning camera shots. Next time he does it, I'm going to fucking stuff him in a used Portaloo."

My lips twitched. "Who is it again?"

"Lucas Grant. A bit of a newcomer. The bastard has talent and charisma for sure, but Viola's on another level, and his fragile ego cannot stand it."

Blood rushed to my ears. "Did you say Lucas Grant?"

"I did."

That piece of shit had gotten a part in a hit show after he'd screwed over Aria? She didn't tell me that. "Do me a favor and send the Portaloo off a fucking cliff."

"You know this guy?"

"I can't go into details, but he hurt someone I care about."

"Interesting, considering I found out he used to date Aria Howard," Theo mused. "He likes to tell anyone who will listen that she fucked up his chances of working with Wesley."

That scummy bucket of rancid turds. "Make sure that Portaloo is stuffed to the gills with sheep shite before you stuff him in it."

Theo snorted. "Oh, you have it bad, old boy, don't you?"

"It's not about me."

He considered this. "I only have to tolerate one more week

of directing this thing. I'll come up with something fun to express my appreciation for Lucas's abhorrent behavior."

I smirked at the thought. Theo was devious when he wanted to be. "Keep me posted on that."

"So, what are you up to, my friend? Other than defending a lady's honor."

I rolled my eyes. "I'm hanging tight on the request of my agent. There might be some movement on the Forster movie."

"That's good. You're at the castle?"

Glancing around the beach house, I lied, "Aye. Still here."

"Well, I might see you soon, then. Once I'm done here, I'm flying back to Ardnoch to work on that damn script."

"Still giving you problems?"

"Being here has shaken some ideas loose, but I like the peace up north. Besides, before I left, I made the acquaintance of this young widow from Thurso. An ex-gymnast, if you can believe. Wonderful girl. Very flexible. It's a bit of a trek to bed her, but she does this thing with—"

"I don't need to know the details, you dirty bugger."

"Oh, that's right. I forgot you like your sex wrapped up in romance and commitment. Sometimes I don't know why we're friends."

Chuckling, I reminded him, "You called me."

"Yes, well, despite your appallingly saccharine need for monogamy, you are quite a bit less of a prick than most of my other acquaintances."

"High praise indeed," I snorted.

"Oh, fuck, they need me back on set. I haven't even finished my sandwich. Don't be surprised if the next time you see me I've wasted away because soul-sucking fiends known as actors have nourished themselves on my blood and bones."

"Goodbye, you melodramatic bastard."

"Yes, well, fuck you too."

"Talk soon."

"Tell Ms. Howard I was asking for her," he snuck in with laughter in his voice before he hung up.

"Bawbag," I muttered.

I was just reaching for the television remote when the sound of the front door closing brought me to my feet. Anticipation filled me as I strode quickly through the house toward the entrance. As I entered the foyer, I drew to a halt. Aria stood at the door wringing rainwater from her ponytail. Water drops clung to her eyelashes and wet her plump lips. Her olive cheeks glistened with rain, and her soaked shirt clung to her tight nipples. My skin heated and all my blood traveled south.

This woman was a craving I'd never experienced before.

I'd read about it. Damn, even the characters I'd played had experienced it.

But me? Nah. As a teenager, I'd been like any teenage bloke and was sex obsessed.

Since then, I'd definitely wanted the women I'd had relationships with, beyond sex. But I'd never felt like I was on the verge of losing control of my senses every time they walked into a room.

Not like with Aria. And I couldn't explain it. It wasn't rational.

I wanted her like I'd wanted no one. Wanted to feel her skin against mine, be inside her hot, tight body, needed to kiss every fucking inch of her. All the damn time.

"I didn't take a jacket," she huffed as she squeezed the last of the water from her hair. "I was less than thirty seconds from the castle to my car and then just a few seconds from the car to the house and then—oh!" She startled as I hauled her against me, her hands dropping to my shoulders. Her wet clothes dampened mine, but I was more focused on the warm, soft body beneath them. Whatever she saw on my face made her eyes widen in understanding. "Oh. But ... I'm all wet." She closed her eyes, half smirking at her innuendo. I grinned and squeezed her closer. "You know what I mean."

"I do." I brushed my lips over hers, unable to resist any longer. I could taste some kind of fruit lingering on them and she smelled of fresh air and an ambrée perfume. My dick hardened. "And you're about to get wetter."

EVERYTHING HAD BEEN GOING PHENOMENALLY. If I'd thought our first few times together were a fluke, this was proving otherwise. After she led me to her large bedroom that overlooked the water, we'd gone at each other like savage animals. Perhaps we'd settle soon enough into our attraction, but once we'd pushed past Aria's insecurities that first night, we were too bloody hot for each other to slow down.

Until five seconds ago, when I'd stopped midthrust, suddenly desperate to have Aria on her hands and knees. I'd made the demand and tried to manhandle her into position, lost to my lust for her. However, her shoving my hands off in distress was like a bucket of ice-cold North Sea water being thrown over every inch of me, including my cock.

"Hey, hey." I reached for her arms. "It's okay, we'll stop, we'll stop."

She grew still, her wide eyes and vulnerable countenance making my chest ache. I kneeled between her thighs as horror and embarrassment filled her expression. "Oh, God. Let's just ... I'm gonna ... I'm ..." She tugged on her wrists but I held on.

"Talk to me. What just happened?"

Annoyance now seeped into her embarrassment, and I watched the telltale signs of her getting ready to throw up her barriers. "Maybe this is just too much work for you. I'm sure you can find one of the members to satiate your needs."

"I'm sure I could," I agreed patiently.

Her eyes dimmed, but she stubbornly tilted her chin. "Then you can go."

I wanted to kiss the stubbornness right out of her. "If that's what I wanted, I would have been in a different woman's bed every night since I got here."

"Brag much?"

I shrugged. "I'm just stating facts. But it's not what I want. You see, my cock has very particular tastes, and right now he's only satisfied by a complicated, prickly estate manager. In fact, he was in the middle of finding something well beyond mere satisfaction when everything went fucking pear-shaped. We'd both quite like to know exactly what happened." I smoothed a hand down her arm. "If you don't like a certain position, it's fine. We don't have to do anything you don't want to do. But just tell me that. Don't shut me out."

Aria's lips parted as she studied my face. I wondered at the bastards who'd bedded her, how they'd treated her. It made me want to rip off their dicks. Absurdly, not just because they might have treated her so poorly, but because they'd touched her in the first place. I didn't think of myself as the alpha caveman type, but I certainly experienced a tight, horrible feeling in my chest that pointed to possessiveness.

"I ... um ..." She lowered her eyes, looking mortified. "I ... it's not that I don't like that position ... I ..." Aria covered her face with her hands and every part of me wanted to cuddle her against me. Tugging on her wrists, I gently eased her hands down and ducked my head so she had to look at me.

"Talk to me, gorgeous."

She exhaled slowly, shakily. "L-Lucas made a few comments about my ass and now I'm worried if you take me like that, all you'll be thinking about is how fat my ass is."

Lucas Grant was a dead man.

I didn't know how or when, but I was going to make him pay for what he'd done to Aria. No one would know the confident, efficient, capable, strong, smart woman who strutted around the castle like she owned it hid a well of insecurities and fear. All because of Lucas Grant and his ilk.

Sheep shite in a Portaloo off a fucking cliff was too good an end for the bastard.

Trying to rein in my anger, I sat back on my heels. "Show me."

Aria looked horrified. "What? No."

"I've seen your arse, Aria. We've had sex several times and I've buried my face in your pussy." I grinned at the dirty look she gave me. "But we need to deal with this face-on, so to speak. Turn around and show me that fine arse of yours."

She crossed her arms under her tits, and my cock twitched at the sight. "Nope."

"I'll go first." I offered, spreading my arms. "I'll show you mine."

Amusement glittered in her eyes. "I've seen yours and it's rock hard from the gym—you know, the place you spend half your day in. Maybe if I did more than swim a few times a month, we wouldn't be having this conversation."

The irritation and fury at Lucas still lingered, so I stated, "Let's get this straight. I am not Lucas Fucking Grant. He's an arsehole who more than likely got off on trying to make you feel like you weren't worthy of him. You're probably not the only woman he's done it to. That's about him. Not you. So turn around and show me your arse so I can prove that I love it."

Her lips twitched as she huffed out a groan of acceptance and then reluctantly, so slowly it only made my heart race harder, turned around on her knees and sat back on her heels. I swallowed hard at the sight of her exaggerated curves. At the long, graceful line of her back as it narrowed, then swooped down into her perfect heart-shaped arse. Her dark hair tumbled in silky disarray across her smooth olive skin, and my fingers twitched, desperate to touch her.

"North?" She glanced over her shoulder.

Heart pounding, dick throbbing, I bridged the distance between us until my chest pressed to her back and she could feel how hard I was. She gasped as I slid my hand around her belly and down between her legs to find her clit.

As I tormented her, her breathing grew shallow and fast. I rubbed my cock between her ass cheeks, grinding on her. "If I have to tell you this every time I take you to bed, I will ... But you are perfect. A fucking goddess. And you and your body set my blood on fire, woman. I can't get enough." I kissed the side of her neck as my fingers moved faster, harder over her, and she whimpered with her coming orgasm. "Sometimes I wonder if I'll ever get enough of you," I confessed, and suddenly Aria cried out, shuddering against my touch.

As she tried to catch her breath, I smoothed a hand up her back and whispered in her ear, "Can I fuck you on your hands and knees now?"

There was a moment's hesitation, then, "Okay."

"Are you sure?" I pressed. "I only want this to be good for you."

"I'm sure," she said with more conviction seconds before she moved forward on her hands and knees, presenting her luscious arse to me.

I groaned as I caressed the curvy globes, my thumb slipping until she gasped in surprise and glanced over her shoulder at me. My voice thickened with need. "Maybe one day you might let me take you here?"

"I've never ..." She shimmied her arse against me, and I grunted. "Maybe. But for now, don't be greedy."

Chuckling on a huff of desperate need, without preamble I guided my cock to her pussy, then gripped her arse cheeks, and thrust in.

"Oh!" Aria cried out, steadying herself.

"You all right?" I asked hoarsely because my entire being was centered on the heat squeezing my cock. Fuck, I wanted to take her bare.

"Yes, yes, don't stop."

So I didn't.

The sight of her taking me, her back arching, the way she pushed into my thrusts with mindless want sent me too close to the edge too soon. I wanted her to come first, like this, to prove she was so lost in what was between us that her insecurities would disappear. Lucas Grant and every prick who had come before him weren't in this room with us, in her mind, poisoning the way this felt. I reached out, wrapped her hair around my fist, and gave it a gentle tug, testing her.

Her pussy rippled around me as she moaned, arching into the next drive of my cock.

Something bigger, more dangerous than satisfaction, slammed through me, and my grip on her tightened. I tugged a little harder.

Aria cried out as her pussy clamped around my driving dick and throbbed, convulsing around me in tight squeezes that cut off the blood to my brain. I let go of her hair to grab her hips, pumping harder, faster into her climax until she wrenched my orgasm from me.

"Aria!" Her name exploded from my lips in a growled yell of disbelief, my mind momentarily blanking as pleasure consumed me. My hips shuddered as I came and came and fucking came.

Fuuuuuuck.

I think I might have spaced out for a few seconds.

My limbs were warm and loose as I pressed my lips to Aria's damp upper back before I pulled out of her.

Then I kissed her delicious arse for good measure and gave it a gentle smack. "This is my arse now, princess."

She let out a huff of laughter as she collapsed onto the bed and turned, her hair clouding around her face, her tits trembling. Her low-lidded eyes smoldered with pleasure and amusement. Her voice was huskier than ever. "Honestly, I can't even argue with you after coming that hard."

Smug, pleased, I grinned. "Good to know that I now have a way of winning every argument with you."

Aria rolled her eyes, and I laughed as I reluctantly jumped off the bed to deal with the condom.

When I returned from the bathroom, tenderness filled me at the sight of her drowsy expression. I tugged on her hand, and her eyes opened. "You need to eat something."

"I'd rather sleep." She yawned as if to prove her point.

The woman worked too hard. Determined, I tugged harder. "Eat first. Then sleep."

Hearing my tone, she groaned and pushed up off the bed. "Okay. But I hope you're cooking."

Chuckling, I hauled her onto her feet, copping a feel before I helped her into her robe. She only rolled her eyes again at my antics, but once I'd pulled on my jeans, she followed me downstairs, where I proceeded to force her to sit and do nothing while I made a pile of French toast for my woman.

My woman.

Three nights together and already she had me thinking that way.

I knew Aria wasn't thinking that way.

This was just casual for her.

But I already knew it wasn't casual for me.

I was hooked.

And in big fucking trouble.

EIGHTEEN
ARIA

I couldn't remember the last time I'd floated into work in such a good mood. Worries over Allegra's continued distance got shoved to the back of my mind. Not even the link my mother had sent me to a website for a new diet fad bothered me, and the million things I knew I had to do at work made me anticipate instead of dread it.

All because last night a generous man had made me feel beautiful and sexual, then fed me, then gave me another two orgasms before insisting on holding me as we fell asleep in bed together. I should have told North to go back to the castle, but it was raining and the truth was, I loved every minute of falling asleep in his arms. It didn't mean anything other than I was appreciative. I'd permitted myself to enjoy North Hunter.

And I felt like a new woman.

North snuck into the castle first when we pulled up. I waited five minutes and strolled in on my cloud of happy. I beamed at Wakefield and called good morning to him. If my cheery greeting surprised the man, no one would know. Wakefield was the world's best butler. He could keep a neutral expression through anything.

I'd barely settled into the office when he knocked on my door, bringing me my morning coffee. Beside the cup was a small plate. "Mrs. Hutchinson made her famous shortbread last night, and I took the liberty of procuring some for you."

I grinned at Wakefield. "She forced you to bring it to me, didn't she?"

"Yes, she did, Ms. Howard."

Chuckling, I took the plate and coffee. "Thank you, Wakefield."

"Very good, Ms. Howard." He retreated from the office with a nod.

Eyeballing the shortbread, I murmured, "What the hell." I'd burned calories last night. My skin heated remembering the way North had powered into me and the way I'd turned mindless and wanting beneath his hands. Never in a million years did I think I'd be able to get out of my head long enough to let go this much in bed. Honestly, it was more than a minor miracle. I didn't think I could switch off like that for just anyone.

Making yummy noises as I ate my shortbread, I logged into my work inbox and swept over the subject lines of the first few emails. One caught my eye because it was from an address I didn't recognize and the subject line was ***Urgent: Ardnoch Estate Inquiry***.

Clicking it open, it took my brain a second to catch up with my body because my heart was already racing with incredulity and anger.

The email read:

To Whom It May Concern,

It's incumbent upon me to make you aware that your estate manager, Aria Howard, is an overweight smear on the reputation and image of such an illustrious club as Ardnoch. Nepotism is an ugly thing when it puts your reputation at stake. You may want to rethink the hiring of an intellectually deficient fat girl that Lucas Grant dumped. Rumor has it she's as frigid as she is stupid. Not to mention superior, unfriendly, and a bitch to your members. If you want a fat, nasty moron running your estate, have at it. But I think we both know Ardnoch deserves better. We're paying a lot for membership. Don't you think we should get what we're paying for?

Yours sincerely,

A Disgruntled Member

THE WORDS *FAT*, *frigid*, and *moron* kept jumping out of the email at me as I scanned it again and again, trying to make sense of it. My cheeks burned with rage and mortification as I cross-checked the email with our members' files. There was no match. Racking my brain, I tried to think if I'd had an unpleasant encounter with any of the members, but none sprang to mind. The only person was North, and while I may not fully trust him, I didn't for one second believe he'd send an email like this to anyone.

The other option was that it wasn't a member. However, my email address wasn't public. Of course, that meant little. Caitlyn got a hold of it, so clearly anyone could.

But this person knew exactly what buttons to press if they wanted to hurt me.

Why were people so goddamn awful?

My mouse hovered over the delete button, but ultimately I was smart about it and created a new folder in my inbox and filed the email away.

Just like that, the anonymous troll had ruined my amazing morning.

I jolted in my seat as my desk phone rang. The screen told me it was security. Wonderful. What now? "Aria speaking," I answered tonelessly.

"Ms. Howard." Walker's familiar gravelly voice sounded down the line. "Have you seen the news this morning?"

I felt a pang of worry as I brought up my web browser. "No, what's going on?"

"We may need to prepare for the paps returning to the estate. North Hunter is in the news again."

I hit the speaker on the desk phone so I could free my hands to type. Sure enough, as soon as I searched North's name, new headlines appeared on the screen. I scanned them, my pulse racing on his behalf. Someone had leaked the CCTV footage of the night North's friends attacked the homeless man.

"Does North know?"

"I don't know. Have you seen the footage?"

I wasn't sure I wanted to. "No."

"Be prepared if you do. It's difficult to watch."

Sucking in a breath, I clicked play on the video. Someone had digitally circled a young boy as he stood back from the others who beat on Gil MacDonald. I'd heard the story directly from North, but actually seeing it, seeing how small he was, broke my heart. I watched as he dove into the crowd of boys, pushing them off the man and getting into a rough tussle with whom I assumed was Darren Menzies. The other boys joined in, beating North. Gil took that opportunity, just as North had said, to run, but the boys abandoned their fight with North to chase after him. North staggered to his feet, clearly badly beaten, and chased after them. The footage switched to a different CCTV camera where you could see Darren chasing Gil into traffic. I flinched as the van hit him.

"Oh my God," I whispered, my heart aching for North.

The article focused on exonerating North, but it didn't matter. They were dredging it up again, making him relive this thing that had scarred him deeply.

"You all right?" Walker asked.

"I hate the tabloids."

"Aye, me too." He sighed heavily. "Look, all the articles I've read are apologetic and favorable toward North. This might be a good thing for him."

"For his career," I corrected Walker. "Not for him. This is just making him relive it all again." Realizing my tone and words gave too much away, I was a little sharper as I said, "I'll contact Mr. Hunter and make sure he's aware. You, Jock, and the team should prepare for visitors at the gate."

"We're on it."

After we hung up, I stared at my cell phone. I didn't want to call him to explain this. It needed to be face-to-face. They could do without me at the castle for one day. I could answer my emails from home, and anything else Wakefield could deal with. I was five minutes away if they needed me. Decision made, I gathered my stuff and hurried upstairs to North's room. When he opened the door, he was wearing workout gear.

He seemed surprised to see me so soon. "I was just heading to the gym."

"We need to talk," I told him solemnly.

———

I'D DECIDED North's well-being was more important than my professional reputation, and I wouldn't overanalyze that either. Without explaining myself, I told Walker that North would be at my place if they needed us. Sloane's partner didn't make a big deal out of it, but I had no doubt he'd tell Sloane later. We wouldn't have told security, but with the paparazzi most likely on their way, Walker and his team needed to know where North was. I informed Wakefield I'd be working from home today and to call if he needed me.

Then I'd waited in my car for North as he packed an

overnight bag. He appeared in the gray morning light, face grim, and my agitation grew. I just wanted to get him to my place to make sure he was okay. The anonymous email I'd received that morning paled in comparison to what he was going through.

A while later, we sat together on my couch, North staring out toward the water with a mug of hot coffee between his hands.

His cell had been ringing nonstop since we left the castle. They had just woken up in the US, so it had taken them a little longer to hear the news. First his publicist, then his agent called, then a lot of friends who had abandoned him these past few months. Cara, apparently, had been trying to get him back before this, and she called so many times, it compelled North to block her. I didn't overanalyze how satisfied I felt by that.

His inbox, in general, was filled with apologies.

"What are you thinking?" I asked quietly.

His gaze flicked to me, and I hated the weariness I saw there. "That I can't believe this is being dredged up again."

"It's different this time," I told him gently. "Everyone can see you tried to stop it."

"You watched?"

I nodded grimly.

"Fuck." North shook his head, agitated. "You shouldn't have had to see that. No one should have. Gil's family shouldn't have to see it. The fucking tabloids don't care who they hurt."

An alarming surge of tenderness and admiration filled me. North didn't care if this cleared his name. He cared if people could be hurt seeing the video. The police had reported the footage missing from their evidence archives, so someone had been paid to steal it.

He put down his mug and stood, pacing beside me. "Who would leak that? Who would do such a thing?"

"Who would gain from it?"

North halted and looked sharply at me. "I would." His expression tightened, and he yanked his phone off the table. "No, no fucking way."

"North, talk to me." I stood, grabbing his wrist before he could dial whoever he was planning to call.

"It's like you said. Who would gain from it? I would. The studio would rehire me and everyone on my team would make a lot of money if this spy franchise were to take off."

Understanding, I still didn't remove my hand. "But you can't go accusing anyone because you won't ever know for certain if one of them got hold of that footage. All you'll do is cause more drama and strife among your team. It's done now. It's out. As difficult as it is, you have to make peace with that."

He glowered, but I knew it wasn't at *me*. Then North's expression changed as quickly and dramatically as the Scottish weather. Pain etched his features. "I feel like I'm going to spend my whole life paying for that night. And maybe that's the way it should be."

Without thinking, I clasped his face in my hands, the bristle of his unshaven cheeks prickling my palms. "You did nothing wrong. You tried to save a man. But you were just a child, North. And you have to learn to forgive yourself."

He wrapped his hands around my wrists, but not to pull away. Instead, he leaned his forehead against mine and closed his eyes.

I stayed there with him, holding him, letting him take whatever comfort he could from me. And despite all my alarm bells ringing that I was allowing intimacy I wasn't ready for to deepen between us, I could not pull away.

NINETEEN
ARIA

"Who were you as a teenager?"

I looked up from the soup and sandwich I'd thrown together for a late lunch to find North studying me curiously. It had been an emotional morning, and North had taken a walk on the beach for some fresh air. I'd stayed back, to give him time to think, and so I could work through the emails piling up in my inbox. I also spoke with Lachlan to update him on the situation after Jock called to tell me that a few paps had arrived at the gates. There weren't as many as the first time because apparently, the paparazzi were only interested in you if the world was hating on you.

I couldn't lie to my boss, especially since security already knew, so I told him North was with me. "It might be difficult for me to ask him to leave if this is a problem for you," I told Lachlan. Thankfully, Lachlan was perfectly understanding.

"It's nobody's damn business why North is at your place. It's complicated for you because your social circle includes the people in this industry. I know this isn't in character for you and I know you won't make a habit of it, so I can only assume you and North have become friends. That's not my business."

Friends.

What an inadequate word for whatever we were.

By the time North returned, I'd cleared the work that was a priority, glad for the distraction. And I couldn't think about the awful email I'd received this morning. Clearly, someone out there wanted to hurt me, and there were a few people it could be, but they weren't worth my energy. I'd wanted to focus on making sure North was okay without overthinking why his welfare was so important to me.

So we chatted as I put together lunch. I updated him on the security situation, and he curled a lip in distaste at the mention of the media.

Then we settled in to eat, which brought us to now and North's out-of-left-field question.

"What do you mean, who was I as a teenager?"

"Well, I was the kid burying his trauma with drive. I wanted out of my tiny part of the world and I wanted to make something of my life. So I didn't focus on what I didn't have. I focused on what I wanted. We didn't really have cliques at school, anyway, but I guess you could say I was the guy who was friends with everyone. Academics, theater kids, the athletic kids, the rich kids, the not-so-rich kids. And I did every extracurricular thing under the sun, so I didn't have to think about anything but school."

While there was an intensity to North beneath his cocky charm and humor (it especially came through in his acting work), I actually couldn't imagine him as that driven type A student he'd described.

"Um ... well, I was academic." I shrugged. "I liked school. And I was on the swim team. Montana, my high school boyfriend, was a linebacker for the school football team, so between my dad being Wesley Howard and Montana being a jock, I was just accepted as one of the popular kids. But I wasn't a cheerleader or the prom queen or anything like that. I was more reserved, not shy, but not overly gregarious. Mamma is such a flamboyant character, loud and attention-seeking, that I think I deliberately wanted to be the opposite."

North frowned in thought. "Did she embarrass you?"

"No." I shook my head. "I mean, it embarrassed me that guys I went to school with had the hots for her and always wanted to hang out at my place, hoping to see her in a bikini. She wasn't around enough for the opportunity, thank God. I think it was more that everything always had to be—*has* to be," I corrected, "about her. I love my mother, and there is goodness in her, kindness and empathy, and I know she loves me and Allegra. But she can be self-involved. When I was a kid, everywhere we went, it was all about Mamma. As I got older, that was uncomfortable for me. We'd go to a family gathering to celebrate my aunt's birthday or to a friend's party to celebrate their anniversary, and Mamma would make sure she was the center of attention. She'd do an unscheduled speech that turned into an Italian serenade or a solo dance. All that energy and beauty ... people are drawn to her. Everyone else just fades into the background.

"For my eleventh birthday, I'd asked to spend the whole day with my father. Just me and him. That year he'd been gone a lot and I missed him. Allegra was nine months old, and when Dad was home, he obviously wanted to spend a lot of time with Ally. I don't know if wanting my dad's time hurt my mother's feelings, but she had a meltdown the morning Dad and I were supposed to leave for our daddy-daughter day out. Dad ended up canceling to take care of Mamma, and our date never happened.

"At my sweet-sixteen party, she got drunk because she was depressed that she was old enough to have a sixteen-year-old and she made a speech in front of all my school friends about it, complimenting me with one hand and reminding everyone how I didn't inherit her rocking bod with the other. Dad was furious. Hauled her out of there and gave her hell. He's always hated the way she talks about my physical appearance, and it was one of the biggest fights they ever had. Mamma got hysterically upset and blamed me for my dad's reaction. Montana and I left the party. My own birthday party." I released a surprised huff. Where had that vent come from? "Anyway ... I guess that's the reason I tried to be the opposite of her."

North scowled. "No offense, princess, but your mother sounds exhausting. I've never met her, but I've seen her on talk shows, and she's a big personality. However, that sounds like more than a big personality. That sounds like narcissism."

Defensive at his harshness, I glowered. "She's not a narcissist. She's just self-involved."

He held up a hand. "I meant no offense, and I'm just mad on your behalf."

My prickliness relented. "It's fine. I ... just ... my parents weren't perfect, but no parent is. And at least I didn't lose mine." I gave him an empathetic look.

North sighed. "You don't have to accept their failings just because some people grew up without parents."

"Actually, I do," I disagreed. "I don't want to live my life resenting them for the mistakes they made. Mamma is trying to be there for us in a way she didn't back when I was a kid, and maybe it's too late for me, but I appreciate she wants to try." I laughed humorlessly. "How did we get into this? Let's change the subject."

"Okay." North pushed his empty plate aside and leaned forward. "Let's go really deep."

I braced myself.

"What's your favorite movie?"

Relieved, I rolled my eyes with a laugh. "You can't ask a director's daughter that question. There are too many choices."

"Tell me just one."

I considered it. "I can tell you my favorite movie that I've only watched once because it hurt too much to watch again, or I could tell you my favorite comfort movie that I watch all the time."

"Tell me both."

"Greedy."

He gave me that sexy, boyish smile. "You know it."

"Ang Lee's *Lust, Caution*. When I was dating Preston, he insisted I had to see this movie, so we streamed it, and I couldn't talk for an hour after it. I didn't want to cry in front of Preston, so I sat there"—I gestured to my throat—"choking on these sobs. And I got up in the middle of the night and locked myself in his bathroom and cried in secret hours after we'd watched it."

North searched my face. "Why didn't you want to cry in front of him?"

Pain flared in my chest at the reminder of the man I'd thought I loved but whom I looked back on and realized I'd hidden so much of myself from. "I didn't know it then, but I know why now." I shrugged unhappily. "He didn't make me feel safe. Not even safe enough to cry in front of."

North lowered his eyes. "Jesus Christ, Aria ... why did you put up with that?"

I stiffened. "Because I thought I loved him."

At my tone, North met my gaze again. "I didn't mean that as an attack. I just wish ... you deserve so much better."

"I ignored the warning signs, so it's as much my fault as his." I shrugged. "What's your favorite movie?"

He looked as if he wanted to say something else, but in the end, he just grinned and said, "The movie I tell the press is *The Deer Hunter*. The real answer is *Toy Story*."

Just like that, the tension broke between us as I burst into laughter.

HOURS LATER, as we lay naked in bed on our stomachs facing each other, I watched North's drowsy expression as I caressed his back lightly with my fingertips. Despite the emotional upheaval of the day, I'd kept him distracted.

We talked more about my life growing up in Malibu and his life growing up in Scotland. We shared our food likes and dislikes, talked about books and TV shows and music. Conversation was easy and fluid.

I wasn't going to overanalyze just how easy it was.

Or how good it felt when North took me to bed and spent hours loving my body.

I thought he was almost asleep, so it surprised me when he suddenly asked, "Do you think you made the right decision coming to Scotland after what Lucas and Caitlyn did?"

Part of me wondered what made him think of them, but I didn't want to dwell on that either. I didn't want to imagine that North thought of me beyond our casual sex arrangement. Because it didn't feel casual.

Today it had felt the opposite of casual.

"At first, I wasn't sure," I replied quietly, wanting to push back the momentary flicker of panic. "I didn't know anyone. I couldn't stop thinking about Lucas, anyway, and nothing seemed to have changed except my location. But one Sunday, I went on a hike to see some of the area for myself. It was a beautiful summer's day, and I'd been following this footpath through the woods when something flashed up ahead, off the beaten path. So I followed and found myself in a field. A field of purple heather." My mind drifted to that day. "There was no one else there. The air was the freshest I'd ever breathed, and the birds were chirping, bees buzzing. The sun was perfect on my skin. I lay down among the heather and everything just stopped. Lucas disappeared from my head. Mamma wasn't there to give unsolicited advice. I wasn't worrying about Allegra. People weren't demanding things from me. And I could hear myself for the first time in what felt like forever."

North's eyes were open now, staring intently into mine. "And what did you hear yourself say?"

"That I was lost," I whispered. "But maybe here was where I could find myself again. So I stayed in Scotland, hoping that I would."

North reached out to brush his thumb over my lower lip. "For what it's worth, I'm glad you stayed."

My throat thickened with unwanted emotion, and I hurried to swerve from what he might or might not say regarding our ... whatever we were. "What about you?" I blurted out. "Have you ever been somewhere and just known that's where you were supposed to be?"

Thankfully, North went with it. He released my lip, but only to caress my arm with the back of his fingers. His gaze followed his touch as he told me, "The first time I went on stage. Nothing had ever felt so right before. I knew from that very moment that's where I was meant to be. Acting is in my blood."

Dismay filled me. But I shoved it back to be a good friend to him. "This whole experience hasn't made you want to walk away from it?"

He shook his head grimly.

"Then don't. If it means that much to you, then don't. Someone changed things today, North, and you have to put aside why, or your anger at why, and be selfish for once. See it as an opportunity. If you want your life back, it's time you made a public statement and told the world what happened in your words, on your terms."

He looked at me so long and so intensely, I didn't know how he would react to my advice. However, finally, North nodded. "I think you're right."

TWENTY
NORTH

"I might as well be here alone, old boy."

I glanced away from the TV screen, not even aware of what was on, surprised to find Theo smirking at me from the treadmill next to mine.

"What?"

Theo let out a huff of amusement. "I was talking about that the gymnast and how, unfortunately, I think I'm going to have to let her go despite her considerable talents." Sweat dripped down his temple as he hit the speed button on his machine to slow to a walk. "And I was going into great detail about those talents, so much so my trainer left here redder than a lobster. Despite my lascivious gym conversation, you, apparently, find the TV ads more interesting than a woman who can touch her toes while I stand and deliver, and can wrap herself around me like a fucking pretzel. Pun intended."

"You're pure filth, you know that?" I decreased my speed, too, hoping to find a machine away from him so I could ignore him in private.

"I'm heartbroken." He deadpanned as he hopped off the machine. "I'm losing my gymnast."

"Because she wants more, and you're a randy playboy who wouldn't know what *more* meant if it bit him on the arse."

Theo raised an eyebrow. "Unlike you, who is so clearly daydreaming about your luscious American."

I cut him a warning look.

But he wasn't wrong.

Two weeks. That was it. Two weeks, during which I spent most of my nights at Aria's beach house while I got my career back on track. With help from my publicity team, I posted a video to Instagram explaining the leaked footage and what exactly happened to Gil MacDonald and my part in it. I felt sick to my stomach doing it, but Aria had been the one behind the camera, reassuring me as I told a story I'd never meant to tell anyone. The response was overwhelming. The public who had condemned me now hailed me as a young hero, which made me want to upchuck.

So I switched off the internet again and let my team deal with it. All I needed to know was that within a week of posting, the studio green-lit *Birdwatcher* with me as the lead. Considering what they'd put me through, I'd requested they send the personal trainer I'd begun training with before everything went tits up to Ardnoch.

I'd have to leave the estate soon enough to start filming, so I wanted to stay as long as I could.

Because of her.

Aria.

I was addicted to her.

As if reading my mind, Theo stared stonily at me as I stepped off the treadmill. "Please don't tell me you're maudlin enough to think yourself in love with her?"

"Fuck off and let me work out," I grumbled before striding over to a rower.

"That means yes." Theo followed. "It looks like it's incumbent upon me to teach you something you should have learned long ago. Great sex does not equal love. Endorphins might trick you into thinking otherwise, but I'm here to tell you they're just chemicals lying to you. Your cock loves her vagina, mate. That's all."

I sighed heavily and asked no one in particular, "Why the hell are we friends again?"

AFTER FINISHING MY WORKOUT, I left Theo to agonize over his never-ending screenplay and made my way to Aria's office. At her distracted-sounding "come in," I entered to find her staring at her phone and biting her nails. The posture of anxiousness was unlike her, and my gut knotted a wee bit. Her mood affected mine way more than I should be comfortable with, but I couldn't bring myself to feel anything but happy that I'd found Aria during one of the toughest moments in my adult life.

And I never wanted her to be anything but happy too. I closed the door and strode across the room. "Hey, what's wrong?"

She blinked rapidly as if surprised to see me. "Oh. I'm ... what? Is everything okay?"

"You tell me." I settled my arse on her desk. Today she wore a short-sleeve silk blouse that accentuated her curves. Her hair was down, something I noted she'd been doing more often lately. It fell in straight, silky strands around her perfect face. My attention snagged on her full mouth and I fought the urge to steal a kiss. Or ten.

Her eyes glinted with amusement as if she knew my thoughts. "I'm fine. What brings you to my office?"

I wanted to push, but I also had to run the conversation I'd had with my agent this morning by her. "Forster wants me back in training ASAP."

Aria's expression turned annoyingly blank. "So you're leaving?"

Frustrated that she was still hiding herself from me, I buried it because I didn't want to push too hard. "I hoped it would be all right with the club if my trainer comes to Ardnoch."

Still no reaction. Just efficient estate manager mode. "You know your membership includes a plus one. We can accommodate your personal trainer. May I ask for how long?"

"About a month, and then I'll have to leave to go train with the stunt team."

She raised an eyebrow. "You're doing your own stunts?"

Was she worried about me? I smiled at the thought. "Not all of them. But some. I want to be as believable as possible. Matt Damon *was* Jason Bourne. Daniel Craig *was* James Bond. Those are the kinds of performances I want to live up to."

She nodded, lowering her eyes. "Well, be careful."

"That's why I'm training." I leaned in and nudged her leg with my foot. "So, why were you biting your nails when I walked in?" Was it because I was leaving in a month? Was she going to use it as an excuse to break things off between us? Because I wasn't giving up that easily.

Aria opened her mouth to speak, hesitated, shifted uncomfortably, and then let out a long, exasperated sigh. I tried to wait patiently through it.

Then she grabbed her phone off the desk and waved it in agitation at me. "I'm worried about Allegra."

Not what I'd been expecting, but I also wasn't surprised. Aria had already told me things were strained between them but had gone into little detail. "What's going on?"

"It's stupid. I'm being stupid." Her eyes brightened with tears. "It's just hormones."

Aria's period had arrived last night, so we'd hung out,

made out, but not a lot else. Which was more than fine with me. She hadn't quite realized we were acting like a couple in a relationship, and I didn't intend to enlighten her until she was already too deep in.

I lowered to my haunches to force her to look at me. "You can tell me anything, princess."

She flicked a manicured hand near her eye and chuckled unhappily. "I'm acting like a baby."

"That's for me to decide," I joked, smoothing my hands over her thighs in reassurance. "Come on, tell me what's upsetting you."

Fiddling with her phone, she took a minute before meeting my gaze. And at that moment, I felt myself falling into her. Falling for her. Because there was nothing more important to me than taking away the sadness I saw buried in her eyes. My hands tightened on her and my words were thick as I pushed, "Talk to me."

"Maybe it is stupid ... but ... Allegra always used to tell me she loved me in her texts." Her voice broke a little as she dropped her phone onto the desk with a thump. "She hasn't said it since I refused to help her with dropping out of college. I thought things were weird, but not so weird that she wasn't talking to me. Does that make sense?"

I nodded, pressing closer.

"She hugged me when she left. I thought we were okay." Without thinking, she sought my comfort, sliding her hands over mine. I turned my palms up and tangled my fingers through hers. "But she's so distant. She just posted a picture from the South of France. She's there for spring break and never mentioned to me she was going to an entirely different country. Oh, God ..." She tugged on her hands, but I wouldn't let her go. "I sound about ten years old."

"You sound hurt," I disagreed.

"I am." Fresh tears brightened her eyes. "What? I'm only

worthy of my family's love as long as I do exactly what they want me to do for them? That's how Mamma has made me feel my whole life, how the guys I've dated made me feel ... I never thought Allegra would treat me like that."

An ache scored through me. I hated that Aria was hurting. And I wanted to promise her I would never make her feel that way, but I knew it was not the right time to broach the subject of our relationship. Yet I wanted to fix this for her. "I'm going to give you the same advice you gave me. Speak up."

She frowned. "What do you mean?"

"Sometimes people are so caught in their own shit, they don't know how deeply their actions can cut others ... until it's pointed out to them." I brushed my thumbs over the tops of her hands, trying to soothe her. "The girl I met hero-worships her big sister. Loves her. And no one is doing Allegra any good by treating her with kid gloves because she went off the deep end once." Aria had confided in me that Allegra had gone off the rails a while back and ended up in rehab and therapy after a dodgy hookup with a drug dealer who turned out to be Sloane's ex. "You all have to accept that she learned a big lesson from that night with Sloane and start treating her normally. Which includes calling her on her bullshit and telling her when she's hurt you. Call her."

Aria considered me, the frown between her brows intensifying. "What if I did hurt her?"

"Maybe you did. But you guys need to talk about it because this is eating you up. Nothing is more important than family, princess."

New emotion sharpened her expression, and her grip tightened in mine. I knew that was for me. Empathy, not pity. And if I wasn't mistaken, admiration. My chest suddenly felt too tight, and I had to swallow the urge to tell her how I felt. "Call her." I moved to stand to give her privacy, but Aria refused to let go of me.

She licked her lips nervously. "Will you ... will you stay with me while I call her?"

Hope—big, terrifying, brilliant fucking hope—filled me at her request. "Of course," I answered gruffly.

And so I settled back on the edge of her desk while she dialed her sister's number. Aria absentmindedly traced a pattern on my knee with her free hand as she waited for the call to connect. Then her gaze moved to mine and she mouthed in disappointment, "*Voicemail again.*"

"Leave a voicemail, then," I whispered.

She looked hesitant for a second and then said, "Hey, Allegra, it's me. Look ... I wish you'd pick up, but since I have a feeling you won't ..." She exhaled shakily. "I'm sorry if I hurt you. I really am. But you need to know you're hurting me too. I"—her fingers curled sharply into my knee but I didn't mind —"I didn't know that your love for me depended on me giving you everything you want, but I guess that's true. Every time I tell you I love you and you don't say it back ..." Her face crumpled and she sucked in a breath. My heart lurched, and I grabbed her hand. "It just ... it hurts. It reminds me of all the times Mamma withheld those words unless I acted like she wanted me to act. She does that to you, too, so you know how it feels. I've always tried to be more for you than a big sister ... but maybe I fucked up. Maybe I hurt you and so you want to hurt me back. I don't know. I just wish you'd talk to me." She disconnected suddenly and looked up at me with shimmering eyes. "Oh, fuck, I shouldn't have done that. I'm the grown-up. I'm not supposed to burden her with my feelings."

I tugged on Aria's hand until she stood and pulled her between my legs so I could hug her to me. She looked so sad and lost as she rested her palms on my chest, and I wondered if she could feel how fast my pulse raced. "You're not her parent, Aria. You're her big sister. Stop trying to protect everyone's feelings, including your own, and let yourself feel whatever the fuck it is you feel." Then I kissed her, pouring my emotions into the kiss until she melted in my arms and kissed me back with a hunger that ignited my blood. It took everything within me to gentle our embrace, to pull back, slow down, and just offer comfort.

Finally, I released her. She panted as she stared at me in round-eyed surprise. Almost as if she felt everything I wanted to say in that kiss. But it scared me to push too soon. So I smiled, caressed her lip with my thumb, and promised, "It's all going to be okay."

TWENTY-ONE
ARIA

It had been exactly twenty-six hours since I sent that voicemail to my sister, and I'd heard nothing from her. Not even a text. No more posts from the South of France on her socials. Nada.

My gut had only stopped churning while I hung out with North last night, but as soon as he wasn't around to distract me, I was back to my gut gnawing anxiously. Even though North assured me it wasn't, I couldn't help but worry that it was wrong of me to put my emotions on Allegra. As much as I loved my mother and father, I finally had to admit to myself that they'd never been the most stable sources of love. I knew my dad adored me and he'd even taken my side against Mamma, but he'd also chosen her feelings over mine on many other occasions, and he'd spent a good portion of our lives not physically there.

As for Mamma, if I was honest with myself ... she'd made me feel unworthy of love as much as she'd made me feel loved. It was confusing. And I hadn't ever dared to admit it to myself, but ... I couldn't trust her. I couldn't trust her love.

But Allegra ... as a little girl, her whole being lit up when I walked through the door. She'd showered me in adoration and love without wanting anything but my love in return, and it had healed something within me. Her love was the reason I'd stayed in LA when I wanted to leave. That was the truth. And I no longer felt resentment now that I could admit that I'd stayed as much for myself as for her.

So having her take that one pure source of love away from me ... it didn't just hurt, it fucking killed. She wasn't a kid anymore. She could inflict damage, and that scared the shit out of me.

My work phone rang, yanking me out of my maudlin musings. The screen told me it was security. After North's public statement, the paps promptly disappeared from the estate gates and things had been quiet the last week. "Aria speaking."

"Ms. Howard." Jock insisted on formality. "We have Jared McCulloch, Sarah McCulloch's cousin, at the gate, asking permission to enter."

I frowned. "For what reason?"

"I'm afraid he's got some bad news for Sarah."

MY HEART RACED in sympathy for Jared McCulloch as soon as I met him in the reception hall. I'd seen the young farmer in passing in the village and knew from Sloane, who knew from the Adair women, that Jared was a bit of a ladies' man. He'd arrived in Ardnoch four years ago to live with his grandfather Collum McCulloch and his cousin Sarah. Collum McCulloch's family had farmed the land north of Ardnoch for generations. The McCullochs had insisted for centuries that they used to own land south of Ardnoch that bordered Adair land. It wasn't a huge piece of property, but it was coastal.

It was Adair land now, and Lachlan's members, including myself, had homes on it.

The farm still existed northwest of the village. Apparently, things had been frosty between Lachlan and Collum but had eased somewhat a few years ago when Collum saved Lachlan's and Robyn's lives. It wasn't friendly by any means, but I knew Lachlan respected Collum.

Now his grandson's handsome face was etched in haggard, restrained grief.

"We've called Sarah down. She's on her way. I'm very sorry for your loss."

Jared nodded, swallowing hard, and I did him the courtesy of not forcing him to speak.

"This way." I turned on my heel and heard him following me as we passed two lounging members who stared at us in curiosity. Jared was dressed in jeans, muddy boots, and a plaid shirt with a padded vest. Glancing over my shoulder, my heart twinged at how lost and dazed he looked.

The staff elevator was just beyond the dining room where a few members sat, including North and Theo. North happened to look up as I passed, and I saw his smile turn into a frown as I marched on.

We stopped at the elevator just as the doors opened to reveal a concerned-looking Sarah and a white-faced Agnes who'd gone upstairs to fetch her.

"Agnes, can you take Jared and Sarah to your office?"

"No." Sarah stepped out of the elevator, her jaw set with uncharacteristic stubbornness as she stared at her cousin. Her cheeks drained of color. "No." The word turned to a plea.

Jared made a hoarse sound and bridged the distance between them. He yanked her roughly into his arms. "I'm sorry, sweetheart," he forced out. "Granda's gone."

"No," she whimpered, shaking her head frantically. "No."

"I'm so sorry." Jared visibly forced back tears.

"No!" A wail of grief exploded out of Sarah as her knees buckled, and I covered my mouth to hold in an empathetic sob, tears blurring my vision as Jared held her up. He crushed her to him as she sobbed loudly against his chest.

I knew from Agnes that Sarah's mother had died when Sarah was a little girl and Collum raised her. She'd lost more than a grandfather when Collum McCulloch died of a heart attack that morning. She'd lost the only real parent she'd had.

A touch at my hand startled me, and I turned to find North and Theo at my side, clearly drawn from the dining room by Sarah's cries. "Her grandfather died," I whispered.

North's expression tightened with sympathy, and he squeezed my hand.

"Come, come now." Agnes rested an arm around the grieving cousins. "Let's go into my office."

I wanted to tell them I was here if they needed anything, but the words wouldn't come as I watched Jared steady Sarah while they stumbled away. My heart hurt so badly for them.

"I'm surprised the mouse has a man," Theo muttered.

North glowered at his friend while I cut him a dark look. "He's her cousin." What I wanted to say was that perhaps the asshole could show an ounce of compassion for once, but I couldn't get away with talking to a member like that. I'd sniped at North, but that was different.

Theo nodded and stared after the retreating cousins. He frowned, gazing after them for a second too long before he pivoted and strode back into the dining room.

"He ... he means nothing by it. He's just not good with emotional displays," North explained haltingly.

"He's unkind," I disagreed. "I don't understand why you're friends with him." Shrugging off my annoyance, I glanced back down the hallway where the McCullochs disappeared. "Poor Sarah. Collum was more like a father to her."

North tightened his grip. "Are you okay?"

"Yeah, I'd like to know the answer to that too," a familiar voice said behind us.

I whirled, heart racing harder to discover Wakefield standing next to Allegra. She looked beautiful but tired, her clothes a little disheveled. She shrugged, her expression wary. "We didn't want to interrupt."

A fresh round of embarrassing tears stung my eyes. It was all too much. "What are you doing here?"

Allegra's tears spilled freely forth. "I came to tell my big sister that I love her."

TWENTY-TWO
ARIA

Mamma had so many outbursts in public that I'd grown embarrassed if I showed emotion or if someone else expressed passionate sentiment in front of others. However, when I looked back on the day's events, I'd realize that maybe I'd loosened up a little from having distance from my mother. Sarah and Jared's grief had been public, but I'd felt nothing but empathy for them and couldn't care less what the members thought, even though my priority was supposed to be their comfort and pleasure.

And when my little sister told me she loved me after traveling to get to me just to say it, I hugged her tight in the middle of the castle hallway while she burst into tears and held on to me like she used to as a kid.

North had pressed a reassuring hand to my back and whispered he'd check in later, and Wakefield had departed with him. I'd gotten Allegra calm enough to take her to my office, and I sent for refreshments because she looked exhausted.

"I'm sorry I upset you so much," I told her, feeling terrible that I'd put her through the emotional wringer.

Allegra wiped at her cheeks with the tissues I'd given her as she sat across from me in a guest chair. "Don't. Don't apologize for giving me the truth." She sucked in a watery breath. "You know, as awful as I felt listening to your voicemail, I was kind of relieved too."

"Relieved?"

"You and Dad have been tiptoeing around me since rehab. You deciding not to help me drop out of college was the first sign that you were starting to treat me normally."

Confused, I hesitantly asked, "Then why have you been so distant?"

Allegra scowled. "Because I'm a brat who couldn't see past my own nose."

I raised an eyebrow. "Allegra, you're not—"

"I am a brat. An impulsive brat who conned herself into thinking she was so mature because of everything she'd been through. But listening to you on that voicemail ... I realized I was doing to you what Mamma does to us, and I was horrified." She looked horrified.

"You're not Mamma," I assured her. "Mamma wouldn't have gotten on a plane to come and tell me she loved me."

Allegra leaned forward, expression pleading. "I want you to know that I wasn't consciously trying to hurt you. Yeah, I was pissed that I have to stay another semester in LA—hello, brat—but really I was pissed because I left here feeling like everyone else in your life."

"What does that mean?"

She shrugged. "I thought as I got older, you'd become less of a parental figure and more of a best friend. That you'd tell me everything. But until that voicemail, I've felt locked out of what's going on with you. You're so scared to tell people how you're really feeling in case you get hurt that you've even started to protect yourself from the people who love you. So, you telling me I hurt you shocked me."

Had I done that? Had I gotten so closed off like that?

"Oh, God, Ally, I didn't even ... I'm sorry if I did that. I guess I've always been in parent mode with you. Mamma never protected you from her feelings, and I wanted you to have someone whose only thought was to protect you."

My sister grabbed my hand. "I get that. And I want you to know that I am so grateful for the childhood you gave me because I know that it's not the childhood you got. But I'm nineteen, Ari, and a lot of shit has happened to me. You don't need to parent me anymore. I just need you to be my sister."

Understanding, I tightened my hold on her. "I can do that."

"Okay. Then I'm sorry for being distant and making you feel like my love depended on you doing what I want you to do. Because it's so far from the truth. You're my calm in the storm, Ari. I love you better than I love anyone in this world." She smiled as she wiped at her fast-falling tears, and I barely saw it through the tears blurring my vision.

I got up, pulling her out of the chair to hug her tight. "I love you so much."

For the first time in weeks, that worry and tension I'd gotten used to carrying melted away.

Wakefield interrupted not long later, bringing in tea and snacks. After he was gone and I'd forced Allegra to eat and drink, I asked about her trip to the South of France.

"Oh, I went with some people from school. I just wanted out of LA for a bit. But I got good news ... Rhode Island accepted me as a transfer. I start there next semester. And I'm excited. I showed them the glasswork I've been doing, and they're already talking about making contacts for me with some East Coast galleries."

Joy for my sister lit through me. "Oh, Ally, that's amazing. I'm so proud and happy for you."

She beamed, her smile chipping away at the weariness in

her eyes. "I can't wait. I haven't told Mamma and Dad yet. Mamma is going to shit a brick."

"Then she'll shit a brick," I decided. "Nothing and nobody is stopping you from attending the school you want to attend."

"What about you?" Allegra raised an eyebrow, her smirk mischievous. "I noticed North Hunter was holding your hand."

Remembering her words about me shutting her out, I decided to tell her the truth. "We're sleeping together. But that's it."

She did not seem surprised or annoyed. "What? You mean, no strings attached?"

"Exactly. We're purely physical," I lied.

Allegra seemed to see right through my deception. "And does North know that because he looks like a guy who's kinda deep into it with you?"

He did?

Butterflies fluttered wildly in my belly at the thought. "Well ... it's perhaps been a little more than physical. He has helped me with some insecurities I've had since Lucas cheated. And ... he was also the one who encouraged me to be honest with you." Saying that out loud made me nervous to think about just how big an effect North had had on me these past weeks.

Panic tightened my chest.

But Allegra, oblivious to it, continued, "Then it's not just sex. It sounds like you two are in a relationship. I sensed that spark between you. Obviously. Not that I'm taking credit for stupidly locking you in a room all night with a strange dude."

I smirked at her sheepish expression. "We're ... friends. With benefits."

My sister didn't look convinced. "I'd be upset that you're

hiding the truth from me if I didn't know that you're also hiding the truth from yourself."

"Ally—"

She waved me off. "I get it. You don't want to get hurt. So I won't push because I'm just glad you and I are back in a good place. I saw Caitlyn before I left for spring break. She's started doing coffee runs at this place by my school." Allegra glowered. "She keeps trying to have friendly conversations with me, asking why you don't reply to her emails. I just assumed you weren't getting them."

"No. She's been emailing from different accounts. I just keep deleting them."

My sister grimaced. "Ari, that's fucked up. You should tell someone she's emailing all the time. It freaks me out she's started getting her coffee at this place because we both know it's nowhere near Curiosity."

Unease replaced my butterflies. "Do you think it's deliberate? To be near you?"

"She did pretty much go after your life. And she still hasn't backed off. I think you should tell someone."

"I don't want to make a big deal out of it or give her the satisfaction of acknowledging her."

Allegra considered this. "Yeah, I guess ignoring someone like her is probably the best kind of punishment. Still, stay alert. She gives me bunny-boiler vibes."

I nodded, glad I hadn't mentioned the other emails I'd received from the anonymous "member." A second had come in after the first. It was pretty much a repeat of what they'd said before. And I knew if a third arrived, I'd have to share it with Lachlan and security, even though the thought of doing so mortified me.

Brushing those concerns aside, I asked, "How long can you stay?"

Allegra gave me a sad smile. "Two nights, then I need to head back."

"Well, it's two nights we didn't have before."

We shared a loving look, and as I thought about poor Jared and Sarah who'd left here in a state of agonizing grief, I'd never been more grateful to have Ally close, physically and emotionally.

North was right.

There was nothing more important than family.

TWENTY-THREE
NORTH

As I stood staring around at the people crowded into the Gloaming—a pub, restaurant, and hotel owned by Lachlan and Arran Adair—I felt a sense of melancholy that was about more than the occasion that had called us there.

Despite the bad blood that reportedly had existed between Adairs and McCullochs for generations, Lachlan had insisted on celebrating the life of local farmer Collum McCulloch in the two-hundred-year-old building they'd renovated. He'd invited the entire village to attend and all around me were people, not just taking advantage of the free food and access to alcohol, but sharing stories about Collum. They were celebrating the man.

Friends and neighbors brought together by one person.

Over the past few weeks, friends who'd gone quiet resurfaced, calling and texting. Not one to hold a grudge, I'd responded to those I genuinely liked. However, standing in that pub in a tiny village in the Highlands, I'd never been more aware of how few loyal friends I had.

Unbelievably, Theo could be counted among the most

genuine. Even more unbelievably, I maybe even missed his presence now that he'd returned to London.

There were my foster parents. They sincerely cared about me.

But that seemed to be the list.

I'd been so focused on building a career that I hadn't bothered to nurture any real friendships. As I chatted with Walker, I considered he'd make a good mate. He hadn't been able to trace anyone to my threatening letters, and no others had arrived since. But I could see from the determined glint in his eyes he wasn't quite ready to give up on the mystery yet. It was a pity he couldn't be lured away from Ardnoch because he was apparently the best private security out there.

I could make do with friendship instead.

For the first time in a long time, I wanted to put down roots.

Glancing across the room at Aria as she chatted with Sloane and Monroe Adair, I knew she was partly the reason my perspective had changed. Of course, being temporarily ostracized from Hollywood had kicked off my introspection, but Aria had only emphasized to me how important connections were. She'd been like a new person since she and her sister had sorted out their issues, even if she'd been sad to see Allegra return to the States. I'd always known the importance of family. Losing mine had made sure of that. But somewhere along the way, I'd allowed myself to focus elsewhere.

But now that I'd found someone I wanted to be around as much as I did Aria, I felt that itch beneath my skin, that driving force that had gotten me where I was as an actor. Now it was focused on her. On a life with her.

When I was old and gray, would any acting award or accolade make up for the fact that I was alone?

The thought filled me with dread. Not just the alone part ... but the part where Aria wasn't old and gray at my side.

Fuck, I wanted that. Aye, I wanted roots, but more than that, I wanted mine to be entwined with Aria Howard's.

My eyes raked hungrily over her back. She wore a black dress with a skirt that flared out from the waist, and I'd imagined sliding my hands beneath it from the moment I saw her.

"Things seemed to have turned around for you." Brodan Adair sidled up to me and Walker at the bar, drawing me out of my overwhelming realization.

Like his brother Lachlan, Brodan had retired from acting. Unlike his brother, Brodan had been more than a good-looking action star. He was taken seriously and on the road to an Oscar win when he gave it up to come home, marry, and become a father. We'd seen each other around on the award ceremony circuit, but we'd only exchanged a few words here and there. I held out my hand. "Nice to see you."

"Aye, you too." He shook my hand. "I'm sorry about what you've been put through. I hope Hollywood has come crawling back on their knees."

I grinned. "They have that. I'm in training at the moment for my next role. Filming starts in a few weeks." It was true. Aria had already commented that she could see a difference in the breadth of my shoulders. I didn't want to bulk up too much, but I needed a lot of upper body strength for some of the stunts.

"Good. Glad to hear it." Brodan gestured around. "What brings you here?"

I forced myself not to look at Aria. "Aria and I are friends. She wanted to pay her respects, and I thought I'd keep her company."

He and Walker exchanged a knowing look I pretended not to see.

"Collum seems like he was quite the character."

Brodan frowned. "He was always a crabbit auld bastard to

me, but I have to forgive him because he saved my brother's and Robyn's lives."

"Aye, what happened there?" I asked.

But before Brodan could tell me, a hush fell over the room. I turned to see what had drawn everyone's attention.

Standing in the doorway was the man I'd seen usher Sarah McCulloch from the castle that fateful morning two weeks ago. Sympathy scored through me as Jared McCulloch looked around the room, dark circles of grief under his eyes.

People seemed to wait with bated breath as his gaze landed on Lachlan.

Then he determinedly crossed the room. Lachlan drew himself up as if preparing for a confrontation. But Jared merely held out his hand to shake. "I'm going to do what my grandad wanted to do but was too stubborn to admit he wanted ... bury that damn stupid feud."

Lachlan pressed his lips together, his eyes looking suspiciously bright. He clasped Jared's hand in both of his. "Despite everything, I admired the hell out of Collum. And I'll never forget what he did for me and my wife. His loss is felt deeply."

Jared swallowed hard and nodded his thanks.

Clapping a hand on his back, Lachlan embraced the younger man and turned him toward the bar. "Let me buy you a drink."

"Sometimes my big brother is a pain in the arse," Brodan murmured at my side. "But then he goes and does shit like that, inspiring the rest of us to be better men, which only makes him an even bigger pain in the arse."

I chuckled softly as the volume again increased. The Gloaming had been built in the square with a large car park for visitors out front. The historical architecture and design of the village appealed to tourists as much as we celebrities staying on the village outskirts. Everything predated the mid-twentieth century, and dominating it all, near the Gloaming, sat a medieval cathedral.

Shops, restaurants, and bed-and-breakfasts scattered throughout the village on quaint row streets. Castle Street was the main road off the square that led out of Ardnoch toward Ardnoch Castle and Estate. It was an avenue of identical nine-teenth-century terraced houses with dormer windows. Many of the homes had been converted into boutiques, cafés, and inns. I'd only ventured into the village a few times, but I'd been struck by how picturesque it was.

The Gloaming itself was like most old pubs in Scotland. It had low ceilings with dark wooden beams, a large fireplace, and traditional furniture with a modern twist.

Aria stood with Monroe near a large table occupied by the Adair family. And they were an outrageously braw-looking bunch. I spotted Eredine, the Pilates, yoga, and mindfulness instructor from Ardnoch. I'd taken a few of her classes over the last year. According to Aria, she was engaged to the youngest Adair brother and pub co-owner, Arran. He sat at her side, his arm wrapped around her shoulders as they chatted with the couple opposite them—an attractive redhead and a bearded man who shared too much of a resemblance to the Adair men not to be one of them. Since I knew Arran, Lachlan, and Brodan, the man had to be Thane Adair, and the woman at his side was presumably his wife Regan.

Beside them were three kids. One I knew was Sloane's daughter Callie, and the other two were dark-haired, a boy and a girl. I didn't know who they were, but they clearly belonged to the Adairs. And tucked into the corner was a man I knew because he'd followed Lachlan Adair everywhere as his body-guard back in the day—Mackennon Galbraith. He held a baby in his arms while the striking woman at his side, whom I knew was Arrochar Adair, sat chatting with Lachlan's wife, Robyn, who also cradled a young child.

Monroe held her and Brodan's son. The Hollywood star who gave up acting for the childhood sweetheart he'd reunited with had fascinated the world, and I remembered the paps had hounded them for a while. But Brodan hadn't given up Hollywood entirely. He'd turned his hand to screenwriting, producing, and directing. He'd found a way to have everything he wanted by returning to his roots. To the Adairs.

They were a big, growing family. Close as could be.

I felt a pang of envy watching them.

My eyes moved to Aria. "Excuse me," I muttered and crossed the room to place a hand on Aria's back.

She glanced up with a surprised smile of welcome. "Hey. You okay?"

I nodded. "You?"

"It's sad, but it's also really amazing to see how someone's life can affect others. All these people came out to say goodbye to Mr. McCulloch. There are famous people who can't inspire that level of emotion."

Her words hit a wee bit too close to home. Who would truly miss me if something happened to me?

At my flinch, her eyes widened. "North—"

A bell rang out around the bar, cutting her off, and we all turned. Arran Adair now stood behind the bar, drawing everyone's attention. "I just want to thank you all"—his voice boomed around the room—"for coming here today to celebrate Collum and the indelible mark he's left on Ardnoch. I'm sure he'd be mortified by the attention, which just makes me glad we did this all the more."

Everyone chuckled and raised their glasses with a "Hear! Hear!" A glance at Jared showed him smirking too.

"Aye, Collum was a gruff man. But he was as stable and loyal and as certain of who he was as any man I've ever known. He *was* Ardnoch. So, while this is a sad occasion, I know Collum wouldn't want us to be sad. Because he was a farmer.

He was connected to nature, to the circle, to the passing of seasons more than any of us. He'd say that this, his loss, was just life, after all. So raise a glass to Collum. Raise your glass" —Arran lifted his—"to life. And to the circle of it." His gaze moved across the room and landed on Thane and Regan.

"To life!" everyone cheered.

Aria stiffened at my side, and I learned why when she leaned into Sloane and asked, "Regan's pregnant?"

Sloane and Monroe exchanged a look, and Monroe smiled. "We just found out yesterday."

Aria's face lit up at the news, and she excused herself before drifting off to offer congratulations.

I was distracted from my intense awareness of the woman when Eredine came over to say hello. Eredine had a serene quality that matched well with her occupation. Originally from the States, she'd picked up a slight Scottish inflection in her accent. She asked how I was doing after the scandal, and because of the sincerity she exuded, I didn't mind talking about it with her. Her fiancé, Arran, quickly joined us, however, who turned the conversation to their wedding, happening in a matter of weeks. His pointed need to remind me that his fiancée was taken amused me. Either he was so infatuated with Eredine he couldn't see past it, or I was doing well at hiding my obsession with Aria.

Soon enough I'd understand exactly where Arran was coming from when, a half hour later, I turned from chatting with Walker and Sloane to see Aria at the bar. With Jared McCulloch.

Their heads dipped toward one another, and a shot of jealousy cut through me.

Before I could let rationality catch up with my testosterone, I wound through the crowded bar and approached Aria just in time to hear Jared say, "If you really want to make me feel better, we could get a room upstairs."

Fury heated my blood, my neck growing hot as I sidled up between them and slid a possessive arm around Aria's waist. "I don't think so, mate. She's taken."

Aria tensed against me, turning solid as a brick wall, and before she could speak, Jared exhaled wearily. His pupils were dilated, and I could smell the whisky on his breath. "Ignore me. I'm drunk. Sorry."

Pity killed my territorialism. "You all right? Do you need someone to see you home?"

"I'm fine." He waved me off and stumbled from the stool. I moved to steady him, but he jerked away from me before weaving his way around the villagers. Arran suddenly appeared in front of him, placing a hand on Jared's shoulder. The farmer seemed to relax at Arran's touch, and I turned to Aria, assured someone was taking care of the grieving man.

That assurance died under Aria's wrathful glare.

Fuck.

"Ari—"

"I'm taken?" she hissed angrily. "I'm not a piece of property you can pee around."

Before I even had a chance to defend myself, she shoved past me and stormed through the crowd toward the exit.

Fucking great.

Hurrying after her, I didn't catch up until we were out the door. "Aria!" I reached her just a few steps away from the bar's entrance, not caring if there was anyone around as I tugged her toward me.

She stumbled in her heels, and I steadied her, taking hold of her biceps. Aria pushed at my chest and it felt like it was caving in. "Aria, please."

Her face was flushed, but I could see right through her. This was more than being pissed at me for acting like a jealous boyfriend.

Panic flared in the back of her eyes.

"I'm not yours. You get that, right?"

"Did you want to fuck him?" I snarled, hurt beyond bearing by her rejection.

"Of course not." She huffed, shoving my hands off her. "But I'm also not your girlfriend. I thought I made that perfectly clear."

The caving-in feeling worsened. "Aria," I exhaled her name hoarsely. "You and I both know there's so much more going on here than just sex."

That trepidation I saw on her face hit red alert status, and I muttered a curse as she took a few steps backward, retreating from me. "No."

"No?" I followed her. "Just no? That's it? That's all I get?"

"We had a deal," she insisted. "Don't do this."

"Aria, I—" The squealing of tires cut me off, and my eyes flew in the sound's direction.

It took my brain a second to make sense of what was happening, but horrified understanding dawned just in time.

An SUV was careening off the road, heading at speed directly toward us.

Instinct took over, and I yelled Aria's name as I threw my body at her. I had the presence of mind to turn my back as I wrapped my arms around her, taking the majority of the impact as we hit the ground.

Blood rushed in my ears. The sound of a growling engine and Aria's cries were muted and far away as the wind knocked out of me.

"North, North!" Aria's hands smoothed over my chest, her concerned, frightened expression coming into focus.

Tires squealed again, and I glanced over her shoulder in fright, only to relax marginally as the SUV reversed and sped off. The sight of Walker running into the road jolted me, and I realized the commotion had drawn people from the pub.

"Did you hit your head? North?" Aria's fingers were on my face now. "North, say something."

My mind reeled as I gaped up at her, and the first words out of my mouth were, "Did someone just try to fucking kill us?"

TWENTY-FOUR
ARIA

I t was hard to determine whether North was okay because he wouldn't stop asking if I was all right. After the initial shock of someone driving their SUV at us, all he cared about was me.

"I'm fine," I assured him. My knee throbbed, but I'd only scraped it when North had thrown us out of the way of the vehicle. He was the one who'd taken the impact. I'd run my hands over the back of his head, searching for bumps or injuries, as his hands coasted up and down my waist. As if he needed to touch me. To be reassured that I was alive and okay.

It frightened me how concerned I was that he was hurt.

And I was even more frightened that someone had just tried to run us over.

"Right." Walker marched to our sides, pushing through Lachlan and his brothers, who'd surrounded us protectively outside of the bar. "I've given the license number to a contact. He's running it."

Walker had been fast enough to run after the SUV to get the make, model, and plate, but he hadn't seen the driver. North didn't want the police involved, considering he was just recovering from being in the news, so Walker agreed to handle it privately.

"You're sure neither of you saw the driver?"

I shook my head. "I didn't even know what was happening until North hauled us to the ground."

North grimaced angrily. "I didn't see. It took me a second to even realize what was happening, and then I was focused on getting us out of the way. It looked like a Defender."

"It was," Walker confirmed. "A very old one. Hopefully, we can track down this person with the plates."

"Unless they're false plates," Lachlan threw in.

The men talked among themselves, but I watched North and caught the winces he made as he shifted. "You are hurt."

"My back." He shrugged but winced again. "I'm fine."

Huffing at his lack of concern for himself, I got behind him and lifted his T-shirt. A bruise was already forming on his left shoulder. "You knocked your shoulder pretty badly. We need to get back and ice it."

"Aria—"

"Look"—I stormed around to face him—"you not only hit the ground but you had me on top of you, and I'm not exactly a delicate flower."

His eyes narrowed. "Don't."

What? It was true. Despite the few inches of height and muscle he had on me, we probably weighed about the same. Maybe I weighed more.

"I'm just saying, if you're pretending you're okay to save my feelings, then that's dumb."

North slid his hand around my neck to cup my nape, something he'd taken to doing when he wanted my full attention. "Let's get this straight: to me, you are a delicate fucking flower. You could throw me to the ground a hundred times a day and I wouldn't fucking complain. In fact, take that as an invitation. I am fine. But you have a skinned knee, so we need to get back and deal with that."

Heat flushed my cheeks, and I was so glad I wasn't a blusher because I could practically feel the Adair men grinning behind me.

"As entertaining as this is," Walker interrupted, "we need to get you back to the estate. Security is on their way to escort you." He studied North grimly. "This could be related to the letters."

North scrubbed a wearied hand over his face while confusion filled me.

"Letters? What letters?"

I KNEW it was hypocritical of me to be angry at North for hiding the creepy letters he'd been receiving (for years, apparently) considering I'd told no one about the anonymous emails ... but that didn't make me any less pissed.

North explained everything as the security team drove us back to the estate, and I grew more alarmed by the second about what had just happened to us. Someone had really, truly just tried to drive their car into us. To injure us.

To injure North.

I'd insisted on one of the physical therapists looking over North as soon as we arrived at the castle, and that had given me time to work myself up into quite the state. Pacing my office, my mind whirled. Overwhelmed. By the intensity of my fear for him.

As much as I wanted to deny it ... I'd stupidly developed feelings for North. While that might not sound like a bad thing, considering how great we were together, we were in this weird, otherworldly bubble in Ardnoch without outside

forces or leading ladies or ... legendary directors he wanted to
work with.

However, as soon as North stepped off the estate to start
filming in two weeks, that would be it. My insecurities would
rear their ugly heads and I'd destroy our relationship. I'd inflict
pain on him because I couldn't trust him.

I didn't want to hurt North.

But I couldn't let this go on.

The thought of never kissing him again, never seeing that
wicked smile as we rolled around in bed, was an agony I was
not prepared for.

A sob welled up and out, and I stumbled into my seat,
shoving the pain back down, making choked, whimpering
sounds that shocked me. For two years I'd barely cried at
anything, and since getting involved with North, my emotions
had flooded to the surface.

Oh my God. How had I let this happen?

I didn't know how long I sat in dire contemplation
before North strode into my office without knocking. Wariness and grief filled me as I watched him lock the door.
When he turned to me, I tried to memorize his handsome
face. How the light caught silver striations in his beautiful
gray eyes.

North's expression hardened. As if he could read my face,
my mind ... "No," he bit out, the word guttural.

I stood and rounded the desk in the opposite direction,
leaning my ass against it for support as we stared at each other
like two opponents. "How was PT?"

"I don't want to talk about PT," he huffed impatiently. "I
want to talk about that look in your eyes."

"We have to end this," I blurted out.

His jaw clenched, and I tensed as he stepped toward me.
"No," he repeated.

Somehow I knew he'd make this even more difficult, and

fury cut through the horrible ache in my chest. "You don't get to decide," I snapped.

"I bloody well do." He crossed the distance between us until our chests almost touched and my fingers curled around the edge of the desk. "I don't want this to end. And I don't think you do either." North cupped my cheek, and I wanted so badly to buss into his touch, but I held back. "Aria, I know today was frightening, but I have a security team. I'm safe. You're safe. I'll make sure of it."

I shook my head frantically. His scent, his heat, was overwhelming me like always. Tingles awoke between my legs. My skin felt hot. "It's more than that. We were fighting before the attack ... I ... I told you that I cannot date an actor."

His eyes flared. "I'm a man, not a fucking actor. Acting is just what I do. I can't believe after everything we've been through—"

"Been through?" I guffawed angrily, feeling literally and emotionally cornered. "We've been living in a goddamn luxury bubble in the middle of nowhere in Scotland! This isn't the real world, North. In the real world, I could never know if you were with me for me or because of what you could get from me."

"What I could get from you?" he hissed, his lips almost touching mine. "All I want is this." He pressed a hand over my heart, his expression fierce, frustrated.

And suddenly, knowing that this was it, that this would be our last intimate moment together, I wasn't ready for last night to be the last time I felt him inside of me. "No. All you want is this." I crushed my mouth over his as my hand slid inside his jeans to stroke him.

His growl of need vibrated through me and then North slid his hands under my ass and lifted me onto the desk. As I plucked at the fastener on his jeans, he shoved the skirt of my dress up to my waist. Then he curled his fingers around my silky underwear, yanked them down my legs, and dropped them as I pushed down his jeans and boxer briefs. North held my gaze, his angry and wanting, as he checked my readiness, fingers searching gently, slipping inside me with ease. His nostrils flared at finding me hot and wet, and he groaned against my mouth before kissing me again, licking at my tongue with his, deepening the kiss until I was breathless with need.

My fingers clawed at his ass, trying to hold him closer, and North gave in, guiding himself to me.

Nudging before pushing in.

He grunted as my heat surrounded his tip, and he broke our kiss to look me in the eye as he thrust all the way in.

I fisted his T-shirt, my inner thighs drawing up tight against his hips as he pulled out and thrust back in. Hard. Desperate.

My lips parted on a cry, my head falling back as the sensation tightened deep within.

"Look at me," North demanded as he anchored my hips in his hands. "Look at me, Aria."

So I did. And seeing the emotion in his eyes, I wanted to close myself against it. But I couldn't. No one made me believe I was as wanted and needed as him, and selfishly, I had to enjoy that one last time. To remember the way he made me feel.

"North ..." His name was a plea.

His jaw clenched, his grip on me tightened, and he began to thrust. Hard, deep drives punctuated by my growing cries. I had no awareness of where we were or if anyone could hear us. All that mattered was him.

"I'm close, I'm close," I panted.

His lips crushed over mine as he gentled his drives, teasing me, making tears prick my eyes. Especially as he pressed kisses along my jaw, down my throat. "This will never be over for me, princess," he whispered hoarsely in my ear. "Never. You're in my blood," he growled, his hips quickening as he felt my inner muscles tightening with my coming release. "You always will be."

My climax hit, my heart pounding as pleasure exploded through me. I throbbed around North in powerful waves, and he cried out against my throat as it brought him to release. He pulsed inside me, shuddering with the force of it.

Quickly, however, reality set in.

A chill skated over my body, and grief clawed at my throat.

North released a long exhale that shivered across my skin. He squeezed my hips before raising his head to look at me.

When I lowered my eyes, unable to bear the feelings he wouldn't hide from me, North muttered a curse and pulled out.

"I didn't wear a condom," he said as he pulled my skirt down to cover me before fixing himself.

My heart raced, but not at the news we'd forgone protection. "I'm on the pill, remember? And I'm sexually healthy."

"So am I." He exhaled shakily. "Aria, please look at me."

I owed him that. To not be a coward. Pushing off the desk, I smoothed my dress, ignoring my underwear lying on the office floor or the feel of his cum between my thighs.

North shook his head, fists clenched at his sides. "Walking away from this is a big fucking mistake."

"I would end up hurting you, or you me," I whispered, too emotional to speak louder. "I'd rather it end now like this."

"I don't want it to end," he stated simply.

Heartbreakingly.

A huge part of me wanted to fly into his arms and beg him to forgive me so we could just go on as we were.

Yet I knew how drastically things were about to change once he started filming again. I knew all my bitter insecurities would destroy us. Or ... my faith in him would be misplaced and he'd hurt me. As long as he was acting, my old wounds wouldn't allow me to believe he wouldn't eventually try to use me. Or cheat on me with a future beautiful leading lady.

Rational or not, I didn't trust him.

And my distrust would come between us.

Staying strong, I lifted my chin and looked him square in the eye. "It's over, North."

His expression was winded, like I'd just punched him in the gut.

Self-flagellation gripped me tight as his eyes brightened, seconds before he gave me an angry nod and slammed out of my office.

The sound of the door banging against the jamb seemed to echo and echo inside the space that I'd used as a cage to protect me.

Locked up tight.

Where no one could hurt me.

Except myself.

I covered my mouth with my hand to silence the sobs that wracked my body.

TWENTY-FIVE
NORTH

U sually when I'm on stage or when the camera is on me, I can slip into character like a superhero outfit. Suddenly, I'm no longer North but the very soul of someone else entirely.

To start, we were shooting the film in sequence, and in London where my character, Daniel Stone, has his carefully cultivated life as an intelligence officer blown up. Daniel is not spy thriller suave. He's a frosty motherfucker, assassin-level emotionally shut down, and part of his character journey over the franchise will be him reluctantly beginning to be part of the world again. To *feel* again.

All I felt, however, as I delivered my lines was panic.

I had not slipped into Daniel like a well-fitting outfit this morning. To be honest, Daniel chafed. Daniel was the equivalent of wearing a mohair suit infested with fire ants. Okay, maybe that was a slight exaggeration, but today's scenes weren't going well.

Why the fuck did Daniel chafe?

I tried to push through it, to rely on my skills to get through the scenes, but I knew by Blake's expression as he approached me after calling cut that things were not going well.

"A word." He nodded his head toward the far corner of the soundstage, and I followed him. Cast and crew moved around us doing their jobs, hopefully not paying attention to the fact that I was about to be chastised by a director who'd fought hard for me to play this role.

While we'd be shooting some action scenes outside on the streets of London, those weren't for a few weeks. For now, we were at Elstree Studios where our set builders and art department had created impressive versions of an MI6 office, a members-only club, and Daniel's sterile London flat. We were using two soundstages, and before we left London, we'd film out of sequence in one of the indoor tanks because I had an underwater fight scene.

As soon as we'd found a private, dark corner, Blake whipped around and stared at me incredulously, hands on his hips.

I blanched. "I know."

"You do?" Blake feigned shock. "Great. Do you want to fill *me* in on why you're acting like Daniel has chronic constipation?"

In Blake's thick New York accent, the insult almost made me laugh, but I knew that would worsen the situation. "I'll get it. I'm just a wee bit rusty."

"Well, whatever is fucking with your mojo, fix it, and soon. The street action scenes are scheduled to an inch of their life, coordinated meticulously with the BFS and Met Police. There is no waiting around for you to switch into character."

"I know." My voice hardened. "I've got this."

Blake gave me an appraising look and nodded before clapping me hard on the shoulder. "You're talented, man. You've got that 'thing,' that quality that makes you great. But that 'thing,' whatever it is, it's not showing up with you. Find it again. Fast." He strode off on the unspoken warning, leaving me to stew in my apprehension.

I'd had my ups and downs in romantic relationships, and while I'd always cared for my girlfriends, I could honestly say that whatever was going on with a woman had never infected my work.

Until now.

It had been four weeks since Aria broke things off. Four weeks since I'd left Ardnoch. I couldn't stay there, so I returned to London with my trainer, and filming started two weeks ago. After we were finished in London, we'd travel to locations in Europe and Asia for the rest of the five-month shoot.

Before Aria, I'd been excited about this movie. This was the part that could launch me into superstardom.

Now I felt like I was missing a limb.

Aria was the reason I'd lost my *thing*, whatever the fuck it was.

I'd promised myself when the day came that she ended our arrangement, I'd fight for more. I didn't.

I let hurt and rejection win.

I didn't fight for her. For us.

Now I understood what all those miserable bloody love songs were talking about. The cliché about days seeming darker, empty, every second meaningless ... it was all true. Cliché, for a reason. Without Aria, I felt exhausted by life. But if I didn't want my career to go down the toilet along with our relationship, I needed to buck the fuck up.

"That's a wrap for today!" Blake called out. "See you back here tomorrow morning at six a.m.!"

I left before anyone—costars, director, producer, writers —could stop me to talk. As I grabbed my gear and pulled out my phone, I saw I had a text from Theo. He was filming a TV show here in London.

At the Roebuck, if you fancy a drink.

The Victorian pub in Southwark was a ten-minute drive from my apartment on St. Katherine's Docks and a favorite haunt of Theo's. There were plenty of exclusive clubs in London that would welcome Theo Cavendish through their doors, but he seemed to eschew fashionable clubs. That's why his membership at Ardnoch was so surprising. When I'd said as much, he'd replied, "No amount of celebrity contamination can mar the beauty of somewhere like Ardnoch."

I tried not to be offended that he considered me celebrity contamination.

I quickly typed a reply, *Be there in an hour.*

It would take me that long to get there from the studios. But I could do with a drink after the day I'd had.

When I walked into the Roebuck later that evening, I found Theo in the laid-back pub, legs outstretched, gesticulating with his hands as he told a story to two women he'd attracted. The thought of having to be sociable pissed me off, and I almost turned and left. But Theo looked up at that moment and nodded at me. He turned back to his companions and said something with that playboy smile that turned people into infatuated idiots.

Whatever it was, the women stood, grinning and waving at him as they crossed the bar to sit with another group.

Gratified by their departure, I slid into the seat opposite Theo. The pub was busy, the bar area packed with people. My friend was nursing a whisky.

"You look like shit," he greeted me pleasantly.

"It hasn't been the best day."

"Tell me about it. Did you know the Roe is becoming a celebrity hangout?" He leaned forward in his seat. "Those girls were telling me Angeline Potter's been in here this week. I'm telling you, that woman is stalking me."

The British actor and rom-com sweetheart, whom I did a movie with back in the day, was a member of Ardnoch, and according to Aria, she spent a lot of time there. I'd been lucky enough to avoid her so far because once she got talking, it was difficult to get away. She was kind of self-involved.

"I didn't know Angeline was interested in you."

"Cornered me at the fucking estate last Christmas under the mistletoe. Never one to let a lady down, I obliged her with a grope." He seemed to consider this. "Ah, actually, I think I went down on her in the restroom."

I grimaced. "You think?"

"I was drunk. But it would explain why she keeps sliding into my DMs and stalking my favorite pubs. I am excellent at cunnilingus."

I stood up abruptly. "I need a drink."

Theo gave me a smug grin. "Don't be jealous, old boy. Some of us are just gifted."

I flipped him off and his laughter followed me to the bar. People had turned to stare as soon as I'd walked into the Roe, but as if used to the odd celebrity spotting, they'd returned to their conversations and food. However, they parted for me at the bar, giving me friendly smiles I returned. Usually, I didn't like to take advantage of my well-known face, but I was hungry and in need of a drink, so I allowed them to skip the queue as the bartender came over for my order.

"Loved you in *King's Valley*," the bartender said as he poured me a pint.

"Thanks, mate. I appreciate it."

"On the house." He pushed the pint toward me.

I slid money along the bar as a generous tip. "That's very kind, thanks."

The bartender took the cash with a pleased gleam in his eyes. "Cool. We'll bring your burger over when it's ready."

"Did you order food?" Theo asked as soon as I returned to him.

I nodded. "I'm starving."

Theo considered me. "You do look like shit, mate. What happened?"

After taking a refreshing chug of beer, I explained the day's woes to my friend.

He exhaled wearily when I was done. "I don't even want to acknowledge it because you know I find romance tiresome, but has this got anything to do with the luscious Aria?"

"You know it fucking does," I grumbled. "I'm a bloody coward who ran away from the first problem we encountered."

"Her breaking it off is rather a big problem, though."

I glowered at him. "I should have fought for her. Now I'm like the walking fucking wounded. I try to be Daniel, but I can't stop thinking about her, so I'm always North."

"Is it because you miss her or because you're worried about her? There is a big difference."

"I know you'd quite like it to be the latter," I huffed. "But nothing has happened to either of us since the attack. Nothing came of it." The plates on the Defender that tried to mow us over were false, so we couldn't track the vehicle to the attacker. "There's been no more letters. Everything has gone quiet." I'd been checking in with Walker several times a week just to make sure. With no leads, there was no choice but to carry on with life as I knew it.

Life without her.

The pain in my chest flared, and I rubbed it absentmindedly as I took a sip of beer.

"How are the rest of the cast? Have they noticed you bungling it?"

"Blake has. We had a word. But everyone else is just going with it. Eden doesn't join us until Berlin." I referred to my costar and leading lady Eden Gabriel, a French actor who'd smashed international barriers to find global fame. We'd met months ago at a table reading and she'd flirted her arse off with me. I'd been seeing Cara at the time, so I wasn't interested.

Now I feared I'd never be interested in any other woman ever again.

Aria Howard had fucking broken me.

Not that I'd admit that aloud. There were only so many hits I could take to my ego and masculinity.

"Ah, Eden Gabriel." Theo swirled his drink. "She's rather beautiful."

"I'm not going there."

"I'm not advising you to." My friend leaned forward. "My number one rule is never fuck anybody on your film set. Costars, crew, no one. Too much money involved for the drama it invites. If the attraction is great, you can always fuck them once the film wraps."

"Nice to know you have some principles," I replied sarcastically.

"You are in a charming mood." He grimaced. "Okay, I'm only saying this because I find you more tolerable than most people, but—fuck, I can't believe I'm saying this—have you considered a grand gesture to win your lady back?"

Surprised he was trying to give me romantic advice, I raised an eyebrow. "Grand gesture?"

"Yes. You said the reason you broke up with the delightful Ms. Howard is because she has trust issues. Why don't you prove you trust her beyond any doubt? Perhaps in doing so, she'll feel moved to reciprocate."

Huh.

My mind raced as I considered his advice and what I could do that would break through Aria's walls.

What I did know was that I couldn't go on like this.

Every day had become about missing this woman. The only solution was to get her back.

I opened my mouth to thank Theo, but a deep, American voice cut me off.

"Cavendish!" A tall, familiar bloke with dark hair and light eyes appeared at our table and clapped a hand down on Theo's shoulder. "Imagine seeing you here."

It took me a second, but the reason for his familiarity became clear.

Preston Holden, of all fucking people.

"Preston." Theo gave the American a tight-lipped smile. "What brings you here? I hope you lot aren't trying to infiltrate my local?"

"Your local what?" Preston frowned, still wearing that shit-eating grin.

Theo sighed wearily. "Never mind."

"Okay, then." Preston's eyes flicked to me, away and then quickly back. "Fuck, man. North Hunter." He gestured to me excitedly and then held out a hand across the table. "Nice to see you again."

"He was talented, so I helped him get an audition for my dad's movie and he got it. I surprised him by showing up to set one day and found him fucking his costar in his trailer. He dumped me while he was still inside her. Cheers to being told that you were no longer of use and that I was getting fat while he's literally inside his beautiful costar."

Aria's words blasted through my mind as I stared at this motherfucker who the entire world loved with his acting accolades and Oscar.

Appetite gone, I stood up, staring stonily at him. "I'm afraid I can't say the same." I looked down at Theo, whose eyes had rounded comically. "You can have my burger. I'm leaving."

"Wait, wait." Preston held up his hands defensively,

expression confused. "What happened? Did I do something to offend you?"

Staring at his pretty-boy face, I wanted nothing more than to smash my fist into it. But I wouldn't. I did, however, want him to know that I knew he was scum. "We have a mutual friend in common. Aria Howard."

Something like uneasiness flickered in his expression, but he brushed it off with a lazy smirk. "Oh, yeah, Aria. I don't have a problem with Aria. If she has a problem with me, that's not my issue."

Arsehole.

I glanced at Theo. "I'll see you around."

"Oh, I'm done here for the evening." Theo pushed to his feet. "I'll walk you out."

Without another look at Preston, I turned to leave.

Then the fucker said, "It's bad enough Wesley Howard won't work with me now ... I should've known that frigid bitch would go around tarnishing my reputation. I guess that's what I get for pity fucking a fatty to get to her daddy."

A red haze of fury clouded my brain and before I could stop myself, I whirled around and slammed my fist into his face. All my weeks of training hit the actor with such impact he might as well have run headfirst into a brick wall.

His legs buckled and he crumpled to the pub floor.

Gasps filled the room and then stunned silence as Preston groaned, semiconscious, blood gushing from his nose.

"Out, out, before the phone cameras appear." Theo rushed me, physically hauling me from the pub before anyone could snap a photo of me standing over Preston's prone body.

A glance back inside saw his security team appear out of nowhere to help him. One of them glared at me, daring me to come back. Preston was conscious, so the urge to run back in and deck him again was strong. Even if I had to go through his security guys to get to him.

A hard smack on my back stopped me.

Looking dazedly at Theo, I found him grinning, highly entertained. "Feel better?"

My knuckles throbbed. "Marginally."

"Well, the prick deserved it for maligning Ms. Howard. It's fuckers like him that make women feel bad about their luscious bodies. Fat, indeed." He scoffed. "Her body is a thing of beauty." He cut me a look. "You lucky dog."

"Do you want smacked in the face too?"

"I'd rather you not mar its perfection." He smoothed a hand over his cheek. "You almost killed the bloke."

A knot tightened in my gut at the thought. "Do you think he'll press charges?"

Theo snorted. "And have the entire world know North Hunter took him out with one magnificent, movie-worthy punch? No. Absolutely not. He's too much of an egomaniac for that. Aria dated that wanker? What the hell was she thinking?"

Irritated, I ignored his question. "How do you know him?"

"At the Oscars when he won. The arsehole is obsessed with status and seemed overly impressed by my father's title. Which, of course, made me despise him. Which, of course, made me a tantalizing challenge to the little prick." He let out a loud whistle, causing people passing us to look. "I am going to relive you decking that fragrant man swine over and over." Theo patted me on the back again. "You just graduated from tolerable to slightly likable."

"I can die happy." I wished I could be satisfied by the encounter.

Instead, it filled me with restless energy.

Theo's apartment was in Mayfair, so we went our separate ways. I walked the thirty minutes back to my flat. It was a two-bed with an open-plan living area. The main room was a light-filled space with a wall of windows. A balcony stretched along the building so I could enjoy my waterfront view of the Thames.

I used to love this place, but it didn't feel like home anymore.

Because I'd forgotten the agonizing lesson I'd learned as a child.

Home wasn't a place.

Home was the people.

Aria ... Aria was my person.

After icing my hand for twenty minutes and pacing my apartment as I planned, I marched into my bedroom and hauled a box out of the cupboard. Inside were all my journals. Every journal I'd kept since I was a teenager.

Rounding my bed, I pulled my current journal out of the bedside drawer. Taking a breath, I flexed my throbbing hand and wrote down the events of the day, along with my thoughts.

My longing.

My love.

Hesitating, I held the journal over the box.

I was basically handing *me* over. Everything I'd ever felt for the last seventeen years was in this box. It was me, stripped bare.

Give her your trust, Theo had said.

Well, this was trust on a level I'd never given to anyone.

I dropped the journal into the box and strode into the kitchen to find packing tape.

TWENTY-SIX

ARIA

Spring was slow in awakening this year. The breeze skating over the North Sea still held a wintry chill, ruffling my hair and sprinkling goose bumps over my bare arms. It was May, but you wouldn't know it.

The sun peeked through the gray clouds above, spilling pale gold rays across the sky and dappling the dark waters before me.

I stared unseeing, feeling my blouse billow, my hair blowing back from my face. A sudden urge to run into the water and just swim until I could do nothing but float away on the waves swept over me. Seagulls cried in the skies above as if they could sense how empty I felt. It was strange how painful *empty* was. By its very definition, emptiness should feel like nothing.

But the hollowness in my chest triggered soreness to radiate out to every part of me. Even my gums ached. My cheeks. My jaw. My whole body was tense because it was afraid I would shatter apart now that this void had opened inside me and weakened my foundations.

Ironically, missing North hurt worse than any of the horrible shit my exes had said and done to me.

"Ms. Howard!" I could hear a voice calling my name over the squawking of the birds overhead.

Turning, I looked toward the dunes that led onto the estate and back to the castle. Before North, I'd rarely ventured away from the castle without telling anyone where I was going. Every day since he'd left, if the weather permitted, I'd sneak out at lunchtime to be by myself on the private beach.

Sarah McCulloch stood in her housekeeping uniform at the top of a dune. She waved. "Ms. Hutchinson is looking for you, Ms. Howard!"

Back to work, then.

Hoping for a distraction, I nodded and headed up the beach. Sarah turned and left well before I could reach her. I didn't take offense. Upon her return to work two weeks ago, I noted a marked difference in her. While still reserved, the shyness that caused her to blush like a schoolgirl seemed to have been stomped out by the brittleness of grief. I could see it in her eyes. The light there had dimmed.

But she'd insisted on coming back to work, so I had to let her do what she needed.

As soon as I hit the path again, I brushed as much sand off my feet as possible and slipped into my heels. It was a ten-minute walk back to the castle and in the flat shoes she wore, Sarah was way ahead of me. By the time I reached the entrance, Wakefield was there to hold the door open, and I entered the great hall to find it empty of members.

"Is there something wrong?" I asked the butler.

"I don't believe so, Ms. Howard. A package has arrived for you. It's in Mrs. Hutchinson's office."

"A package?"

"Yes, Ms. Howard."

Agnes hopped to her feet a few minutes later when I knocked on her open office door. She rounded her desk and gestured to the box sitting on it. "This arrived for you twenty minutes ago. It says it's for the *urgent* attention of Ms. Aria Howard."

Frowning, I crossed the room and looked down at the label.

It was handwritten.

And I knew the handwriting.

My pulse raced. "Who left this? When?"

"A courier. Twenty minutes ago," she repeated, her brows drawn together. "Would you like security to open it fir—?"

"No," I cut her off much too abruptly. "I mean, no. I'll just take it to my office."

"It's rather heavy."

I picked it up to discover she was correct. "It's fine."

My legs trembled as I hurried out of her office to escape more questions. Blood rushing in my ears, I barely noted anyone as I moved as swiftly as possible to my office. As soon as I got inside, I dumped the box on my desk and quickly locked my door. Then I kicked off my shoes and approached the package like it was an opponent I was about to face in the ring.

North's handwriting stared back at me.

What could he have sent?

Why would he send me something now?

He'd left a month ago. According to Walker, he was already filming the spy movie in London, and there had been no more letters, no threats, no leads on the incident with the Defender. In fact, North was without a private security detail while he was back in the city he now called home, despite Walker's recommendation that he at least have a bodyguard with him at all times.

Idiot. Why didn't he have a bodyguard?

And what was this damn box?

Shaking with nerves and excitement, feeling more alive than I'd felt in the last four weeks, I cursed the Scot for doing this to me. For making me feel so much.

Then I tore open the box and frowned.

Books?

I picked up the first one and flipped it open.

My breath caught at the familiar scrawl of his words on pages that had been dated at the top.

Not books.

Journals.

Disbelief coursed through me as I pulled out journal after journal. I flipped through them quickly, searching the dates, and soon realized he'd sent me every journal he'd ever written. There were entries from when he was a boy.

And that first journal was his current one.

Tears blurred my vision as I practically collapsed into my office chair and clasped the book to my chest. With a deep breath, I blinked away the emotion and flipped open the journal to read about the last few months from North's perspective. The tears I'd tried to hold back rolled down my cheeks as I saw myself through his eyes. How I'd become his confidante, the person he felt at ease with more than anyone. The person he looked forward to seeing every day. The woman who excited him. Who made him feel like a teenager again. I felt my cheeks heat at the mention of how phenomenal the sex was, though, thankfully he didn't go into too much detail.

My chest ached at his admission that his favorite part was lying in bed afterward, talking about stupid things and big things ... watching me sleep. He said he loved to watch me sleep, relaxed and warm at his side. To be the one privileged enough to see me at a moment so few people got to.

I grew angry with myself as I read about his subsequent hurt when I broke things off. The feelings of rejection. Of abandonment. Yeah, that killed. I hated how his hurt turned to self-flagellation. How he blamed himself for not trying harder to convince me to be with him.

Then his last entry made my stomach twist.

MAY 2

Today was a shit show of the highest order. Daniel continues to elude me, and there's no other explanation for it—missing Aria as much as I do means I'm unable to separate myself from the part. My love for her, my grief, is all-consuming. Therefore, I can never be anything but North. It pissed Blake off. His silent warning means I'm on thin ice. I have to find a path to Daniel.

Surprisingly, the best advice I received today came from Theo. He suggested I show Aria that I trust her implicitly, hoping that in doing so, she'll reciprocate my trust. I was just considering that it might actually be good advice when, to make the day an epic shit show, Preston Holden walked into the pub we were in. I should have taken the high road, but I wanted that smug bastard to know I knew he was scum. Decking him had not been in the plans, and hopefully he doesn't press charges, but I found some satisfaction in watching the bastard bleed. Mostly, it made me feel empty. He deserved to get hit, but I'm not proud of doing it. It came from a place of anger at myself more than anything. I walked away from the woman I love. Like a fucking coward.

But Theo's right. I won't give up. Before I can find my way to Daniel, I have to find my way back home. And my home is with Aria.

She needs to know that.

A SOB BURST out of me as I closed the book and pressed it hard to my chest. That emptiness inside was already filling just from his words, from this tangible connection to him. God, I missed him so much.

I stood, staring at the journals. Everything he was, was in here.

Every private thought he'd ever shared with these books.

All here.

And he'd handed them over to me.

Trusted me.

My fingers skimmed over the leather-bound journals that catalogued North's life for over a decade and a half.

He loved me.

He really did.

I sucked in a sharp breath. Because I believed him.

And I didn't need to read through all of his thoughts to cement that belief. He could keep some things to himself. Everyone deserved to have thoughts be only theirs. Hands shaking with my decision, I repacked the journals into the box. Now that I thought about it, I was a little angry that he'd taken the risk of sending this when anyone could have broken into the box and sold the contents to the tabloids.

There was no way I was sending them back via courier.

No.

I'd just have to return them myself. Along with the reciprocation of the faith North had placed in me.

Decision made, my first call was to my boss.

My second call was to my dad.

"Hey, sweetheart," he answered. "It's good to hear from you. Your mother's been calling, and she says you keep sending her to voicemail."

"Dad, I need a favor," I said, not addressing my mother's complaint.

"Oh?"

"Can you find out if the film crew for Blake Forster's current production is still in London?" I could have called Walker to ask, but I didn't want anyone acquainted with North to know about my plans.

"Uh ... sure, I guess. Can I ask why?"

"I need to know ASAP."

"Okay. Again, why?"

"There's someone on the crew I need to talk to."

"I'm going to need more than that, sweetheart."

I sighed, fearing his judgment, but not enough to not get what I needed from him. "North Hunter is the lead, and I have something of his that I need to return. Immediately."

"Aria ..." My dad's exhale crackled the line. "Maybe you should steer away from actors for a while."

"Dad ... I won't explain who North is or what's between us. I just need your help."

"If he hurts you—"

"Dad."

"Fine," he grumbled. "But this better not mean we're losing you to Scotland permanently."

I smiled, staring out my office window at the castle grounds, but I didn't answer because I was suddenly excited to discover if that was a promise I couldn't keep.

TWENTY-SEVEN
NORTH

"**C**ut!"
     I blinked, coming back to myself as Blake Forster stepped into the scene. My head throbbed and the stuntman, Dec, I'd been fighting, pulled me to my feet. "Staircase caught you there." He looked past the cameras to the crew. "Medic."

"I'm all right." I dabbed at the shallow cut I'd sustained when Dec had thrown me against the stair banisters on the set.

Blake took in the minor injury. "We're switching out with your stunt double, so get that looked at." Then he grinned as he smacked my arm. "That was perfect. Whatever rage you're channeling, keep it up."

My "rage" was actual fear manifesting as fury. As soon as I'd sent Aria my journals, an overwhelming terror of rejection and abandonment flooded me. It didn't take a fucking psychologist to work out where the fear stemmed from.

The result was that I'd been on edge for the last few days, so I'd poured it all into the movie. There was nothing else for it. As soon as I stepped off camera these days, my gut churned as North. But finally, I had tapped into Daniel, and his gut didn't churn. It was a nice reprieve.

Walking with the medic, we cleared the cameras and I rested my arse against the buffet table so she could reach me to clean my cut.

"It doesn't look too bad," she murmured as she sterilized it.

I nodded, my fingers curling into the table as my gaze drifted over her shoulder toward the scene they were resetting for my stunt double, Mick. White beneath the soundstage lights caught my eye.

Aria.

She stood tall in jeans, a white shirt open loose over a black strappy top that clung to her curves. She wore her hair down.

This was sexy, casual Aria that people didn't get to see often.

I blinked rapidly, cursing that I was actually starting to hallucinate her. But then she turned as if looking for someone, and I saw the security pass hanging around her neck.

Aria was here.

Anticipation rushed through me. "Excuse me," I muttered distractedly to the medic, gently extricating myself from her to go to Aria.

My movement drew Aria's attention, and our eyes met across the room. She was here. She was really fucking here. Hope shortened my breath. By the time I reached her, I was practically bloody panting.

Her gorgeous eyes were bright in the dim light as she searched my face as if cataloguing it. "I—I'm so mad at you for mailing something so private. Anyone could have found those journals."

What?

Okay.

Disappointment crept in. That wasn't what I'd expected her first words to be. My throat closed.

"So ..." She stepped into my personal space, her perfume filling my senses. "I brought them back, personally."

What did that mean?

My fingers flexed at my sides with the urge to touch her.

At my continued silence, Aria's brows drew together as if in pain. "North, I am so sorry for pushing you away. And if you still want me ... I want to try something real with you."

Relief and euphoria flooded me, my grin splitting my cheeks. "Aye? Really?"

Aria smiled big, too, so beautiful she made my chest ache. "Really."

She'd barely said the word when I'd hooked my hand around her nape to crush her mouth to mine. The feel of her lips, her taste ... it was *right*. No woman's kiss had ever been more right than Aria Howard's. I kissed her like we'd spent years apart instead of weeks. I kissed her as if we were the only two people in the room, not giving a shit about the cast and crew around us.

When we finally broke for oxygen, I clasped her precious face in my palms. "Can you stay? If it were up to me, we'd walk out of here right now, but we have a few more hours of filming—"

"I can stay," she assured me, leaning in to press another kiss to my mouth. "I missed you."

"You have no idea," I told her gruffly.

"Actually, I do."

I laughed with self-deprecation. "The journals. Right."

"I only read the most recent one. I don't need to know every thought you've ever had, North. Some things should just belong to you. But it meant a lot that you trusted me with those."

This woman.

I wanted to tell her I loved her right there and then, but

not with everyone else around. Pressing my forehead to hers, I whispered, "Thank you."

"Back at you, babe," she whispered.

I FORCED myself not to jump all over her as soon as Blake wrapped for the day. It turned out Blake knew who Aria was because Wesley was the one who got her access to the set. I didn't introduce her as my girlfriend because I wasn't sure yet how she wanted to play this, but the kiss probably gave us away. Afterward, I escorted Aria to a restaurant for a bite to eat before taking her back to my place. The whole time, my blood thrummed hot with the prospect of getting her alone. It felt like I hadn't touched her in so long.

We talked over dinner about how we'd make the long-distance thing work while I was filming because now that she wanted to be in a relationship with me, I was wary of any kind of distance between us. Aria seemed certain it was time she started taking back her personal life and not work weekends at the estate, which would free up time to fly out to see me. I wanted to pay for the flights, but she was adamant about paying her own way. Between her savings and trust fund, money was certainly no object for her. I imagined she was worth a lot more than I was.

I didn't care.

None of it fucking mattered.

All I cared about was getting to see her any chance I could.

We'd make this work.

I'd fight like hell to make this work. And I was starting to believe that Aria would too.

All my thoughts of making leisurely love to her went out the window as soon as we got into my flat and my woman jumped me. Aria pulled at my clothes, her kisses desperate and hot, and I couldn't have denied her even if I wanted to.

Our clothes scattered through my living space and into my bedroom like a trail of bread crumbs until we were naked and she was riding me like an Amazonian queen, taking what she fucking wanted.

By the time I returned to the bedroom after disposing of the condom, Aria sat up against the pillow, one long leg bent at the knee, her arms flung over her head, olive cheeks dewy from our lovemaking. Her eyes met mine, and she didn't rush to cover her body. Instead, her gaze invited me to look my fill. She trusted I wanted her. That I found every inch of her spectacular. It made me feel good to make her feel good about herself. God, I loved her.

Blood rushed to my cock, and her eyes lowered as my semi went full mast. "I could stare at you all fucking day, woman."

She gave me a sultry smile, and I suddenly knew this was who Aria had been before Preston and Lucas got in her head. Confident, sexy, sexual. She'd found her way back. "You too."

I grinned as I swooped down to pick up my jeans to pull the pack of condoms out of the pocket. Aria watched as I rolled one on.

Putting a knee on the bed, I climbed over her as I caressed my hand up her smooth leg, ripping the duvet aside to trail my fingertips across her silky inner thigh as she spread her legs to accommodate me. Hovering over her, I watched her face as I slid two fingers inside her wet heat. Her eyes lowered as she shifted her hips against my touch. Her lips parted with an excited gasp, making me thirsty for them. I kissed her. Deep, hungry, and she slid her arms around my back, drawing me closer.

Removing my fingers, I braced my hands on either side of her shoulders and nudged between her legs. Releasing her from the kiss, I stared into those gorgeous eyes filled with trust I did not take for granted, and I pushed inside her.

Aria brought her thighs up around my waist and slid her hands down my back to grip my arse as I thrust. She moaned, and the sound throbbed in my dick at the same time her fingers clenched into my arse cheeks.

I pulled my hips back, a teasingly slow withdrawal, and then groaned as her tight heat squeezed me when I pushed in.

"Yes," Aria panted. "Yes. Only you feel like this."

Satisfaction mingled with emotion, and even though every nerve ending was screaming at me to fuck her, I didn't. I wanted to make love to her.

Gripping her thigh, I yanked her hips higher, changing the angle of my thrusts, as Aria released her hold on me and slid farther down the bed. "Fuck." She panted as I dragged out of her painfully, pleasurably, slowly, until only my tip was inside. Her hands clenched into the sheets as she held my gaze. She had to see everything I felt. Had to know how much I loved her, adored her, but she didn't look away. And that gave me hope. I found her clit with my thumb as I moved, and her eyes widened as she tilted her chin back and whimpered.

Fuck, yes.

I circled her clit harder.

"North." She gripped my waist now, fingers biting into me. "North, please."

Knowing I was at the breaking point, I increased my thrusts, fucking into her, her generous tits trembling with my every drive. Her whimpers grew into moans and needy pants, making me harder. So fucking hard.

"Am all I you need?" I braced over her, hips snapping as the desire to come overtook everything. "Because you're all I need."

"Yes!"

"I love you, Ari. I love you so fucking much," I gasped, needing her to come because I was about to lose it.

Her nails dug into my back. "North ... ahhhhh!" She threw her head back in a cry of pleasure as I felt her inner muscles throb around me as she came.

"Aria!" I roared as the power of it tore through me, my hips jerking against her as I ground my cock into her, wanting to feel every single lingering tug of her climax.

I fell over her, my lips against her damp skin as I breathed heavily into her neck and shuddered, my cock still pulsing.

Finally, I lifted my head to meet her stunned gaze. Tears filled her eyes as she clasped my face in her hands and kissed me gently, reverently. When she released me, it was to snuggle against my throat and wrap her arms around me.

Catching my breath, I held her tight and promised myself it was okay that she hadn't told me she loved me back.

I could be patient.

TWENTY-EIGHT
ARIA

I t was unusual for me to be off the estate on a weekday at lunchtime, but here I was, attempting to have more of a life. A month ago, I'd reluctantly left North in London and flew back to the Highlands to have a serious chat with Lachlan about the hours I worked. My boss had never asked me to take on the overtime and responsibilities that I had, so he seemed relieved that I was creating boundaries for myself.

"We have a management team capable of running the estate at the weekend," he'd reminded me. "That's how the place ran before your arrival."

I still worked longer hours than most during the week, but those extra hours created a guilt-free zone for me to leave early on Fridays to catch a flight to London. They'd just moved locations, though, so last night I'd arrived back in Inverness from visiting him in Berlin. We didn't always get a lot of time together on those weekends, but I was used to hanging around a film set, having worked as my father's PA when I was in college. So I was cool to watch North do his thing until I could get him all to myself. The days they didn't need him—when they filmed elaborate stunts with the stuntmen—were my favorite.

We'd spent some glorious hours in bed. And in the shower. And up against the wall. Over a dining table ... My skin heated just thinking about it.

"I think we're ready to go at the end of the month. Do you think we're ready?"

Realizing Sloane had directed a question to me, I blinked out of my aroused stupor. "Ready?"

We sat in Flora's, a café on Castle Street, with Monroe having lunch. Brodan was taking care of their baby boy, Lennox, this afternoon so Roe could catch up with me and Sloane. Sloane was friends with both of us and that friendship had brought us together. Thankfully, Monroe had a sincerity and kindness I felt I could trust. North was teaching me to lower my barriers again to let good people in. It helped that I hadn't had any more weekly reminders from Caitlyn that friends like her existed. Things had grown quiet on that front, and it was bliss.

"My bakery." Sloane smirked at me. "Where were you just now?"

"Nowhere." I took a quick sip of tea, not meeting her eyes.

She snorted. "Yeah, I've been to nowhere. Walker's usually in nowhere. Naked."

I rolled my eyes. "What were you asking me about the bakery?"

"That it should be ready to open by the end of the month."

Considering she was so organized she was ready to go now, I thought it sounded more than doable and said so.

"Oh, I'm so nervous thinking about it."

"People will flood to it, Sloane," Monroe assured her. "And opening it for only a few days a week is so smart."

"Yeah, I hope so." Sloane eyed me suddenly. "Enough

about me. Let's talk about you and nowhere. How was Berlin?"

My decision to date North was an enormous step for me, so we'd agreed to contain our relationship to just our friends and family. Obviously, I was on North's set every weekend, so they all were aware, but the crew also knew better than to gossip about the cast. At least in any way that could reach the public. So I'd told my family (Allegra was happy for us, my dad was worried and wary, and Mamma kept badgering me about when she would meet North), and Sloane, Monroe, and the Adairs, but no one else officially knew. Well, North had told Theo Cavendish. I still wasn't sure about that guy, but North fully explained what happened with Preston in London, and I was glad Theo had the presence of mind to get North out of there. And he'd said nice things about me. So maybe there was a beating heart in the aristocrat's chest, after all.

"It was great." I bit my lip against a secret smile. "We saw little of the city, but it was great."

"Oh, I know what great means." Sloane wiggled her eyebrows comically. "So, is it getting serious?"

At her words, I heard North's deep voice in my head.

I love you.

Inwardly, I flinched and lowered my eyes so my friends couldn't see my panic. I'd read it in his journal before I flew to London, so I knew that's how he felt. Having him say it while we made love was one of the most beautiful things that had ever happened to me.

But for some stupid reason, I could not say the words back.

He hadn't said it since ... until last night. He'd gotten a cab to the airport with me and after we kissed for an inordinately long time at the drop-off point, he'd said he loved me.

My anxiety had clenched a fist around my throat and I couldn't get the words out. Couldn't reciprocate them.

Even though I felt them.

So I kissed him again. I'd poured everything I felt into that kiss and hoped it was enough for now.

But I noticed the glimmer of sadness in the back of his eyes when I walked away, and my chest had ached ever since. The thought of hurting him shredded me.

"It's serious," I replied quietly. "But I still have some issues to work through." Clearly.

"Do you want to talk about it?"

Monroe's phone vibrated on the café table and she threw us an apologetic look. "It's Brodan. One second." She lifted the phone, tapping the screen a few times, and then her expression tightened.

"You okay?" Sloane asked.

But it was me Monroe looked at. Something about her wary, sympathetic countenance filled me with dread. "Brodan just sent me a link to a newspaper article."

Oh, God.

I nodded nervously, and Roe handed her phone over. Taking it, I scrolled, and as I did, my hands shook.

The tabloid article headline was SCOTS ACTOR FINDS LOVE WITH HOLLYWOOD PRINCESS.

"Shit," I murmured, my gut roiling.

There were photos of me and North in Berlin. Holding hands walking down the street. Kissing passionately at the airport.

I stopped at one picture. North was holding my face in his hands and staring at me with such adoration it made me want to cry. Until that moment, I didn't think I'd ever fully processed the way he looked at me. Like a man in love.

Now everyone knew it.

Those feelings no longer belonged to just us.

The article said an anonymous source close to the couple told the *Daily Mail* that we were very much in love and had been dating for several months since meeting at Ardnoch Estate. They also said North had spent time in LA with my family, and we were all very close and talking about moving to LA together.

It was just lies pulled from speculation and guesswork.

Someone on the set had betrayed us for cash, of that I was certain. Everyone else who knew about us, I trusted.

I really did.

But now North and I were out there. My chest tightened and I felt a little dizzy as I dropped Monroe's phone on the table. When North left me ... the world would find out. I'd be humiliated all over again.

Sloane's hand covered mine, and she asked me if I was okay. I nodded, unseeing, reeling from the violation of my privacy.

"I've been there, Aria," Monroe said quietly. "The paps came after me and Brodan when he retired from acting. If you need to talk, I'm here."

My cell rang in my purse, and I knew it was him before I even pulled it out to look at the screen.

"It's North," I murmured.

"You should answer. He's probably worried," Sloane insisted.

Part of me didn't want to answer. I wanted to run away and hide and not deal with any of it. However, I knew that would hurt him, and I think I'd hurt North enough already.

"Hey." The word sounded croaky to my ears as I answered.

"Gorgeous." North sounded out of breath and panicked. "Did you see the news?"

"I did. Just this second."

"Are you okay?"

My heart hurt that the first thing he'd thought to do was check in on me. "It's not ideal."

"Look, Aria, I am so sorry. I'm getting on a plane right now to come to you."

"No." I stood, pushing away from the table to walk out of the café for more privacy. Outside on the street, I could hear him better as he rambled on about needing to be with me to make sure I was okay. "No," I repeated. "North, you can't walk out on filming. And not for something that we both know was an eventuality." It was true. If I intended to be in a relationship with North, it would eventually become public knowledge. Even if he was just a regular Joe off the street, at some point, our faces would find their way online. Because of me.

Because I was Wesley and Chiara Howard's daughter.

I was the problem. Not North.

"It had to be someone on set." He cursed. "I'll have a word with Blake."

"Don't." I shook my head, turning to look back into the café where Monroe and Sloane watched me with obvious concern. Their genuine worry soothed me a little. "North, we didn't hide our relationship from the film crew. That's on us. We just have to roll with this now."

He was silent for a few seconds. "As long as this doesn't make you want to run away from me, I'm fine with the world knowing about us. I'm more than fine. I'm in this, Aria, so for me this was always going to come out."

"You're right. It was."

"So, we're okay?"

Hating that I'd made him uncertain about us, I assured him, "We're more than okay. In fact, there's this one leaked photo that I kind of want to frame."

North's relieved chuckle warmed me all the way through. "Aye, I'm partial to a few myself. You're so fucking beautiful."

My cheeks heated. "I don't deserve you."

His voice was gruff with emotion when he replied, "You deserve the best, and so you make me want to be the best."

Tears filled my eyes and I blinked rapidly, trying to hold them back. Maybe those three little words were difficult for me to say, but I needed him to know how I felt. "You are the best, North. The best man I've ever known."

He exhaled sharply, his breath crackling down the line. "You would say that to me when there's nearly a thousand miles between us."

I grinned. "I'm cruel that way."

"I can't believe I have to wait a week to show you my appreciation."

I shivered at the thought of what that might be. "I can't wait."

We spoke a little more and when we hung up and I turned back to the café, I marveled how just the sound of his voice could bring me back from the brink of panic and fear.

TWENTY-NINE
NORTH

"**N**orth!"

I halted on my way to my trailer. Today's shoot was a wrap, and I just wanted to grab my phone, get back to my hotel, order room service, and call Aria. Yesterday was the closest she'd ever come to pronouncing her feelings for me, and it pissed me off we were in different countries.

We'd talked again last night and exchanged several texts, but I wanted to hear her voice again.

I was impatient to hear her voice.

Instead, I turned to find my costar, Eden, hurrying toward me. We were both still in costume. She was in the glittering green evening dress her character wore in the scene where we first meet. The Gallic beauty had arrived on set yesterday, and so far, our scenes were going well. Our characters had chemistry, which was great for the movie. But I knew when a woman was giving me the come-on, and I was trying to make it clear I wasn't interested without having to explicitly say it.

The brunette reached for me and pressed a manicured hand to my arm. Aye, she was technically beautiful, but she did nothing for me.

I was almost inured to physical perfection. I'd been around so much of it in this industry that it was nothing new. A person had to have something more to them to make me feel intense about them.

Like Aria.

She'd had me by the balls since we'd met.

The thought of her brought a small smile to my face, and Eden mistook it. Her fingers tightened on my arm.

"Let's change and get a drink to celebrate a good day."

"That's a kind offer, but I'm just going to head back to my hotel room."

Eden flashed me a predatory grin. "Why don't you invite me to join you?"

There it was. I half admired the European forthrightness and confidence. I liked how few hang-ups the French had about sex. But right now, it made things awkward. I gently extricated my arm. "I have a girlfriend."

Her perfect brows drew together. "Wesley Howard's *daughter*?"

So she'd seen the articles online. "Aria. Aye."

She shrugged. "*D'accord*. You know where to find me if you grow bored with your American."

I gave her a thin-lipped look and promptly walked away.

By THE TIME I got back to the hotel, all thoughts of Eden had fled. I wanted to shower, order room service, and call Aria. However, when I returned to the hotel, the manager stopped me.

"Mail arrived for you, sir," he said before handing over the envelope.

A chill skated down my spine at the familiar font. And lack of address. "Was this hand-delivered?"

"A courier delivered it, sir."

I murmured a thank-you and walked away, almost afraid to open the letter. Sucking it up, I ripped into it and pulled out the piece of typewritten paper. And some photographs.

I wonder if she knows who you really are. You don't deserve her. You don't deserve anything.

My pulse jumped at the sight of the photos. They were taken inside my London flat. Whoever had broken in had smashed my Golden Globe and BAFTA awards.

As I got into the elevator, I hit Walker's contact on my phone. He picked up on the third ring. "Walk, I have a problem." I explained the note and the photographs.

"That's it," he replied. "I'm sending you a list of recommendations for private security and you're going to pick someone I can have flown out to you tonight."

My gut clenched, but I knew he was right. "What about my flat?"

"We need to call the Met and have them look into it. This person might have left behind prints."

"I think we should put protection on Aria until we know what we're dealing with," I suggested, hating the thought of putting Aria through that but needing to know she was safe. "This letter obviously refers to her."

"Aria's off the estate right now."

I stumbled to a halt just as I got out of the elevator. "What do you mean she's off the estate?"

"She left the estate two hours ago. She's running an errand for Lachlan in Inverness. I'm sure she's fine, North, but I'll send someone after her if it'll make you feel better."

"Aye, aye, it'll make me feel better." I continued to my room and noted the housekeeping cart was outside it and the door was open. Great. I just wanted into my fucking room. Something had been wedged in the door to keep it open.

A prickle on my nape gave me pause.

I glanced down the corridor both ways, looking for other housekeepers. Then I looked back at the door and the ice bucket that propped it open.

Why would housekeeping need to prop open the door?

"Walk ... the letter didn't have an address on it. The hotel said a courier service delivered it, but ..." I pushed open my door without stepping inside and saw my clothes had been strewn everywhere. And sitting in an armchair facing the door, waiting for me, was someone I hadn't seen in years. Understanding crashed over me, and I swayed with the immensity of it. "Walker ... I know who's been sending the letters."

"Who?" he barked in my ear.

"Barbara Benny. Darren Menzie's mum."

"Who? How?"

"Because she's in my hotel room." I hung up the phone as I stepped into the suite. Somehow, deep down, I think I'd always known the letters were about what happened to Gil. What we'd done as boys. What I'd failed to stop Darren from doing. I must have moved the ice bucket because the hotel door clicked quietly shut behind me.

THIRTY

ARIA

Lately, I'd been feeling restless. Not with my life in Scotland—I loved my life in Scotland, even more now that I was starting to have one outside of my job. But being without North for most of the week left me feeling a little unmoored. Like there was something I should be doing and wasn't.

It manifested itself in ways such as wanting to be out of my office more and volunteering to drive to Inverness to drop off a contract renewal with the estate's solicitors. It was pretty urgent, and Lachlan had intended to drive it over since it would be quicker than mailing it. But I'd offered instead. So that's why, instead of ending the day driving ten minutes home, I was driving an hour toward the city before the solicitors' office closed.

Feeling out of sorts was probably the reason I answered my mother's call, twenty minutes from my destination. I'd been avoiding talking with Mamma as much as possible, making excuses to cut her off when she started asking about North or complaining about Allegra moving to the East Coast after the summer. Now I was trapped in a car with her musical accent filling the interior.

"You've been avoiding me," Mamma stated right away.

"I have not," I lied. "I've just been busy."

"*Sì, sì*, getting your papa to call in favors so you can be on the set of your new boyfriend's film. A man I still have not met. Did you know he played a serial killer in his last movie?"

I rolled my eyes, my hands tightening around the wheel. "It was a TV show. And he's not actually a serial killer, Mamma."

"I know this. But it is a very dark part to play. What does this say about him?"

Oh, for God's sake. "What does it say about Dad that he made a movie about an alien that was a serial killer? Or an assassin? You remember he made those, right?"

Mamma tsked. "I'm your mamma. I can be upset that I haven't met this man. And he's a Scot. Scots are earthy. Not sophisticated."

"Untrue. And especially about North." I tried not to let her irritate me. "Anyway, how are you?"

"Uh, well, one of my daughters would prefer to flee to the other side of the country than be near me, and the other fled across the ocean to start a life with a Scotsman."

My agitation simmered. "One: Allegra is going to one of the best schools in the country, not fleeing *you*." *It's not actually about you, Mother!* "Two: I moved across the ocean to start a career for myself. North was just a happy bonus two years later."

"And what of your *papà*? Me? Do you not want to be close to us?"

I wasn't going down this road with her again. "You know that's not true. You and Dad have your lives. We have ours. We make time for each other. That's how families work."

"Don't condescend to me, Aria." Mamma sniffed haughtily. "Anyway, I want to know more about this North person. For a start, what kind of name is North?"

"My mum told me I was named after the North Star because they knew I was all they would ever need ... to find their way. That I'd brought them together on the right path. I was their true North."

An ache squeezed my chest at the memory. "A beautiful name," I replied huskily. "North is a beautiful name."

"Hmm. You sound like you like him very much. If that is the case, you need to take better care of yourself, coccolona. I've been looking at his relationship history, and he has dated very beautiful women. The last was a pop star. Those pictures of you online, coccolona ... you need to lose some weight. Did you not get the link I sent you about the diet plan my friend has used? She says it works wonders. I was thinking—"

"Stop!" I yelled, angrier, louder than I expected.

In fact, I hadn't expected to say it at all. But the word exploded out of me.

Hurt that I hated she could inflict scored through.

"Aria!" Mamma snapped. "What is the matter with you?"

"What's the matter with me?" I huffed. Finally, it seemed, I was at the end of my tether with my mother. "What's the matter with you? North loves me. *Loves* me. And he loves my body. Unlike you, he loves me the way I am."

"U-unlike me?"

"Yes." Okay. So we were doing this. My hands shook around the steering wheel as I continued. "North has helped me gain back the confidence you helped take from me. Do you know that you're partly the reason that I hated looking in the mirror for so long? That every comment you've made about my weight over the years has shredded my self-esteem, bit by bit? You've made me feel like I wasn't lovable, that there was something wrong with me. You want to know why I avoid your calls, Mamma? Because who wants to put up with someone trying to change them all the time? Who has the heart that can bear that kind of hurt from their own mother? Am I not lovable to you as I am? Do I need to be fixed for you to love me?"

Silence greeted me at the end of the phone.

Then a sniffle and a quiet, "No, coccolona, of course not."

"And that. Don't call me that. Do you know what it's like for your mother to give you a pet name that means *cuddly*? You call Allegra your treasure. And I'm cuddly. You might as well have named us 'the daughter you're proud of' and 'the fat one.'"

"Oh, Aria," she whimpered. "You know that was not my intention. At all. You're my coccolona because you were such a cuddly baby. That is all. I promise."

"Somehow, after you disparaged my body and told me to lose weight to keep my man, I find that hard to believe."

She said nothing for so long that I thought maybe she'd hung up. But suddenly she exhaled shakily. "Your papà was right. He tried to tell me. I thought I was doing the right thing. I thought I was helping you to be happy. I just wanted you to be happy. But I put what makes me happy on you. I am a vain woman, *tesoro*. I know this of myself. It's not something I am proud of, but I promised to always own who I am. I put my obsession with my body on you, and I am sorry. I never intended to make you feel unloved."

Shocked at the apology, I was silent.

"*Tesoro*?"

"I'm processing," I replied quietly. "I honestly expected this to turn into an argument."

"My first instinct was to yell at you and hang up ... but I am trying to be better. I'm not a perfect person or parent. I know that. But I am trying to be more involved and to listen."

"Okay." Her uncharacteristic reasonableness made me

brave. "And we appreciate that, Mamma. But if you can hear a little more truth, I have something else to say."

She sucked in a breath. "All right."

"Allegra and I aren't kids anymore. We have grown-up lives. Decisions to make. You have to accept that sometimes the decisions we make won't be about you ... but that doesn't mean we don't love you. Because we do love you."

She sniffled again, and I knew she was crying by the shakiness of her words. "Okay. I will try to see it that way. I just ... I want to spend more time with you girls. I'm trying." What she obviously still wasn't getting was that it wasn't that it was too late, but we had our own lives now to prioritize, the way she'd prioritized her life over us.

"We'll all just try." I finally settled on diplomacy.

"Sì. We'll try. And no more coccolona or comments about your weight. I promise."

"Thank you."

"I love you, Aria. You know this, sì?"

An ache flared across my chest. "I love you, too, Mamma." For better and for worse.

We chatted until I arrived in the city. After hanging up with Mamma's promise to come to Ardnoch soon, I felt so much lighter. My relationship with my mother would never be perfect, but I'd finally stood up to her and the world didn't end.

She was shockingly contrite about the whole thing.

All this time, I'd been afraid to tell her to back off.

It was true what they said. Fear of the thing was often worse than the thing itself. Now I just had to hope that she stuck to her promise to stop commenting on my body.

I was just nearing the parking lot when my phone rang again. Seeing Walker's name I answered immediately.

"Aria, where are you?"

The fact that Walker had used my first name alerted me. I

tensed. "Just about to stop in at the solicitors' office in Inverness. Why?"

"Turn around and head back to the estate. Don't get out of the car."

"Why? What's going on?" I got into a different lane at the next roundabout so I could turn myself around.

"North received another letter at his hotel, and whoever is sending them is in his room with him right now. I've got hotel security heading up to him. But you were implicated in the last letter, so I need you back at the estate."

Fear coated my palms in slick sweat. "The person threatening North is in his hotel room? Right now?"

"Aye, but security is on their way. Just come home. I'll update when I know more."

"Walker—" My voice shook. "Please don't let anything happen to him."

"He'll be fine."

He had to be. North had to be okay. "I think I'm going to be sick."

"Breathe," Walker coaxed. "Just breathe in and out."

"He better be okay," I murmured, tears thickening my throat. If anything ever happened to North, I realized it would change me forever.

He'd already changed me forever.

THIRTY-ONE
NORTH

Barbara's eyes narrowed as I crossed the room to stand before her. "Dae ye ken who ah am?"

"You're Darren's mum." I stuck my hands in my pockets not quite knowing what to do. She'd always been a small woman, and even when we'd been kids, her face had a rough haggardness that suggested a difficult life. It was worse now, her skin etched with wrinkles. She looked much older than her years. Her hair had thinned to a wispiness, and she'd scraped it back into a ponytail, her scalp visible in patches all over her head. Dressed in a housekeeper's uniform, I understood how she'd made it this far to my suite.

"You've been sending the letters."

"Aye." Her hatred seeped from her pores.

"Why?"

"Tae fuck wi' ye."

"You've been following me? Found out where I lived?"

She nodded. "Ah leaked the story tae the press and thought, finally, ye were gettin' whit ye deserved. Ah even stayed in Ardnoch, jist tae mak' sure ye were miserable. But then someone posted that lying video online aboot ma Darren, and ye started tae get yer career back."

I stiffened, rage simmering in my gut. "Did you drive that Defender into me and Aria?"

Barbara lifted her chin. "Ah did."

"You could have killed Aria," I seethed.

"Aye, and ye'd be hurtin' like ah've been hurtin' fur years!" she screeched so sharply, I flinched. "Couldnae believe it when ah saw ye oan TV. The laddie that pit ma laddie away, no only livin' his life but gettin' fuckin' famous. How's that fair?"

"I didn't put Darren away," I told her calmly. "His actions did."

She stood up, her hands clenched at her sides. "Ma Darren wis jist a wee boy."

"Who your partner abused so fucking badly, Darren became nothing but anger, and he inflicted that anger on others."

Her eyes brightened. "That's no true."

"It is true." My guilt gave way to reality as I remembered hiding in Darren's closet when Barbara's boyfriend came home drunk. Barbara was in the living room, watching TV. I remembered being terrified as her boyfriend beat on Darren while she did nothing. And then sick to my stomach when I realized he was sexually abusing him too. I'd found a baseball bat in Darren's closet and burst out of there to stop him. It didn't matter that I'd helped my friend. I'd seen his shame. Darren spiraled from that moment on, his misdeeds growing darker, and our friendship splintered.

I wasn't to blame. The events leading up to Gil MacDonald's death had started long before that night. "You knew, didn't you? You knew what he was doing to Darren, and you didn't stop it."

"Ah dunno whit yer talkin' aboot. Am here tae face ye fur

puttin' ma wee laddie away. *You* betrayed him an' he died in prison because o' *you*."

"I did betray him," I admitted. "I betrayed him because it was the right thing to do for an innocent man who was killed in the most horrific way."

Barbara's lips trembled with her fury.

But I continued, "But you betrayed Darren, too, long before I ever did. We wouldn't have even been there that night if you had just protected him."

"Ahhhh!" she screamed, her face contorted and mottled as she pulled a knife out of the inner pocket of her jacket and flew at me.

I only had a second to register the weapon and lean back, swiping my hand up to bat away the knife. Pain flared down the center of my palm where it cut me open, but I didn't have time to think about it because she slashed at me again. I stumbled back, dodging her enraged stabs and swipes as I tried to find my feet.

"Ye killed ma laddie!" she screamed over and over, her words cracking and hoarse. So overcome with her fury, she lunged with too much force and lost her footing, enough for me to sidestep her and grab her wrist. It was against everything I was to hurt a woman, but Barbara Benny was gone. All that was in her was crippling self-loathing she'd misdirected at me.

I snapped her wrist back and she dropped the knife with a howl of agony.

Then suddenly security was in the room and pulling her away from me.

"Are you okay, sir?" a man in a black suit asked, his face blank with stoic professionalism as his colleagues cuffed Barbara Benny.

"I need a medic." I gestured to the blood gushing out of my hand. "But otherwise, I'm fine." And despite what had occurred, I realized I was.

"Ah should've come after ye when ye were a boy! When they took ye away!" Barbara cried. "Ah should've ended ye then!"

Everything Barbara had done to me was so she didn't have to face her own guilt. All these years, I'd believed that what happened to Gil and what happened to Darren were my fault. That I could have done better to stop it. But I was just a boy. And I'd tried.

Barbara had sat back and let a monster destroy her son.

It wasn't my fault.

Anguish and relief thickened my throat as I finally, finally let the guilt go.

THIRTY-TWO
ARIA

I t was a bad day to visit the set.

North had ... well, *warned* wasn't the right word, but he'd told me last night that they were filming the love scene between him and his costar Eden. The French actor had rubbed me the wrong way from the moment we met because she flirted with North right in my face. North's ambivalence soothed my irritation, but I think I'd underestimated just how much watching them kiss was going to bother me.

In fact, I lasted two seconds watching him make out with the other woman before I quietly slipped away and let myself into North's trailer. Just the sight of him clasping her face, the way he clasped mine when he kissed me, was enough to split my chest open.

It was June. The film had moved location to Rome, and several scenes—that didn't require a car chase through the city —were being shot inside Cinecittà Studios. Despite June not being Italy's hottest month, it was a scorcher outside, and I was grateful for the AC unit in North's trailer.

But not the quiet. In the quiet, I had time to think about

his lips on hers. Her hands running down his chest, clutching at his ass.

I'd dated actors before.

I understood the business.

Actors had romantic scenes with other actors. Most of the time, it meant nothing. Though it had meant something with Preston and his costar. However, I knew North would never do that to me. So my possessiveness shocked me. I didn't know if it was a product of being cheated on or if it was just because it was North.

Since Barbara Benny's attack, we'd grown closer. North's palm needed stitches, but otherwise, he was good. Although I'd had to return to Ardnoch two days after it, we'd never been emotionally closer. Barbara was facing prison time. She'd admitted to attacking us with the Defender and to sending the threatening letters. Neither of us knew if she really thought she could kill North by coming to his hotel room. It was obvious, however, that he'd become her obsession and it probably always would have led to a rage-filled confrontation.

We'd decided to put it behind us. The threat that had hung over North was over, and I'd noted a difference in him. He admitted to me that seeing Barbara, remembering her culpability in what had shaped her son, had relieved him of a lot of guilt. And I could see that lightness in him.

We found a rhythm again, traversing the challenges of a long-distance relationship, and I think, doing it well.

Despite everything he'd had to deal with, and how busy he was, I never felt like I wasn't a priority to North. His early-morning texts and late-night phone calls made me feel like I was the first and last thing he thought about. Every day.

My trust in him was growing.

So ... why was I so freaking jealous of this stupid love scene? I couldn't let him see it affected me because this was

North's job. His career meant so much to him, and I wouldn't have my insecurities getting in his head while he was trying to do his job.

Mind made up, I left the cool interior of his trailer and made my way back to set because I didn't want him finishing the scene to find me gone. Thankfully, I discovered my not being there wasn't an issue because they'd closed the set for the scene where North and Eden's characters made love. One of the camera crew informed me that only a small crew remained inside, along with an intimacy coordinator.

Still, I waited impatiently for the scene to be over. When the sound stage doors finally opened, I followed members of the crew back inside. I ignored the knot in my gut at the sight of Eden walking off set in a robe. North was in nothing but boxer briefs, shrugging into a pair of pants. His athletic build had filled out during the making of this film, his already broad shoulders now impressively exaggerated against his narrow waist. The muscles in his back rippled as he pulled on a shirt, and I decided not to focus on the fact that Eden Gabriel had most likely felt those muscles move beneath her hands during their scene. I really tried. But when I tried, I kept thinking about how physically perfect she was and how her belly probably didn't jiggle when North moved over her.

I closed my eyes and looked at my feet as a wave of anxiety threatened to take hold.

Fuck.

I needed to get a grip.

What the hell?

Forcing myself to focus, I took a few calming breaths and looked up. North talked with Blake for a few seconds, nodding along with something he said.

Blake patted him on the arm and then called, "Break for lunch! Be back here in thirty!"

North scanned the crew until he found me and then strode in my direction. My eyebrows rose at his determined expression, and I let out a little gasp of surprise when he hauled me against him and hugged me like I might disappear.

At first, I welcomed the embrace, but worry seeped in the longer he held me. Pulling back, I searched North's eyes, and saw fear and remorse in them. "What's wrong?"

He cupped my nape in his hand and rested his forehead on mine. He whispered hoarsely, "I'm sorry."

"North ... you're acting. I know that."

He lifted his head to nod reluctantly but smirked sadly. "If it was you ... kissing, touching another guy ... I'd fucking hate it. I ... don't know if I could do it."

The confession made me feel a million times better. I smiled, resting my hands on his chest. "Yeah, you could. Because you trust me. Like I trust you."

"North!" Eden's voice stopped whatever my boyfriend's reply might have been, and we turned to find her approaching now dressed in jeans and a tee.

Anyone could see we were having a moment, but Eden Gabriel only had eyes for my guy. My fingers curled into his shirt, and I could tell by the soothing stroke of his hand down my arm that he felt my tension.

With slinky Gallic flirtatiousness, Eden sashayed up to North and ran the tip of her finger down his arm. "That went well, did it not?"

North sidled a little closer to me. "Aye."

My lips pressed together at his blunt one-word response.

She seemed unfazed, cocking her head as she ran her gaze up and down his body. I had apparently ceased to exist.

Eden was caressing his shoulder now, and I was seconds from ripping off her hand. "Those scenes are usually so awkward, but you made them so easy. We're natural in the bedroom together, no?"

Was she fucking kidding me?

"Eden, I'm standing with my arm around my girlfriend who you haven't looked at once and are deliberately trying to provoke," North said calmly but matter-of-fact. "Now I'd appreciate when we're not filming that you don't touch me. Okay?"

Her jaw popped out like she couldn't believe what she was hearing, and honestly, I was surprised too. Most men I knew, even the best ones, avoided confrontation as if their lives depended upon it. Even Montana, who was a great high school boyfriend, would get squirrelly and nonresponsive when another girl hit on him. It used to upset me. Why couldn't he just man up and say "I have a girlfriend so don't do that"? You know why? Because he enjoyed the attention.

But North?

I was coming to find that North Hunter was a unicorn.

"I, uh ..." Eden, for once, looked uncomfortable and unsure as her eyes flicked between us. "I did not mean to be inappropriate. If the shoe was on the other foot ..." Flustered, she waved a hand. "It won't happen again." Eden shrugged and walked away.

Until North called her out, I wondered how many times Eden had flirted with someone in front of their partner. Was it just because no one had ever told her no?

North turned to me and raised an eyebrow at my expression. "What's that look?"

I curled my fingers into his shirt. "It's the 'my boyfriend just made me so wet, I'm going to need him to take care of it' look."

His eyes flared and a second later, my hand was tight in his as he practically hauled me off set toward his trailer. Laughter threatened to burst out of me and did when he gently shoved me up the three short stairs. Inside, North spun me around, his mouth crushing down on mine as we stumbled back into the wall. Something fell off it and crashed at our feet, but neither of us was paying attention.

I felt his warm, rough hands on my outer thighs as they brushed my skin, pushing my skirt up to my waist. With an almost animalistic grunt, North curled his hands around the fabric of my underwear and tugged, the sound of them tearing away from my body and the sudden air between my legs increasing the heat between us to a combustible level. He'd just ripped my underwear off. A deep tug in my belly made me moan with want.

Our lips collided in biting, nipping, licking kisses as we both reached for the closure on his jeans. He shoved them and his boxers down to his ankles, freeing his cock, and I watched as he took his wallet out of his back pocket and retrieved a condom. As he rolled it up his straining arousal, I licked my lips in anticipation. No one felt like North. No one ever would.

"I want it hard," I pleaded, the trickle between my legs amplifying my already excited state.

"I'll give it to you any way you want," North assured me, his voice guttural with promise. And promise he did. I gasped as he gripped my legs, spread them, and thrust up into me.

"North!" I cried out in pleasured shock, his throbbing heat overwhelming me. Every feeling, thought, all my focus was on the sensation of his thickness inside me, and I struggled for breath as my body tried to adjust and relax. It was as if every nerve was inflamed, and a minuscule shift between us sparked a tug of delicious tension I immediately sought more of.

North, however, held still against me, breathing heavily as he stared into my eyes with such love and longing.

And a hint of satisfied possession.

I pushed my hips against him, and his grip on my thighs became almost bruising.

"I need you," I whispered.

His control snapped.

As North hauled me up, I didn't think about how heavy I was or if this was awkward. I wrapped my legs around him. Holding tight, I panted with excitement as he pounded us into the wall, thrusting into me hard, gliding in and out of my snug channel. The trailer rocked with the force of his drives as he pounded me into the wall, and I loved every fucking second.

I felt his thumb press down on my clit and I blew apart, my cry of release triggering North's. He threw his head back, his eyes on me, his muscles strained as he gritted his teeth to muffle the sound of his climax, and my inner muscles clenched around him as he throbbed with release.

North fell against me, his lips on my shoulder, his chest against mine, my arms still locked around him. He turned his head and kissed my neck.

"Ye werenae jokin'." His accent thickened with lust as it sometimes did. "Ye were soaked, princess."

His hot mouth hit my throat and he groaned. I shivered at the feel of his tongue as he scattered wet kisses upward toward my ear. Then North whispered, voice hoarse, desperate almost, "I love ye so fucking much."

Joy, fear, adoration, longing, relief, anxiety. I felt it all as I tightened my arms around him and kissed the top of his head. I tried to open my mouth. To say the words back ... but they wouldn't come.

It made little sense because the one emotion I felt more than all the others was love.

I loved North.

Why couldn't I say it?

Tears pricked my eyes. Especially when he lifted his head to look into them. I sensed and saw his disappointment. But he didn't condemn me for my weakness. Instead, he kissed me with such tenderness, it only made me feel worse.

Was I broken?

The thought terrified me.

Because if I couldn't say it to North ... there was no hope of me ever saying it ever again.

THIRTY-THREE
NORTH

Walker proposed to Sloane at her bakery opening. She said yes!

Walker proposed to Sloane at her bakery opening. She said yes!

The text from Aria made me smile as I chugged a bottle of water. Blake was filming a scene between my costars for the rest of the day, and I was enjoying downtime overlooking the gorgeous Lake Como.

Hot sun beat down on my back as I replied.

Happy for them. I'll need to text Walk.

It didn't surprise me Walker had proposed to Sloane at the grand opening of her bakery. Aria told me last weekend she thought his proposal was brewing.

Monroe is holding an impromptu engagement dinner for them tonight. I might miss our call.

My gut twisted. Not because she'd miss our nightly call, but because I wished I were going with her. A friend's engagement dinner sounded like something you were supposed to do as a couple. These things never bothered me before. I'd missed girlfriends' birthdays, for goodness' sake, because of filming schedules.

The difference was that Aria was my home, and I felt like together we were making a place for ourselves in Ardnoch, even if I couldn't be there all the time. I didn't want to quit—I loved acting too much. But it would take me a while to get used to being so aware of missing out on life events with Aria.

Maybe if she'd tell me she loved me, it wouldn't bother me so much.

I was trying to be patient, but fuck, it stung every time I said it and she didn't say it back.

Sighing, my fingers flew over my phone screen.

> No probs. Enjoy yourself. We'll talk later.

Tomorrow we flew to Japan for the last of our location shoots. It was too far for Aria to come visit, so I wouldn't see her in person for a month. I didn't know how I'd handle all that time apart, especially with things feeling not quite settled between us.

Aria sent me a blowing-kiss emoji. In return, I snapped a selfie with my back to the lake and a view toward Tremezzo and sent it to her.

Barely a few seconds later, she replied,

> Well, now I'm turned on and you're not here to do anything about it. Thanks. Asshole.

I barked a laugh and typed back,

> You're welcome, gorgeous.

Still smiling, I turned to lean on the wall, staring out at the sun glistening like diamonds across the water. Fuck, I missed her. I stood there for a wee while, enjoying the epic beauty of my location for a bit. They didn't need me for the rest of today, which meant I wasn't on camera again until Tokyo, so when my belly grumbled, I decided to take myself off.

I walked up the quaint narrow paths that wound through the mountains between red-tiled-roofed buildings of terracottas, pinks, and yellows. Flowers and lush green vegetation bloomed on wrought iron decorative balconies with old-fashioned lamps hanging off shopfront doors. No one even looked at me, even though the residents knew we were filming, and there were plenty of tourists around. It was great. I felt almost normal for once.

Among the stores were a few trattorias to choose from, and I stepped into the cool shade of the nearest one to order a zucchini pasta dish.

Eating it in peace, enjoying the normalcy, the solitude, I would have been annoyed by the buzz of my phone in my pocket if I hadn't thought it was Aria.

It wasn't.

The text was from my publicist.

> These photos went online an hour ago and are already all over the internet. My advice is to ignore and not make any statements on your socials. I'd advise Aria to do the same.

What now? I tapped on the link and let out a stream of muttered expletives. Heart pounding, I scrolled through the images and the article on a gossip-rag site. The headline read **LOVE RAT? IS KING'S VALLEY ACTOR CHEATING WITH COSTAR?**

Fuck.

Someone had taken photos of me and Eden at the restaurant here in Como last night. We'd dined with three of our costars, Blake, and the producer Garry. But at one point, I'd left our table to answer a call from Aria, and Eden had approached once I got off the phone. After I'd told her to back the fuck off, Eden had been easygoing about it. Now that she wasn't flirting with me every chance she got, she was funny and good company. She'd made me laugh about something, and I hadn't even noticed she'd touched my arm as she smiled up at me. In another photo, I was leaning in to hear what she was saying over the loudness of the music at the restaurant, and it looked like she was whispering intimately in my ear. I hadn't touched her, but from the angle the camera took the shot, it looked like my hand might be on her hip.

Fuck, fuck, fuck.

Any fool could see this was no evidence of my cheating, but the insinuation was enough for panic to take hold. Even though this was bullshit, it was still intended to humiliate us. To humiliate Aria.

Hands shaking, I called Aria to give her a heads-up. To talk it through.

It went straight to her voicemail.

Could she have seen the article already?

Frantic at the thought of her seeing those pictures—and her experiences with her exes coming back to bite us in the arse —I hurried to set.

Pulling Blake aside, I told him I had an emergency at home and that I'd meet them in Tokyo.

Blake cursed. "For fuck's sake, another emergency?"

I stared stonily at him, not in the mood to expand on the situation, even though he was my boss. "I will make it to Tokyo in time," I vowed.

"Fine." He waved me away. "I'm holding you to that."

I left without another word.

FIRST, I had to endure the helter-skelter drive from Lake Como to the airport. I'd told my driver I needed to get there as soon as possible, and he took me very seriously. It was like being in a real-life *Mario Kart* game. To put it into perspective, the drive to Malpensa Airport is typically an hour and forty minutes from Bellagio, and he got us there in an hour.

I tipped him big for his haste and the thrill. The fear of dying certainly kept me distracted from my fear of losing Aria over stupid, misleading photographs and false rumors.

That panic resettled at the airport. Fortunately, I got there in time for a flight that was taking off in an hour. Unfortunately, there were no direct flights to Inverness. I had to fly into Edinburgh and then hop on a private flight to Inverness from there.

Throughout the day, I tried calling Aria, but she wouldn't pick up and I was growing pissed off as well as fearful. You didn't just shut a person out when something like this happened. Every time I got angry at her, though, I reminded myself of her past. Of how she'd been treated and how easy it was for her to believe that she was temporary, easily thrown away.

Not essential.

If only she knew. I was trying to make her see how essential she was to me, but I guess I was failing.

By the time I reached the estate, it was late in the evening, and I was exhausted, hungry, and trying not to believe that this frantic trip wasn't a giant waste of time.

The guards checked my ID, called up to the estate, and then let my cab through. An underbutler welcomed me at the main entrance. I planned to walk to Aria's beach house from there, but when I strode into the castle, my pulse jumped at the sight of her marching through the grand hall toward me.

She was still here, working late.

Her expression was wary, surprised.

"You haven't been answering your phone." My angry voice carried across the hall.

Her step faltered, but she recovered, straightening her shoulders with determination. She had her estate manager's face and voice on as she said to the butler, "Thank you, McGill. I'll see Mr. Hunter in my office."

The butler nodded and strode off, but my eyes were on Aria. "Well?"

"My office," she said pointedly, and I curbed my impatience as I followed her through the grand hall.

Her hips swayed from side to side, and I wanted to grab them and pull her back into me. Wanted to whisper in her ear how desperately I needed her and feel her capitulate in my arms.

Fists clenching, I didn't do any of that.

She was acting like I'd done something wrong, and I braced for the confrontation.

However, as soon as her office door closed behind me, she whirled, eyes wide, expression apologetic. "Oh my God, North, I didn't mean for you to come all the way here. What about the film?"

I deflated a wee bit. "I was finished for the day. We meet in Tokyo on Thursday to start filming again. Why didn't you pick up your phone?"

Aria closed her eyes as if in pain. "I ... I just needed some time."

"You saw the photos."

She opened her eyes, apology bright in them. Not accusation. "I did."

"You ... believed them?" I practically choked on the words.

"No!" She bridged the distance between us, resting her hands on my chest, and I couldn't help but curl my hands around her upper arms. To pull her close. Breathe her in. "North ... I didn't believe you'd cheat. I promise. But ... but a miracle didn't just happen to me overnight. Okay? My first thought when I saw those photos was, why wouldn't he want Eden? Maybe he is just ... using me," she whispered. And even though I could see the shame in her expression, I was furious.

"What the fuck do I need to do to get it through to you I want you for you?"

Aria flinched. "I ... I can still hear their voices in my head. I'm trying, but ... I don't want them to win. God." She tried to shove away from me, but I wouldn't let her. "Stop!" Tears filled her eyes, and this thing built in my chest, making me feel like it might crack in fucking two from the pressure. "You deserve better than this. This relationship shouldn't be a goddamn chore. It's too much work for you. Look at what it's doing to you! You just flew here from Italy to check on me."

I gave her a little shake. "Do you love me?"

Her face crumpled immediately, and my heart lodged in my throat as she nodded and sobbed. I'd never seen her like that. I'd seen her sad and upset ... but never this. Tears stung my eyes because her pain was my fucking pain, and I wrapped my arms tight around her. "Then we just keep working at it," I promised her hoarsely.

"I-It's too much for you."

"I decide what's too much for me." I clasped her face and bent close. Her eyes were a brighter green with the sheen of tears in them. "I would go to the ends of the earth for you, Aria Howard. Because I am in love with you."

Her fingers curled around my wrists, her voice shaking with tears as she whispered back, "I'm so in love with you, it scares the hell out of me."

Relief unlike anything I'd ever felt eased the pressure in my chest, and I leaned my forehead against hers. "One day it won't scare you," I vowed. "One day, it'll be as easy as breathing. I won't stop until you believe with every inch of your being that I love you for you and there's nothing else I want in return but for you to love me too."

Somehow, I had to find a way to make her believe that for good.

Thirty-Four
ARIA

"Okay, for a Saturday morning, you look exhausted."

I glanced up from my coffee mug as my little sister sauntered into the kitchen. She looked beautiful and well-rested and I envied her. "I went to bed at midnight but got up at four to video call with North. They were shooting early in the morning and then shooting a night scene, but he had a separate shoot with a whisky company he's signed a promo deal with. So he had an hour between noon and one ... which is four in the morning, our time."

Allegra grinned as she moved around the kitchen, making coffee. "And you couldn't just wait to talk to him another day?"

"That was us waiting." I groaned, resting my cheek on my palm. My eyelids were so heavy. "His schedule has been full out since he flew to Tokyo two weeks ago. His new brand partnership with Horus, the watch designer, started. They wanted him to do some promo in Tokyo. So did this Japanese whisky company."

"Are they doing early promotion on the movie while he's there?"

I shrugged. "I think he said he had a few interviews with some influencers over there. Long story short, he's so busy, we've barely talked." And I missed him so much. It had taken a lot to be truly, truly vulnerable with North, but I knew deep down I owed him that. He'd been nothing but genuine and loving with me. My insecurities, my deep-seated fears, were not his fault. I was working to be better about not letting them win.

Allegra arriving in the Highlands for summer break was a wonderful distraction. Mamma was set to arrive in a week, and Dad even had a break in his schedule to spend a month with us. We'd all be in the same house for the first time in years, and I was looking forward to it. Mamma had not made one disparaging comment about my body since we'd had our honest conversation, and I answered her calls more now. She still liked to complain to me about Allegra not wanting to spend time with her, but overall, our relationship felt healthier.

"I was thinking, once I've had another five million coffees, maybe we could take a trip to Aberdeen today. Do a little East Coast college wardrobe shopping?"

Allegra's brow wrinkled as she slid into the breakfast nook beside me. "Isn't that a long way to go for shopping?"

"We could get the train from Inverness. Stay overnight. Maybe have a cocktail or two?"

My sister nodded. "That does sound good, but I think you should see something first." She slid her phone along the table.

I scowled. "Nope. No. Every time someone says that and passes me the phone, there's something not good at the other end." I'd avoided googling anything that might bring up articles about me and North. I didn't have social media accounts since deleting them when I broke up with Lucas. And North's team ran his, so it was mostly work-related stuff they posted for him. Now and then, he'd post something a bit more relaxed from location. But nothing about us because he didn't want to fire up the online storm again.

"Okay, crabby." Allegra tapped her phone screen, and it lit up to show a paused video of North. "But I really think you're going to want to see this one."

I looked my sister in the eye. "You promise this won't hurt me?"

She gave me a small, tender smile. "I promise, big sis."

Tapping the screen, I watched as a pretty interviewer asked North something in Japanese. A voice off-screen translated it, and I tensed at the question.

"Now that you're dating legendary film director Wesley Howard's daughter, does that mean we can expect you to star in one of his upcoming movies?"

North looked relaxed, even though this question was like the boulder in our relationship, rolling toward us, picking up speed, readying to crush our love to death.

"No," North answered, a smile in his voice to soften the bluntness of his answer. I sucked in a breath as he continued, "As much as I admire Wesley as a filmmaker, I don't believe in mixing business with family. Aria is my family, and she's Wesley's daughter."

"Oh my God," I whispered, shocked.

The translator restated his response to the interviewer, who asked another question.

"Does that mean you're saying you'll never work with Wesley Howard?"

North shrugged casually, even though his next words most certainly were not casual. "Aria's the one. So, no. I'll never work with Wesley Howard."

My eyes flew to Allegra, who grinned like a Cheshire cat while blood pounded in my ears. "Where did you find this?"

"It's all over the internet. Western media picked it up. The headlines are SCOTS ACTOR WILL NEVER WORK

WITH LEGENDARY DIRECTOR and NORTH HUNTER SAYS HE'S FOUND THE ONE." Allegra shook her head in joyful amazement. "Boy, when he makes up his mind about something, he doesn't hold back, huh?"

"Oh my God."

"Is that all you're going to say?"

Before I could respond, my phone chimed. I reached over to pick it up.

"Who is it?"

Joy filled me as I swiped the screen to see the text from our father. "It's Dad." He'd sent the link to North's interview with just three words:

> I like him.

"He really loves you, Ari. For real."

I nodded, unable to control the stupid tears spilling down my cheeks. They wouldn't stop even as I swiped at them.

Allegra scooted around the bench and pulled me into her arms. "I'm so happy for you."

Holding tight to her, I cried with pure relief.

I'd given my heart over to North so completely, in a way I never had to anyone. That meant his love had the power to break me, and for too long, that's what I'd focused on.

I hadn't focused on the fact that his love had the power to heal me, too, and I was so grateful that when I truly, deeply fell in love with a man, it was with North.

He *was* a freaking unicorn.

And he was all mine.

THIRTY-FIVE
NORTH

I was beginning to think maybe Aria had some kind of news filter on her phone so she wouldn't see any articles relating to either of us.

The Japanese interview I'd done had exploded beyond even what I'd imagined. While some articles called me arrogant for daring to say I didn't want to work with Wesley Howard, most were in raptures over me calling Aria "the one." My publicist was loving the positive media and subsequent polish to my reputation. For her, it was great that I was being linked so seriously to such a well-respected Hollywood family.

Yet that wasn't why I'd said what I said.

I said it because it was true, and I never wanted Aria to doubt that I was with her for her and only her.

But we'd exchanged texts since the blowup, and she hadn't said a word about it. The eight-hour time difference made it difficult to call without scheduling it, and I'd already gotten her out of bed before the crack of dawn to catch up. We'd finished filming a night shoot, and it was just past midnight in Scotland. I couldn't call her now.

I'd banged up my shoulder during a stunt and I wanted

nothing more than to return to my hotel room and soak in the tub. And try not to fixate on the fact that Aria hadn't mentioned the interview. Some of my costars, including Eden, had given me a friendly ribbing today. Theo had texted:

> You are a brain-addled sickening romantic and this ridiculous behavior is going to end badly for you. I honestly do not know how we are acquainted.

I'd looked up old-fashioned insults and replied:

> You are an ultracrepidarian.

The meaning of which: a person who gave unwanted opinions on subjects they had no personal knowledge of.

Theo shot back:

> Okay. You're somewhat tolerable again.

I'd snorted at that and accepted the good-natured banter from my costars.

But by morning, with my shoulder gowping and no word from my girlfriend, I was in a bad mood. As excited as I was about the movie, I was tired and ready for it to be done. My agent had sent me a bunch of scripts over the last few months, and I was interested in several of them. But I was determined to take a few weeks off to spend time with Aria after this film wrapped before deciding on what was next.

When I let myself into the hotel room, my head was down as I rubbed my shoulder. The last thing I expected when I looked up was Aria, in a white summer dress that highlighted her olive skin, sitting on the sofa, her long legs crossed.

Waiting for me.

What the ... "How? When? Why?"

After the hotel in Berlin had let Barbara slip past security, my team had made sure this hotel's security was top fucking notch.

Thank God, they were apparently wrong.

Anticipation thrummed through me as she stood and bridged the distance between us. "The hotel manager recognized me and is a fan of our coupling. About an hour ago. And I had to fly all this way to tell you something really, really important." Reaching me, she slid her arms around my neck, pressing her soft, warm body to mine.

I wrapped my arms around her waist, relaxing instantly now that she was here. All of a sudden, everything felt right in the world. Aye, I was a sappy arsehole. "What's so important it couldn't wait?"

Her lips twitched as her eyes searched mine. There was no guard up in her expression now. No barriers. Her love for me was clear to see. "I needed to tell you that you're 'the one.' My forever. That I'm honored to be your family. That you'll always be my family too. Always."

Too much joy swelled in my throat. I couldn't hold back my tears, and I didn't give a fuck. Because I had been waiting a long time to find my family again. Twenty-three years of searching. Now she was here.

In my arms.

My family. My home.

THIRTY-SIX
ARIA

I didn't know what I'd expected when I returned to LA. Certainly not to feel nostalgic. Yes, this was my hometown, but a lot of hurt had happened here. However, instead of feeling all of that, I remembered driving to Beverly Hills with my friends and hanging out on Rodeo Drive, our lives so different from other kids. But those were the moments when the differences didn't feel bad. We felt lucky. And happy. We weren't thinking about absentee parents or the pressures of living up to successful moms and dads. We were privileged and enjoying it for once.

I wanted to remember *that* Aria, the one who was grateful for her privilege and her sweet boyfriend and funny friends to spend her hot summer days with.

Strolling down Rodeo, I had to admit that the scorching sun was nice when you didn't have it all year round. It beat down on my back as I looked in the window of Jimmy Choo. My hard-earned cash had mostly been spent on airplane tickets these past few months, but I was in a good mood, and the übercool rose gold sunglasses in the window called to me.

Screw it.

I strode in and sighed at the heavenly AC that cooled my skin. A retail assistant was at my side in seconds and I was out the door, popping on my new sunglasses within five minutes. Mamma would be so proud I was spending money on designer stuff. Well, she would be if she wasn't so pissed at me right now.

She, Dad, and Allegra were currently at the beach house in Scotland while I was in LA for the first time in over two years.

"Oh, of course! You fly to California as soon as your entire famiglia fly to Scozia for you!"

It was true. I had followed North to LA for a week while my family was in Scotland. However, I'd spent two weeks with them, and I'd spend more time with them when I got back. But North had wrapped filming on *Birdwatcher*, and although we'd had some alone time, my family was kind of smitten with him. He loved it. And I loved that my mother cooed over him like a proper mom rather than flirting with him, that my dad showed him respect and admiration, and that Allegra teased and laughed with him like a little sister.

I loved giving North that.

But I also wanted him to myself for a week.

He was taking meetings in LA—two for movies and one for a TV show. To my surprise, North had wanted my opinion on the scripts his agent sent him, and these were the three we whittled it down to.

While he took a meeting this afternoon, I'd promised him I'd be fine doing a little shopping and not much else. I won't lie—after running Ardnoch almost twenty-four seven for the last two years, I didn't know what to do with downtime. I was restless.

I wandered through Beverly Hills, crossing Wilshire to go to a gelato place Allegra had recommended. While waiting in line, I felt a burning on my cheek and turned to see a tourist snapping a photo of me before noting I'd seen her do it. She blushed and hurried quickly away.

That was new.

When I'd lived in LA, no one recognized me. I wasn't an actor, and I'd only ever been photographed attending my father's premieres. People in the industry knew who I was, but I wasn't a household name. But being called "the one" by North Hunter had made me recognizable.

After our first night out at a restaurant here, photos of us showed up online. I guess the public loved a love story, but they also loved the drama of watching one fall apart, and I had a horrible feeling we'd never stop being interesting to the tabloids until we did. Fall apart, that is.

Shaking off the dread that accompanied the thought, I reminded myself I lived in a place designed for privacy, and eventually, everyone would realize North and I would not fall apart. They'd grow bored. Once we'd been married a few years and started having kids, they'd move on.

I blinked. Startled by the thoughts that just so easily entered my mind.

That's how secure in our love and relationship I was.

I truly believed North was my future.

My phone beeped and I pulled it out of my purse. A text from North:

> Meeting's over. It's hot as fuck. Let's go christen the pool.

I texted him I was on my way.

He replied,

> You know by christen, I mean fuck, right?

Laughing, I told him I'd somehow managed to crack that

code. Feeling high on my happiness, I grabbed my gelato and headed back to my rental car. We were staying at my parents' place in Malibu while we were here, and I'd dropped North off in Century City for his meeting. Now it was time to pick him up for more uninterrupted sex. Seriously, my family had hogged so much of his time while we were in Ardnoch that I'd had to sneak into his suite during office hours for some sexy time. Very professional of me.

I'd parked in a garage near Rodeo Drive, my flip-flops echoing off the concrete walls as I walked. After placing my new purchases in the back of the car, I changed into sneakers because driving with flip-flops was asking for trouble.

Barely a second after I shut the driver's-side door, the passenger side opened, and I sucked in a breath of frightened surprise as an intruder got into the car and slammed the door.

Then she turned to me.

Dislike warred with wariness, the nape of my neck tingling in warning as I came face-to-face with Caitlyn Branch for the first time in over two years.

"What the hell do you think you're doing?" I yelled. Had she been following me?

Caitlyn smirked, and I noted her appearance with increasing unease. She'd dyed her red hair to a shade of dark brown that matched mine. A golden fake tan covered every inch of her, and her eyes were now green instead of brown. Contacts. "It's good to see you too, Ari."

"Get out of my car, Caitlyn."

Instead, she stuck a hand in the large purse she carried and pulled out a gun.

It felt like my heart stopped for a good few seconds before it raced. The sense of unreality made my head spin.

She rested the gun to my forehead and at the cold press of it, nausea crawled through me. This wasn't happening.

This couldn't be happening.

"It's Ariella. And we're going to take a nice little drive, right?"

At her sweet tone, I stared at her with incredulous horror. "Have you lost your damn mind?"

"I just want to talk." She lowered the gun to her lap. "Now, you're going to drive toward Little Tokyo."

My gaze dropped to the gun. "Why?"

"Because I've been trying to reach out for two years, Ari. Trying to get my best friend back. I've been waiting for this moment. Now no one can stop us from being together. Like we're supposed to be."

This wasn't a joke. My stomach somersaulted. Gazing into her eyes, I saw she truly believed that. "Caitlyn—"

"It's Ariella!"

"Ariella ..." My tone was soft, coaxing. "I don't know what you think is happening here, but just let me go. You don't want to get in trouble for this."

She scowled. "For what? Talking to my best friend?"

Oh, hell. "For holding me at gunpoint."

"This?" She waved it. "This is just to make you listen. I don't want to shoot you."

I nodded. "Good. Good. So let's just take a second. We can talk without the gun."

Hurt tightened Caitlyn's features. "I don't want to shoot you ... but unless you come with me and let me have my say ... I will blow your brains out."

THIRTY-SEVEN
ARIA

Caitlyn forced me to throw my phone out of the car on the Santa Monica Freeway before we continued driving to a storage facility on the edge of Little Tokyo, down by the LA River. We could see the city skyline to our left, mountains to our back, and there were not enough people around for me to feel safe. In any way.

Once we parked in the empty lot outside, Caitlyn forced me out of the car.

With the gun pressed to my back, Caitlyn swiped a card over a machine at the entrance to a large one-story building. Inside, it was cool from the AC. We were inside a long corridor of dark gray walls with garage-like doors all along it.

"Keep walking." She nudged the gun into my back, and I forced my shaking legs to walk. I was glad for my sneakers because I wasn't sure I wouldn't have broken an ankle in heels. My legs trembled so badly.

Halfway down the corridor, Caitlyn commanded I stop and then she punched in a code on a keypad by one of the doors, and it rose along the ceiling. Shoving me inside, I gaped as she hit a light switch and a small storage room was revealed.

But there wasn't just "stuff" stored in here.

Among piles of boxes and crates of household items and a rail of clothing was a single bed tucked into the far right corner with a pink comforter and decorative pillows on it. Beside the bed was a small table and lamp.

I had to get out of here.

I whirled on her, but it was as if she knew how I'd react because now her gun was pointed in my face. Her expression hardened.

"Sit on the bed. Now."

My heart hammered so hard I swear it hurt as I stumbled backward toward the bed. Feeling the mattress against the back of my legs, I slumped down onto it. "What are you doing, Cai—Ariella?"

"I'm kind of living in my storage unit. I thought that was obvious." Caitlyn waved her free hand around. "Why pay crazy LA rental prices when this is warm, safe, and ventilated? And no one will interrupt us here."

Oh, fuck. Refusing to let her see my terror, I lifted my chin in defiance. "You plan to keep me in here? Other people must rent the surrounding units."

She nodded. "They do, but I have a gun, so I'm pretty sure you'll keep quiet if anyone stops by. This is just until you see things my way, you know."

"And what way is that?"

Caitlyn considered my question, the gleam in her eye suggesting she was delighted to have my full attention. "That we're supposed to be integral pieces of each other's lives." She laughed incredulously. "It boggles the mind that you can't see we're pretty much the same person, Aria."

"How is that?"

"Look at us." She turned to glance at a mirror that hung on the wall above a chest of drawers. "We look like sisters."

Dyeing her hair and wearing contacts to look like me.

Taking my job at Curiosity. Sleeping with Lucas ... Allegra was right. Caitlyn had been single white female-ing me.

"Do you want my life?" I forced out.

She turned back to me. "Your life is my life. We're connected." Caitlyn lifted a hand to her temple, grimacing. "Everything feels itchy and ugly in here without you around. Why did you leave me?"

"Cai—Ariella ... I ... let me go. We'll find someone for you to talk to. I'll help."

"Talk to?" She frowned. "I'm talking to you, aren't I?"

"I mean someone who can help you."

"Help me with what?"

At her genuine confusion, I realized she had no awareness of her own mental health issues. Or at least she was in denial about them.

I attempted another tack. "Why don't we leave here and go grab dinner and talk?"

"I tried that!" Caitlyn suddenly yelled, and when she raised her arm, her sleeve pulled back to reveal flashes of cuts and scars along her arm. "I've been trying to talk to you for two years! But you punished me for Lucas, and I don't know why! I don't know why you left me when I was just trying to be close to you!"

Considering the possibility that Caitlyn was self-harming, I attempted not to get angry at her. She needed help. I just didn't know how to get through to her. "How is keeping me in here making any of this better?" I asked calmly.

She shook, her breathing calming. "This is only temporary. Okay. Just until you realize how important it is for us to be together." Caitlyn sat on the end of the bed, and I tried not to look at the gun in her hand.

"Let me tell you about my life for the past two years."

For the next half hour, I endured the inane retelling of her life in LA without me. About the men she'd fucked because she was sure they were the kind of men I'd fuck. About Allegra being a disrespectful little sister (it took everything not to bare my teeth at her calling Ally her sister), and about how much she missed me.

"So many unanswered emails. I thought maybe it was that stupid job in Scotland keeping you from me, so this year I started sending anonymous emails pretending to be members." Her eyes widened. "I didn't believe anything I said in them, but I wanted them to fire you so you'd come home."

Understanding dawned. "You sent those awful emails about me?"

"I stopped after two because they made me feel so bad for saying those things. But I only sent them for your own good." She leaned forward, expression pleading. "You have to know that everything I do is for you. For us. When I realized how much Lucas had hurt you, it was my hurt too. So the night before he had this big audition, I laced his food with ground pistachio."

Oh my God. Lucas was fatally allergic to nuts. All nuts. "What?"

Caitlyn shrugged. "He's fine. I took him to the ER. But his face and hands were red and bruised from the swelling and he couldn't make his audition the next day. He lost out on the job." She laughed like she'd played a hilarious prank rather than almost killed someone. "He deserved it for taking you away from me. See?" She beamed. "This is why I wanted us to have this time together so you can see that I'm on your side."

"I see that," I whispered, sick to my stomach.

"Good. Good." Caitlyn's eyes brightened with tears. "When you welcomed me into your life, made me your friend even though I was a nobody, it was a lifeline, Ari."

My chest squeezed with sympathy despite the awful circumstances. Maybe if I could get her to talk to me, really talk to me, I could make her see this was wrong. "How so?"

"I ..." She shrugged. "I don't want to think about my life before you."

"I'm trying to understand. Maybe if I knew what your life was like, I'd understand why we're here right now."

She considered this. "Okay." Her gaze dropped to her feet. "I'm a foster kid. My dad took off when I was about seven and then, when I was about nine, they came and took me away from my mom."

"Why?"

"She was a drug addict."

"I'm sorry."

Caitlyn looked at me with those strange contacts. "I moved from foster home to foster home, and when I was fourteen, I was at the mall with my friends and I saw my mom." She gave a huff of bitter amusement. "She was clean. Turns out she'd been clean for two years and she never bothered to come get me. She told me that looking after a kid was too much responsibility and she was afraid if she took me back, she'd fall off the wagon with the pressure."

Dear God. Suddenly, Caitlyn's frantic desire to keep a hold of our friendship made perfect sense. She had intense abandonment issues because of her childhood. But why me?

"I'm so sorry, Caitlyn."

She flinched and whispered, "It's Ariella now."

"Ariella. Will you tell me more? About your life before LA?"

And so she did. Her story was one of a cycle of abuse and abandonment that made my heart hurt for her, for other kids like her.

A story that made me fearful that I was about to be the next victim in the cycle.

THIRTY-EIGHT
NORTH

I could hear my heart. It felt like it was inside my throat, banging like fuck in there. "I'm telling you, something is wrong."

"Dad, I agree. Aria would never take off like this and not pick up her phone. She'd find a way to contact us," Allegra said, her young face tight with worry on my phone screen.

When Aria didn't arrive in Century City six hours ago, I'd tried calling her only for it to go straight to voicemail. Two hours passed, and I was growing frantic, so I returned to the Malibu house in case she'd returned home for some reason. The rental wasn't at the house, and neither was Aria.

"We should call the police," I bit out.

Wesley scowled, worry pinching his brow. "While I agree something isn't right, I think it's too soon for the police. Aria's rental could have broken down somewhere, we just don't know."

Chiara's face suddenly appeared on my screen in between her husband and daughter. "Why don't you try that cell thing where you can find someone by tracing their phone?"

Fuck. Why hadn't I thought of that? "How do I do that?"

"Oh, oh, I know!" Allegra hurried out of frame, but I could still hear her voice. "You can track a cell through the phone number!"

Under normal circumstances, I'd find that horrifying. "Really?"

"I'm just getting"—Allegra's voice grew nearer until she was back on screen—"my phone. Give me a second."

We all waited impatiently until her face lit up. "Got her!" She showed me a map on her phone screen. A red pinpoint hovered in a certain spot, but I couldn't make out an exact location.

"Can you zoom in?"

"Sure." She zoomed in and frowned. "It looks like she's parked on the Santa Monica Freeway." Allegra frowned as she looked at me. "That can't be right."

Fear churned in my gut. "I'll check it out. Is there anyone you can think of ... who would"—I could barely think it or about the possibilities—"who would want to hurt Aria?"

Chiara clung to her husband. "No, I ..."

Wesley shook his head, expression grave. He looked at his youngest daughter. "Allegra?"

She bit her lip, frowning in thought. "Well, there is one person, but ... there's no way ..."

I snapped, "Allegra, who is it?"

"Ari's ex-friend, Caitlyn Branch. I told Ari at the time that I didn't think her behavior was appropriate. It was like she was trying to take over Ari's life. You know, the whole cliché single-white-female thing."

"How does that make her a threat?" Wesley asked.

Allegra shrugged. "I'm not sure it does, but she's been emailing Aria constantly since she left LA. And she's been coming around this coffee shop at my school to talk to me. I've told her to back off, but it's like talking to a brick wall. She ... seems a little delusional."

"Unstable?" Wesley pressed.

"I hate to use that word, but ... yeah."

"Why didn't Aria tell me about this?"

"I think she thought Caitlyn was harmless. She could be still."

"Enough," I cut in. "Send me the link to that map, Allegra. I'm going to follow her phone. While I'm doing that, you look into this Caitlyn Branch person." I glared at Wesley. "And I don't care about goddamn privacy. If I don't find Aria with her phone, we are calling the police."

Aria's father nodded. "Take my car. The keys are in a lockbox in the garage. Code is 5478."

"The fact that you're letting him drive your Aston Martin scares the shit out of me." Allegra looked ready to be sick. "Please find her, North. Please."

I nodded abruptly and hung up.

Adrenaline pumped through me as I hurried through the mansion. The garage sat on the part of the mountain that faced out toward the road. I didn't even process the dark red Aston Martin other than to be grateful for the way it hugged corners as I sped toward LA.

THIRTY-NINE
ARIA

"I'm tired." Caitlyn looked weary and her voice was hoarse from all the talking she'd done for the last five hours. There had been moments of silence while she ate a bag of potato chips and then used a Porta Potti in the corner, much to my horror. I was trying not to think about my bladder because there was no way I was peeing in this storage room. "But I can't sleep because you might leave."

That panic set in as the walls of the small storage unit seemed to draw closer. "Are you really going to make us stay here all night?"

"Just until we can figure this out."

She had no idea what she was doing. This impulsive thing she'd done. "How did you know I was in LA?"

"Online photos." Caitlyn scooted back along the bed until her back was braced against the wall and she handled the gun with both hands. "I guessed you'd stay at your parents' house, so I waited there all night and followed you into the city."

"North will be looking for me."

Her expression turned icy. "We'll talk about him in the morning."

"Cai—Ariella—"

"No. He's a problem for me, okay."

Confused, I asked tentatively, "Do you see something romantic happening between us?"

She scowled. "No. It's not like that. But men destroy female friendships. We let them. And it's so stupid because after the marriage and the babies and we're older and our kids have fled the nest, we're back to needing our friends. So many of us get so caught up in the husband-and-babies thing that we push our friends away, and we're left with nothing. I won't be that person, Ari. I won't abandon my friends." Tears glistened in her eyes. "And I don't want them to abandon me." With her free hand, she swiped at her tears, and I saw the scars on her arm again.

In the hours she'd been talking about her life before she met me, there was no mention of self-harming.

"What is that?" I asked, pointing to her arm.

Caitlyn lowered it, looking guilty. "Nothing."

"Ariella—"

"I said it's nothing."

Back in high school, Montana and I had been close friends with a girl named Kelly Goldie. Her mom was an actor and her dad was a plastic surgeon. They were never around, but Kelly behaved as if she didn't care. She enjoyed her life. Until around fifteen, when Kelly changed from being this bubbly, perky cheerleader to being sullen and angry. She pushed us all away. I tried harder than anyone to get through, but when I saw her covering up cuts on her arms and asked her about it, she stopped talking to me altogether.

And I let her.

I didn't push.

I didn't try to find out what the hell had happened to her.

When I was working at Curiosity, Kelly's death made the

news because of who her parents were. She'd committed suicide.

It weighed on me for weeks after and I wasn't sure why.

Until now, looking at Caitlyn's scars.

I felt guilty for not trying harder with Kelly. Maybe that wasn't rational. Maybe nothing I could have done as a teenager would've helped. But I hadn't even tried.

Seeing similar cuts on Caitlyn's arm made me see her as something more than a bad person who was holding me hostage. I saw Kelly in her. I saw her pain.

So I considered a different tack. "Why ... why is my friendship so important to you?"

"Isn't mine important to you?" Her lower lip trembled with hurt.

I sidestepped her question. "I asked you first."

She considered this. "I'd met some famous people in LA before you. I looked up to them, admired them, but they were assholes. They thought they were better than me, than everyone. When I found out who you were when we worked at Curiosity, I was so shocked. You were so fair to everyone. I mean, you were a little intimidating because you're a total boss lady, but I admired that. You helped me switch careers. You supported me. The more I got to know you, the more I wanted to be your friend. You grew up with this amazing family who loved you, and people respected you. And when you befriended me and took me under your wing, I thought ..." She brushed impatiently at a tear that fell down her cheek. "I thought that meant I must be worth something."

Caitlyn was lost. I knew what lost was like, but this was lost on a whole other, extremely painful level. I believed she could find herself again, but she needed help. And she wouldn't get that help if she went to prison for holding me hostage at gunpoint in a storage facility.

I realized to get through to her, I needed to be honest with her. Vulnerable, even. Tell her things that I wouldn't tell her under normal circumstances. "My life isn't perfect. I have a good life, but it's not what you think it is. And I'm not a perfect person you should put up on some kind of pedestal."

"Right," she scoffed.

Anger flared in my gut, but I shoved it down. "You think because my parents are famous and we had money that it made our lives perfect? My parents love me, I know that, but they didn't raise me, Caitlyn. A series of nannies did. And when Allegra came along, I was ten years old, and I began to parent her, so I never really had a normal childhood on multiple levels. I had to see my parents' relationship splashed across the tabloids because the world didn't want to believe they were so in love. I had friends gossiping at school about whether my mom was cheating on my dad. I had friends jerking off to photos of my mom. Tell me that's not weird."

Her lip curled with a flicker of amusement.

"I had a mother who loved me but made me feel fat and ugly with her constant need to mold me into a mini version of her."

Caitlyn's amusement died.

"I had boyfriends who only dated me to get to my father and made me feel worthless when they were finished with me. I had friends betray me."

Her gaze lowered.

"And because of that, I built up walls and shut out everybody. Including my family. And I almost lost someone I love because I didn't know how to tear down those walls once they were up. When I did, strangers splashed photographs of me all over the internet and picked apart my appearance and questioned why the guy I love loves me back. Half of them are rooting for me, and the other half want it to fall apart just so they'll have something juicy to read on the way to work the next morning. Do you know what it's like to fall in love with the whole world watching and waiting for you to be humiliated again? My life is not perfect, and *I'm* far from perfect. But I *choose* to focus on what makes my life *good*. So should you. Because you're worth something to this world without my approval or my friendship."

"So you did abandon me," she whispered. "You deliberately abandoned me."

"You betrayed me when you slept with Lucas," I explained gently. "I didn't want to be friends with you anymore."

Her look singed me to the bed. "Isn't that a stupid thing to say to someone with a gun?"

I pushed through my fear. "You're not going to shoot me."

"I might."

"No, you won't."

Desperate tears filled her eyes. "I might!"

And I knew at that moment that she wouldn't. "Caitlyn—"

"It's Ariella!"

"No, you're Caitlyn. That little girl who has fought through so much to still be here deserves to be acknowledged. Don't abandon her."

I knew almost immediately I'd pushed too far, and my heart lurched in my throat as she pushed off the bed, pointing the gun in my face. "You don't know shit! You're trying to confuse me with lies! But we're the same! We're the same!" Tears streaked down her face, and I was terrified. Terrified she'd pull that trigger.

"Please," I whispered. I hated her for making me beg.

My plea seemed to calm her. In fact, her face smoothed into a surreal mask that alarmed the hell out of me.

"Good. Good. This has been a great start," she said, as if we were finishing work for the day and not that she was holding me hostage. "But I need some air. I think I'll drive around for a while. We wouldn't want your rental sitting out there for someone to find. I'll be back in the morning." She waved to the bedside cabinet. "There's some food and water in there."

"Don't." I stood, and she immediately trained the gun on me again. "Don't you dare leave me here."

"Oh, Ari ..." She cocked her head as if I was the sweetest thing. "Don't you get it? We're never leaving each other again."

But two seconds later, she stepped out of the storage room, gun aimed at me as she punched the code on the keypad and waited for the garage door to close.

Tightness crawled across my chest as panic set in.

This wasn't happening.

How could this be happening?

North. North would find me. I nodded, shaking so badly my teeth rattled. North would be looking for me right now.

She couldn't do this.

She couldn't get away with this.

Calm down, I commanded myself. *Stop panicking*. I inhaled slowly and exhaled. Over and over, until my shaking decreased. Then I searched the rolling metal door, looking for weakness. I hammered against it. I tugged on it. Time passed —I didn't know how much, but I dripped with sweat from my attempts to get the damn door open. For a while, I yelled in the hopes that someone would show up and hear me.

Voice hoarse, I sat down on the bed and gazed around the room, letting my rational mind take over. I was Wesley Howard's daughter, and I was North Hunter's one and only.

Between the two of them, they'd find me.

And if they didn't and I had to face Caitlyn tomorrow, I had to come up with a plan to disarm her so I could save my damn self.

FORTY
NORTH

Aria's phone had been abandoned somewhere on the Santa Monica Freeway. I was done waiting around after discovering that. I called the rental car company to track her rental while Wesley called the police.

The company had just called to tell us the car was found, abandoned in Glendale.

Standing in the hotel suite we'd commandeered, I stared hard at Wesley, Walker, and Wesley's private security team, trying like hell not to succumb to that splintering feeling in my head and chest.

Aria had been missing for twenty-four hours.

The first few hours I'd tried not to panic.

My gut told me something had happened to her, and I felt like a useless prick waiting around, doing nothing.

Wesley had contacts in the LAPD. He chartered his private plane to fly him and his team over from Scotland. Walker had insisted on coming too.

A knock on the hotel room door had me rushing toward it. Wesley hurried at my back and greeted the two men in suits on the other side.

"Frank, Pete, thanks for coming." Wesley ushered them in. Aria's father's eyes met mine. "These are the detectives I told you about."

"Any news?" I barked.

The taller of the two raised an eyebrow, but the shorter man shook his head. "We've sent officers out to Glendale. They'll canvas the area while we pursue leads elsewhere. According to Wesley, Aria told you she was shopping on Rodeo Drive?"

I nodded.

"We're pulling footage from traffic cameras and parking garages in the area. We'll hopefully hear something soon." The short man turned to Wesley. "We're looking into Caitlyn Branch. We have officers out interviewing colleagues at her last job, a restaurant called Curiosity."

"So you really think if we find Caitlyn, we'll find Aria?" I couldn't even think about what that woman could be doing to Aria while we stood around in this fucking hotel room.

"It's our only lead at the moment until we get the footage from the parking garage. So far, we haven't been able to track Caitlyn down. She's unemployed and was evicted from her apartment a month ago. We've got men staking out both places in case—" A shrill beep cut Pete off, and he whipped out his phone. We waited with rising fucking impatience as he swiped at the screen. Then, "Got her."

My heart lurched into my throat. "Aria?"

Pete nodded and passed around the phone. "Parking garage camera picked her up walking to her car."

Wesley and I looked at the screen together. Pain and fear and longing filled me at the sight of Aria rounding her car to the driver's side. She seemed to be doing something at the side of the car for a few seconds and didn't notice the woman approaching the passenger side. My breathing stopped as the woman turned to look over her shoulder, as if making sure no one was watching, and then she got into the car.

Wesley tapped the screen, rewinding it a few seconds before pausing it on the woman's face. "That's her," he snarled angrily. "That's Caitlyn Branch."

"What now?" I demanded.

Pete took his phone back and replied with too much calmness, "Our guys are already using traffic cameras to follow the car."

"Fuck!" Wesley spat in a fury. "I will fucking destroy this bitch if she hurts my girl!" His gaze seared through Pete. "You might want to find her before I do."

Or before I did. I felt almost numb with fear as I reassured him, "We'll get her back. She'll be okay."

Because there wasn't another option.

If anything happened to Aria, I'd never get over it.

Walker gave me a stoic nod before he turned to Pete. "I'm Walker Ironside, private security."

Pete nodded. "I've heard of you, Mr. Ironside."

"I take it you have officers out there, following the information analysts are sending them from the traffic cameras?"

The detective nodded.

"Me and Wesley's team are going out there, and I want you to patch us in."

"Our officers are on it."

"No offense, but your officers are not military trained. We are." Walker gestured to the security guys at his back. "We're going to be the ones who recover Aria Howard."

Frank opened his mouth to protest, but Walker cut him off. "If the LAPD fucks up this rescue, you'll be dragged over the coals for it."

Pete sighed and nodded.

Walker looked back at Wesley. "I'll get her back safe and sound," he vowed.

"I'm coming," I insisted.

"You're not trained."

Fury filled me, my accent thickening with it. "Ah've just spent the last six months training with men who have elite military background. Ah ken ye think Ah'm just a stupid fuckin' actor, but I ken how tae handle maself."

"You're also emotionally involved," Walker stated with annoying calm. "If you get in the way, this could go tits up."

"And you're no' emotionally involved? This is Aria, for fuck's sake."

"It's different. I can compartmentalize."

"Aye, and if you come home with another bullet wound, Sloane will have ma arse. So I'm coming."

"Let him go," Wesley said wearily. "Please ... just ... just get out there and find my damn daughter."

Walker glowered at me for a few seconds, then bit out, "Fine. But if you get in my way, I will knock you out for your own good."

Heart pounding with anticipation and adrenaline, I nodded. "That's fair."

FORTY-ONE
ARIA

There was no way in hell I could sleep. I'd been afraid to drink any of the water or eat any of the food Caitlyn had supplied in case it was drugged. Instead, I'd sat curled up on the bed for hours until the pressure on my bladder was too much, and I had to use the Porta Potti.

The storage facility was cold, so I'd drawn the blankets around me and stared at the garage door, my mind whirring with a plan. As soon as I heard her approaching the next day, I'd brace myself at that garage door and lunge at her before she had a chance to draw her weapon.

It was a stupid plan, but it was the only one I had.

I attempted not to think about North and my family, about how worried they were. If it was North or Allegra or my parents who had gone missing, I'd be losing my goddamn mind.

There was no way to know what time it was when I heard the slam of a door and the footsteps out in the corridor. Caitlyn had brought me here around noon, and if I were to guess by the gnawing hunger in my stomach, I'd say more than twenty-four hours had passed since then.

"It's me!" Caitlyn called, her steps slowing.

I pushed off the bed and hurried over to the door, bending my knees ever so slightly, bracing to tackle her.

My pulse raced at the sound of her inputting numbers on the keypad outside, and then the garage door shuddered to life. It was heavy. No wonder I hadn't been able to budge it. My eyes darted to the ground, searching for Caitlyn's feet.

But nothing.

Tense, I waited as the door lifted to halfway. Still no sign of her.

Finally, when it got to chest height, I saw she was on the other side of the corridor, her back to another storage door. Gun in hand, pointed at me.

The door cleared into the ceiling, and I stared balefully at her.

She smirked. "I thought you might be a bit testy after your night in a new place, so I thought it prudent to put a little distance between us." Caitlyn waved the gun. "Back up, sit on the bed."

I'd never felt truly violent toward anyone before. But at that moment, I didn't care if she needed help. I wanted to rip off her face.

Backing up until I hit the bed, I sat down, spine rigid.

Caitlyn sauntered in and threw a white paper bag toward me. "Croissant from your favorite patisserie."

I didn't even look at it. She huffed. "Please tell me you ate and had something to drink." At my silence, she scowled. "You have to look after yourself. Eat." Caitlyn pointed the gun at me. "Now."

I'm going to end you. Seething, I picked up the bag and pulled out the buttery croissant. It *was* from my favorite place two blocks from Curiosity. Yet it tasted like ash as I forced myself to swallow, praying she hadn't drugged it.

"That's better." She sighed, relaxing her gun hand. Today

she wore her hair in a tight ponytail, and I could see the white lines around the margins of her hair where she'd missed with the fake tan. "Today I'm going to tell you about my childhood. I think it's important you hear about it so you understand just how alike we really are."

What? Confused, I reminded her, "You told me yesterday."

Her eyes narrowed. "No. We didn't speak yesterday. But we are today. You see, we're so similar, Ari. My dad is a world-famous director too. My mom is a model. My little sister is the apple of their eye. Of mine too. There's an age difference, so I kind of raised her."

Oh my God. "Caitlyn, you're confused. Don't you remember what you told me yesterday? About being in foster care. About your mom."

She blinked, stupefied. "No, I think you're the one who's confused. My life is exactly like yours! My childhood is exactly like your childhood. Privileged, with parents who loved me, but the pressure to live up to them, you know. I understand you better than anyone because of it, Ari."

I gaped at her, probably more terrified at that moment than in the last twenty-four hours combined.

Caitlyn was gone. She'd fully immersed herself in delusion.

"Do you want my life?" I whispered hoarsely, fearing that ... "Are you going to kill me?"

Tears filled her eyes. "I would never hurt you unless you made me. Don't make me. Just ... be with me. We're like sisters. Soul mates. I can be a better sister to you than Allegra can, and you can be a better sister to me than mine can. We'll share everything. I just ... I just need you to stop pushing me away." Agitated now, Caitlyn stood, anger morphing her despair into something ugly. "And he has to go. North. He'll only come between us like Lucas did." She pointed the gun at me. "I only slept with Lucas to be close to you, and you punished me for it."

I could feel my panic rising, my breath shallowing as I really, truly began to understand just how far gone Caitlyn was. But I grabbed hold of that anxiety and tried to talk myself through it. If getting Caitlyn to admit the truth of her reality had not worked (in fact, it seemed to have pushed her further into her delusion), then maybe agreeing with her would. "I'm sorry," I lied. "I took my anger out on the wrong person."

Her arm dropped, gun at her side. Hope gleamed in her fake green eyes. "That's right." A small smile teased her mouth. "Thank you."

"You were my best friend," I continued the lie. "I thought Lucas was trying to take you away from me and you were letting him."

"No." She shook her head frantically. "How could you think that after all the emails I sent?"

"I didn't get them. I didn't get any emails. I swear."

Caitlyn frowned at the deceit. "I thought you said you did."

"No. I would have reached out if I thought you were trying."

"So this ..." She glanced around at the storage facility. "I didn't need to do this?"

"No." I stood slowly, disbelieving it could be this easy. "Yesterday, I was just so mad at you for not trusting me either, for bringing me here when we could have talked."

"You told me to get out of the car." Caitlyn eyed me carefully.

"Because I hadn't heard from you in two years." I turned the tables on her. "You disappeared from my life for two years. I didn't know you were trying to reach out, and I assumed because you slept with Lucas that you didn't want me to reach out." Maybe if I could talk her in circles, confuse her, she'd drop the weapon.

Rubbing at her temple with her free hand, I could see her confusion but also her longing for me to want her.

"You're right," I pushed gently. "You really are the only one who can understand me. I'm the only one who can understand you."

I would never know or understand Caitlyn. Why she'd fixated on me. Perhaps she needed to believe that my privileged childhood with beautiful, talented parents had been idyllic. Perhaps, after everything she'd been through, she just wanted so badly to be like me, but also maybe to be loved by someone like me.

"Let me come to you." I lifted my arms as if to hug her. "Please, let me come to you."

Her shoulders slumped, gun still in her hand but relaxed at her side. I tried not to look directly at it as I took one step forward and paused. Caitlyn nodded, tears slipping freely down her cheeks now.

Heart in my throat, feeling like any second she might put a bullet in my brain, I tried not to let my fear show as I bridged the distance between us and wrapped her in my arms. She was shorter than me, and she buried her face in my neck as I squeezed her tight and ran a soothing hand down her back. Murmuring calming noises, I tensed ever so slightly when she brought her arms up around me. One fist clenched onto my dress while the cold press of metal touched my bare skin as she rested the gun against me to return the hug.

"It's okay," I whispered, pulse increasing as I prepared to fight. "It's okay."

Then I struck.

I yanked her head back by the ponytail and then wrapped my hand around her throat, squeezing tight as I turned to grab her gun hand. I got hold of her wrist and pushed her arm away, the gun away, as I squeezed her throat, my nails digging into the skin.

Her face turned purple, her eyes huge with rage, and I startled as the gun went off, a bullet blasting into the ceiling.

Releasing her throat, I got purchase on her shoulder and yanked it back in the wrong direction. I heard something pop as she screamed, and the gun clattered to the ground.

I scrambled toward it, even as I felt her claw at my back, her nails raking down my skin so hard, I knew she drew blood. Then my hair. She pulled so hard, but with a rage I didn't know I had in me, I screamed and shoved her with all my might.

As I straightened with the gun in my hand, I turned to find her sprawled across the floor, hair askew and throat bright red, holding her dislocated shoulder. I pointed the gun at her and fear widened her eyes.

"Move." I gestured to the bed. "Now!"

Whimpering in agony, Caitlyn crawled over to the bed and turned to face me. Her tear-streaked face made her seem like the victim.

"Code to the door or *I'll* blow your brains out."

"P-please, don't leave me in here."

"It's only until the cops arrive. Code. Now. Or I will shoot you and tell everyone it was self-defense, and they'll believe me since you fucking kidnapped me!"

She flinched and then nodded, crying hard. "0508."

My birthday.

Sick to my stomach, I walked backward out of the unit, gun on her the whole time as I input the code to close the doors and step back like she had.

"Please, Ari. Please!" she wailed pitifully.

Tears thickened my throat. I didn't know if they were for her, for how lost she was. I think they were for her. She was so lost, and I wasn't. And I hated her. But I also felt unbearably sad for her too.

Tears flowing down my face, I turned and ran toward the exit. I had to find North. I had to let him know I was okay.

Bursting out of the doors, I squinted against the bright sunlight, the afternoon heat that told me it had definitely been more than twenty-four hours since Caitlyn took me.

I scanned the empty lot before me.

Hurrying out onto the blistering pavement, I tried to think. Think. Think. *Think*. There had to be a business around here with actual people in it.

"You know, you really should have run."

At the sound of Caitlyn's voice, I turned slowly around but with the gun raised. To my horror, Caitlyn stood before me with a gun gripped in her hand.

She stared at me like I was the most disappointing person she'd ever encountered. "There's a safety in each of the storage facilities so people don't get locked in. A keypad. It was hidden by a pile of boxes. I mean, you wouldn't have gotten out because you didn't know the code until today. But I got out."

"And there was another gun in the room?" I asked, my knees shaking as I forced my hand not to. I didn't want her to see my fear. And to think just seconds before, I'd actually felt sorry for her.

Caitlyn smirked. "There's a hole in the floor beneath the bed. You wouldn't have found it." Her smile fell. "I can't live in a world where you don't want to be with me, Ari."

"Caitlyn—"

"It's Ariella." She narrowed her eyes. "And I misspoke: You can't live in a world where you don't want to be with me."

FORTY-TWO
NORTH

The last traffic camera to pick up Aria's rental was in Little Tokyo.

We'd arrived half an hour ago and had been driving around, searching for the car registered in Caitlyn's name. No luck so far. But my gut ... my gut told me to keep looking.

"Let's do another circle," I said from the back seat.

Suddenly, Walker's phone rang. "Ironside," he answered immediately, and I leaned in to listen.

"And we're just learning this now? Fuck. Got it." He hung up and turned to Jack, one of Wesley's guys. He drove while Walker sat up front in the passenger seat. "Caitlyn Branch is really called Daniella Smith. There's a storage unit under her name in Little Tokyo." He glanced down at his phone. "Take the next left."

Jack floored it as my pulse raced.

Perhaps part of me thought it was a long shot, wishful thinking, that we might be days trying to find where Caitlyn —Daniella—had taken Aria. Yet as I sat forward, hands braced on Walker's and Jack's seats, searching the street ahead, I couldn't fucking believe what I saw in the distance.

"That's her!" I'd know her anywhere. "Is she—"

"Holding a gun." Walker unbuckled his seat belt and whipped out his own gun. "And so is Caitlyn. Sit back!" He barked at me as he wound down his window. "Jack."

Jack, to my shock, slowed as we approached, but before any of us could do anything, Caitlyn's body jerked, the gun falling from her hands as she flew off her feet and hit the dirt.

Aria had shot her.

It seemed to happen in slow motion.

Until Jack hit the brakes and Walker jumped out with the rest of the security team and surrounded Caitlyn.

"Aria." Relief made me almost unable to move, my limbs so heavy with it. But then she turned to squint at the SUV, as if looking for me.

I jumped out of the vehicle, my heart threatening to bang out of my chest as Aria's face crumpled at the sight of me. The gun fell from her hand, clattering to the ground, and she swayed like she might pass out.

Then I had her in my arms, my embrace probably too tight, but she clung to me, hands pulling desperately at my shirt. "I've got you, gorgeous. I've got you."

Her sobs shuddered through my body, and I tried to take it all, tears wetting my eyes as I pressed a hard kiss to her head. "I've got you," I whispered over and over again, maybe to reassure me even more than to reassure her. "I won't let you go. I'm here."

The sound of sirens grew louder, approaching from a distance. But I kept my back to Caitlyn and Wesley's men.

"Did I kill her?" she whispered, trembling so hard I feared she might shatter completely.

I glanced over my shoulder and met Walker's gaze.

"She's alive. Shoulder wound," he reassured.

"No. She'll live."

Aria sagged in my arms but seemed to plead, "She was going to kill me. I had to."

"I know. Hush." I held her tighter. "You're so brave. I'm so proud of you. And I've got you now. I'm here," I repeated thickly. "Always here."

FORTY-THREE
ARIA

Two Months Later

Ardnoch, Scotland

"Y ou will be fine, sì?" Mamma held me at arm's length, her beautiful eyes filled with concern as she catalogued my every feature.

An SUV waited in the driveway of the beach house to take Mamma to the airport. While Allegra had left a few weeks ago to set up her new apartment in Providence, just a few minutes' walk from RISD, Mamma had stuck around longer than usual.

As ready as I was for her to leave, I'd attempted over the last few months to be patient with her. What happened to me had disturbed my parents more than I could have imagined. Dad stayed a few extra weeks in Scotland just to make sure I was recovering. Allegra insisted I take Zoom meetings with her therapist, which I did for her sake.

Now Mamma was finally heading back to LA to her own life.

"I'll take good care of her," North vowed as he slid an arm around my shoulders to draw me into his side.

Mamma nodded. "I know, I know. But what about when you are working?"

"Then she'll take care of herself." He grinned at me, and I melted at his sexy, admiring smile. "She's proven she's more than capable."

Eventually, after a few more reassurances and several more hugs, my mother reluctantly got into the SUV that drove her away.

"I love her ... but God, it'll be nice to have this place to ourselves." I cuddled into North. "I can't believe we have a whole six weeks alone before you start work." After a few online meetings (because North didn't want to leave me either), he'd decided on his next project, a television show filmed in Glasgow based on a series of Scottish crime novels. Part of me wondered if North had chosen the project to be closer to me, but he promised he'd chosen it because it was the one that called to him the most. Moreover, it fit into his schedule while *Birdwatcher* was in postproduction for the next nine to twelve months. So there was a good year to eighteen months before North would need to do the press tour.

"And filming is only scheduled until Christmas." North pressed a kiss to my temple. "I can't wait."

I grinned as we watched the SUV disappear out of sight. "You haven't even started filming and you're already wishing it over?"

"I'll miss you."

"You'll see me every weekend." I turned in his arms. "But let's not think about it while we actually have uninterrupted time together." We had the entire weekend to ourselves. "What do you want to do first?"

North chuckled, a wicked gleam in his eyes. "Oh, I can think of a thing or two."

"Yeah?" I gently shoved him toward the door. "Then what are we waiting for?"

"I THOUGHT Sundays were for sleeping in?" I teased as I hiked behind North, who checked his phone for his bearings.

After a delicious Saturday spent mostly in bed, North had woken me up at the crack of dawn to tell me he had a surprise for me. He'd then instructed me to wear comfortable clothes and hiking boots.

Now we were in the middle of nowhere, walking through woodland.

"We're almost there," North muttered. "I think."

I laughed, and he shot me a cheerful smile over his broad shoulder.

The truth was, I didn't care where he was taking me as long as we were together. Being kidnapped and almost murdered by my ex-friend put life into perspective. I'd already decided to work my ass off to deserve North and to make sure he knew I had every faith in him. But when I saw him in Little Tokyo, his face a pale mask of terror mixed with relief, I knew there was no one else in the world I wanted to find me whenever I got lost.

Somehow, having never fired a gun before, I hit Caitlyn in the shoulder. She lived but has been charged with kidnapping and attempted murder. The district attorney concluded that Caitlyn should be hospitalized, and if she responded well to treatment, she would face a lengthy prison term.

I hoped she got better, for her sake. I truly did. However, I felt safer knowing that if she did improve, she'd go to prison.

It was hard to keep the story out of the press, and I found

myself caught up in a media storm all over again. Thankfully, North could handle it and we had Ardnoch to retreat to on the days I felt like I couldn't.

I still woke up in the middle of the night from nightmares, and North always woke up with me. He held me while I tried to fall back asleep. The nightmares bothered him as much as they bothered me, but Allegra's therapist told me they were normal. Eventually, they would dissipate.

North had practically moved into the beach house, but Lachlan had told me a member who owned the beach house three down from us wanted to sell. I hoped to broach the topic with North. See if he would be interested in buying the house together. Of course, it was a big move, and I was totally putting myself out there by even suggesting it ... but I felt brave.

Smiling to myself, I watched my handsome boyfriend as he stopped, frowned at his phone, and then looked to his left. His cheeks were unshaven, and just staring at them reminded me of this morning and the rasp of his whiskers against my inner thighs.

Heat swirled low in my belly. "Hey, boyfriend, any chance we're lost?"

He looked at me, a slow grin lighting his face. "We're here." With a wink, he stepped off the path that hikers had created in the woods and started walking through the trees on our left.

Bemused, I followed and as I did, a sense of familiarity tingled through me. "Wait," I called out to his back. "I know this place."

Then suddenly we were out of the trees and standing in a field of purple heather.

My field of purple heather.

North turned to gaze at me, and my breath caught at the

love in his expression. "I asked Lachlan where your field might be ... did he get it right?"

I nodded, emotion thick in my throat. "This is it."

He took off his backpack, keeping his eyes on me as he unzipped a pocket ... and pulled out a dark blue velvet jewelry box.

Shock, joy, anticipation, love, so much love, flooded me as North dropped his backpack and walked toward me with that box in his hand.

"North?" My eyes flew to his from the box.

He swallowed nervously. "You once told me that this is where you realized you were lost and that maybe staying in Scotland would help you find yourself again."

He remembered.

He remembered everything.

"I wanted to bring you back here because I know what it feels like to be lost." North stepped closer to me. "I've been lost since I was seven years old."

Tears for that little boy who'd had so much taken from him burned my eyes.

"Until you," he confessed. "And I think what you felt here that day was fate. I think fate kept you here for me. To find me. So we could stop being lost together. Will you stay?" North got down on one knee and opened the box to reveal a stunning large oval diamond within a cluster of smaller diamonds set in a diamond-shaped platinum clasp. It looked old Hollywood and was so me that I was momentarily dazzled by its perfection. North continued, drawing my eyes back to his, "Will you stay found with me, Aria? Forever?"

I nodded, lowering myself to my knees. "Forever."

Relief and joy filled North's face and then he kissed me, hard, hungrily, our lips parting in laughter and tears, until finally he let me up for air. But only to slip the diamond on my ring finger.

"Do you like it?" he asked, caressing my finger with his thumb.

"You couldn't have picked anything more perfect." I reached for his face, the diamond winking in the late September sun. "I couldn't have picked anyone more perfect. I'm so lucky you picked me back."

North closed his eyes as if in sweet agony before resting his forehead on mine. A cool breeze fluttered over our skin as birds sang the perfect engagement song. Peace, a sense of utter rightness, moved over me, and I knew North felt it too as we kneeled in blissful silence, together, connected.

Home among the heather.

EPILOGUE
THEO

This was Scotland for you. Only a few short hours ago, the sun had been shining, glinting off the North Sea. I'd even taken a bracing walk along the private beach on Ardnoch Estate.

And now the evening sky, usually still bright so far north at this time of night, was dark and foreboding. Rain lashed my suite windows, and I could see the waves crashing against the beach beyond.

It made me think of Gothic tales and tragic love stories.

It made me think of the reason I'd escaped to Ardnoch.

I exhaled heavily, for once feeling the prick of isolation. North wasn't here to throw back a whisky with. It was strange arriving at the estate and not having Aria Howard greet me. I'd gotten used to the woman, and she was far prettier to look at than Lachlan Adair.

However, my old friend North had managed a miracle and actually persuaded the woman to have a life outside of Ardnoch Estate. I liked them. But fuck, they were annoying with their sickening lovey-dovey ways.

Fools too, I thought broodingly.

It would end badly. All love affairs ended badly.

I should know.

"God, I'm bored." I groaned, flopping down on the gargantuan bed. I would call up Clarissa but I got the distinct impression my call would be unwelcome. I think it was the text she'd sent calling me a colossal prick that tipped me off.

Shame. She was an ex-gymnast and still incredibly flexible.

I wondered who else was staying on the estate and whether there was anyone worth fucking. I desperately needed the distraction.

See, I had writer's block.

I'd felt it coming for months. The last script had been a struggle in between filming projects for other people. Yet writing was the thing I enjoyed most, and I couldn't bloody come up with anything worth a damn.

If I couldn't come up with anything while living in a castle on the Scottish coast with violent waves and forlorn wind wailing against the windows, then I was absolutely, positively fucked.

Truly.

In the arsehole.

With a pen that had run out.

"Bloody hell." I pushed off the bed, determined to find something to occupy my desert-dry, barren, ignominious excuse for a brain. Grabbing my room key off the side table, I strode to the door and yanked it open—

"Fuck!" I clasped a hand to my chest in fright at the sight of the woman standing on the threshold with her fist raised, as if to knock. "I almost defecated in my trousers, thank you very much." I glared at her.

Then frowned because she was familiar.

It was the mousy housemaid. Sarah, wasn't it?

Her pale cheeks had turned a mortifying shade of red as

she lowered her hand and blinked at me like she'd never seen a human before.

"May I help you?" I snapped impatiently.

If possible, her cheeks darkened, and I almost felt a tiny bit guilty. Just a smidge.

But then she surprised me by throwing back her shoulders. "I—I'd like to speak with you, Mr. Cavendish."

I searched her gaze, curious despite myself, and was shocked to discover she had stunning eyes. They were the clear and green like the jade waters of the Verzasca River in Switzerland.

She was always scuttling around the castle, trying to be invisible, that it was any wonder I hadn't noticed.

At my perusal, she nibbled nervously on her lip.

"Well?" I grimaced. Shy women were not the most comfortable creatures to be around, and I had places to be, someone to find to fuck away the monotony of my colorless, toneless, creatively dry existence. "Sarah, is it?"

The housekeeper gaped. "Aye. Sarah McCulloch."

I gestured for her to hurry up.

"Oh. Um... May I come in?"

Raising an eyebrow, I leaned against my door, arms crossed over my chest. "Wishing to follow in the boss's footsteps, my love, and bag yourself a member?" I smiled darkly at my innuendo.

Sarah swallowed hard, a spark of something that might have been annoyance flaring in her eyes. "That's not why I'm here."

I pushed off the doorjamb. "Why are you here?"

She licked her lips again, looked me straight in the eye, and stated with more confidence than I'd expected, "We have business to discuss, Mr. Cavendish."

***

Want more from Theo and Sarah?
THROUGH THE GLEN (THE HIGHLANDS
SERIES #3)
Out February 1st, 2024

**He's a cynical, world-weary Londoner. She's a shy Scot.
They might seem like opposites, but a few weeks in the
Highlands will bring them together in ways they can't
imagine...**

Theo Cavendish is the second son of a British viscount, and
he's spent years running from the aristocratic world he grew
up in. Betrayal and loss taught him lessons he's not quick to
forget. As an award-winning screenwriter and creator, Theo
prefers to throw himself into the world of film and television.
He moves from one project to another, never really letting
anyone truly know him.

As a housekeeper at the exclusive Ardnoch Estate, shy Sarah
McCulloch feels invisible most days. No one really knows her,
and they definitely don't know she's a bestselling crime writer.
She dreams of seeing her series on screen and believes only one
person can develop it for television. On the day she quits the
estate for good, she shares her secret with club member, Theo,
and asks him to consider her books.

Sarah never expected him to say yes or to show up on her
doorstep ready to write with her. Or that weeks spent locked
up in her cottage would lead them to form an intense but
undeniable connection. A bond that Theo is not sure he's
ready to accept, even though he can't bear to be without her.
However, when they finally venture out of their bubble, Theo

finds he'll have to battle more than his own demons to protect Sarah from hurt. For he's got another fan, one intent on bringing the darkest elements of his most famous script to life. And unless he can figure out this real-life antagonist's next move, Theo could be in danger of losing Sarah forever.

OUT NOW

Curious about the Adair Family?

HERE WITH ME
The Adair Family Series #1

SETTLED in the tranquil remoteness of the Scottish Highlands, Ardnoch Estate caters to the rich and famous. It is as unattainable and as mysterious as its owner—ex-Hollywood leading man Lachlan Adair—and it's poised on the edge of a dark scandal.

AFTER NARROWLY ESCAPING DEATH, police officer Robyn Penhaligon leaves behind her life in Boston in search of some answers. Starting with Mac Galbraith, the Scottish father who abandoned her to pursue his career in private security. To re-connect with Mac, Robyn will finally meet a man she's long resented. Lachlan Adair. Hostility instantly brews between Robyn and Lachlan. She thinks the head of the Adair family is high-handed and self-important. And finding closure with Mac is proving more difficult than she ever imagined. Robyn would sooner leave Ardnoch, but when she discovers Mac is embroiled in a threat against the Adairs and the exclusive members of the estate, she finds she's not yet ready to give up on her father.

DETERMINED to ensure Mac's safety, Robyn investigates the disturbing crimes at Ardnoch, forcing her and Lachlan to spend time together. Soon it becomes clear a searing attraction exists beneath their animosity, and temptation leads them down a perilous path.

While they discover they are connected by something far more addictive than passion, Lachlan cannot let go of his grip on a painful past: a past that will destroy his future ... if the insidious presence of an enemy lurking in the shadows of Ardnoch doesn't do the job first.

Printed in the USA
CPSIA information can be obtained
at www.ICGtesting.com
LVHW031042231124
797431LV00050B/2233